Fairest Creatures

Fairest Creatures

KAREN TAYLOR

Published in the UK in 2021 by Garrison
An imprint of Leamington Books
Edinburgh, Scotland

leamingtonbooks.com

Distributed in the UK by BookSource, and Leamington
Books

ISBN: 9781914090370

Production Editor: Peter Burnett
Typesetting: Joshua Andrew
Editorial: Ambrose Kelly
Cover Layout: Cavan Convery
Cover Image: Janine Wing

Typeset in Garamond, Maradona Signature and
OldNewspaperType.

Printed and bound by Imprint Academic, Devon.

For Alex

From fairest creatures we desire increase,
That thereby beauty's rose might never die,
But as the riper should by time decease,
His tender heir might bear his memory;
But thou, contracted to thine own bright eyes,
Feed'st thy light's flame with self-substantial fuel,
Making a famine where abundance lies,
Thyself thy foe, to thy sweet self too cruel.
Thou that art now the world's fresh ornament
And only herald to the gaudy spring,
Within thine own bud buriest thy content,
And, tender churl, mak'st waste in niggarding.
Pity the world, or else this glutton be,
To eat the world's due, by the grave and thee.

William Shakespeare

Creature

July 27, 2019

The place reeked of chemicals. It was only now that she fully appreciated this. Before, she could just smell, taste even, the sharp, spicy odour of something he'd eaten at lunch, or dinner. He hadn't been back for a while. She figured it must be getting late – there was a line of artificial light under the door. The rest of the room was in darkness – not the pitch black that made her gasp in fear when she first opened her eyes. She'd become accustomed to that and could make out shapes. To her right she could see the heavy folds of a stage curtain, a sturdy tasselled cord at one end. The curtain skirted parquet flooring. She imagined the swish it would make as it was pulled across to reveal – she didn't want to know what it might reveal.

Her neck ached; the leather choker, which was fixed around it, cut into her skin when she tried to move her head, forcing her to look forward at the door, with its thread of light her only clue to the passage of time.

How long had she been clamped to the chair? A day? Two? The cold steel enveloped her. Its high back chilled her scalp, her limbs numb against its flat, wide surfaces. If she'd been here less than a day, the chemical smell could be chloroform. Maybe that's what he'd used to drug her. A tear fell from her eye and it felt like a release. She let another fall, secreting it slowly. She couldn't sob – the gag in her mouth, the choker around her neck, the belt secured fast around her waist – put paid to that. But she still had this one liberty and she wondered why. What did he want her to see?

Two dark spots broke the line of light. She inhaled sharply, involuntarily jerking back her head. Letting her head tilt back forward, she watched the spots move. Could he see her? Her heart was hammering, causing darts of pain as it beat against its incarcerated chest. Her breath quickened. The dark forms moved away, restoring light.

The scene was shifting behind the door. She could feel it. Her body and nerves were so taut they picked up every micro movement in the atmosphere.

A key struggled in what was probably an old lock. The door opened and he stooped to pick up a candelabra – seven of eight slim candles alight.

He nudged the door shut and walked towards her.

'How are you settling in?' he said, with a look of concern. 'I know this can't be easy for you.'

He pulled a phone from his pocket. 'I have something for you.'

It was hers, and he watched for her reaction.

'I wouldn't wish to raise your hopes. We're on airplane mode here. It's untraceable and will be disposed of. But, I thought you might appreciate some messages from home.'

She closed her eyes and shook her head as if being forced poison.

He pressed her forefinger to the screen. Had she given him her password?

'You were more forthcoming last night,' he said, answering her thoughts. 'Share the messages with me. Read them to me.' Removing the gag from her mouth, he placed her finger on the messages icon.

'Mum, where are you? I've been trying to get hold of you all evening.' The words came out in a hoarse whisper. He reached for a bottle of water on a side table. She shook her head, although each word caught and burned in her throat. 'Can you text or call.'

She opened the next message: 'Mum, please call. I'm getting worried now.'

And the next: 'Mum. just call will you. I'm scared.'

She paused to look at him, but he just nodded encouragingly, like a kindly doctor or teacher.

'I've called the police. Sorry if I'm over-reacting.' She looked away and let her finger fall from the screen.

'Love you,' he said, picking up the phone and continuing for her. 'I'm waiting up for your call. Love you. Stay safe. Love you.'

She closed her eyes and bit her lip hard, so hard that she broke skin. I'm dead, she thought. The forlorn hope and desperation in those messages filled her with untold grief.

'Did you like your messages? I thought they'd make you feel more at home. Make you feel missed. Loved.'

He purred those last words and she had to force herself not to heave.

'Loved,' he repeated, walking over, bending his head and leaning in close, so close the soft flesh of his cheek brushed hers. She could smell his breath. Cold and fresh this time. He'd brushed his teeth. Somehow that made it worse.

'Look at me.' He tilted her chin upwards. 'I don't want to force you to see me. But you will. I know you will.'

She opened her eyes and he regarded her closely, as if she were a specimen.

'Cobalt blue, near perfection. But your mascara has smudged. Have you been crying? Here, let me fix your face.' He pulled a silk handkerchief from his pocket and dabbed the skin around her eyes.

'That's better,' he said, standing back and frowning in concentration. 'You have two fine lines between those beautiful eyes. I never noticed them before. We'll get rid of those for you. Restore you to your former glory.'

'What do you want from me?' Her tone was neutral, mirroring his own. His demeanour was menacing, but non-violent. She felt she could be a match for him, given the chance.

'A dining companion,' he said, feeling in his pockets. She saw a glint of metal and flinched.

'I'll just lock up first,' he said, jangling the keys as he moved to the door. 'Make sure we're not disturbed.'

She watched him flick through the keys before he found the right one for the lock. It was long and narrow. Took him a while to work it; she'd remember that. Then he picked up the candelabra, walked over to the curtain rope and started to pull it. The curtains were heavy and slow-moving – they didn't so much swish as lumber across the floor.

She was momentarily distracted by the stench of chemicals, which the curtains had contained to a certain extent. Then her eyes rested on the scene before her. A long wooden table, laden with plates piled with opulent displays of food. Candlelight played on crystal glasses – full to the brim with dark red wine. Another candelabra was positioned mid table. He took a box of matches from a side drawer in the table and began to light the candles – one, two, three, four, five, six, seven, leaving the last one unlit.

Figures were seated around the table; candlelight flickered on their faces, creating an illusion of animation. But they were still. She inhaled deeply as he turned, felt for his keys, and walked towards her.

'Would you care to join us for dinner?' he said, a polite smile on his face, before he knelt to unlock the manacle that fixed one of her feet to the chair.

'I'd be delighted,' she replied, smiling as best she could.

June 10, 2019

They'd found the hand in a glass box in woodland just outside of town. It was placed between the exposed roots of an ancient oak, a suitably fairy-tale setting for what looked pretty much like the work of the Sleeping Beauty Killer.

Detective Inspector Brandon Hammett studied the photo, taking in the details of the dried flowers in the skeletal fingers. This could be a new crime, or an old one that the killer had decided to leave as a calling card. There hadn't been any recent reports of missing persons in the Penzance area.

'What do you make of it?' Detective Sergeant Jo Menhenrick had come into the station's incident room, and was leaning over his shoulder, a mug of steaming coffee in one hand.

Brandon eyed the mug, but relaxed, reassured that in all the time he had known Jo Menhenrick she had never put a foot or, for that matter, a hand, out of place. He watched her place her mug on a coaster on the table, well away from the object of his attention.

'I don't know. This crops up – in the style of the Sleeping Beauty serial killings in the mid-90s – with nothing to tie it to. No missing person reports, no domestics, no bodies. Although there were never any bodies.'

Menhenrick moved to the other side of the table and sat down.

'Were you born in the '90s, Jo?' he said, smiling over at her.

'I would have thought with all your old country Southern charm you'd know not to ask a woman her age, Boss.' Jo narrowed her eyes over the rim of her mug.

'In my business, you need to know the details.' Slow, dark blue eyes returned her look.

'I'm not your business, though.' She stiffened a little and took a sip of coffee. 'But, as you asked, I just missed the '90s – it's my 30th this month. Hence the reason I am a little sensitive about my age.'

Brandon relaxed into his chair, cradling the back of his head in his hands. 'We'll have to go out and celebrate. It's a good age to be – I seem to remember.'

'You aren't so old yourself, Boss,' Jo said, raising an eyebrow.

No, he thought. But sometimes, a lot of the time, he felt it.

'Okay, well, let's say we were both babes in arms and way too young to recall these crimes when they occurred. But they're folklore around here. When I pitched up at the station five years ago from Houston, the station chief at the time talked me through what were to the day, and remain, the great unsolved murders of our times. In Cornwall and beyond.'

Jo edged forward to take a closer look at the photo. 'I do remember Reg Maxwell talking about the cases ... how the murders seemed related but were so erratic that it proved difficult to trace the killer or find a motive.'

'Downright impossible, I believe. At least for the MCITs at Newquay. The dismembered body parts would turn up, in differing stages of decomposition, usually weeks or months after a missing person report. The consistent factors were there was always an object, displayed with a single body part, in a glass case. Once, there was a death mask of a young woman called Naomi Foster, with a red rose. Hence the tag, The Sleeping Beauty Killings.'

'Any other consistent factors, Boss?'

Brandon sucked in a breath and bit his top lip. 'His victims were all women, aged 30-35. And all extremely beautiful.'

Brandon picked up the photograph, got up from the table and walked to the incident board. He pinned it up and stood back to consider it. 'The MCIT guys will be all over this. But, you know, there was never an incident in Newquay. We had four local women go missing in Penzance in 1996 within three months. Then it went quiet. One of the women was a lecturer at Penzance Art School, another was an artist's model, the third a potter. All vanished without trace until –' he paused to think. 'Until bits of them turned up – a braid of red hair, a hand clasping a clay goblet, an ear – the most bizarre

16

mutilation of all. An ear with an expensive earring. A very expensive earring, which no one had reported missing.'

Jo stood up abruptly and tucked a lock of her abundant red hair behind one ear. She kept it pinned up for work, but it had a habit of tumbling free. 'This guy is sick. Seriously sick, Brandon. Leaving these tokens ... like a cat leaving a bird's claw by his mistress's chair. He's trying to impress.'

'Yes. But who and why? And why has he reappeared now?'

Jo didn't have an answer. Why would she when no one had been able to find one in twenty-three years.

'You say Newquay will want to take this up? We won't get a look in?'

Brandon cocked his head to one side and looked at her. 'I think you know me better than that, Jo. They've got their work cut out over there mopping up a whole region's escalating crime rates. Would a historic murder case – one that has foxed the best – really appeal to them?'

Jo frowned. 'Probably, Brandon. If it appeals to you and me, why not them?'

'Because they're under-staffed and have quotas to fulfil and, as I said, this has its origins in local Penzance crime. Also, I do have some experience in these types of murders.'

'Go on.'

'There were some pretty nasty ritual killings I was assigned to as a rookie detective in Alabama. I'm not taking any credit here. Far from it. But I was one of the team, and we nailed the evil bastard.' He paused, ran a hand through his thick brown hair. 'He wasn't the first or last fucked up piece of work we had to deal with. But even the UT Police Academy, with its bulging shelves of textbook psychos, couldn't prepare me for this son of a bitch –

'You know, I made some mistakes back then. Underestimated the level of low cunning. Made lazy assumptions.' Brandon paused and looked at his hands. 'Maybe didn't press hard enough, soon enough. If I had, well ... perhaps we would have caught the killer earlier.'

He turned back to the photograph. 'I won't fuck up again. Serial killers like to think they're clever. Unique. And in some respects they are. They all have their tag. But what you learn is they're all attention seekers. They can't help themselves. Sure, they can put their urges on hold for a time – sometimes a very long time – particularly if they over-stretch the mark and get nervous. Perhaps just escape detection. But chances are they'll return. Often to their original killing ground. That said, this could be a copycat killing. The guy – assuming it is a man – would be 23 years older.'

'Older, but not wiser?' Jo joined him to look at the photograph.

'I reckon that's for us to find out.'

Julia

June 10, 2019

Julia Trenowden was in bed when the doorbell rang at 10.30am. She'd been awake since six, packed her son Nick off to school, made breakfast and then slipped back under the duvet for want of anything better to do. The doorbell rang again and she dragged herself up, wrapped herself in a silk kimono and headed bare foot to the door.

There were three people on her doorstep. All, evidently, strangers to one another.

She dealt with the courier first, scribbling a signature on his device in exchange for a shoe box-sized parcel. She reddened at the thought of its contents, before turning her attention to the others as the courier hurried away to his van and next delivery.

'Something nice?' said the second man on her doorstep, the dark-haired, handsome plumber that she'd invited to consider a caretaker position at Hartington Hall. There were many jobs needing doing and, with the cottage in the grounds part of the deal, they could come to a mutually beneficial arrangement. They just needed to 'drill down to the specifics', he had said. And here he was, tool kit at the ready.

Julia smiled at him. 'If I've chosen wisely. Why don't you both come in and I'll join you in just a few ticks.'

'Shall I make us all some coffee, Mrs Trenowden?' said the third person – a woman in her mid to late forties. Sensible shoes, hair smoothed back in a tidy updo, no or nude make-up. Everything about the woman screamed discretion. Julia hoped this wasn't pure packaging. This was all new to her. Like so many things, since Sam had died.

'That would be lovely. And please do call me Julia. Do you need any help finding anything?'

Diana gave a small smile. 'I remember from our interview. Americano, no milk, no sugar, Julia?'

'Perfect.' Julia made as graceful an exit up the stairs as she could, in her unravelling kimono and bare feet. Maybe I need someone to organise my diary, she thought, as she checked her phone calendar and noted the double booking. And someone to deal with the staff. Life, she had come to realise, was a succession of tedious tasks, unless you mastered the art of delegation. Diana Chambers, if she proved herself competent and honest, could run the place, she'd already decided.

They were all back on the doorstep within twenty minutes. Julia had long mastered the art of brisk discourse, when it suited her. Both employees would start the next day, giving them all a weekend to … Julia reached for her cup and took it to the coffee machine … adjust.

She tapped the top of the machine absentmindedly as it dispensed gurgling black fluid into her cup.

It was just her and Nick now. And Nick was at school all day, doing homework into the evening and then on his Xbox or out with friends.

She had to make a go of things – use her gallery to attract the best local talent and, possibly, beyond.

Her phone buzzed and she clicked on the image of a new fan on Huddle. She recognised the ruddy complexion of the local butcher, swiped left and deleted the dating app. There had to be a better way to meet people. At thirty-five she was too young and – she glanced at her reflection in the gleaming stainless fridge door – attractive, to decay, Miss Havisham style, in a crumbling mansion.

Julia had never been one to over think things or wallow in self-pity. She pulled across her iPad and tapped in BetterThanAllTheRest, an expensive upmarket dating agency. She'd throw some money at the project. And, she decided, she'd throw a party at The Hall.

Time to exorcise some ghosts. Time to lift her own spirits.

Brandon

June 10, 2019

'This has just come in.' Jo waved a print out at Brandon, as he sat, ready to drive off in his Skoda. He pulled the gear stick into neutral and turned off the engine, before rolling down the window. Taking the paper, he scanned its scant details and the bleary photograph of Clarissa Bowles, 32. She was smiling lazily into the camera, a headband of flowers in her long blonde hair, a mass of festival goers behind her. Brandon rested his elbow on the open window and looked up at Jo.

'We need more photos. Better ones. And her exact movements since—' He referred back to the print out. 'Saturday night.' He reached for the door handle, levered himself up from his seat and got out of the car. 'Have you – anyone – spoken to her next of kin?'

Brandon was standing now and Jo tilted her chin upwards to face him. 'I didn't take the call – Sarah did, and put this together. The alarm was raised by her flatmate – Renu Randhawa. Clarissa had been on a date. Someone she'd met on the dating app Huddle. Ms Randhawa said she did this periodically – it wasn't unusual. She wasn't around on Sunday morning. Again, not unusual in itself. But she wasn't answering texts.'

Brandon sighed and looked to the side. 'Not a good sign.'

'Phones run out of charge. Particularly when you've been out all night.'

Brandon gave Jo an incredulous look. 'I may be a few years older than you, Jo, but I am aware of the downside of mobile technology.' He ran a hand over his top lip, aware that he needed a shave, unless he was going for full-face furniture. It'd been a while.

'We're losing time while we wonder why she didn't use her new friend's charger, or a mobile one. Or just go home. Clarissa Bowles, a beautiful young woman of 32, has been out of contact for over 24 hours.'

Jo looked him straight in the eye. 'I'm on it, Boss. We'll throw the works at this.'

'Stew can do the leg work, but contact Newquay, get this info out there.'

Jo turned to go.

'You have Ms Randhawa's number?' Brandon was holding the car door open.

She checked her phone. 'Yes.'

'Call her now. We're coming over.'

Renu Randhawa wiped a dusty hand across her brow, beckoning Brandon and Jo in with the other. Her small pottery studio was neat but crowded with materials and works in progress. An oblong of brown clay was slowly collapsing on its spindle.

'Sorry to intrude,' Brandon said.

Renu waved a dismissive hand at the attempted vase. 'It's nothing. I just needed something to do this morning. Something other than look at my phone.'

Brandon followed her gaze to the phone on a pedestal table and then let his eyes rest on her. She was around the same age as Clarissa – early 30s. Small and slim, her glossy dark brown hair hung in braids, framing a face of fragile beauty.

'Why don't you come through to the living room? Perhaps I could make us some tea?'

'That won't be necessary,' Brandon said, gesturing to Jo. 'We won't take up too much of your time.'

Renu brushed aside the beaded curtain hanging across an archway that led into the next room. Brandon involuntarily ducked his head as he passed through into the brightly coloured antechamber. It looked like it should smell of incense or scented candles, but the cold, damp aroma of clay pervaded the space.

Brandon looked around. It was an Aladdin's cave of knick-knacks – brass urns, bowls and hookahs, nestled between ceramics of varying sizes. Wall mirrors tried to create the illusion of space. Renu sat down on a big leather pouf and gestured for Brandon and Jo to take the sofa a few feet away. Their knees practically touched and he could see dark smudges of shadow below Renu's eyes.

'Perhaps—'

'I—'

They began to speak at the same time. Brandon nodded at Renu to continue.

'I sorted out some more photos of Clarissa. Some better ones.' She reached down to a pile by her side and handed them to Brandon.

Clarissa could have been a model. There wasn't a bad photo. The light caught the perfect angles of her cheekbones, the whites of her eyes, the silky sheen of her long, tousled hair. It seemed inconceivable that she was looking for love on a dating app. In one photo, sunlight shone through the fine fabric of her skirt, revealing slender legs.

'She's beautiful,' Jo said, looking up from a framed photo.

'Yes. She worked with nursery school kids. She was an angel. How could anyone—' Renu looked away and then rubbed her eyes, before casting them down. 'She's gone. I know she's gone. I … I can feel it. I—'

Jo reached out and touched her hand briefly. 'I know how hard this is for you. But you can help, more than anyone. Tell us all you know about her date. Was this her first time with him or her?'

Renu flashed a look. 'It was a him.'

'What did she call him? Where were they meeting? How long had they been chatting before they decided to meet? Did Clarissa have anyone else in her life? An ex-partner, perhaps?'

Renu pulled her legs up to her chest and wrapped her slender arms around them. 'There was someone years ago. He broke her heart and, up until the start of the year, she was off men completely. She was happy working with the children. Loved her job. And she helped me in the studio – came with me to art fairs. But she became restless at the end of the year. Her ex had got married, his wife was expecting, she wanted to find someone herself. She thought time was running out. And –'

Jo looked at Brandon, who gave her a discreet nod. 'Go on.'

'She worked at a nursery. Men don't work at nurseries. She had no option but to go online.'

Brandon leant forward, his hands clasped together on his knees. 'Did you worry about her?'

'Yes.' Renu looked him in the eye. 'More than I can say.'

'The man she went out to meet on Saturday. Did she talk about him?' Brandon said.

'Not much. But I heard her talking to him on the phone in her bedroom. They'd been talking for a few days before she agreed to meet him.'

Brandon glanced at Jo. 'Is that usual?'

She nodded. 'On some apps.'

'Clarissa was on Huddle. The women make the first move. It's considered safer. She said his name was David. And that she was meeting him at a bar in St Ives. Ricardo's. I … I called her there a few times that evening. But she didn't pick up.' She was looking down and Brandon could see her hands trembling.

'Just one more thing, Ms Randhawa, before we leave you.'

He caught the look of alarm in her eyes. 'Do you have her parents' number? Other next of kin?'

'There was no one else. Her parents are dead. She was an only child. I was all she had.'

Jo reached out her hand again. 'We're here if you need to talk.'

Renu rose from the cushion with feline grace. 'Thank you.'

'Thank you,' Brandon said getting up from the sofa, his tall frame dwarfing her. He stooped a little and handed her a card. 'And if there is anything else. Call us. Any time.'

She slipped past him, held aside the beaded curtain and let them pass.

'There was one other thing,' Renu said, as the three of them stood at the door.

'Clarissa thought it was a minor thing. But I didn't.'

Brandon narrowed his eyes and waited.

'His photograph. He looked hot. Really cool looking. Any woman – anyone – would have fancied him. But that photograph wasn't verified.'

She was looking Brandon straight in the eye. 'When you enrol on these sites they ask you to have a web photo taken to prove you look like your profile photo. His photo wasn't verified. It could have been an avatar for anyone. Anyone of us standing in this room.'

June 11, 2019

It was 6.30pm and Julia was sat at the kitchen table, topping up her glass of white. She was staring hard into her iPad.

She took a sip of wine and pushed the glass away. 'Diana, I just can't decide. Fancy dress, posh or smart casual. What do you think?'

Diana stopped loading the dishwasher and ran her hands down her apron. 'Fancy dress.'

Julia turned to her with knitted brows. 'You think so? Wouldn't it be a bit cheesy? Hard work for everyone?'

Diana smiled. 'It will be great. And such fun to organise.'

'A lot of work, though.' Julia reached for her glass.

'I'll do the bulk. The boring bits. Not that there will be any boring bits.' Diana had a faraway look in her eye, as if she was already ordering in the champagne. 'You deserve this after all you've been through, Julia. We'll make it a night to remember.'

All she'd been through? A night to remember? Julia tensed and then let it go. Her recent bereavement was common knowledge. Diana was no better informed than anyone else.

'Well, if you don't mind the extra work? We'll need caterers and extra staff, and the place will need a deep clean. We'll have to open up the main salon.'

Julia turned to see Diana smiling confidently, her finger poised on the dishwasher start button.

'Come and join me for a glass, two heads are better than one.'

'It's not really my place.' Diana's mouth was pursed but her eyes sparkled. She pressed the button and the dishwasher purred.

'Nonsense. This isn't Downton Abbey! It's 6.30 and you should have clocked off an hour ago. I need inspiration. If I ask Nick it will be Star Wars, or The Avengers, or blimming Game of Thrones. Although, I suppose, Game of Thrones could be quite interesting –' Julia was imagining herself as the blonde one, her hair cascading over skimpy furs.

Julia went to get up, but Diana anticipated her move and helped herself to a wine glass from the wall cabinet.

'Why don't you go for something glamourous – maybe film stars,' Diana said, pulling out a chair and sitting down beside her.

'Well, yes?' Julia said, absentmindedly pouring Diana a drink, ignoring her hovering hand as the wine rose higher. 'The Golden Age, perhaps?'

'Good idea.' Diana took a sip from her glass and passed it to one side. 'It would keep the timeframe fluid – from the silent movies, through to the '60s.'

Julia narrowed her eyes and took a sip of wine. 'People can go glam, noir, or full-blown Cabaret. I'm loving it.'

Diana smiled and raised her glass. 'I'm so pleased for you. You need this.'

What she didn't need was the pitying, patronising tone of her housekeeper. But now wasn't the time to get oversensitive. Julia gave her a benevolent smile. 'Thank you, Diana. We'll make it a night to remember. For all of us.'

There was a rustling sound by the kitchen door and Julia turned to see her son sneaking past and up the stairs.

'Excuse me, Diana, I need to have a word with Nick. But, yes, let's think on the Golden Age of Film. I'll do some research on costumes.' Julia gave Diana a dismissive nod and got up from the table.

'So will I,' Diana said, getting up and walking over to the sink. She poured the rest of her glass down it. 'Will that be all?'

Julia stopped in her tracks. 'Well, yes, of course. Enjoy your evening.'

Julia knocked at Nick's bedroom door. 'Nick, can I come in?'

He didn't answer, but she heard him put something away and trudge across the floor.

He opened the door, still wearing his school blazer.

'Everything all right?' Julia said, giving him a searching look.

'Yes, of course.' He nodded towards the open door.

'Heard you saying something to the Black Widow about a night to remember. For all of us?'

Julia raised an eyebrow. 'At least come up with a better nickname.'

'Give me time,' Nick said grinning, one hand on the architrave. 'Whoops, here she creeps.'

Nick moved backwards and Julia followed him into his room as Diana bustled past up the stairs to her own one.

'So what were you two hatching?'

'A party.'

'Oh no, Mum.'

'Nick,' she grimaced. 'It will be fun.'

'When is it?'

'I was thinking July 1.'

'So, I've got a few weeks to make my escape.'

Julia cuffed him lightly on the arm. 'You can't leave me too.'

Nick sat down on the bed and started fiddling with his Xbox remote. 'I'll come to the party. If you want me there.'

'Why wouldn't I want you there?'

'Cramp your style? Have you met anyone yet on Huddle? Or that poncy posho site?'

Julia sat down beside him. 'No. That's just a distraction. I'll probably never meet anyone.'

Nick picked open the remote and took out the batteries. 'Have you got spares?'

'In the bottom kitchen drawer, by the dishwasher,' Julia replied distractedly.

'So, Mum, what sort of party is it?'

'Fancy Dress.'

'Oh no.'

'The Golden Age of Film.'

Nick sprung up from the bed. 'Mum!'

'You don't need to dress up.'

'Too right.'

'And you can bring some friends.'

'If they'll come.'

He sat back down and Julia knocked against him with her shoulder. 'Give your old mum a break.'

He gave her a brief smile, before returning his attention to the remote. 'Mum.'

'Yes.' This sounded serious.

'Dad invited me to New York for a few weeks in the summer holidays. You okay with that?'

He'd picked his timing. No, she wasn't okay with that. Any time spent out of her radius made her nervous. But it was his Dad, flaky bastard that he was. What choice did she have?

'In principle, of course. Just let me know the details. In good time.' Maybe it would come to nothing. Or maybe it was for the best? Nick was 15. She couldn't baby him forever.

Julia got up abruptly. 'Now.' She lowered her voice. 'That the kitchen's free. Do you want a snack before supper?'

Nick got up to join her. 'Who's the best son in the world?'

'Let me see?'

Nick was waiting for his answer. The same answer she'd been giving him since he was little.

'You are.'

'Love you, Mum.'

Brandon

June 12, 2019

The wind was slapping cold air and sand in his face as he stood at the foot of the cliffs, watching the forensics paw over the object on the ground. It glinted in the sun, light reflecting off its glass and metal frame. The top was covered in sand: every time the CSIs brushed aside a coat, another formed.

Brandon watched them construct an area around the box, struggling to fix yellow tape in the gale-like conditions. It was a bizarre and macabre exhibit – something that you might expect to find at The Tate or National History Museum. Except the piece of flesh on display was days old.

Al Chapman, the chief CSI, was busying about the scene and signalling for his team to stop taking photos and wrap things up. There wasn't much they could do in a small Cornish cove, in inclement conditions.

Brandon moved down to join Al, a wiry guy in his mid-fifties. He must have seen a few pieces of dead flesh in his time, but he was looking perplexed.

'What do you make of it,' Brandon said, standing next to him, not exactly shoulder-to-shoulder. Al was a small man.

'It's an ear. Small. Looks female. Young. Doesn't show signs of age.'

'Just death.' Brandon gave him a sideward glance.

'Can't say until the lab examinations, but decomposition suggests the ear was removed from the body quite recently. A few days ago, max. Less than a week.'

Brandon looked to the sky and then down at the sand and the fluttering tape, before his eyes rested on the box. 'I see.' This was in sharp contrast to the skeletal hand that had launched the murder enquiry. They still hadn't been able to link the DNA to any missing persons. Brandon was beginning to think that they might never – given that the hand could be twenty-three years old. But they were trying. Going through the files and contacting bereaved relatives.

Al looked at him. 'You think this is the work of the Sleeping Beauty Killer? If it is, the person who has lost an ear is unlikely to be alive.'

Brandon continued to gaze at the box. 'Were you in the force when the killings took place in 1996?'

Al nodded: 'Cut my teeth on them. This is similar in so many ways.' He paused.

Brandon turned to him. 'What's different?'

'The timing. The girl – young woman – has only just gone missing.'

'We don't know who the ear belongs to.'

They were facing each other now.

'I think we do, don't we? Clarissa Bowles, the nursery school teacher who's missing.'

Brandon turned to the crime scene. 'The sooner the remains are identified the better. Let's move this along sharpish. The victim could still be alive.'

The words sounded hollow and he could feel Al's eyes on him.

'Okay, let's tidy up here now. Get the body part back to the lab,' Al instructed his team.

Brandon watched them swoop in. A SOCO lifted the box and deposited it in a secure container.

'The other -- thing – in the box. A shell?'

'A conch,' Al said, standing back as the box was ferried past and up the cliff steps.

'Can you send the photos over asap and the DNA results.'

'We'll have Clarissa Bowles DNA?'

'Of course,' Brandon said.

Al's features relaxed a little. 'It's not pretty is it?'

'No.' Brandon turned to go. 'And, if you are right about the timing, we need to get a move on. Time's not on anyone's side.'

July 27, 2019

Her smile was as stiff as the frozen ones around her. She was seated at the far end of the table, the furthest from the curtains, which he had drawn. To her left were four bodies propped up in high back dining chairs, the closest to her barely recognisable as a human corpse. It was taking every ounce of self-control to retain her nerve.

He was forking a piece of fish from his plate, his eyes, momentarily, off her. She noticed that the body to his right, her left, was in better condition than the rest. The blonde hair was still long, if not luscious, the flesh pale, but relatively plump. She looked like her photos in the papers. The realisation made her gag and she circled the spaghetti on her plate, round and round.

When she looked up she met his gaze.

'Is it to your taste?' he said, dabbing the side of his mouth with a heavy linen napkin.

'It's delicious. Just the right amount of saffron.'

He put down his napkin and clasped his hands together. 'I am so pleased, my love. I do try. And—' He had a slightly coy, if not bashful, look on his face. 'No more than 300 calories per portion. Not fattening in the least.'

'That's very considerate of you.' She'd eaten less than 30 of those calories and they'd caught in her throat. She took another forkful – conscious of the need to preserve her strength, concentrating on the scent of jasmine emanating from the candles. The longer she played his game, the longer her chances.

His hand reached for the decanter and he poured wine into

the glass of his companion on his right. The legs of his chair made a polite ahem of a scrape as he rose from the table. 'Can I tempt you with a little more? This is a rather special vintage. Chateau Margaux 1993?'

She nodded. If he'd wanted to drug her, then there were numerous other ways. He wouldn't spoil the wine.

His hand brushed hers as he took her glass and poured. His fingers trembled, the wine splashing over the rim, droplets trickling down the crystal.

'You look so beautiful in this light.' He used the napkin wrapped around the decanter to wipe her glass. 'Here's to you, my lovely. My immortal beauty.'

'Here's to us.' She raised the glass to her lips and drank. The wine tasted good. It would have been so easy to drain the glass and relax into the situation. But that wasn't going to happen. Not while she had breath in her body.

'To us.' He clinked her glass and walked back to the other end of the table. His dinner jacket was perfectly laundered, not a crease in the fabric.

'You will think me remiss. But no pudding tonight.' He was smiling at her – flirting – and she took a gulp of wine. 'Best we both keep a clear head and healthy constitution for tomorrow.' He was a handsome, slim man, well-preserved for his forty or so years. He'd obviously worked at it. But his eyes looked tired; speckles of red circled the pale blue irises.

One of the flames was flickering, a candle coming to its end. He blew it out. Just that one extinguished source of light darkened the room. The masklike face of the redhead second on his right, fell into shadow, a row of bracken teeth just visible.

She took a sip of wine before looking up at him. 'Tomorrow? What plans do you have?'

He smiled and lounged back in his chair. 'Nothing too taxing, my dear. First, I want to make a study of you. At your finest. You are so very beautiful. Never forget that. I won't let anyone forget that. Ever.' A tear formed in his eye and he looked away.

Folding his napkin, he placed it on the table before rising from it. 'And then, my precious darling, I will walk you through my gallery. Introduce you to—' He was turned away from her, his hands clasped together behind his back. 'I would like to introduce you to someone special. Someone I admire so very much.'

It was difficult to keep still – she shifted in her seat. Her eyes roamed the room. Was this the time?

'Let's call it a night,' he said, turning suddenly and striding towards her. He'd felt her energy and unease. She'd have to be careful.

'Do you want me to help clear the table?'

'No.' His voice was curt, his body close.

'Please—'

'Bear with me, darling, bear with me.'

'I can't sleep in that damn thing. I—'

He had steered her to the chair. Hadn't pushed her, or grabbed her, but she could feel his force. It would be futile to protest.

He clamped her wrists to the arms of the chair first and then strapped the leather belt around her waist, before kneeling to fix her ankles to the metal legs. Bile rose in her throat and she wondered if the food would come up, and whether this would be a good or bad thing.

'Don't think unkindly of me,' he said, rising to his feet and gently lifting her chin so she looked him in the eye. 'It's for the best. Trust me.'

'Please, no,' she said, as he went to fix the leather choker around her neck.

'I will never hurt you. I only want the best for you.' He snapped the clasp shut.

There was a bottle of water on the side table, next to the gag. The gag was new – freshly laundered peach silk. The colour of flesh.

'Could I have a sip of water, please?'

'Of course, my darling. Whatever you desire.'

He held the bottle to her mouth and she took a long draft. He didn't take his eyes off her neck. When a little water spilt from her mouth, he took away the bottle.

'I'll come and see you in the night.' He took the gag and tied it around her mouth, the material soft but suffocating.

'Good night, my darling.' His lips brushed her ear. 'Trust me. I won't fail you. Trust me.'

Julia

June 13, 2019

'Quite a looker,' Jake Nayler was peering over Julia's shoulder as she read The Times Online at the kitchen table. She clicked out of the other window – BetterThanAllThe Rest.

'Yes,' Julia agreed, studying the photo of Clarissa Bowles, whose severed ear had been identified by the forensics. 'Just terrible.'

Jake moved in closer. 'Says she'd been using a dating app. What would a hot woman want with one of them?'

Diana Chambers, who was cleaning out the spices cabinet, clanked down two jars. 'Times have changed, Jake. Dating has changed – maybe being god's gift you hadn't noticed.'

She gave him a daggers look, which Jake returned with a full beam smile. 'I didn't know you cared, Di.'

Julia edged back her chair. Jake took the hint and returned to his leaky tap.

'Are they saying it's the Sleeping Beauty Killer? Diana asked, one arm deep in the cupboard. She pulled out a sticky jar of homemade chutney. 'School Fayre 2015,' she said, tangling it above the collection of rejects. 'Do you want to keep it for … sentimental reasons?'

Julia wrinkled her nose and went back to the screen. 'Yes. They're linking it to the SBK – as they're calling him. Bears all the hallmarks. Body part, displayed in a glass box, no other remains.'

'Who's working on the case?'

Diana's hands were still in the cupboard, ostensibly tidying, when Julia turned to her. 'DI Brandon Hammett. Our local detective. He's heading up the murder team out of

Penzance, with support from the Major Crime Investigation Team in Newquay.'

'A serial killer back on the loose.' Jake was polishing the tap with a cloth.

'It would appear so.'

'You take care, Miss. Any worries, you know where to find me.'

'Thank you, Jake,' Julia said, twisting round to face him. 'It's so reassuring to have you here. Both of you.' She made a point of looking at Diana, who was still on the stepladder, head in the cupboard.

'Does the CSI get a mention?' Diana had closed the cupboard and was coming down the ladder.

'Yes.' Julia had returned to the screen.

Diana came up behind her: 'Al Chapman.'

'You know him?'

'He was on the case in the mid-'90s. He was young then, but made his presence known.'

'How?'

'Always there at the scene. Mentioned as part of the team, when the analysis came through. They didn't wear the white suits they do today – and he stood out.'

'Did you fancy him, Di?' Jake said from behind. They didn't turn around.

'You must have been very young yourself, Diana. Well-remembered.' Julia said.

Diana had one hand on the back of Julia's chair, her eyes on the screen. 'I remember all right. Those were times you don't forget.'

Diana's leg touched her thigh, before she moved back a few feet. 'Coffee, Julia?'

'That would be lovely. There really isn't anything else in the news this morning.'

'I'll be getting on then.' Jake was hovering. 'Unless there's anything else needs doing?'

'Best tend the garden. The orchard, in particular. There will be a lot of windfall fruit after the recent gales. Do help yourself and, of course, leave some for Diana and put a basket out for passers-by at the end of the lane.'

'So thoughtful. Thank you.' Diana called over from the coffee machine, as Jake walked past and out of the kitchen. When he was out of earshot she added: 'Do you want to make a start on the party arrangements?'

'There are a few other things I should be getting on with first.'

The lines between Diana's brows tightened. 'Of course.'

'Let's run through some ideas this afternoon. If you have a few minutes?'

Diana smiled and placed Julia's cup of coffee beside her. 'I do.'

Julia waited for her to leave the kitchen before returning to her computer screen. She clicked on BetterThanAllTheRest and scrolled through the latest offerings. She was never short of 'fans', but there were few that attracted her. She didn't consider herself fussy, but there were limits. Just as well when she considered some of the dates she'd already been on. She thought back to her Falmouth Art School days when it really was 'raining men'. Now the pool, although not exactly a puddle, wasn't the sea with the promised plenty of fish.

Her eyes were glazing over and she was considering diverting to film star costume searches when a profile caught her eye. Axel Fleming, 46. He was good-looking, if a little stiff. Blonde hair, greying at the temples. Intellectual metal rim glasses. A tidy, close shaven beard. He described himself as a boring Swede, looking for someone to excite him.

He listed finance as a profession, so was likely to be loaded. Julia wondered whether she could meet his criteria. Her confidence had been knocked recently. If she was honest, she had always lacked confidence with alpha males. It was easier to have second-raters fawn over her, rather than meet the high standards of a real match. He was attractive, well-educated and rich. Not unlike herself. And he said he was boring. Let her be the judge of that.

Brandon

June 13, 2019

Two feet hung from the tree, the hem of a flimsy dress tangled around the ankles. The sun was setting, its low beams obscuring his vision. She was a way off, maybe 30 metres or so, and the grass was a metre high. But he ploughed through, heart beating fast and loud.

He had to get to her before it was too late. Cut her down, give her mouth-to-mouth, make her well again. But she wasn't getting any closer. The sun was blinding him now, the grass making it hard to move.

The field was deserted – no vehicles on the dirt track, which wound its way past the copse and up the hill where the outlier shacks slouched in half shadow.

He looked ahead and up. A low branch caught his leg causing a dart of pain; but nothing like the stab in his chest as his eyes caught hers. Her head was bowed, her eyes stared down. He was six feet two, but not tall enough to reach and release her. So he scrambled onto the raised mossy roots, stretched out, felt the cord, with its hard tight knot and slipped back. Slipped again and again, falling to his knees, scrambling back up. Even though it was too late. It was always too late. He raised his head slowly and looked into her eyes. Still blue, but darkening like the sky.

He woke sweating, his heart beating wildly, and reached for the packet of cigarettes on his bedside table. He wouldn't go back to sleep. Not after one of these dreams. It had been a while, but he didn't need a shrink to know why the nightmare had returned.

He glanced at his phone – 3am – pushed back his duvet

and swung out of bed. Cigarettes and lighter in one hand, he gently opened his bedroom door and snuck down the landing and up the stairs to his attic studio.

Moonlight flooded through the velux window. He opened it, lit up and took a long drag. It was a clear night, the stars out, the full moon reflected on the sea. He took another drag and turned back to the room and the comfort of his leather armchair

Brandon didn't consider himself a spiritual man. He'd loved the music and drama of gospel in the Alabama of his youth, but he'd maintained a sceptic's eye. Could always spot a phoney; had come across enough opportunistic preachers in his time. But these dreams. The ones with Jessica. He couldn't fathom them. His wife had died of cancer, in hospital. Nothing he could do. Nothing a preacher could do. So why … he dragged on his cigarette … why was she always hanging from that tree. That very tree, in the most miserable, godforsaken armpit of Alabama, where it had all happened and where he had managed to make a difference.

There was only one way to block out the noise. He got up and picked up the Stentor from the small wooden table. There were other fiddles. Fine ones. But the Stentor was the friend he needed right now. He placed its belly under his chin; his stubble had grown into something resembling a beard and it brushed the wood. He picked up a bow and teased the strings so they hummed a lullaby. He was conscious of the hour – although the room was sound-proofed and Chelsea slept well.

He'd left the canvas Rachel had been working on in the alcove by the window. She'd left in a hurry for London. Hardly surprising – so many unresolved issues with her. And, he hated to say it, with her boyfriend. Maybe they were right for each other? Hard to say. He pulled the bow down hard and struck the strings in quick succession. Time would tell. Right now, he was facing the biggest challenge of his life. Who would have thought the same killer, in a different guise, would stalk his turf again.

Julia

June 15, 2019

It was unmistakably him. He didn't even look older than his photograph, as all the rest had. Axel Fleming looked better. The glasses were off. As was the stiff selfie smile. Julia took a breath, smiled and walked towards his table.

He rose and stretched out a hand. 'Julia, I'm delighted to meet you.'

He whipped around to pull her chair back from the table.

'Thank you,' she said, descending gracefully. What was it about her that made everyone treat her like royalty? Or maybe that was just his way?

She noticed a bottle of wine in an ice bucket by his side.

'I took the liberty,' he said, following her gaze. 'Chablis? I seem to remember you saying you liked it.'

'Perfect.' She let him pour, reflecting on the many messages they'd exchanged before this first meeting. It was a wise strategy. The Huddle dates had crashed and died on inadequate research.

'Tell me about yourself,' he said, after she'd taken a few sips of wine.

'I think we've covered most of the bases.' She could have kicked herself. He was meant to be the boring one.

'Let's rest at base camp a while then. That suits me. I am the boring Swede, after all.'

Julia gave a polite laugh. 'And I'm tasked to excite you.'

He looked at her with his cool blue eyes. Eyes that warranted their own insurance policy; like Betty Grable's legs. She'd researched her for the movie party.

'I'm excited already.'

Julia felt a frisson herself and took another sip of Chablis. 'I assume you've googled me? Read about—'

'No.' He was still looking into her eyes, his wine untouched.

'Really?'

'Really.' He averted his gaze and picked up his glass. 'I like to hear things, as you English might say, from the horse's mouth.' His own English was impeccable; fluent with just a touch of an accent. 'In explanation, I've spent many years in research. Researching hot shot executives, masters of the universe, and their lawyers, as well as the financial markets. Few people live up to the expectations of their public personas. I learnt all I needed to know about you from your profile and our messaging.'

'Well.' Julia took another sip of wine. He certainly wasn't boring. If this was base camp, way to go. 'You said you wanted someone to excite you.'

He smiled and waved a dismissive hand. 'That was just a tease.'

'I am, sadly, the stereotypical poor little rich girl.'

Axel leaned back in his chair. 'Not anymore. I guarantee, not anymore.'

Julia looked up at him. She'd broken her golden rule – don't blurt out. Never complain, never explain.

Julia put down her glass and looked him in the eye.

'You can talk through things as little or as much as you wish. I'll listen. But that was then. I'm here for the now. The Happy Ever After. How boring is that?'

Julia laughed 'We'll find out.'

June 16, 2019

Brandon was staring hard at the piece of paper in his hand. 'Fancy being my plus one?' he said as Jo swept past with an iPad.

'Eh?' she said, placing the device on the incident room table and turning to face him.

'A party invitation.' He gave her an ironic look. 'Fancy dress.'

Jo threw back her hand and laughed. 'Go on, Boss.'

'The Golden.' He raised an eyebrow. 'Age of Film.'

'You're just selling it to me, Boss. Whose party?'

'Julia Trenowden's.'

'Fits the profile. Sounds swanky. When?' Jo started to peel off her jacket.

'July 1 – nightmare.'

Jo gave a short laugh. 'All work and no play, Boss!'

'Well, possibly, but the last party I went to organised by Julia Trenowden was murder.' He looked at his hands.

Jo folded her jacket over her right arm. 'The Arthouse opening wasn't a rip-roaring success, granted. But this could be like the roaring twenties. You could be Al Capone. I could be a gangster moll.'

'So I take it that's a yes, then?' Brandon pushed back his fringe and looked at her.

'We could do with some light relief, couldn't we?'

'You call this light relief?'

'Well, beats what's just come in.'

Brandon's head shot up. 'Go on.'

'Another missing person report. Rebecca Morley, 34, café owner.'

Brandon put down the invitation and joined Jo at the table. She touched the darkened screen of her iPad and tapped in the code to reveal a photo of a young woman standing at a counter displaying pastries, salads and sandwiches. Ringlets of golden hair tumbled over tanned shoulders.

'I know her,' Brandon said, stroking his beard. 'Jesus. I know her – been to Becky's Café many times. When was she last seen?'

'Yesterday. Café was closed this morning – one of the staff called the station. Said it was unlike her – not telling anyone.'

'Does she live alone?'

'With her brother, Nathan Morley. He wasn't picking up either when Lena Lewandowski called.'

'You have his number?'

'You bet. And his address.'

'Okay. Let's pay him a visit. And then you can check out Ms Lewandowski.'

Brandon's phone buzzed and he clicked on a text. 'Al Chapman. He reckons he's picked up something interesting on the Bowles DNA.' Brandon tapped a quick reply before nodding at Jo. 'I'll deal with him later. This could well be a live lead.'

Brandon parked the car outside the Old School House in a Penzance side street. It was a granite building converted into one and two bedroom flats. It took a while for Nathan Morley to open the door of his ground floor apartment. He emerged bare-foot and bare-chested in pyjama bottoms, scratching a head of wavy dark hair.

'Yes?'

Brandon showed his card. 'Nathan Morley?'

He nodded his head.

'Is your sister, Rebecca Morley at home?'

'She'll be at the café.' He pulled himself up straight. 'Is there a problem?'

Brandon looked down and then up. 'We're just checking on a call from an employee of the café. Rebecca didn't show up this morning. Lena Lewandowski called the station when she couldn't get hold of her.' Nathan stepped back and thrust a hand against the doorframe. 'I'll go check her room.' He disappeared into the dark hallway, navigating two bikes and a pile of boxes,

They could hear him knocking lightly on a door and then banging harder. 'Becky, you up? Becky?'

Nathan was back with them in minutes. 'The bed's made. She hasn't slept in it. Does this look bad? Oh God, is this bad?' His mouth was screwed up, one palm against his forehead, the other hand on the doorframe.

'Can we come in?' Brandon held his gaze.

Nathan moved to one side. 'Yes, of course. Of course.'

The living room was a man cave; empty beer cans on the floor by the sofa, takeaway cartons on a soiled coffee table.

'I had some mates round last night for poker,' Nathan said in explanation. 'Becky was out.'

'Where?' Brandon said, standing in the middle of the room, Jo by his side.

'On a date. I don't know where, exactly.' He brushed aside a few cushions and an empty bag of crisps on the sofa and gestured for them to sit.

'A date? Someone she knew?'

Nathan pulled out a wooden chair from under the table and sat down. 'She'd hooked up with someone on Huddle.'

'First date?' Jo asked.

'Yes, or at least I think so. She'd been chatting and messaging him, so I think this was the big night.'

'Did she tell you where she was going?' Brandon was leaning forward, arms on his legs.

'The Lido – they were going for a coffee at the Jubilee Pool and, if things were cool, they were going to go from there.'

Brandon glanced at Jo. 'Did she call you? Text? Say how it was going?'

Nathan got up suddenly. 'Where's this going?'

'We need to get a clear picture of your sister's movements. Has she contacted you?'

He went to the bookshelf and picked up his phone, tapped in his code and scrolled. 'One text. She said he was really nice and they were going for a drink, maybe supper.'

Brandon was on his feet. 'Anything else?'

'Look for yourself?' Nathan handed him the phone and began to pace the room. 'God. God – this is bad. This is—'

'There could well be an innocent explanation,' Brandon said, handing the phone back. 'Call her.'

Jo rose to join them as the faint ring tones on Nathan's phone stopped and Becky's cheery answer phone voice came on.

June 16, 2019

The waitress came over with one americano for Brandon and a latte for Al Chapman. Sun streamed in through the glass-fronted Lido café, and Brandon shielded his eyes with a cupped hand as she placed the cups and saucers. He'd already spoken to the girl – Scarlet Pierce – about last night. Got a brief description of Becky and her date. He'd arrived after her. Didn't order a coffee – although he sat while she drank hers. Scarlett didn't get a close look. Didn't hear his voice – Becky did most of the talking – and then they left. Not through the main exit, but out through the glass slide doors, which led to the patio and the pool.

Al waited until she'd left the table before continuing. 'I found some interesting DNA on the body part. As you know, we found clay particles and sand – the clay from her work, the sand most probably came from the cove where the box was found. Although, it could suggest the victim had been to another beach. Cross contamination. But there was something else.' Al picked up his coffee cup and took a luxurious sip, wiping a finger across his upper lip where some froth had settled. Brandon smiled. The man had an innate feel for substance contamination.

'I'm listening.'

'Gamma Hydroxybutrate.'

Brandon raised an eyebrow and took a sip of coffee. 'GHB. Figures. The date rape drug of choice.'

'Except, the SBK isn't raping them.'

Brandon blew out and narrowed his eyes. 'I'd like to know how you worked that one out from an ear.'

'All the body parts have been handled and presented with care. None have revealed any trace of semen, bruising or another person's DNA.'

Brandon continued to look at him.

Al took another sip of coffee, wiped his mouth with a paper napkin, and pushed aside his cup. 'You have to realise I was there at the start. I know his style. His technique. I could write a thesis on it.'

Brandon suspected he probably already had. He certainly had his opinions. 'I've read the files.'

Al looked at him.

'Many times.'

'And do you feel you know him?'

Brandon looked Al in the eye. 'I know his public persona. Like that ear, like that hand, we only know parts of a unique person.'

Al folded his napkin into a tight square and placed it in the saucer, spilt coffee fanning out through the tissue. 'Any other missing person reports?'

Brandon hesitated before answering. Rebecca Morley wasn't a missing person – yet. 'No.'

Al got up to go. 'Thanks, for the coffee. On me next time.'

Brandon watched him leave via the open slide doors. Saw him weave, unobtrusively, through the patio tables and chairs, the diners oblivious to the remarkable abilities of this non-descript, middle-aged man.

Creature

July 28, 2019

He'd come to her just past six in the morning. She'd read the time on his watch as he untied the gag around her mouth and unclamped her hands. The door to the hallway was open and lit by bright sunlight – the wings of a bird fluttered outside the small, lead-framed window. The scene filled her with unease – a snatch of freedom before the walk to the gallows.

He'd brought a bowl of soapy warm water with him, as well as a mirror, flannel and towel.

'I'll leave you a few minutes,' he said, turning away.

She leant over and took a swig of water from the bottle by her side. And then another and another. The wash and brush up could wait. Her reflection eyed her warily from the mirror. She looked okay – for someone in her situation. But how long before he considered some sort of intervention? She'd thought long and hard about his motives and intentions. He was obsessed with looks. Hers were fading fast in this airless tomb – how long before she was propped up, rather than clamped, to a chair? The mirror's frame was solid silver – deadly, if wielded with intent.

When he turned she was preening herself in its glass. He stood back and watched her, a smile slowly forming. 'You look adorable.'

'Did you tint the glass? It's very flattering.'

'Nonsense. The mirror doesn't lie. You look lovely.'

'It's beautiful. Antique?'

'I believe so. It was my mother's.'

'She has fine taste.'

'The finest. Are you hungry, my dear?'

She placed the mirror face down on the side table and smiled at him. 'Ravenous!'

'I am so pleased. I have prepared a delicious, but simple, spread for us in the kitchen garden. It is such a pleasant morning, I thought we could eat outside.'

The news took her by surprise, and she rested a hand on the table to steady herself. This could be trap, of course. But outside – away from the stench of death, which contaminated everything – was a treat she hadn't anticipated.

Her fingers rested on the mirror. She thought about picking it up, but left it.

'Come,' he said, taking her by the hand. I'll show you my secret garden. Everything is crafted from my own hands. From the seeds of last year's crops grow the fruits of today.'

'Wonderful.' She squeezed his hand when he hesitated by the table and the mirror. He gave her a sharp look, but continued to walk towards the door, still holding onto her, exerting just the slightest of pressure.

All she could see was sky from the window. Was she by the sea? It made sense – a remote seaside pile. She mentally flicked through the ones she knew – wondered if she might recognise this one. They'd reached the end of the stone floor passage and a wide stone staircase, which spiralled up into a turret. To their left was a wooden door. He turned the key in its lock and jerked it open to a bright sunny day. She was lost in the moment: the scent of roses, the cheery sunflowers that lined the ancient wall and the radius of yellow courgettes in freshly turned soil. In a sheltered corner, there was a small round table laid for breakfast. An antique lace cloth covered all but the ankles of the white legs. A cake stand bearing pastries and French toast, a jug of milk, and dishes of butter and jam, circled a porcelain teapot.

He released her hand and pulled back a chair for her to sit on, dusting off a few fallen leaves. It crossed her mind to grab the teapot and fling it at him. But she had to get her bearings. Timing was key.

'Shall I pour?' His eyes never left her.

'Please.'

'What a lovely walled garden. It's enchanting,' she said, as he moved the teapot away.

He stood with the pot in his hands, and lowered his eyes. 'Thank you. That means a lot to me. This garden is special. It's a haven. For no one but you and me.'

A light breeze ruffled the edges of the lace. In the far distance, she heard the sound of a ship's horn.

They ate in silence, allowing her to consider her surroundings. At the far end of the garden, beyond the vegetable patches and rose beds, was an old iron gate, covered in ivy.

'Would you like me to walk you around the garden?' he said, putting down a butter knife and leaving one piece of toast on his plate.

'Finish your breakfast first.' She took a mouthful of toast, savouring its delicious combination of butter and jam. No food could taste better.

A bee buzzed around the jam before settling on his plate. He picked up a water glass and captured it, watching it bash itself against the sides.

'I've finished.' He got up from the table and came round to her, helping her up and taking her arm. He started to walk with her like a gentleman in a Jane Austen novel. She remembered the film Pride and Prejudice with Zombies, and thought of the others indoors. It was a surreal scene; the vegetable patches pretty and uniform, the roses pruned to perfection, the sunflowers silent spectators.

When he stopped at the iron gate, she could see slivers of blue and green through the gaps in the ivy and metal work. His hand increased its pressure on her arm.

'There's nothing beyond,' he said, letting go.

He walked the few feet to the gate and rested against it, all the while gazing into her eyes. 'Nothing beyond. Nothing at all.'

Brandon

June 17, 2019

Brandon was sitting at a small table in the corner of The Turk's Head staring into his pint. Jo was with her Huddle date at a table near the door. So far, so bland. He was a bog-standard bloke of around 40 and seemed impervious to Jo's attempts at flirtatious flicks of her hair and animated anecdotes. Brandon had concerns about this investigative avenue. Sure, Jo was a good-looking woman, but he had doubts about the killer falling for such a blatant honey trap. The man had escaped detection for over 23 years. He knew his way around women – beautiful women. Would today's technology be his downfall? Jo reckoned it might.

Stew came back from the bar with two more pints. This kind of undercover work had its advantages. He took a sip.

'You've got some froth on your beard, Boss,' Stew said sitting down.

Brandon ran a finger across his upper lip. Nobody likes being told that.

'How's it going with lover boy?' Stew wasn't convinced about the strategy either.

Brandon lowered his voice. He'd perfected the art of speaking just below a room's ambient noise a while back. 'I'll bring her in after we've finished these.'

Stew rolled his eyes. 'Dumb idea. The killer wouldn't agree to meet anyone in an enclosed space like this, with all manner of witnesses. You've already got a photo of him on your phone and he's chatting on, totally oblivious.'

'I agree, he's not our man. But this is Jo's first date. A practice run. She's new to all this.'

'My heart bleeds for her. But the SBK – he's too smart to fall for a pretty girl, with a good line in chat.'

'What makes him so different from the rest of mankind?' Brandon shook his head and grimaced. 'The thing is, Stew.' He hunched over the table. 'This is how people meet today. End of. I met my wife at a bar in Austin 16 years ago. That's rare now. Even in Texas. In many respects, the killer is no different to you and me. He will have been forced to adapt. Young women are wary of pick-ups in public places. Also—' He glanced over at Jo's table. 'How handy is it for a predator to have a whole stack of profiles to scroll down. He's got all he needs to know. Looks. Age. Interests. Profession. Status. Our killer is out there – I doubt very much it's the guy sitting at that table with Jo right now – but he's out there and on a site and dating app. It's not the only way we can flush him out – but it's a pretty solid one. The man has been lucky so far in avoiding technology – no CCTV or apps in his glory days – now he will be adopting it for his needs. At some point Jo will register on his radar. If she hasn't already.' Brandon looked over at her.

'She sure scrubs up well,' Stew said, following his gaze.

'I'll put her out of her misery.' Brandon started to text, pressed send and picked up his beer.

Across the room, Jo had adopted a concerned expression; looked like she was making her excuses.

'Classic brush off,' Stew said, grinning at Brandon. 'And he don't look too pleased.' The guy was already at the exit, jacket over one shoulder, the other shoving open the door.

Jo finished her drink before coming over. 'I'm not a betting woman, but I wouldn't say this was our killer.'

'Why's that?' Brandon said, smiling at her as she stood looking down at him. 'No chemistry?'

'Zilch,' Jo said pulling up a chair.

Julia

June 17, 2019

'You look a million dollars.' Diana was standing behind Julia, who was appraising herself in her bedroom mirror.

Julia pursed her lips. 'You don't think I look a little Greta Garbo before she slipped off to be alone?'

Diana gave a polite laugh. 'You look like Grace Kelly in her prime. The dress is just perfect – the epitome of glamour.'

Julia turned round to face her. 'Diana, you are too kind. Thanks for finding the stockist. The dress really is to die for.'

The specialist stockist that supplied the shimmering gold gown had been at the bottom of a list created by Diana. At the top was a costumier who specialised in carnival and high-class hooker bling. Julia had flicked through Diana's endless suggestions before finding something suitable.

Diana stood there admiring her handiwork.

'Have we had any more acceptances?' Julia changed the subject to another at the forefront of her mind. A few people still hadn't responded, including her best friend Rachel, who'd gone quiet. 'I know most people will have emailed me direct, but I thought—' She thought that the expense of sending out flash, gold-edged invitations would have tempted a few more people to the post office.

'I haven't checked today's post yet,' Diana said, giving a small smile of encouragement.

'Is Mr Fleming coming?' Diana had picked up Julia's jacket and was brushing it down, ready to hang in her wardrobe.

'Try and stop him!' Julia was smiling again.

Diana swung round. 'Who's he coming as?'

'Jay Gatsby.'

'That's not strictly Golden Age. The Redford version was in the '70s.'

'I know, I know, Diana. But it suits him to a tee.' She was smiling broadly, thinking about her new charming man.

'Yes,' Diana agreed.

'Who are you going as? Have you decided yet?' Julia had slipped out of the dress and stood in her bra and pants.

'I will be needed at the door,' Diana said, looking down and reaching over to take the dress.

'Nonsense! We have agency staff. You must join us as a guest.'

Diana busied herself with the dress, covering it with the protective polythene it came in. 'I'd rather not, Julia. I'd prefer to enjoy the spectacle from the side lines.'

'You can bring a friend, of course.' Julia was pulling on a t-shirt.

'Thank you, you're too kind. But I'd really rather not. I will enjoy myself just as much, if not more, watching you all having a good time.'

'Well,' Julia said, sitting down and wiggling into her jeans, 'Ensure you have a few flutes of champagne. And, of course, take a day's holiday in lieu of the overtime.'

'That is very generous.' She was standing at the door, forcing Julia to edge past her to make an exit.

'Have you decided what shoes to wear yet? Diana said, to her back.

'No. Next task of the day.'

'I think I know the perfect stockist,' she heard Diana say as she walked along the landing to the stairs. Her phone pinged. It was her best friend Rachel. 'I'm thinking of coming as Mrs Danvers .' Julia burst out laughing and typed, 'Nooooo. :D.'

June 17, 2019

It was two days since Rebecca Morley had gone missing and there were no leads. Not on Rebecca or Clarissa. Brandon ran a hand over his chin, felt tightness in his neck and shoulders. They'd gone through Clarissa and Rebecca's dating app contacts. There were no cross-overs – although they each had one match who couldn't be accounted for. The profiles had passed the standard mobile phone verification check. But that was an easy thing to fix with a burner phone. Not so easy were the image verifications. There were two men, one blonde, the other dark, who couldn't be traced, although their images had been approved via an online camera comparison. The killer had employed some tech trickery, suggesting he was either computer savvy, resourceful or rich.

Brandon was staring into the ether when Jo came into the incident room to join him.

He flinched when she placed her iPad on the table.

'Sorry, didn't mean to startle you.'

'I'm just a bit on edge – feel I'm working against time and a different kind of evil.'

'Is that why you've grown a deliverance beard?' Jo was smiling at him.

He smiled softly back: 'I'm not the one who needs to look pretty, Jo.'

'Not even for the party?'

'Especially not for the party.' He got up from the table. 'I'm not in the right frame of mind for socialising. Too much on my mind.'

He walked over to the incident board and looked at the

photo of the box with the dismembered ear. 'Have you been able to trace the suppliers of the box?'

'No,' Jo said, coming up alongside him. 'And, believe me, I've tried. I've been all over the web. They're unique. The metal frames are probably hand-crafted or antique.'

'I guess he wouldn't have used them if he thought we could buy them from Amazon.' Brandon gave a mirthless laugh. 'He's smart.'

'And rich?'

'I would say so. Someone with a taste for the finer things.' He turned round to face Jo. 'I've been thinking about bringing in a psychological profiler.'

Jo nodded.

'It's all right us making these assumptions, but it could help. We need help. The man is playing cat and mouse with us. He's avoiding CCTV, slipping through safeguarding checks, not drawing attention to himself in any way.'

'No witness descriptions,' Jo added.

'With the barrage of publicity following his last two dates things are going to get that much harder for him.' Brandon clicked on his iPad, bringing up an image of Rebecca Morley.

'Do you think she's still alive, Boss?'

Brandon shook his head. 'Dunno. Nothing has turned up yet. Perhaps? They're combing Millennium Woods and Kynance cove as we speak. Personally, I'll be surprised if anything is found in the two places he's already used. He'll have to change tack if he's to keep in the game. His old haunts are on our radar. Women are going to be wary of dating apps.'

'If they weren't already,' Jo said.

Brandon's nodded and then glanced at his phone, which had buzzed a text. He read the message and returned to Jo. 'A profiler could help us identify his next moves.'

'Do you know of one?'

'Yep. The best.'

Brandon's phone buzzed again and he frowned in concentration.

'Important?' Jo said.

'They've found a shoe in a glass box. Fits the description of what Becky was wearing on her date.'

'Where?'

'The steps of Gingerbread Cottage in Newlyn.'

'Any?'

'No. No body part.'

'So he's already changing tack?'

'A little. Testing the wind.'

'Gingerbread Cottage?' Jo looked at him. 'Are you thinking what I'm thinking?'

'Yep,' he said as his phone started to ring – Al Chapman's name on his screen. Brandon raised one eyebrow. 'He's always one step ahead – sees himself as a psychic as much as a pathologist.' He tapped the green button. 'Yep, just heard. See you there.'

'Want me to come along?' Jo said.

'No point at this stage. Keep going through the CCTV, see if anyone registers. Check on Becky's last movements ... I'm clutching at straws here.'

'Sure.' Jo stopped to look at her own phone. A new fan on Huddle had popped up. She enlarged his image.

Brandon peered over her shoulder. 'Maybe you shouldn't respond.'

Jo tutted and clicked on his profile. 'I'm a detective. And I have excellent back-up. He's cute too.'

Brandon smiled. 'Don't go anywhere until you check with me.'

'I'm not your daughter.'

'No, but I'm your Boss. You can engage with him, sure. But no hook-ups until we can arrange proper support.'

'I hear you, Boss.'

'Take care, eh,' he said, before heading for the door.

The SBK was toying with them. The visual analogy was as subtle as a neon sign blaring Ginger Bread Cottage, get your baker's shoe here. In reality, the house plate was small and cutesy, the place more Swiss chalet than gingerbread.

The inhabitant was not according to folklore either. Mrs Hayes was a slender woman in her mid-forties, rather than a wrinkled old crone. A teenage daughter, in cut-off mini shorts, stood on the doorstep with her.

'When did you notice the shoe?' Brandon said, addressing the woman.

'Half an hour ago,' said Mrs Hayes, glancing at her daughter. 'Jade was about to go to school.'

Brandon looked at her clothes. Cut off shorts, cropped top. 'School?'

'Yes.' Mrs Hayes crossed her arms. 'I told her to stay back with me, till you came. You might want to ask her direct, or something. She changed clothes. She's a teenager.'

'What time did you leave the house?' Brandon asked the girl.

'8.30. It's a short walk to school. Tavistock House.'

A private school in Newlyn. It was beyond Brandon's pocket, and St Piran's in Penzance suited him and Chelsea fine.

'You called the station at 9.00.'

Mrs Hayes jumped to her daughter's defence. 'She thought it was a prank. Or maybe a present. Took some photos of it for Instagram. She wasn't to know. One of her followers said it looked like the shoe the missing girl had been wearing. And the glass case … well, that's what he puts them in, isn't it?'

Brandon nodded and then turned when he heard a car pull up. It was Al Chapman. He got out of the car, beeped it shut and walked towards them, pulling gloves from his white suit.

'Am I a little overdressed?' he said, glancing at the girl and the shoe on the ground.

Brandon gave a grudging smile. 'I wouldn't say so.'

He turned back to Mrs Hayes. 'Has anyone else touched the shoe and the case?'

'No. Just Jade.'

Al took this as a cue to kneel down and examine the evidence. He didn't touch it – just moved his head around, recording details, before taking some pictures and standing back up.

'I'll get a container from the car.' He paused. 'It's a beautiful thing. She must have put some thought into her outfit for the date.'

The idea had occurred to Brandon too. The shoe was new, fancy evening wear – lilac suede, with an intricate arch of green and lemon tapestry flowers on the upper.

'Wouldn't say they'd stock this on the high street,' Al said, returning with the container.

'Anything else suspicious?' Brandon said to the women, before putting out his palm to stop Al lifting the case. 'Anyone hanging around outside. Did you hear a car pull up? A bike? Chatter?'

'Nothing out of the ordinary. I had the radio on while I was making sandwiches for Jade. Not that she's likely to eat them!' She rolled her eyes.

Jade shrugged. 'I had my earphones in. Sorry.'

Brandon took a few photos of the shoe from different angles, before nodding at Al to do his business.

'If there is anything that occurs, Mrs Hayes, Jade, then phone the station. Thanks for calling this in, so promptly.'

'Want a lift back to the station?' Al asked, as they walked away from Gingerbread Cottage.

'Got my car round the corner.' He'd decided against blocking the already crowded and narrow street with the Skoda. No CCTV again. Who'd have thought you needed it in such an idyllic setting. Cobbled street, cute cottages, crime-free.

'Got any theories, Brandon?' Al said, as he opened his car door.

'A few. And you?'

'Yes. Perhaps we can meet again for a coffee, after we get the DNA confirmation.'

His confidence knew no bounds.

'If there's anything you want to tell me now – never been a better time,' Brandon said fixing him with his cool stare.

'Nothing that can't wait. I'll be in touch.'

Brandon gave the car roof a soft tap before Al drove off in his Toyota Prius.

He walked down the lane and turned right onto a small road that led to the seafront. Sitting on the low wall that hemmed the promenade, he pulled out his phone, tapped in a message and pinged the shoe photos to Jo. Then he took a piece of paper from his pocket and tapped in the number written on it.

Suzanna Fitzgerald picked up the phone after four rings. 'Yes.'

'DI Brandon Hammett. Ms Fitzgerald. Can we talk?'

June 17, 2019

Suzanna Fitzgerald was a tall woman in her mid-fifties. Red boxy hair framed a pale freckled face and sharp green eyes. She oozed professionalism; her elegant Georgian town house the product of it. Brandon had driven straight to Truro when she'd agreed to speak to him.

'I was expecting you to get in touch,' she said, leading Brandon down the hall, with its original artwork and into a large garden room at the rear; expensive bi-fold doors opened out onto a well-tended garden.

'I do it all myself,' she said, watching Brandon standing and admiring the view. 'It's my passion.'

'It shows,' he said, turning slowly to face her.

'Please.' Suzanna gestured to a chair.

'Thank you.' Brandon took a notepad from his jacket and sat at the table.

'Coffee?'

'I'm fine, thanks.'

She pulled out a chair and joined him at the table. 'You're young, behind that beard.'

Brandon smiled. 'Well, I wasn't around when the Sleeping Beauty Killer was first in town.' He paused and looked up at her through his fringe. 'I'm sorry, I didn't mean to be rude.'

Suzanna burst out laughing. 'I could say I was a child at the time, but you wouldn't be here if that was the case.'

Brandon nodded. 'True.'

'You need my experience?'

'Yes. Your notes from the original case and your thoughts on this one. Will you come on board?'

She nodded. 'I want to find the killer as much as anyone involved in the investigations. I feel I know him. Maybe I got too involved last time. It was a while before I took on another case.'

'I heard.' Brandon paused. 'Do you think it's the same person? Or a copycat?'

Suzanna looked at her hands. 'It's a little early to say. The boxes and body parts are his hallmarks.'

Brandon leaned forward, resting his arms on the table. 'Something just came in. Two hours ago.'

'He's speeding up. I wonder why?' Suzanna looked away, caught up in thought, and then met his eye. Her eyes had a hypnotic quality – windows into his soul, not hers. 'What came in?'

Brandon was overstepping the mark. He hadn't run this past MCIT – they might think Suzanna Fitzgerald wasn't their girl – might have preferred him to discuss developments with them first. Fuck it. 'Rebecca Morley's shoe – the one she was wearing on the night she disappeared. It was left, in a glass case, on the doorstep of Gingerbread Cottage in Newlyn. A schoolgirl found it and her mother reported it.'

Suzanna leaned back in her chair and gave a mirthless laugh. 'Playful.'

'Unlike him?'

'Rather coarse for the SBK. And there was no body part?'

Brandon shook his head.

'That would be out of character.'

'Which may mean this is someone else?'

'Or he wants us to think it is.'

'You think he's that clever and conniving?'

'Let me tell you a story.'

Brandon smiled. 'I'm all ears.'

'But, first, some refreshment.' Suzanna got up, walked over to a work surface by the door, picked up a tray and brought it over. She poured two glasses of what looked like fresh lemonade and passed one to Brandon. Brandon went to refuse, but met her gaze.

'Let's take our glasses of Vitamin C out into the garden, for a top up of Vitamin D.'

'Do I look like I've got scurvy?' Brandon gave an incredulous look.

'Indulge me. My children have flown the nest. Nurturing is what I do best.'

When they'd settled outside at a weathered metal table, Brandon took a sip. It tasted good.

'Not so bad,' Suzanna said, watching him over her own glass. 'A little sugar takes the edge off the sharpness.'

Brandon nodded and took another sip, before resting the glass on the table.

'The SBK would approve of homemade lemonade.' Suzanna was mixing hers with a glass stirring rod.

'You think so?'

'I know so. The man – and I do think he's a man – is a gentle, refined soul.'

'Which puts him at odds with his MO?'

'Indeed. Which leads me to believe he's suffered significant trauma.'

'What sort?' Brandon took another sip of lemonade.

'Bereavement. Probably at a young age – childhood or adolescence.'

Brandon leaned forward. 'You get this from his victims? Their age?' He paused. 'Are we talking about an ex-girlfriend? Unrequited love? First cut is the deepest and all that?'

Suzanne sat upright, her eyes trained on him. 'Women. A woman, clearly features. But this has to stem from more than a distressing love affair. This is a cut which refuses to heal. He's still in pain.'

'Do you think that's why he's attacking these women – hoping revenge will make things better?'

'He's not attacking them.' Suzanna looked at him over her barely-touched glass and reached to top his up.

Brandon waited for her to continue and then broke the silence. 'He's not attacking them? I think the evidence so far suggests otherwise.'

'Let me rephrase. He doesn't think he's attacking them. And, the evidence also shows no signs of violence. The body parts are clean, well-preserved and presented with care and taste.'

Brandon felt something on his tongue, and discreetly crunched on a lemon pip. 'So what is he doing? What does he want with these women?'

'To protect them. To save them.'

Brandon sucked in a breath. 'Save them from what? They all had good lives – careers, friends, beauty.'

'On the surface, yes, these women would be the envy of many. And yet—'

Brandon said nothing. His pen rested on his notepad.

'And yet, he recognised something in them. Or thought he did. And decided to come to their rescue.'

'Like a dark prince.'

'Like a lost soul.'

Brandon cocked his head to one side. 'Lost soul?'

'A lost soul, looking to create a Happy Ever After.'

Brandon blew out. 'Which, of course, he can't. It's a warped narrative on a loop.'

'Yes.'

'And he can only keep indulging himself – and his white knight fantasy – because? Can you help me here?'

'He has money. The boxes, the props. Or he's very clever. Or both.'

'What do you think?'

'Both.'

'And looks?'

'I would say he has charm – whether via his appearance or his personality. These women were drawn to him. They certainly weren't repelled by him.'

Brandon squinted. 'Rebecca Morley was seen chatting animatedly with a man who, more than likely, was the SBK at the Lido in Penzance the night she went missing. She'd exchanged messages and calls with him. So that would make sense.'

Suzanna leaned forward. 'What did he look like?'

'The waitress wasn't able to give a good description. He was turned away; she didn't hear him speak.'

'Hair colour?'

'Fair, but it could be dyed, obviously. And he was sitting – difficult to get an idea of his frame.'

'She didn't see them leave?'

'No. They left through the side doors that lead to the patio. Not through the main exit. He picked his time.'

'Clever.'

'We've established that.'

Brandon's phone beeped.

A text from Chapman. 'We found a toenail in the silk lining of the shoe. It's Rebecca's.'

'Something important?' Suzanna said.

'A toenail. Found in the lining of the shoe.'

'Rebecca's?'

'Yes.' He was watching for Suzanna's reaction.

'She must be dead. I can't imagine he would remove the nail if she was alive.'

Brandon nodded lightly. 'So you think it's his work?'

'Yes. The nail hidden away from the sight of the mother and daughter who lived at the cottage. He would have wanted to spare them. But he knew the forensics would find it.'

Brandon stood up. 'I best be getting back to the station.' He felt for his jacket on the back of the chair. 'Thank you for your time. I'd like to run things past you, as they come in – get you up to speed on developments so far – if you're happy with that?'

Suzanna got up from the table. 'Yes. I want, I need, to work on this case. It's a story that needs resolution. We have a resourceful, manipulative and damaged man who will keep on killing women, keep on reliving his own trauma, until we stop him.'

Suzanna paused before continuing: 'When a child's history involves suffering a significant trauma, they are unable to mature and can remain stuck in that specific developmental stage where the trauma occurred. This developmental impairment leads to emotional dysregulation in adult life. It affects their judgement and ability to regulate their emotions in a rational and balanced way. The structure of the personality is altered. They grow up in a confused state; forming healthy relationships with others is challenging.'

Brandon looked her in the eye. 'I'll be in touch. Send over the files we have so far. If you could reciprocate? That would be extremely helpful. And thanks for the lemonade. Real good.'

Suzanna stepped away, reached up to a cupboard, and pulled out a plastic flask. She poured the rest of the lemonade into it and passed it to Brandon.

Brandon smiled. 'Thank you,' he said taking the flask and walking to the door. Clouds were gathering as he left the house, head down, deep in thought.

Brandon

June 17, 2019

Thirty minutes later Brandon was at St Piran's Secondary School sitting before his daughter's form teacher, her words hitting him like shore breakers. Jeanette Major had requested a meeting because of slight concerns over Chelsea's recent behaviour.

A clock ticked loudly on the wall behind his head, reminding him of all the other things he had on that day. He let her talk, observing the frame on the desk between them. It displayed a photo of an amiable-looking couple in holiday clothes and a girl, around five, with a determined, toothy smile. The forty-something woman across the table stopped talking and fixed him with the same smile, even more potent today with its coating of red.

Brandon leaned forward, resting his arms on his legs. 'I hear what you're saying, Jeanette.'

She continued. 'As well as Chelsea's insistence on wearing make-up and rolling her skirt up far too high, there are other issues. Homework in late, or not at all. Some unexplained absences from class, or late reports. It's a constant drip drip of low-level disobedience. Chelsea is, of course, as charming as ever when challenged.' She paused: 'Is everything okay at home?'

Brandon brushed a hand across his mouth. 'Thanks for letting me know, Jeanette. I'll have a word with her. Is there anything I can do?' He looked into the questioning eyes behind light-framed glasses. They didn't register alarm, just disquiet.

'No, not at the moment. Just a word, I should think. Quite often that's enough.'

He'd wondered why Chelsea hadn't been asking for help with her homework; he'd hoped she didn't need any.

Brandon stood up, feeling for the coat he'd draped on the back of his chair.

'Thank you for coming in at such short notice, Brandon. I'm sure we can nip this in the bud.'

Jeanette remained seated at her desk, making Brandon stand like a schoolboy waiting to be excused. He was reminded of his first day at St Piran's twenty-one years ago – standing in the Head's office with his mom, the new kid in town with the yank accent.

She hesitated before saying: 'Is Chelsea missing her family and friends in Texas?'

Brandon shrugged on his coat. 'I wouldn't say so. We've been back in Penzance for five years or more – since her mom died.'

Jeanette nodded sympathetically.

'We have little family in the States now. Chelsea's grandma, my mom, is here, as you know. And her grandaddy keeps us all amused.' Brandon smiled, thinking of his pop and his legendary stories.

'If there isn't anything else?' he said.

'There is one other thing, now you're here.' She gestured to Brandon to sit down, but he remained standing. 'I just wanted to thank you for sorting out our little drugs problem last term. The police presence at the school gates was very reassuring. Have the culprits been sentenced?'

Brandon felt in his pocket for his car keys. 'Thankfully, that county line has been severed. At least for the time being. But be alert to any suspicious behaviour – either from your students or people hanging around outside during school hours. Descriptions, photos – the best visual information you can provide. And, of course, call the station immediately.'

He made for the door, but Jeanette beat him to it.

'Thanks for letting me know about Chelsea,' he said. 'It's easy to miss these little signs.'

'Yes. Yes, it is.' Jeannette met his gaze as he passed through the door and out into the corridor.

He gave a small smile as he left, feeling the pressure of those eyes on his back as he walked away.

Chelsea. She'd coped so well since her mom had died. She'd seemed fine. Were things going to change now she was fifteen? He couldn't see it, but Jessica would have known if something was up.

When he was clear of the entrance he put in a call to the station. Jo was out, presumably following up leads. He beeped open his car, took off his coat and slung it in the back, forgetting there was a greasy burger carton on the seat. Glancing at the clock, he reversed out of the carpark. He'd head straight back to the station, check on things.

Fumbling in the glove compartment for his packet of cigarettes, he pulled one out and lit up, steering the car with one hand onto the main drag. He felt for a CD in the side pocket and slipped it into the player, allowing himself to be transported back to the Alabama of his youth and the company of the old boys who played in the waterway bars. He'd sat amongst them often enough, legs dangling over the side of the jetty, his pop drinking and chatting, while someone played the blues.

It wasn't a bad place to be. For him, much of the charm of Penzance was the water and the music and the gentle rhythm of life. It was a lifestyle he would protect as best he could. Pulling up at a set of red lights, he turned on the windscreen wipers. It was raining again.

Creature

July 29, 2019

'I feel sad today.'

How to answer that? It had come apropos of nothing – like a solitary drop of rain on a fine day.

'I wanted to show you my gallery, but I don't know now. I don't know.' His brow was creased and he rubbed it with the back of his hand, before glancing back up at her.

'I've been looking forward to it.' She returned his gaze with an encouraging smile. 'So much. I thought we could finish our breakfast and spend the rest of the morning there.'

She folded the napkin on her lap and placed it beside her plate. This was the second morning they'd spent together in the garden. Yesterday's breakfast had been clouded by her interest in the gate. She wouldn't make that mistake again. She'd had plenty of time to consider it – back in the room, back in the chair, back at the table with his grotesque guests, and the inedible food all cooked to his idea of perfection.

'This jam is delicious. From the garden?'

He waved a dismissive hand at a trowelled crop of land to his left. 'The strawberry patch – a poor harvest, dug up and ready for next year.'

He lifted a piece of toast to his mouth and then dropped it back on his plate. 'When you're ready, my dear, when you're ready. Don't mind me. Of course I will take you to the gallery. It just makes me a little nervous.'

'Nervous?' She took a bite of toast. And then another. She was going to eat as much as she could, while she had an appetite.

'Silly, I know. Childish. Forgive me.'

She smiled. 'Nothing to forgive. Your work means so much to you, of course you will be nervous.' She reached over for another slice of toast and buttered it quickly.

'You make me happy.' He was smiling at her, as she wiped away a droplet of jam from the side of her mouth. 'Seeing you happy, is enough for me.'

She buttered another slice of toast, smeared it with jam and passed it to him.

He gave a gentle wave of his hand. 'You have it my, dear. Watching you is satisfying enough.'

He followed close behind her as she climbed the turret stairs. She didn't turn her head as she passed the small windows embedded in the stone walls, but caught, from the corner of her eye, visual clues. The curve of a small cove, the yellow of bracken against green; sky, endless sky.

His arm circled her waist when they reached the top of the stairs. He inserted and turned a key – he had so many keys – and pushed open the heavy door. Another hallway, but lighter this time; lined with paintings and shuttered windows on one side, doors on the other. Taking her arm, he walked her to the middle of the hallway and a set of wooden double doors, the sort you'd find at a banquet hall. The thought made her flinch.

He squeezed her arm and took a breath. 'Nervous too? Don't be. I want you to be brutally honest. If I've failed. If I can improve – let me know. I want to learn – I have so much to learn.'

She doubted that, thinking of Chairman Mao and his Hundred Flowers Campaign, which invited ideas and criticism and ended with carnage. Never had there been a better time to lie through her teeth.

There was no smell. It was her first thought when they entered the long, oak-panelled room. Portraits lined the walls. Faces looked down at them like they do in stately homes. They were majestic. Like the portraits of a master, each was different, but had a distinct style.

She walked towards the first portrait and he let her. It was as if in this room, in this realm, she was queen and he was her subject.

The portrait was amateurish, but showed promise. The style tight and derivative. A brass label nailed to the bottom of the frame dated it June 1996. Beauty of the Lake. The subject was seated on a felled tree trunk by an expanse of water, blonde hair cascaded down her shoulders and arms. Her dress was pale blue, dappled with light that filtered through trees. Her face was pale, with just a touch of pink on the cheeks and lips. The eyes were the colour of her gown, a shade darker than the lake. He'd striven for serenity and achieved resignation.

'What do you think?' he said, at last.

She turned to see him clasping his hands together.

She'd hoped for more time to compose her reply. 'It's extraordinary.'

He moved forward a few feet. 'In what way?'

'It's like she's with us in this room.'

'That's what I intended. I wanted to bring her to life. So we could celebrate her. Always.'

'What's her name?'

He looked away and then down at his hands. 'It pains me to say.'

Had she blown it? 'Then don't. Don't. The portrait speaks for itself. She speaks to us.'

'Yes, yes,' he agreed, following her as she moved to the next painting.

'Beautiful,' she said, and meant it, to a certain degree. The setting was stunning – a red-headed woman in a forest, part of the forest, in a dark green and lilac gown.

'You like it?' He'd moved closer; she could smell sweat.

'I love it.'

He hesitated before asking: 'More than the first one?'

'Difficult question.' Damn right it was. She couldn't show favouritism. 'They each have different qualities – one is light … ethereal. The other darker, more intense. It reminds me of—' Should she draw comparisons with a master? Or would he want to be original?

'Reminds you of?' Too late.

'Elements of William Blake's The Forest. Of course, that was a tapestry and this is oil on board, but each conveys the depth and … magical intensity of woodlands.'

His head was bowed.

'The lush, timeless beauty. The promise of renewal as new life pushes through the earth,' she added.

He looked up. 'Blake's Forest is a favourite of mine. The influence was unintentional – but many are. Those seeds of ideas that ferment and come to fruition, in the most unexpected of circumstances.'

He was looking more confident. Was that a good or bad thing?

They moved to a third painting. A nude. She glanced at him, but he was unabashed. It was just a different artistic form to him.

'It's a life study with stunning numinosity,' she said, with all the authority she could muster.

He let out a sharp exhalation. 'I tried. I try so hard to do just that. I—'

He walked back to the doors, rested his forehead against the wood, and stood there for a minute.

He turned and looked her in the eye. 'Can we leave it for now? Come back tomorrow. I would like to think on what you've said. Process it. And then we can resume our tour, tomorrow? Does that suit you?'

'Yes.' It did. She glanced at the 'others', made some mental notes, before walking towards him.

He reached out both hands and she took them. 'Thank you. You understand. I didn't think anyone ever would.'

She swallowed and then looked him in the eye. 'I do understand. Trust me.'

'With all my heart.'

'And soul?'

He gave a short sigh. 'I lost that some time ago.'

When they left the room she was surprised that he turned right towards the set of stairs at the other end of the hall. She gave an imperceptible gasp of fear. Or was it excitement? They were moving away – far away – from the room, with the chair and the bodies. Could anything be worse?

There was no door to the stairs, just a small landing, from which the steps wound up and down. He led her up, allowing her to look, unnoticed, through the turret windows. She recognised the coast line – the distinctive Gurnard's Head promontory, the white house on the clifftop, docile horses feeding on grass, framed by hedgerows of yellow gorse. She knew where she was.

The staircase opened out onto the top floor. Two of the three shuttered windows were partially open to air the space.

'I hope this isn't a rash decision,' he said, letting go of her hand, but blocking the stairs.

There was no answer to that and she let him continue.

'You don't like sleeping downstairs.'

She caught his eye, and he glanced away.

'There is a room, next door to my studio. It's yours, if you'd prefer.'

She'd prefer to go home. To rip the sheets off the bed and escape through the windows. See her son. Calm his terror. Live again. But her choices were few. Right now, she had to choose between a metal chair or a mental case.

'I'd like to see the room, please.'

He smiled and took her hand. The room was charming and spacious. Lemon toile wallpaper, voile lace curtains at the shuttered window, a petite French dressing table and a small, draped, four-poster bed. A woven cane backed chair was in the corner, by a side table and small wooden tapestry stand.

'I'll take it,' she said, smiling, glancing up to gauge his reaction.

He smiled back. 'There is a catch.'

There had to be.

'You allow me to paint you while you sleep.'

'I'm not sleepy.'

'Later. When you are.'

'And will you sleep?'

'I rarely do.'

She walked over and examined the tapestry stand. She ached to do something. Tapestry would be a perfect diversion. 'Do you have any material?'

'Of course. I'll get you a selection. You know how to weave?'

She smiled. 'I'll learn.'

'I have books in the library.'

She swung around. 'Brilliant.'

'I'll take you after lunch,'

Lunch. Her stomach lurched.

'In this wing? In your studio, perhaps? Here?'

'I've prepared something we can eat in the orangery. It's my favourite room. Temperate. Lush. Scented with lemons, oranges and orchids. Brassavola nodosa: Lady-of-the-Night.'

She touched his arm and he stiffened, before relaxing. 'It sounds heavenly.'

'It is,' he said, looking at her. 'It is heaven.'

June 21, 2019

It was past midnight when the call came in. He'd been dozing; a notebook fell off the bed when he reached for his phone. It was Stew, on night duty at the station.

'There's been another delivery.'

Brandon sat up straight. 'What do you mean, delivery?'

'Not Amazon,' Stew chortled.

'Not funny. What is it?'

'A glass box. Same old.'

'You been drinking?'

'No. Had a call from a barman at the Turk's Head, though. He was clearing up outside around eleven and saw this box – under one of the tables. Except, it wasn't just a box.'

'Get to the point.' Brandon ran a hand through his hair. They'd put Stew on a whole bunch of courses. He seemed to be getting worse.

'A hand. A skeletal hand.'

'And?'

Brandon sighed. 'He usually includes another item in his packages. It was dried flowers last time.'

'The barman didn't go into much detail – said there was a bit of old paper in the box.'

Brandon bit his top lip. 'Okay. Phone Al Chapman, tell him to get his guys to the pub ASAP. I'll meet him there. What's the barman called?'

'Toby Jenkins. I told him to stay put and guard the box.

'Good.' Stew was functioning on his usual low-level wattage.

There was a chill in the air – Brandon turned up the collar of his jacket as he got out of his car and crossed the road to the pub. A sign declared the Turk's Head the oldest pub in Penzance. Stepping into the low-ceilinged, cramped interior, he wouldn't argue with that. It was built for working men who drank in huddles. Not hopeful singletons on Huddle, more suited to perching on high stools in sleek, back-lit bars.

Brandon made his way through the thin corridor that led to the kitchens and outside area. It was quiet. He was the first to arrive. Or maybe not – Al was already there, crouched, camera in hand, torch pointed at the box on the floor.

'Good evening Detective Inspector,' he said, without turning.

Could he smell him? Brandon hadn't washed before coming out.

The barman, Toby Jenkins, greeted him. 'I called as soon as I saw it. Looks just like the one in the papers.'

'Thanks,' Brandon said, crouching down to join Al. Two SOCOs had come into the garden and were unrolling their yellow tape.

'Is this really necessary?' Brandon looked at them over his shoulder. 'There's no one to cordon off here, other than the ghosts. We'll be done by daybreak.'

Al nodded. 'The DI's right. Leave it for now.' He waved a hand around the area. 'See what you can pick up.'

The SOCOs went about their business, setting up a lamp and scouring the ground, tables, hedges and patio burner stands for evidence.

'Thoughts?' Brandon said, shifting to put more weight on his left leg.

'A hand from the same body that turned up ten days ago and started off this whole business. The state of decomposition doesn't suggest a new corpse.' Al edged closer and lifted the lid off the box with his careful, gloved fingers. 'It's the right hand – matching the left one we have.'

Brandon shifted his weight back onto his right leg. 'And the document?' He was looking at the piece of parchment paper in the skeletal hand.

'Well, I'm a pathologist, not a poet, but I can see that it looks like a piece of verse. Shakespeare, if my expensive education stands me good.'

Brandon moved in, reaching out a hand to steady himself. Al was balancing on the floor like a yogi, and Brandon wasn't going to suggest – although he darn well felt like it – that Al just pick up the box and put it on the table.

Al began to read the verse:

'And summer's lease hath all too short a date.
Sometime too hot the eye of heaven shines,
And often is his gold complexion dimmed;
And every fair from fair sometime declines,
By chance, or nature's changing course, untrimmed;
But thy eternal summer shall not fade,
Nor lose possession of that fair thou ow'st,
Nor shall death brag thou wand'rest in his shade,
When in eternal lines to Time thou grow'st.
So long as men can breathe, or eyes can see,
So long lives this, and this gives life to thee.'

Brandon stood up before his legs gave up on him. 'Sonnet 18. The first part – the more famous part – has been ripped off.'

Al turned his head to look at him, wobbling slightly on his haunches. 'Very impressive, Detective Inspector. Do you know the first bit, the bit our killer decided to edit out?'

Brandon looked to the heavens for help. 'Don't quote me verbatim, but, it goes something like … Shall I compare thee to a summer's day? Thou art more lovely and more temperate. Rough winds do shake the darling buds of May.'

Al got up to join him. 'I'm impressed. Did they teach you that at the University of Texas Police Academy?'

'No.'

They looked at each other, but Brandon wasn't prepared to bear his soul to Al. Not now, likely never.

'Pub quiz over. How it's going over there?' Brandon turned his attention to forensic officer Nadia McGowan who was picking up a cigarette butt with tweezers.

'Nothing out of the ordinary. We may find traces of DNA on the stubs and the empty glasses and coasters.'

81

Brandon nodded. 'Okay. I'll probably pick up more from the staff tomorrow. Someone may have seen the killer enter the gardens, with a bag, possibly, and even place the box beneath the table. But—' He stopped Al from butting in. 'I doubt whether he would have done anything obvious likely to raise suspicions.'

He turned to Toby. 'How long would you say the box was under the table?'

'Not long. It was a pleasant summer's evening. We had a lot of people in. I was clearing the tables on and off from noon. That box wasn't there much before eight.'

'Did you notice anyone suspicious? A lone man? With a bag?' Brandon watched him struggle to recall.

'The crowd were mostly couples. Some groups of four or five. A few people on their own, looking like they were waiting for others.'

'And of those, how many usually get up and leave before their friends arrive?'

'Not many. Maybe people who've been stood up.' Toby looked towards the far side of the garden. 'There was a guy sitting over by the fence. He was turned away from the garden – which is unusual, because most people waiting have their eye on the entrance.'

'What did he look like?'

'Late forties. Baseball hat, loose rugby shirt with the collar turned up. Not sure about his trousers.'

'Did he have a bag?'

'Not that I could see. He may have tucked it away against the fence.'

'What time did he leave?'

'It would have been before nine. I was on bar duty for a bit and when I went back out into the garden he wasn't there. Just an empty beer glass.'

'I guess that glass has been washed?' Al cut in.

'Probably. They stack and wash on a rota. He left early, so chances are it was washed.'

'Did you see him leave?' Brandon said.

'No. The bar was busy.'

'Okay, thanks. I'll stop by early tomorrow, speak to the rest of the staff. Someone may well have seen him leave. But you've been incredibly helpful, Toby. Well observed. You can go now.'

The clouds parted and allowed the moon to shine through. The metal edges of the box glowed in its rays.

'I'll get this back to the lab.' Al knelt down and put the box into a plastic container. The contrast between the plastic Tupperware and the aesthetic beauty of the metal-edged glass box was stark.

The SOCOs were finishing up too. Nadia was waiting to cordon off the garden area after they left. 'We'll come back in the morning – may have missed something in the dark.'

Brandon nodded in agreement and turned to Al. 'How soon before we get the DNA results?'

'Should be quick. We have the other hand, of course, although it hasn't been identified. If this is, as I suspect, from the same body, then our work won't take long. Just a case of finding out whose body they belonged to. And that's your department.'

Al turned away.

'If it's not from the same body?' Brandon said to his back.

'It will be. I'll guarantee that.'

June 22, 2019

'Mirror, mirror on the wall, You're still the fairest of them all.'

Jake Nayler's reflection was leering at her and Julia swung around, almost tripping over the hem of her golden gown.

'What the hell are you doing?'

Jake smiled and ran a hand down the bedroom doorframe. 'You said you wanted me to fix that rattling window. The one that's been keeping you up at night.'

Julia turned up her palms in apology. 'Sorry to snap, Jake. I forgot. What time is it?'

'Ten. You want me to come back?'

'No. No. Give me a minute.'

She thought he'd move away from the door, or turn his back so she could slip out of her dress and change, but he stood staring at her.

'It's a beautiful dress,' he said. 'It suits you.'

Julia turned back to the mirror. 'Thank you. I wasn't sure – that's why I was trying it on again. I didn't know whether I could—' She paused. She was talking to a handyman not a girlfriend. But confidantes were in short supply. 'Pull it off.'

'What are you talking about? You look hot.' He wiped his brow theatrically and grinned at her. 'You got a date for the party?'

'Yes.' Julia smoothed an imaginary crease in her dress.

'Well, don't look so happy about it!' Jake's eyes were laughing at her.

'I am happy.' She forced a smile.

'That foreign bloke?'

'Axel, yes.'

Jake held her eye. 'He's a lucky guy.'

She glanced away and summoned up her lady of the manor patter. 'And you, Jake. Are you bringing a young lady?'

'You might say that. Or she might.'

Julia gave him a questioning look.

'I've been trying to dump her for a while. But she's clingy. She's been pressurising me to bring her along. So, what can a chap do?' He shrugged his shoulders.

The elephants in the room were shuffling around looking awkward.

Julia reached a hand to her neck, before looking back up at him.

Jake stepped forward. 'Do you need help with the zip?'

She certainly did. But would this be the point of no return? Axel was lacking in one important department. Was he gay? He didn't act gay. But his hesitant flirtations left her crippled with longing and insecurity.

Jake didn't wait for an answer. He came up behind her, undid the hook and pulled the zip down mid-way. She let the shoulder straps fall off and watched him in the mirror as he raised his head and met her eye. He moved back when he heard footsteps on the landing. Diana. Julia turned round and pulled the straps back up as she arrived with a set of fresh towels. She didn't seem surprised to see them together.

'Jake is going to fix the window frame.'

Diana didn't say anything, just bustled past into the en suite and started to stack the towels.

'You left your tool kit outside the door,' she called out, 'I almost tripped over it.'

Jake looked at Julia. 'I'll go fetch it. Get started.'

'And I'll get changed.'

'Wouldn't want to spoil that beauty,' Jake said, as he walked to the door, glancing over his shoulder at Diana who was standing, in the en suite, her arms folded.

Diana moved aside as Julia went into the bathroom to change. 'Let me help you,' she said, leaning down to pick up the hem of Julia's gown, before shutting the door.

June 23, 2019

Suzanna Fitzgerald was wearing a bright, patterned kaftan; a generous slit revealed her long, slim legs as she walked. A straw hat cast a shadow on one side of her face, giving her an air of mystery. It was a hot day and they were in the garden again. She was pouring him lemonade. Not asking this time. It was good to be in the company of someone who had him sussed.

'Poetry. That's new.' Suzanna was looking at him from below the brim of her hat.

'Turn up for the books. The poetry books.'

Suzanna smiled at his stab at humour. 'It's different.'

Brandon leaned forward. 'Is this significant?'

'Could be.' She waved away a fly hovering over the jug of lemonade. 'Shall I compare thee to a summer's day? The sonnet is a bit of a cliché.'

'It had to be if I knew it,' Brandon said, smiling.

'You knew it from the less famous lines. I wouldn't have done.'

Brandon looked down and then took a sip of lemonade. 'So, are you suggesting that this isn't the work of the SBK?'

'Just a feeling, at the moment. The message in the verse is blatant. It's about a beautiful person. A woman, most likely. And how time will, inevitably, diminish that beauty. Unless—'

'Unless?'

'Someone intervenes. Someone immortalises the subject.'

Brandon rested his hands on the table and studied them.

'And summer's lease hath all too short a date.
Sometime too hot the eye of heaven shines,

And often is his gold complexion dimmed;
And every fair from fair sometime declines,
By chance, or nature's changing course, untrimmed;
But thy eternal summer shall not fade.'

He glanced up and met Suzanna's eye. 'He's protecting them? Preserving their beauty?'

'That may be his MO, but would he spell it out? It seems out of character.'

'And the body parts don't belong to either Clarissa Bowles or Rebecca Morley. We don't know who those hands belong to.'

'They belong to the same person?'

Brandon wiped a hand across his mouth. 'Yes. We have had the forensics report. But they don't match the DNA from the victims who are missing now or those who disappeared in 1996. Of course, the '90s DNA is less reliable. But, regardless, we are none the wiser.'

Brandon glanced at his phone. There was a text from Jo.

'Anything important?'

'No. But I best go. We're trying to trace the boxes and some of the old artefacts. It's a laborious business.'

Suzanna got up. 'I'm sure it is.'

Brandon rose and walked with her through the doors into the kitchen. 'In summary. This last box seems out of character?'

'A little,' Suzanna corrected.

'But the difference is worth bearing in mind?'

'I'd say so. Two boxes. Two hands from a body, which can't be identified. A ham-fisted – excuse the expression – message. One which lacks the subtle sophistication of the SBK.'

She paused, but held his gaze. 'I could most definitely be wrong and, of course, it's been a while since he has been killing. He may have changed his approach.'

'But you don't think so?'

'No.'

'Thanks for your time and the lemonade.' Brandon was at the door, a hand shielding his eyes from the sun.

'A pleasure as always. I hope I've been of some help.' She stood on the doorstep, smiling gently, analysing him. It was in her job description, but that didn't make him feel any more comfortable.

'You have. You've added another dimension. I'll be in touch.'

Brandon walked to his car, replaying the last lines of the sonnet.

'But thy eternal summer shall not fade,
Nor lose possession of that fair thou ow'st,
Nor shall death brag thou wand'rest in his shade,
When in eternal lines to Time thou grow'st.
So long as men can breathe, or eyes can see,
So long lives this, and this gives life to thee.'

Was it a cliché? Or simply something so profound and beautiful that it deserves timeless recognition? If the sonnet wasn't sent by the SBK, it came from someone who understood him. Or thought they did.

June 23, 2019

It was getting on for midnight and Brandon put down the fiddle he'd been playing badly for the past twenty minutes. He couldn't concentrate. Usually the music would carry him away into the moment. But not tonight. There was too much unfinished business to attend to.

Top of the list was Chelsea. She was at his mom's. Again. He felt he was neglecting her – but he'd sort that, once the murder investigations were over. If they ever were. They'd got themselves a psycho with literary pretensions. Breaking the mould. Maybe Will Shakespeare would have been able to fathom the creature, but Brandon sure couldn't. Poetry, ornate caskets and artefacts, bits of dead flesh. All the ingredients for a Shakespearean 'play'. But a nightmare for him.

He picked up his Stentor again, stroked its strings, let the music voice his frustrations, watched his shadow play against the living room curtains. It dipped and lurched as if it was setting the pace and he was trying to keep up. He was tired, that's all. And he couldn't sleep – but that was a good thing; he didn't want to waste time in dreamless slumber. He'd be out there now, hunting the guy down himself, if he could. If the law allowed. He gave the strings a few short strokes, before opening up for a lament. The wood was damp against his chin, he'd been pressing too hard. He relaxed his jaw a little and played out some lazy last chords.

The phone rang as he was packing away his fiddle. He tensed immediately.

'Hi Mom.'

Bad news. It had to be at this hour.

He paused, listening. 'Don't panic. What time did you notice she wasn't at home?' He let her stumble out the details, could hear the fear in her rushed, breathless words.

'Have you called her? Okay. Stay put. Tell Pop to calm down.' His father was banging around in the background. 'I'll go out in the car. Don't worry, Mom. I'll find her. Keep your phone on and charged.'

Brandon clicked her off and then phoned and texted Chelsea. No response. He went onto WhatsApp, holding his breath as he waited for her details to come up. She hadn't been on there since 7pm. It wasn't looking good. Sweat seeped through his pores, his heart raced. Calm down.

Surely the sick bastard wouldn't abduct a schoolgirl? Not his type. He had a type, they'd established that. But he was a killer and Chelsea was the daughter of the DI hounding him. He pushed aside the thoughts. They weren't helping.

He snatched up his car keys and then stopped, sat back down and turned on his iPad. Find My iPhone was the best tracking device at this stage. In the gloom of a kitchen with just a few remaining down lights, the map on the computer glowed with a kind of magic. The familiar streets of Penzance shifted into view, woken from secret dreams. A green dot blinked in one of them – Bread Street. What the fuck! Had some homeless mugger got her phone? Or worse. He had a sudden vision of Chelsea, make-up on, no glasses, blind as a bat, skirt rolled up to her knickers alone and frightened in some backwater basement. He headed out into the night.

Waves were lashing the sea wall as he drove along the promenade. A huge spray leapt the wall and doused his car, blinding him momentarily. He clicked on the windscreen wipers and kept moving, hugging the kerb which lined the sea front B&Bs before taking an early left into town. The wind was buffeting the car's chassis – there was a storm brewing. Storm Someone's Name. The road curved up to the top of Market Jew Street. He cruised it, wary of the shadowy figures in the shop doorways, wondered if the SBK was lurking there among the homeless. Heart pounding, he took a left down one of the narrow side roads which led to Bread Street. The destination was his trump card. His only card.

The street was deserted – just a few lamplights broke the dark, one faulting and casting neon strobes in the puddles below. Turning off his headlights, he checked his iPad for the green spot. He was close, just a few metres up on the right.

Switching off the engine he got out of the car and opened the boot. He kept a taser in there, for emergencies. In the States, it would have been a firearm, but the taser, in the right hands, would do the business.

There was light coming from a small window in one of the houses. The door was shut, but he could hear noise within. It looked like a shuttered shop – running into disrepair like numerous others in the street, in the town. He tried the door handle – the place was locked. He knocked a few times. No answer. Okay, be like that, he thought, walking back a few paces, before launching himself at the door, kicking it down with three mighty thuds.

'What the fuck!' yelled a guy with bright yellow hair, who leapt out of the way as the door caved in on him. 'Man, who invited you?'

Brandon ignored him and surveyed the room. There were several groups of young people wearing their tribe's garb: piercings, tattoos, holey jeans, lurid hair colours. At the back a band was packing up – looked like another acoustic set was about to come on. It was a lock-in gig. Where was Chelsea?

The place was tiny – a small two-bed terrace which had been reinvented many times. Brandon remembered it being an artisan bakery a few years back. Just in front of the door, running alongside the wall, was a wooden staircase. The smell of dope drifted down, filling his nostrils like in the old Bisto ads. A few heads turned as he mounted the stairs – but no one challenged him. He heard people heaving the front door back shut as he reached the landing.

A heavy curtain was draped across the entrance to a bedroom.

'What do you reckon?' someone inside said. 'Sounded like the door was being kicked in. Maybe we're being raided?'

'Maybe you are.' Brandon pulled back the curtain to see a group of teenagers slumped on big cushions. One of them whipped the joint he was smoking behind his back.

'I'll take that,' Brandon said, his eyes on him.

'Your Dad's here,' Damien said, nudging Chelsea who was curled up on a cushion.

She wasn't wearing her glasses. All manner of thoughts and emotions were coursing through him, but that one detail, that one frigging detail, lodged in his brain.

'Where are your glasses? You can't see without them. Where the hell are your glasses!'

'Dad!' Chelsea sprung up from the cushion. 'Dad!'

'Don't Dad, me, young lady. Get your things together now! Right now! Questions can wait.'

Brandon gave Damien a cutting look. 'If I catch you messing with my daughter again there'll be hell to pay.'

He turned his attention to the two others cowering on the floor. 'Nick – who'd of thought it?'

Nick looked down. 'Sorry, Brandon, it won't happen again. It's just …'

Nick's friend Jack blustered in. 'We really wanted to see this band. They are huge! What other chance would we have got? None if we'd asked nicely.'

Brandon shook his head. 'Don't soft talk me with band chat. It's gone one and you've been smoking weed. You've got a lot of explaining to do to your parents. All of you get your stuff. We're leaving now.'

Brandon brushed aside the curtain and headed down the stairs, the kids in tow. The guy with the yellow hair was at the bottom waiting for him.

'Is this your gaff?' Brandon said, looking him straight in the eye, the kids banking up behind him.

'What's it to you?'

Brandon brought out his badge. 'What's your name?'

He hesitated before replying. 'Luke. Luke Foster.'

'Mr Foster, I want you to close up now and I expect you to report at the station first thing tomorrow.'

'On what charge?'

'Pedalling drugs to underage kids, first up. Be there tomorrow morning. And get a proper lock for the door – you won't be doing business here for some time.'

Brandon went out into the street and beeped open his car. 'Get in.'

Damien moved to walk away, but Brandon called him back. 'And you.'

Damien looked stunned. 'I can walk.'

'Get in.'

He dropped Jack off first, waited for his dad to answer the door and then went on to Damien's.

'Mum won't be up,' he said quietly. 'I don't like to wake her. It won't do you any good, either. She'll be more likely to bawl you out than me.'

Brandon frowned, but let him go.

'Just you two, then?' Brandon said, turning to Chelsea and Nick in the back.

'You best drop me at Grandma's,' Chelsea said, 'My school stuff's there … and my glasses.'

'Why didn't you answer my text, Chelsea?'

Chelsea looked at him from below heavily made-up eyebrows. They gleamed like stick-ons. 'I couldn't see, Dad. I heard the ping, but I couldn't read it.' Her top lip started to tremble. 'Don't be mad at me.'

He sighed. 'I am so mad at you. Don't you ever do this to me again.'

'Sorry, Dad.' Tears were streaming down her face.

Brandon lent over and stroked her hair. 'We'll speak after school. Let's not keep your Grandma waiting any longer.' Brandon had texted his mom as soon as they were out of the lock-in.

She opened the door immediately when Brandon pulled up outside the cottage, Chelsea rushing to her.

'Just you and me then, Nick.' Brandon patted the passenger seat headrest in a sign for him to join him up front. Nick scurried round obediently.

It was a twenty-minute drive from Paul, past Mousehole, Newlyn and Penzance, to The Hall on the outskirts of town. Plenty of time to pick his brains.

'So how many times have you been nipping out for late night gigs and a smoke?'

'Not that often. It's a new thing.'

'Oh yeah?'

'Yeah. Imperfect Storm have just started playing these pop-up gigs. There was one in St Ives before Christmas and another in Bread Street a week back. Jack and I went to that one. This is Chelsea's first. No kidding. And Damien tagged along. He's a strange one, but Chelsea likes him.'

'I know the family well,' Brandon said ruefully.

Brandon felt for a cigarette in his coat pocket. 'Pretentious name – Imperfect Storm.'

'Here, have one of mine,' Nick said, pulling one out and lighting it for him.

Brandon smiled wryly. 'This has got to stop, you know. You've got school tomorrow. You're not even fifteen yet, are you? You'll worry your mom sick.'

Nick turned his head to the side window. 'I don't think she's noticed. I don't think this would even cross her mind.'

They sat silent for a while, both intent on the road ahead, Brandon's headlights full-beam, illuminating the trees and, from time to time, a nocturnal animal.

'It's been a difficult period, hasn't it?' Brandon ventured.

'Nothing changes, does it?'

'What do you mean?'

'It was difficult with Sam. Difficult without Sam. And now.'

'And now?'

'There's a killer on the loose looking to hook up with fit women and my mum's on dating apps. Mind if I have a cigarette?' Nick went to take one.

'Sure do.'

'But …'

'There's only one adult sitting in this car and he's driving you home.' Brandon took a long drag. 'Has your mom met anyone yet?'

'Early days, but there is someone. He's been to the house a few times.'

The windows were steaming up. Brandon rolled his down a little. 'Do you like him?'

Nick turned to the side window again, ran a finger through the condensation. 'I can't really make him out. I like him, well enough. He can be cool – interesting to have around. Anyone would be better than Sam. But he doesn't seem … I don't know. Real.' He drew a smiley face with his finger. 'It's like he has created himself – or a version of himself, he thinks we will buy.'

'He's just trying to impress you, son. Your mom's a fine woman. You can't blame a guy for trying.'

'Could be the dope – mind expanding and all that. And I'm doing English Lit. Forget I said it.' Nick turned back to Brandon. 'But, you know, you wouldn't expect to find him kicking around a ball on the football pitch.'

'Well, that's something in his favour.' Brandon smiled as he studied Nick in the mirror.

They were on the promenade, the waves still bashing the sea wall, tossing seaweed, stones and spray at them.

'Are you going to knock up the house when we get back?'

Brandon had been thinking about that himself. He didn't see there was an awful lot of point. Nick was, despite this night-time excursion, a sensible boy.

'No. I trust you'll tell your mom in the morning. Just don't do it again.' They were turning into the lane which led to The Hall. Even from this distance he could see a light burning in one of the upstairs windows. Was Julia up?

Brandon turned off the car lights as he drove onto the forecourt. 'Turn the security back on,' he said, as Nick hopped out.

'Thanks, Brandon. It won't happen again.'

Brandon waited until Nick had slipped in through the front door. When it closed he glanced up at the lighted window and thought he saw a figure draw away into the gloom.

Creature

July 29, 2019

He'd been as good as his word. She lay on a satin, quilted eiderdown, a fine cotton sheet covered one side of her body, falling artfully away over the side of the four-poster. He'd given her a simple white Victorian nightdress to wear. Her head rested on one of four pillows embroidered with lilac, cornflower blue and yellow flowers.

'Sleep, princess,' he said. And she closed her eyes and listened to the sound of pencil on paper, sure strokes and pauses. Now was the time to sleep. If she could. Under her lashes she surveyed the room. The key was in the door. She drew in a breath. The shutters were open, to give him light, but the window was shut fast. She hadn't had a chance to see what was outside. Whether it was a steep drop. Her arm was beginning to go numb from her resting position and she shifted slightly.

'Are you okay, darling?'

'Yes. Just getting a little more comfortable.'

'Do you need another pillow?'

'No, I'm fine.'

This wasn't as bad as being clamped to the chair in that awful room. But it wasn't a night at the Ritz, either. It would be impossible to sleep. She wouldn't try.

She was drowsy when she woke. The shutters had been closed and the only light in the room came from a small lamp by his

99

easel. Her head felt heavy as she tried to raise it. Had he drugged her? He must have done – she'd only felt like this a few times before. Each time after taking a sedative.

She steadied herself and listened. He was still in the room. She could hear him snoring quietly in his chair. When she raised her head a fraction she could see his pencil in his lap, his eyes closed, his head on one side. The key was still in the lock. The realisation made her catch her breath and her heart began to beat faster. Her mind was racing, adrenaline kicking in. The cotton sheet had fallen on the floor and he hadn't attempted to cover her with it, despite the chill. He had to be asleep. But how deeply? She reached down to the sheet. It would be her alibi, if needed. There were ornate mule slippers by the side of the bed. Would they be a hindrance? Everything, she decided, could be ammunition, and slipped off the bed to pick them up, tucking them into her knickers, still holding onto the sheet.

He let out a low, shuddering snore and she froze. His face was ashen in the dim light – looked like he'd needed the sleep – but he still held the advantage. Every single advantage – apart from the one she had right then. She was awake and he wasn't.

It was four long steps to the door. Three from where he sat, his head lolling, his breathing even and low. She took a first step. He didn't move. And then a second, letting the sheet fall silently to the floor. If she needed it, it was there, just feet away.

He made a smacking sound with his tongue. She stood perfectly still. He cleared his throat and shifted to the side, folding in his legs to get comfortable. The snoring had stopped, but his breathing was still deep and even.

One more step – her foot pressed down on a loose floorboard, which wobbled and creaked and she silently cursed herself. He shifted again and she took the final step to the door.

She put on the slippers and tested the handle. The door was locked. Her hands shook as she took hold of the key. It was stiff, as she knew it would be, having seen him fumble enough times with ancient keys. She wiggled it. Wiped her hands down her night dress and gripped it between finger and thumb, forcing it one way and then the other, until something clicked. A double lock? She turned it again.

Bang!

Something had fallen on the floor. She looked over her shoulder to see his sketchpad splayed at his feet.

Her hands were damp as she turned the key – slowly this time, terrified it could break.

'Darling?'

She pushed the door open and ran, hitching up her nightdress, the slippers slowing her. She flipped them off, but stooped to pick them up. He was at the door as she hurtled down the turret stairs.

The steps were cold and slippery, but she kept running, leaping the last two steps to the archway that led to the first-floor landing.

He was gaining on her. 'Stop, what are you doing? Stop! You don't know what you're doing, darling. Stop.'

She raced along the landing to the door. It had to be open. Please let it be open. He hadn't stopped to lock it when they'd visited the gallery. She threw herself at it, and it swung open, allowing her to rush through, and slam it shut. She leaned hard against it, breathing heavy, as he pounded on the other side, his full force rattling the metal latch. The bolt cut into her back, but it felt loose. Loose enough for her to inch the bar along with one hand, her back still to the door. Each time he pounded the wood, it opened a crack and fell back, allowing her to move the bar further.

He could hear what she was doing. 'It's no good, that bolt won't hold. It won't protect you.'

Her chest was heaving as she pressed her full weight against the door, the metal ripping into her nightdress. One more inch. Just one more fucking inch.

'Open the door, darling. Be sensible. It's for your own good.' His voice whispered against the wood.

In that one unguarded second, she slid the bolt into the bracket and ran. The door at the bottom of the steps was closed and she took a breath before trying the handle. He'd been careless before. Not this time. It was locked fast. She threw herself against it. There wasn't a bolt. She'd seen the door enough times to know that. But no key. No damn key. The hammering upstairs had stopped. He must be taking another route. No time to think it through. She kicked the door again, but it remained firm. Her eyes searched around and settled on the high turret window above. It was small and a potted plant was blocking out most of the light. There was a chance. She stood on tiptoes and moved the pot, feeling for a key. Nothing. She put her hand in the soil and felt around, digging for treasure, before striking something hard. Her heart lurched. Let it be the key. It had to be the key. She'd never been so pleased to see a filthy old piece of metal. Wiping it on her night dress she put it in the lock, resisting the urge to force it. It fitted and she wiggled it gently, letting it find its groove, before turning it to hear an orchestra of music to her ears – the quiet click to freedom.

The garden was lit by a crescent moon and slits of light from the house. She walked swiftly along the stone path, which skirted the vegetable patches, to the iron gate. It was locked, but no matter. She hitched up her dress, grabbed hold of a curve of metal, and pulled herself up to the top, finding footholds in the iron and ivy. As she thought, the gate led to a grassy slope, which fell away to a steep drop and small cove. To her right were the fields she'd seen from the turret windows, the ones that formed part of the coastal walk to Gurnard's Head. She lifted one leg and then the other over the top of the gate, twisted round and climbed down. She still had the slippers, tucked into her pants. Not needed as she ran along the clifftop towards the fields. But on the road. She'd need them on the road home.

Julia

June 30, 2019

Diana Chambers was at the top of a ladder attaching a string of fairy lights to one of the silver birches. She was dictating orders to Jake, who was unfurling the lights from a box. On the patio below a small army of caterers were preparing a hot food area, while others were assembling small round tables and chairs that spilled out onto the lawn.

Julia scratched at her neck. It wasn't like her to feel nervous. But she did. No amount of hired help could detract from the fact she faced this alone. There was also a small whiff of disapproval in the community. Was it appropriate to hold a grand party while women were disappearing on the streets? Dead body parts turning up? She'd been made to feel like Marie Antoinette by one of the school mums, who was, nevertheless, coming to the party. Julia pondered the woman's likely outfit. Audrey Hepburn in the Nun's Story? Julie Saint Andrews in the Sound of Music?

Too late to cancel now. Diana was looking up at the window and Julia gave her a small wave. It had been Diana's project. And she didn't have to even attend! All the fun of putting on a lavish spectacle and none of the play-acting. This was intended as a stage to launch her into a new, exciting era. But she didn't feel excited. Just exhausted at the prospect. She stopped herself from rubbing her neck again – in 24 hours' time it would be sticking out of a showy gown.

Jake had finished with the lights and was talking to a guy they'd hired to do the disco and moving pictures karaoke. He had some rolls of plastic to cover the wiring – Jake's suggestion – he'd wanted the place to look good and be safe. Julia was touched by his concern. And something else. He was wearing a tight white t-shirt and shorts and looked like a Hollywood extra. She'd been grateful that Diana had walked in when she had that morning when Jake had helped her with the dress. It had saved her an awful lot of trouble. But, and she winced at the thought, cost her a lot of potential pleasure. Nothing had happened, or been hinted at, since. It left a gnawing disappointment.

It was the same with Axel: early promise and subsequent disappointment. What was she doing wrong? What was she signalling? Had she lost it?

'The flowers have arrived.' Julia turned to see Diana by the door. 'Do you want to advise the florist?'

The old Julia would have snapped into action, watching and politely correcting the flower arranger. But not today. She lacked inspiration and energy.

Diana was waiting for an answer, her face blank, eyes watchful.

'Yes.' Julia pulled her shoulders back. 'I think it's important. Don't you?'

Diana gave a small nod. 'Your choice of flowers is exquisite. Only you can show them to their best advantage.'

Something caught in her throat and she cleared it before answering. 'Diana, thank you. I was beginning to wonder if they were right. If there were too many? Too few?'

'You can never have too many flowers,' Diana said, straightening her collar.

'That is so true. And, of course, there will be homes for them to go to afterwards.'

Diana sniffed. 'They won't take them at the hospitals and hospices any more. Health and safety. They're for us and our guests to enjoy. And rightly so.' She smiled one of her rare smiles.

'Right,' Julia said, stiffening her back and walking to the door to join Diana.

'By the way, Axel Fleming called,' Diana said as they walked along the landing.

'Oh.' Was he cancelling her? 'When?'

'About an hour ago – just before the caterers turned up.'

Julia felt in her pocket for her mobile.

'We best get down to Blooming Beauties so they can get started,' Diana said, glancing at Julia's hand.

'Of course,' Julia replied, putting the phone back in her pocket.

Brandon

July 1, 2019

Brandon was studying a photo of a piece of expensive jewellery on his iPad. The earring had been left in one of the SBK's glass boxes on July 19, 1996, and no one had claimed it. He'd arranged for it to be sent off to an expert in London to get an idea of its worth and, if at all possible, its provenance.

He swiped to another image – this time one of the boxes. It was driving him crazy trying to source them. Jo had scoured the web looking for stockists – new, old, specialist, antique – and had hit a glass wall. They had to come from somewhere – unless he made them himself. He wanted to get analysis of both the glass and the metal – see if their composition and origin could throw up some clues.

'How's it going?' Jo was standing at the door, a suit holder over one shoulder.

Brandon grimaced. 'Slowly. Very slowly. Nothing to go on. Apart from the identikit of the man at The Turk's Head. Looks like Niki Lauda in the artist's impression. Baseball hat, slim, hunched.'

'It's something, Boss.' Jo hung the suit holder on the back of the door.

Brandon returned to his iPad.

'So, you don't want to see what you're wearing tonight.'

'No,' he said, smiling wearily. 'I trust you in all things sartorial.'

Jo turned to go. 'I'll leave you to it, then. What time do you want to meet up?'

'I think Julia said a seven start. So eight? I'll pick you up.'

'You're driving … to a party?'

'Yes. Don't intend staying too long. Lot on.'

Jo gave him a thoughtful look. 'There's nothing we can do right now. Limbo. Let's enjoy the night – for Julia's sake. She's put a lot of effort into this. And come under some flak too.'

Brandon twisted his neck to look at her. 'Really?'

'Some noise on social media about the inappropriateness of a party at this time. With a killer on the loose.'

Brandon grimaced. 'Book a cab, Jo, Julia had this planned before all this kicked off. She's been through hell and back.'

Jo looked down. 'Rachel coming?'

'I don't know – but I wouldn't be much of a detective if I didn't suspect so.'

'Well, I'm looking forward to it. I can practice my flirtatious moves for my undercover role.'

Brandon looked at her and grinned. 'Perhaps you're taking your new work a little too seriously? Any dates set up?'

'Not tonight. Tonight I'm going over to the dark side.'

'Who are you channelling?'

'Lauren Bacall? Some sassy broad. And you, Boss.'

'You tell me, Lauren?'

'Edward G Robertson as Al Capone.'

'If you say so. Not exactly a looker, Jo. But, I guess, crime ain't pretty.'

He turned back to his iPad.

'I'll book the cab for 7.30,' Jo said, walking to the door.

'Sure. By the way.'

Jo stopped and turned.

'You reckon he'll be lurking?'

Jo's face hardened. 'The killer?'

'Yep. If the party is the talk of the town, as the gossip you report suggests, it might pique his appetite.'

Jo looked at a spot on the far wall. 'Hadn't thought of that. It would be risky for him, wouldn't it?'

'But tempting. All those pretty young-ish things, congregating in a beautiful setting, in all their finery. Just a thought.'

'A good one, Boss.'

'I'll send over a copy of the identikit. See you at 7.30.'

Julia

July 1, 2019

She watched from her bedroom window as the first guests arrived. The cars weren't limos, but there was a real Hollywood feel about the sight of plush motors being ushered in by valets, their occupants stepping out like peacocks, Diana and her attendants at the door to welcome them with champagne.

'We should go down,' Julia said, although she was reluctant to move.

'Not just yet.' Axel was at her side and he touched her bare arm, sparking a delicious sensation. She could have made love to him there and then. But it was out of the question. The teasing closeness, his conspiratorial whispers and glances, were tormenting her. He looked incredible – better than Robert Redford, better than Leo DiCaprio, as Jay Gatsby. His greying hair suited the part; suited his ice blue eyes and cool, Swedish persona. Like Gatsby, he was an enigma.

'You look beautiful, Julia,' he said, smiling at her. 'You deserve to make an entrance.'

'Will you accompany me?' They would look so good together. Her nerves were still jangling, but with exhilaration now. Axel had come good. He'd come more than good – he was magnificent.

'I bought these for you.' He pulled a small box from his pocket and opened it. Julia took a breath – men hardly ever got presents right, let alone something as important as jewellery. She could imagine the look of disapproval on Diana's face as she swept down the stairs wearing something 'not quite right'. She opened the box and they were perfect; discreet diamond earrings, which would add a touch of sparkle and not detract from the shimmering gold of her dress.

'They are beautiful, Axel. Thank you for loaning them to me.'

'They're yours.'

'But I couldn't accept something so—'

'They're yours,' he said, 'Please try them.'

He watched as she fixed them to her ears, a frown of concentration on his face. She twisted her head this way and that in front of the mirror, watching as they caught the light, tucking a fallen lock behind her ear.

'Ready now?' he said, as she turned away from her reflection satisfied.

'Yes.' She picked up her clutch with her phone and lipstick, but put it down again as she noted Axel's look of disapproval.

He opened the bedroom door for her and she walked through and out onto the landing, preparing to make her grand entrance down the stairs. At the top of the stairs, she paused and looked down – people were mingling but starting to turn and look up. Rachel was grinning at her, and touching her wrist, which didn't have a watch, but her message was clear. 'What time do you call this?' What was Rachel wearing? She looked like Jessie out of Toy Story. Her boyfriend was by her side, in a casual shirt and jacket. She couldn't help smiling. As she took the first step, Axel came alongside and tucked his arm under hers, escorting her down the staircase.

Rachel gave her a massive hug. 'Sorry, have I crumpled your dress? You look utterly divine! Who are you?'

'Good question!' She pulled away and looked Rachel up and down. 'I think I may be Jean Harlow, or Hedy Lamarr, or a combination of both or many more. I'm a generic starlet.'

'You look fab.'

'And you?'

Rachel smiled, and slapped her thigh. 'Oh come on?'

Julia gave a puzzled look and glanced at Axel.

'Calamity Jane, pleased to meet you. My name is Gatsby. Jay Gatsby.'

'Pleased to meet you too, particularly as you got my outfit. Honestly, how many female cowgirls were there in the Golden Age of cinema?'

'Only one Calamity, but there was also Cat Ballou,' Axel said, smiling kindly.

Julia studied the man at Rachel's side. He could have been any dressed down Hollywood lead – from Cary Grant to Montgomery Cliff.

He handed her a card.

Julia took it and read: 'Bates Hotel. Norman Bates?'

'The ultimate geek psycho. They don't make them like that anymore.'

Axel appraised the couple before them. Accepting champagne from a waiter, he passed a flute to Julia.

'I'll catch you both later,' Julia said, gliding away, Axel in attendance, to meet and greet her other guests.

The place was thick with people in all manner of costume. In the midst she saw Rachel cosying up to her man. They were well-suited, and it stung. Just a bit. As if reading her thoughts, Axel touched her shoulder and bent his neck to whisper in her ear. 'There's no one in this room to match you. Your beauty and poise is innate.' She would have liked him to wrap an arm around her and pull her close. But he didn't. He never did. In many respects, he was like a Hollywood leading man – a gay one; a handsome, charming walker for lonely stars. It wasn't working. Their relationship, no matter how gilt-edged, wasn't working. She'd got more spark from her husband Sam, particularly in the early days. Her first boyfriend Jago had at least given her Nick, the love of her life. She wouldn't let it wreck her evening, but this couldn't go on.

Diana was at the door letting in a new bout of guests. Julia watched Jake Nayler swipe two glasses of champagne, one for himself and one for his girl, a peroxide blonde in a faux fur coat and tight red dress. He was wearing jeans, a white T-Shirt and red Harrington Jacket, his hair pushed back off his forehead. James Dean in *Rebel Without A Cause*. Perfect. He'd caught her watching and was making his way over, his girlfriend at his side gulping champagne.

'Wow. Belle of the Ball,' Jake said, standing before her, his girlfriend tucking her arm under his possessively.

'Mae West?' said his girl.

'Just because I'm pleased to see Julia, doesn't mean to say she's done up as tinsel town's notorious old tart.' Jake had put her firmly in her place and she moved back, scowling.

'She's Grace Kelly, of course. Pure class.' Axel had moved to defend her. But she didn't need, or want, his protection tonight. She'd been under wraps for too long and, in the immortal words of the Hollywood great, Bette Davis: 'Fasten your seat belts, it's going to be a bumpy night.'

'Excuse me,' she said, giving Jake and the blonde a polite

smile and moving towards the door. Brandon was there in a sharp pinstripe suit, his outfit, for once, accentuating his tall, broad shouldered figure. Jo was at his side in an even sharper, fitted grey suit. Her titian hair was parted on the side, skimming her shoulders in glossy waves. Brandon took a glass of red wine from Diana and walked towards Julia, planting a kiss on her cheek, before standing back to admire her.

'You look lovely,' he said, the simplicity and sincerity of the statement threatened to bring tears to her eyes.

'Thank you. You look – incredible too. Al Capone? You've gone to the dark side?'

Brandon grinned. 'My partner's idea.'

'You look stunning, Jo!' Julia said, and she meant it.

'I scrub up well,' Jo replied, reddening.

'What have you got in the case?' Axel had joined them.

Brandon looked down at his violin case, before raising his eyes slowly to meet Axel's. 'My weapon of choice. A Stentor Messina.'

'You play the violin?'

Julia answered for Brandon. 'He plays the fiddle beautifully. Blues, Blue Grass, Hot Club de Paris. I hope you'll play for us tonight, Brandon?'

'Well, that wasn't on the invite.'

'But, as you've brought your instrument, perhaps you would indulge us?' Axel, extended his hand. 'Axel Fleming. Jay Gatsby for the night.'

'Brandon Hammett, and this,' Brandon watched Axel look at Jo, 'This is Jo Menhenrick. My partner – police partner – and gangster moll for the night.'

'Any particular one?' Axel had turned to Jo.

'I'd say Lauren Bacall, but I don't think she was actually a moll. Just hung out with shady guys.'

'Good answer,' Axel said.

'I hope to see you on the stage later, Brandon.' Julia was looking towards the back of the room and the open French windows, where you could see the garden setting, with its fairy lights and flowers and pretty tables and chairs. 'We've got a disco. But it would be fun for people to do turns. I have a karaoke machine set up too.'

'I think I could be persuaded.'

Julia saw him peer over her shoulder and scan the room. 'Rachel's here.'

He looked at her. 'Good. Good. I haven't seen Rachel for some time. It will be good to catch up.

The four of them looked at each other for a moment, before filing away as couples in different directions.

Two hours later, Julia and Rachel had escaped to the chapel at the top of the grounds for a private chat.

Julia topped them both up with pink champagne and they sat on the bench by the side of the ancient church and looked down the slope to the throng. It was a balmy summer's night and it was magical: people dancing and chatting under the fairy lights and stars, older people seated at tables tucking into food, Nick and his mates hunched over their phones, punctuating the night with peals of laughter.

'So, tell me about Axel? The Ice Prince.' Rachel was looking ahead, but Julia didn't need to read her face. 'I'm surprised he hasn't tracked us to the chapel.'

'Rachel!'

'He's gorgeous, of course. You deserve your Scandiman. You look Hollywood Royalty.'

Julia sighed. 'Look like. Rachel—'

Rachel turned to face her. 'What is it?'

'I don't know.' Julia looked down and then threw back her head and ran a hand through her hair.

'It's like going out with a vision of perfection. A hologram. When I go to touch him, there's nothing there.'

Rachel sat up straight. 'He's frigid?'

Julia shook her head lightly. 'I haven't got as far to find out.'

'Have you snogged him?'

Julia gave a hollow laugh. 'Not even a peck on the lips. The cheek, yes. But not the lips. I can't take this any longer.'

Rachel edged forward on the bench, still watching the performance below. 'How long have you been seeing him?'

'Around three weeks – since the first messages on BetterThanAllTheRest. I can appreciate he might want to take it slowly. That suited me too – at the start. Now. Now it's driving me to distraction. I can't jump on him because I know

113

he'll draw away.' Julia glanced at Rachel and caught her eye. 'I did try. It was humiliating.'

'I can imagine,' Rachel said, wrapping an arm around her waist and giving her a quick hug. 'But he is still stuck to you, like a gooey fondue, so this is his problem. Not yours. And he knows it.'

Julia squeezed her hand. 'Thanks, Rachel. I suppose I'm going to have to start all over again – probably on Huddle. It has a more immediate appeal – not all this match-making with rich blokes that are all a bit suspect. I mean, why would a multi-millionaire want or need to go on a dating site?' Julia turned to Rachel.

'Because everyone does it? Because money don't buy you love?'

'No,' Julia agreed, 'But women swarm around rich, successful guys, like bees round the honey pot. Not even rich ones – just decent ones. If women as much as sense there's an opportunity – a neglectful wife, or better still, a dead one – that guy will be snapped up.'

'It makes sense,' Rachel said. 'I wasn't looking after I lost Oliver, but there weren't many single men around.'

'Apart from Norman Bates down there.'

'Well, he's a bit suspect, isn't he?'

Julia burst out laughing. 'No! You're perfect together.' She took a sip of champagne and topped them both up.

'You think so?' Rachel's eyes were on Brandon, who was chatting to the guy who was doing the sound.

'I thought you and Brandon might be good for each other. But you're not a perfect fit.'

'No. I love Brandon, but as a friend. He is wonderful. Heaven knows why he hasn't met the right person yet.'

'Well, it took him a while to get over the death of his wife and then you exploded onto his scene, and now he has his hands totally tied with the murder investigations.' It was the first time it had been mentioned that evening. Julia had deliberately steered off the subject and Rachel hadn't brought it up – possibly because she didn't want to spoil the atmosphere either.

'God, yes.' Rachel took a gulp of champagne. 'It's just awful, isn't it? And no progress made. The killer is a fox.' She turned to Julia. 'I don't like you going on those apps. The killer used one to meet his last victim.'

Julia grimaced. 'Well, yes. But that was before we knew his game. He's unlikely to try the same trick again. And—' She looked Rachel in the eye and raised a brow. 'I wasn't born yesterday. I would ensure that everything was trackable and people knew just where I was, etc.'

Rachel bolted upright. Axel was walking away from the tables and stage, and up the slope towards them. 'Don't just give Nick the details, tell me too. Or Brandon. Brandon is definitely your best bet. I agree that,' and she lowered her voice, 'Axel is probably not the one. Not if he can't get physically close to you. Just don't do anything rash. You are such a catch. Take your time. Your prince might not show, but you're absolutely lovely, and the right man will. I promise.'

Tears were pricking Julia's eyes and she sniffed to pull herself together. 'Thank you, Rachel. What would I do without you?'

Rachel took her in her arms as Axel approached and whispered. 'I'm here for you – I might be in London – but I'm right at the end of a call or text. Be careful. Not just of bad dates but … I probably shouldn't say it—'

'Go on, quick.'

'Diana gives me the creeps. There is something of the Mrs Danvers about her. I've felt her dagger eyes on me for much of the evening – even up here!'

Julia moved away, giving her a light kiss on the cheek, as Axel rose before them.

'You look like adorable, nattering prom girls. But I thought you wouldn't want to miss our fiddling detective.'

Brandon

July 2, 2019

He saw them coming down the sloping lawn together; Rachel on her own, Julia trailing behind with Axel Fleming. They looked like something out of a film; the women's dresses less fresh than at the start, Rachel's suede one had grass on it, her hat hung at her back like her rucksack used to, her hair had escaped their pigtails. The hem of Julia's dress was damp, there was a spot of mud on one golden mule, tendrils of hair rested on flushed cheeks. Axel had undone his top shirt button and bow tie. He still looked neat – the lengths of his tie rested either side of his collar, as if measured.

It was past midnight and gas burners were throwing out heat and light; the moon a glitter ball. Brandon started to play the opening chords of *Minnie The Moocher*, a tinkling piano and sax played on a backing track, a *Betty Boop* cartoon was on the big screen behind him.

'I'd like to thank Julia on behalf of all of us here tonight for putting on such a wonderful party. And I'd like to invite our Golden Age beauty onto the stage to join me.'

Brandon ignored her mild protestations and helped her up.

Julia was a class act singing *Moon River*. In that dress she looked like she had breakfast at Tiffany's every day. Axel was smiling encouragingly from below. Brandon noticed she wasn't looking at him, her eyes were ranged way over his head.

'I think that's a wrap,' Brandon said, when the last performer left the stage.

'Not so fast, Dad.' Chelsea had picked this time to emerge from her cluster of teens.

'What are you wearing?' Chelsea had poured herself into a

hot pink bandage dress; her platform shoes put the emphasis on elevation.

'Clothes, duh!' Chelsea rolled her eyes. 'From *Pretty Woman*.' Looked like she'd picked one of the earlier scenes, when Julia Roberts was still a working girl.

'You want to do a duet with me?'

Chelsea grinned up at him. 'Does the bear poo in the forest?'

'As a matter of fact, he does.'

'And?' Chelsea was giving him her exasperated expression.

Brandon reached down and helped her onto the stage.

'I'm going to teach you some fundamental lessons about life, young lady.'

He turned to Gus and mouthed, '*Bear Necessities*'.

'How embarrassing,' Chelsea said as the song opened and Baloo and Mowgli appeared behind them. But she didn't look embarrassed. And the song was just right to finish on. It was past two and people were filtering out, saying their goodbyes.

Jo strolled over as they came off stage. 'Glad you came, Boss?'

'Yeah. Reckon I am.'

'Ready for the off?'

'I'll see you back here in ten,' Brandon said, 'Just need to help Gus pack away.'

Chelsea snuggled up to him. 'You were great, Dad. Awesome. Such fun.'

He held her for a while and then let her go, watching her skip away through the tables and out round the back to join her friends. She was still dating the school delinquent – Damien Kane – but life couldn't be perfect. And he wasn't so bad – his sharp eyes and inquisitive nature had helped him solve his last big case. Brandon sat on the stage, swinging his legs, weary all of a sudden. That case was nothing compared to what he was dealing with now. It was straightforward – motives, money, murder, mistakes – this new one didn't tick the boxes in any way. They had a killer that didn't have an obvious MO, and he was patient. They'd been nothing since the shoe turned up at Gingerbread Cottage. He was biding his time.

Gus was rolling up the screen. 'Want a hand getting that into your van?' Brandon said standing up.

'Thanks, Brandon. And the sound system too.' They could

have left it until tomorrow, but there was no use for it now. The last of the guests were at the door. Brandon could see Julia saying goodbye to a couple that looked like Fred Astaire and Ginger Rogers. Diana was still hovering, getting coats and bags.

The sound system was heavy and it took the two of them to walk it around the grounds to the side passage and out onto the forecourt. Clouds were forming, the moon barely visible.

Chelsea and Jo were sitting on the edge of the stage when they went back to pick up the last of the equipment.

'You guys want a lift back? I've got to go through Penzance and Newlyn?' Gus said.

Brandon was grateful for the offer. He was beat and hadn't booked a cab yet. 'That would be great.'

He picked up his jacket from the back of a chair and scanned the surrounds. 'You seen my fiddle?'

'Back of the van,' Gus said, feeling for his keys.

Brandon frowned. 'Okay. Did you put it there?'

'Don't think so,' Gus said, yawning. 'Maybe by mistake?'

He let it go. Perhaps someone trying to be helpful? He could see Rachel at the door and he moved away. 'Just want to say goodbye to Rachel.'

She was peering through the hallway, probably looking for him.

'Your stage coach out front?' He approached her, a small smile on his face.

Rachel returned his smile and flung her arms around him. 'It was so good to see you. I've missed you.'

Her face was burrowed into his chest and he stopped himself from smoothing back her hair. 'Don't stay away so long next time.'

Brandon and Chelsea were the last to be dropped off. They stood on the cobbled pavement outside their terraced cottage and watched the van drive away, Chelsea giving Gus a departing wave.

Brandon picked up the violin case, which he'd propped against the door and heard something rattle inside. It felt much lighter – he hadn't noticed that when he'd swung it out of the back of the transit. He placed it on the pavement, away from the door.

'What is it, Dad?'

'I don't know. Why don't you go open up – go straight to bed.' He pulled the house keys from his pocket and gave them to her.

She put the key in the door and opened it a crack, before turning back to him.

'Bring it inside, for god's sake,' Chelsea said.

'In a minute.' He didn't know what it was, but some instinct was telling him not to bring the case inside. It didn't feel right. It could be fitted with explosives, for all he knew.

'Can you get me some gloves, darlin?' he said.

'Right.' Chelsea knew exactly where he kept them – bottom drawer of the bureau.

She was back in moments. He took the gloves and put them on. 'Chelsea, go into the house.'

'But, Dad.'

'Into the house. And shut the door.'

Chelsea went in without a whimper. She always knew how far to push him. Brandon took a breath and unclipped the case. There was no explosion. That was always going to be unlikely. He gently pulled back the lid, grimacing when he saw the small glass case.

July 2, 2019

Al Chapman was at his house within twenty minutes. He'd called Julia at the same time and asked for the guest list. They'd go through it first thing in the morning. Which was, Brandon looked at his watch, around three hours off.

Chelsea came out of the door with a flask of coffee and two mugs.

'Thanks, darlin',' he said, giving her a nod of dismissal.

Ed was crouched, taking photos and dictating notes. 'Index toe, early stages of decomposition, clear cut through ligament, nail removed.' He got up. 'It shouldn't take long to identify the body part as belonging to Rebecca Morley. The glass case is smaller, but same composition as the others used by the SBK.'

Brandon grimaced. The man was always too presumptuous. But, in this case, he had to be right.

'Why don't you get a few hours' sleep? I'll get the specimens back to the lab and have the checks down asap.'

'You'll get a team round to Julia Trenowden's?'

Al nodded. 'Consider it done.'

Brandon sucked in a breath. 'There was one small mercy.'

Al cocked his head to one side. 'Enlighten me, Detective Inspector.'

God, the man irked him. For all his scientific expertise, Al lacked crucial emotional intelligence, the oil for the engine of discovery and so many things.

'The killer went to an awful lot of trouble to deliver his message. He could have dropped the case off at the party. It would have been easy with all the comings and goings. But he picked an ingenious and risky way to make his delivery, make his point, and not spoil Julia's night. He showed compassion and consideration.'

'And, possibly, that he knows Julia?' Al's small eyes were shining behind his metal rimmed specs. For a second they looked like specimens in glass cases. Brandon shook his head to rid himself of the illusion.

'I think the killer might well know Julia. Either from a distance, as a stalker, or someone closer. I'll keep that in mind when I'm questioning the guests.'

Al gave him a look – a look that resembled something like respect.

Creature

July 30, 2019

She saw the dipped headlights and knew. She was on the B3306 Coast Road, making her way to the Gurnard's Head pub. It was still a distance off, but she could see light in an upstairs window. Her heart began to beat hard and fast. She'd been careful to keep to the side of the road, just in case she had to shrink from view. As soon as she heard the tell-tale sound of the car engine, she moved into a hedgerow. The car passed and she sighed. Yes, he was on the hunt, but there was an awful lot of tarmac to cover and bushes to hide behind.

She moved back out onto the road and quickened her pace. The mules were impeding her progress, but the tarmac was hard and they were, on balance, better than nothing. The road was rising and curving right, and she lost sight of the pub. All was silent apart from the tweeting of birds and the flapping of her slippers. The incline was heavy-going and she thought of finding somewhere to sleep in the fields. The pub was a haven, but he could be there, waiting in the carpark to catch her before she made contact. She'd get to the top of the hill and make a decision.

The decision was made for her. His car was at the bottom of the slope and when she came into view he switched his headlights on full. She turned immediately, kicking off her slippers and forcing her way through brambles to get into a field.

He was chasing along the road, calling out to her and someone else. She ducked into a field of corn, falling to her knees and crawling towards the far side. Grit and dirt stung legs already grazed by thorns. He couldn't find her in there –

not in the dark – and farm workers would be back at daybreak. Her breathing began to slow, and she curled on the ground, stilling her body like a cornered creature in a catatonic trance. It could only have been a minute before she heard his voice again and other sounds, low and snarling, corn crunched underfoot. She got to her feet and ran – even though there was no point – towards a barn on the western edge of the field. It could be open, it could be open, the words were like a mantra as she tore through the hardened, sharp stalks, the dog gaining on her, panting and snuffling as it nosed through the maize. It was snapping at her heels as she reached the door, with its solid metal bolt and KEEP OUT warnings, and she spun round. The dog, baring its fangs, looked set to spring, before being tugged by the rein and drawn whimpering to heel.

'Look at you,' he said. His usual cool demeanour replaced by contempt, hate even. 'If you could only see yourself. The state you're in.'

All pretence was gone. They were two damaged people playing a high stakes game and right now he was winning. Her nightdress snagged on a piece of wood when she got to her feet, and she jerked forward so it tore before she fell into his arms. Distracted, he didn't notice the piece of cloth left hanging from the door.

Brandon

July 2, 2019

It was at times like this when Brandon was glad he had a beard and didn't have to waste time shaving. It was eleven o'clock the morning after, and the fifteenth of 150 guests was just about to join him and Jo in the interview room. Julia had been brilliant. She'd tucked away any personal disappointments, or indeed, horror, and sent him over the guest list with email addresses and mobile numbers. They had managed to arrange interviews for the majority and would mop up the rest later. The first tranche hadn't thrown up any possible people of interest – well, depending what you meant by interest. He'd had a chance to speak to Rachel again and it took a little while to eliminate her from his inquiries.

The door opened and a tall man with greying hair and light blue eyes walked in. Axel Fleming looked remarkably fresh for someone who'd been up half the night.

Fleming looked at the chair opposite to Brandon, who nodded for him to sit down.

'My partner – DS Menhenrick – will join us shortly,' Brandon said, watching Fleming ease into the chair. 'Ah, here she is now.'

Jo walked into the room, slipped an iPad into her bag, and sat down next to Brandon. 'Good morning, Mr Fleming. Are we ready to start?'

Brandon nodded.

'Interview commences 11.05am,' she said clicking on the desk recorder.

'Could you tell me something about your relationship with Ms Trenowden?' Brandon got the ball rolling.

'We're good friends.'

'Friends?' Brandon leaned forward and rested his arms on the table.

'We've been seeing each other. Dating.'

'Is this a recent thing?'

'Yes, quite recent. We met on a dating site – BetterThanAllTheRest – three or so weeks ago.'

'And things are going well?' Brandon was watching him carefully.

'Very well. Julia is a wonderful woman.'

Brandon smiled in agreement. He could understand too, why she would be attracted to Fleming. He was good-looking and sophisticated and, quite likely, rich.

'What made you go on the site?' Jo said.

Fleming smiled. 'You think I don't look like the sort of person who would go on a dating site?'

Jo remained silent.

He gave a small sigh. 'It's not easy meeting the right person. Julia is the right person.'

'You don't meet women in your work?'

He leaned back in his chair. 'All the time. But it's not like I'm at college.' He gave a short laugh. 'I've reached an age where most compatible women are either married, committed or working from home looking after kids. And I'm a busy man. The site is an efficient way to—' He hesitated. 'Meet women.'

'What do you do for a living?' Brandon gave Jo a quick glance.

'I'm a financier.'

'But you're in Penzance now?'

'Taking a bit of a break. I still work from home, but it's nice to get out of the city.'

'Where is home?'

'London.'

'Originally?'

'Stockholm. You caught my accent?'

Brandon smiled. 'Yes.'

'And you're from the States?'

'Texas. We're both tourists, Mr Fleming.' Brandon looked down and opened his notepad.

'What do you know about the local disappearances?' He raised his eyes and Fleming met them.

'As much as anyone who reads the papers. Shocking. I assume this is why you've called us all in?'

Brandon looked down again, before returning his gaze. 'Do you remember the disappearances in 1996? The so-called Sleeping Beauty Killings?'

'Only from what I've heard this time round. The news wasn't covered in Sweden. Shocking as it was. And I was quite young then.' He smiled.

'A student?'

'Yes.' Fleming began to shift slightly in his seat. He looked at his watch. 'If there's nothing else? I can send you my CV, if it's helpful. And, of course, you can check LinkedIn.'

'The CV would be helpful.'

Fleming got up to go.

'If you don't mind,' Brandon said rising from his chair. 'We'll need to do a DNA swab. Just a formality that all the guests are going through.'

'Of course,' he said. 'I'm only too happy to oblige.'

'Interview terminated at 11.27am,' Jo said, before clicking off the recorder and getting up. 'I'll get someone to take your swab.'

The two men stood facing each other in silence, each long second recorded by the mechanical click of the wall clock.

July 3, 2019

They'd done the formal part of the interview at the station, but Brandon wanted to pick Julia's brains in a more conducive atmosphere. The bench by Hartington Hall Chapel seemed like a good enough spot as any – he'd noticed Julia and Rachel there during the party. It also gave him a panoramic vista of the white suits below.

He'd gone to The Hall to oversee the work of the CSIs. They hadn't found his Stentor yet, which pissed him off. He rubbed his neck. It was a minor irritant in the circumstances.

Julia sat by him surveying her domain. She spread out her arms. 'I feel like selling the place. Maybe I will. I'm rattling around in here with Nick away all day and much of the evening.'

Brandon was looking towards the area where the tables were still arranged, but he wasn't seeing anything in particular. Just yellow tape and white aliens foraging.

'You're seeing someone, though? Axel Fleming?'

Julia sighed. 'Yes. But he's unlikely … it's early days. He won't be moving in anytime soon.'

Brandon kept staring ahead. 'Something not right?'

Julia gave a short laugh. 'Everything is right. Too right. Brandon, I don't want to bore you with girl talk.'

He shifted on the bench. 'I am a detective, Julia.'

'Well, Detective Inspector, there is nothing fishy about Axel. He's fine as a date. Charming. Considerate.'

Brandon let her talk into his silence. It suited him. And then she stopped.

'One of forensics is waving up at us.'

129

Brandon squinted. They all looked much of a muchness in their space suits, but he recognised Chapman's cocky stance.

'Best go down. He's looking excited.' Brandon got up and turned to her. She looked pretty sitting there in a white sundress sprinkled with red roses, her hair smoothed back behind her ears, no make-up. She hardly ever wore make-up. Didn't need to.

'Can I join you?' she said.

He held out his hand. 'It's your place. Don't ever forget that.'

She rose and they walked, hand and hand, for a few steps before they let go and continued down the gardens to the others.

Al Chapman was waiting for them by the taped off area.

'What is it?' Brandon said, reading the look of jubilation on Al's face.

'Nadia found an item of female clothing in the cottage. The one, I believe, occupied by the caretaker.' Al looked at Julia for confirmation.

Julia started, before quickly gaining her composure. 'Jake Nayler has a girlfriend. Stacey, I believe. She was with him last night.'

Brandon nodded. 'I spoke to him earlier. He mentioned Stacey Hunter. But you'll take the item to the lab?'

'Of course,' Al said. 'It's bagged and in the van.'

'Isn't that a little extreme?' Julia's arms were wrapped around her torso, her brow creased.

Al gave Brandon a look. 'If you'll excuse us a minute, Ms Trenowden.'

Brandon followed him a suitable distance.

'A pair of panties were found in a holdall, in a corner under the stairs. They're in good nick – unlikely to be used as a cleaning rag.'

'Well. Well done, Nadia, this could be important. If you could get the checks done immediately I'll arrange for Nayler to come in for further questioning.'

Al gave him a look as if he was spouting the frigging obvious.

Brandon walked back to Julia and left him to it.

'Anything significant?' Julia was looking concerned.

'We won't know until after the examination.'

'Do I need to do anything?'

Brandon regarded her carefully. It was an uncomfortable situation. Nayler was, in all probability, innocent – could have been hiding away evidence for all manner of personal reasons. Didn't want to upset his new woman, possibly. Until the DNA was checked, he was in the clear. But it worried him, all the same. He didn't want to leave Julia alone and vulnerable.

She appeared to read his thoughts. 'I have Nick and Diana – and a lethal left hook. Don't ask me where I picked that up from.' She smiled and rested a hand on his arm. 'Jake just isn't the guy.'

Brandon gave her a long, thoughtful look. How many times had he heard people say similar?

'Be alert,' he said after a while. 'Just a precaution. And call me – anytime, you feel the smallest bit uncomfortable.'

'That is good to hear. Thank you, Brandon.'

He could see Al getting into his van, eager to get back to the lab.

July 5, 2019

Two days later Jake Nayler was sitting in the investigation room on the basis of DNA on Rebecca Morley's knickers. Nayler looked mighty cheesed off. The Stentor had yet to pitch up, but a suspect piece of underwear had. Brandon shelved his misgivings and signalled to Jo to start recording.

Jake was lolling back in his chair, Jimmy Shapter, a legal aid lawyer, by his side.

'Shall we get started?' Brandon said, looking him straight in the eye.

Jake smirked. 'Why not. I'm being paid to sit here chewing the fat over a pile of rubbish.'

'You deny hiding the panties in your holdall?'

'Yeah. Why would I?'

Brandon stared him down. But he had a valid point. Why? There were many ways that he could have disposed of such a flimsy piece of evidence.

'Do you also deny meeting Rebecca Morley after a series of messages via Huddle.'

'Yeah.'

'Your phone, Ms Morley's phone and the dating app's records show differently.'

Jake sighed and shook his head. 'I've been set up.'

Brandon passed him a photograph of Rebecca Morley. 'You're telling me that you've never met this woman. Never messaged her on Huddle?'

Jake looked at the photo and frowned. 'I did meet someone who looks like her. A Susanna … Suzy. Can't remember her surname.'

'So you recognise Rebecca, or Susanna, as she called herself, from this photograph. But you didn't recognise her from the photos in the news?'

Jimmy was whispering in his ear.

'I don't get time to read the papers. And she looks different in this photo. Hair shorter.'

Brandon stayed silent. So did Jake.

'Did you go on a date with Suzy? The messages suggest you met up on March 4 at The Lido. The same venue she was last seen at.'

Jimmy went to say something, but Jake raised a palm to quieten him.

'I did meet Suzy, or Rebecca, or whatever the lady liked to call herself. We met at The Lido back in March. We didn't click. It didn't go any further.'

Brandon leaned forward. 'Why?'

Jake rolled his eyes. 'Full of herself. Had all these plans—' He rocked back in his chair and then fell forward, hunching over the table as if poised to say something in the strictest confidence. 'I don't want to speak ill of the dead, but I got the feeling she thought I wasn't good enough for her, but would make a good support act.'

'Did that annoy you?'

Jake was looking at his hands. 'Not particularly. She was too good for me.'

Jo glanced at Brandon. 'But you're a good looking man. And confident. Why would you think that?'

Jake looked at Jo and smiled. 'Well, that's the most audacious chat up line I've ever heard, detective.'

Jo looked ruffled and Brandon stifled a smile.

'You know what she means, Mr Nayler. You don't strike me as being the sort of guy that's shy with the ladies. In fact, your name – or names – are all over Huddle. Which suggests you have some pulling power and front.'

'How many of those other dates have gone missing, Detective Inspector?'

Brandon held his eye, but it was hard.

'Maybe you were waiting to meet the right one?'

Jake blew out and rocked back in his chair. 'Look. I met Suzy … Rebecca, and it was fairly clear from the start that I wasn't her type. Not a 'keeper', that's for sure. She was – is – a successful business woman. Beauty, brains and ambition. What would she want with an electrician? A handyman?' He paused and looked at one hand, a plaster unravelling on his thumb.

'She ran a café. I'm sure your skills would have been useful.'

Jake sighed. 'Yeah. Maybe. We just didn't gel.'

'From the phone records it seems that Rebecca liked you. There were 40 calls from her mobile to your burner between March 1 and April 27. Just one reply.' Jo was reading from notes.

'I didn't kill her. I didn't run away with her. If I'm guilty of anything, I ran away from her.'

Jo looked at Brandon and edged forward on her chair. 'She was chasing you?'

Jake looked her in the eye. 'I guess so. I don't like to rat on a lady – particularly one in trouble – one who can't defend herself. But yes. We weren't right for each other, but I reckon she was desperate.'

'Nathan Morley, Rebecca's brother, said he saw you together at The Vault in the Market Place on March 15. She came home distressed an hour later.'

Jake grimaced. 'I dumped her. I told her it just wasn't going to work. That she should find someone more … like her. I wasn't good enough for her.' He looked to the side, caught Jimmy's eye. His lawyer had remained silent throughout – Jake could handle his own defence.

'Sometimes you have to be cruel to be kind.' He was looking at Jo as if giving her a life lesson.

'That's a cliché, Mr Nayler.'

'Yep – that's what you get from the great unwashed. We weren't right for each other. There was no chemistry. She was needy and I didn't have anything to give.'

'How was she needy?' Jo held his gaze.

Jake twisted in his chair. 'This is becoming more like a therapy session.'

'Answer the question,' Brandon cut in.

'She was trying too hard. Talking too much. In my face. Wanting to know about past girlfriends – current ones. Yeah. She wanted exclusivity and I wasn't ready to give it.'

'She wanted commitment?' Jo said.

'And all the trimmings?'

'What do you mean?' Jo was sitting ramrod straight in her chair.

135

Jake shook his head in disbelief. 'She was getting on … or so she kept telling me. Thirty-four, or something. She wanted a partner. Kids.'

'She wanted you?' Brandon said, watching him closely.

Jimmy went to say something, but Jake shushed him. 'Apparently. But, I felt, it was just about … timing, I ticked a lot of the boxes.' He looked at Jo, 'As far as she was concerned. I was presentable, the right age, had a job with quite a good income. Rebecca – although aspirational, if that's the right word – wasn't rich. The café just about paying its way. If truth be known, my skills would probably have been a bonus for her.' He paused. 'Look. There was nothing personal in our split – I tried to tell her that. She just wanted things I didn't, at this time. I didn't, and don't, want to settle down yet. Until I meet the right person, that is.' He looked Jo in the eye, but she wasn't going to fall for that one.

'Stacey?' Jo said, 'You're not on the dating sites anymore.'

'No and no.' Jake glanced up at the clock. 'Stacey isn't the one. But I'm not looking around at the moment. Got my hands full at The Hall.'

'You weren't at The Hall when you were seeing Rebecca?' Brandon said.

'No. I was living in Heamoor. At a mate's.'

'Name and address?'

'Ricky Mason. 8 Crofters Cottages.'

'Where were you on the night of June 15?' Brandon was leaning forward.

'At home. The cottage on The Hartington estate.'

'Alone?'

'Yes. There was a match on.'

'You didn't fancy going to the pub to see it?'

'No. I've got Sky. And I'd had enough company for the day.' He rolled his eyes.

Brandon remained silent.

'Diana – the housekeeper – had been giving me hell over some minor thing. Stacey was bitching about coming to see my new pad. She was facetiming me, if you want to check my records.'

Brandon nodded.

'I just wanted some me time. Men are allowed that too, aren't they?'

Jimmy smirked.

'How did those pants end up in the holdall under the stairs?'

'Some bugger put them there. Set me up. Why the fuck would I keep hold of a missing woman's knickers.'

'You tell me.' Brandon said holding his gaze.

Jake shook his head slowly. 'I can't help you any further. I'm not your guy.'

'You don't appear to be anyone's guy,' Jo said.

Jake shot her a look, before turning to Jimmy. 'Can I go now?'

'Any further questions, Detective Inspector?'

'Not for now,' Brandon said. 'Where can we reach you, Mr Naylor?'

'8 Crofter's Cottage. My place is a crime scene.'

They'd turned the place over – had found some strands of Rebecca's hair. But nothing which would incriminate Nayler. No one had seen her at the cottage. Or anywhere near it.

Jo signed off the interview and they watched Jake and Jimmy leave the room.

'What do you think?' Jo said, when they were out of ear shot.

'He has no motive, as far as I can tell. And those panties could have been planted. We'll go through his movements on the night of June 15. But I'm not hopeful. What about you, Jo. Thoughts?'

'He doth protest too much, in my opinion.'

'We are questioning him about abduction and possible murder, Jo.'

'Yes – but all this, I want to be free stuff. Why? He's not that young. Why wouldn't he want to settle down?'

'Because, like he said, he hasn't met the right one?'

'Or maybe he's a sad loner?'

'You picked up that vibe?' Brandon raised an eyebrow.

Jo grimaced. 'He came over a bit … creepy.'

'He was hitting on you, Jo. Which, given the circumstances, was a bit creepy.' Brandon smiled.

'I'll check out his alibis.' Jo was reddening. It didn't take much.

'Asap. And, also, let's give some thought to who might have easy access to the caretaker's cottage. Because if Nayler isn't our guy, then someone had the audacity and wherewithal to frame him. The SBK is getting bolder.'

Julia

July 7, 2019

She watched him walk up the drive, shoulders hunched, feet shuffling through the gravel. He took a deep breath, straightened his back and rang the doorbell.

'Come in,' she said, opening the door.

'I didn't know whether to come. But figured that ballcock wouldn't fix itself.' Jake had adopted his default expression – a wide grin.

Julia couldn't help but smile. This 'person of interest' really was an interesting person.

'Shall we have a coffee first?'

Jake stroked his chin. 'Want to take the chance?'

Julia burst out laughing. 'I know I shouldn't laugh. God knows, this whole business is far from funny, but, Jake, I can't see you as a serial killer.'

'Don't look wicked enough?' He did look wicked, and Julia knew she had to watch her step. But she didn't think he was a lady killer. Not in the literal sense.

'Where's Diana?' Jake was sitting at the kitchen table, stirring sugar into his milky coffee.

'Day off, in lieu of the party.'

'Di took a day off?'

'I insisted.'

'Good.' He took a sip of coffee.

'Good?'

His shoulders relaxed and his legs stretched out under the table. 'She will be loving this. Jake Nayler gets nailed by the cops. Wouldn't surprise me if—'

Julia leaned forward. 'Don't say anything you'll regret.

Diana wouldn't want to see you in trouble.'

Jake widened his eyes. 'If you say so. You are the boss.'

Julia got up from the table. 'Want some more coffee?'

'Got anything stronger?'

She gave him a quizzical look. 'I thought you came round to fix the ballcock?'

'I'm feeling stressed. You got anything on this afternoon?'

Nothing apart from organising a mass clear-up of her house. But that could wait for Diana. She was stressed too. The phone hadn't stopped ringing – guests, the police, the press, Axel, Nick's school.

'Wine or whisky?' It was past two. Julia was at the high kitchen cabinet, with its well-stocked supplies of alcohol.

'Both.' He was grinning again and, to her surprise, so was she.

An hour and one bottle of red later, Julia was topping them up with two tumblers of whisky. She was enjoying herself. More than she'd enjoyed herself at the party. More than she'd enjoyed herself in a very long time.

'They should provide beverages at the cop shop, it would make interviewees much more chatty.' Jake reached over and picked up a tumbler. He took a swig. 'That is good, madam. Very good indeed.'

'Talisker Storm.' She took a sip herself.

'Now you've gone through my illustrious family history. How about yours, Mrs Trenowden. Any skeletons?'

Julia scratched her neck. Skeletons? The body in her family closet was still warm.

'The ancestral home will be rattling with wrong-uns, I'm sure.' Julia looked at him over the rim of her glass. 'You don't get this rich on luck and talent alone.'

'Well, you're an angel, Julia. No mistake.'

'As if.' Julia rubbed her neck again. It had been good to hear him talk about his life – refreshing after being surrounded by hyper-active high-achievers. It was easy chat. But the way he was looking at her now crossed a line. Her phone pinged. Axel.

Jake took hold of his tumbler and settled back in his chair, watching her.

She keyed: 'Call you later', sent off the reply and turned back to Jake. He looked handsome, his jaw relaxed, the teasing grin gone, his eyes telling her all she needed to know.

She got up from the table and he shot up too. They stood facing each other for a good few seconds. He wasn't going to make the move. It was up to her. And so she reached out and touched his jaw, her fingers stroking fine stubble. He moved his head and brushed his mouth against her hand.

It had been so long. So long since someone had shown a real interest. Shown desire.

'It's been a while,' she said as his arms circled her and drew her close.

'Too long,' he said, kissing her forehead and then her nose and lips. 'Let's fix that.'

They went upstairs and into the main bedroom and he started to undress her slowly. She let him unzip her dress and pull it over her head, leaving her standing there in her pants and bra.

'I think you should go. This is a bad idea,' she said, turning her head to one side.

'Don't be daft,' he said, pulling her to him. 'This is the best idea you've had for ages. You need to be loved.'

He tilted her chin upwards and she looked him in the eye. 'You can't give me the love I crave.'

'Maybe not,' he said, unfastening her bra and feeling for the zip of his trousers. 'But I can give you the next best thing. And it's exactly what you need.'

He stroked her side as they lay together on the bed, the sheets scrunched up at the bottom of the mattress. She felt girlishly shy, but sated. Of all the steps she could have taken, was planning to take, to make something of her life, this one had been the easiest and most pleasing.

'What you thinking?' he said, edging away to study her.

'Nothing much.'

'Good. That's often the best way.'

He stroked her hair and gave her a kiss, before rolling away. 'I best fix that damn ballcock.'

Julia propped herself up on an elbow and smiled.

'Wouldn't want to upset the mistress of the household,' he said, pulling on his trousers and giving her a quick look over his shoulder.

Julia laughed. 'Indeed.' She knew exactly what he meant. Diana wouldn't be happy if his chores weren't done, despite being called away for urgent business in town.

He spun round and grabbed her hands. 'Don't worry. No one need know about what happened. Or what might happen in future.'

Julia went to speak, but he gave her a quick peck on the lips. He understood.

Her phoned pinged.

'That his lordship, checking up on you?' Jake stood at the end of the bed, grinning. She was so happy to see that grin.

'Yep.'

'Well tell him the water tank will be good as new, so madam won't need to worry about her shower.'

Julia reached for her kimono, which was draped over a velvet cocktail chair by the bed. 'Thanks, Jake.'

He turned to her, one hand on the door knob. 'A pleasure.'

She could hear him outside in the forecourt, getting tools together, and she relaxed into the bed pillows to reflect. This seemed the perfect set-up. Guilt-free sex. He'd been a considerate and good lover leaving no bitter aftertaste. She hoped he would continue to accept the situation. It could only be temporary, while things remained platonic with Axel. She'd give Axel a little longer. She enjoyed his company and now she had Jake for sex, perhaps she could make it work? Or at least make it end, without acrimony on either side.

She hadn't come, which didn't surprise her. She rarely did the first time with a new lover. But she knew she would and the intimacy and stimulus were all there.

Julia was fully-dressed when Jake popped his head around the door to say the over-flow problem was sorted. He threw her the house keys, which he'd used to get into the attic.

'What do you need doing tomorrow?'

Julia crinkled her brow and thought. Well, apart from the obvious. 'The larder door keeps sticking – if you wouldn't mind.'

He smiled. 'Consider it done.'

'You can come back to the cottage, when everything is … settled.' Julia felt it needed to be said.

'Yeah, maybe. Right now, I'm fine at Ricky's. Thanks, though.'

That was a relief. He understood the demarcation and she waved him goodbye with no regrets.

When she went out onto the landing she noticed a glow coming from the next floor. He'd probably left the light on in the attic. She climbed the stairs. The light was coming from Diana's room. Was she back already?

Julia gave a gentle knock. 'Diana? Are you there?'

There was no reply, so she tried the handle. The door was locked. No worries, she had the keys. It felt like an imposition going in to turn off the switch, but wasted energy was one of her bugbears. The key turned easily – either Diana or Jake, on her instructions, would have given it a recent squirt of WD40.

Diana had left a table lamp on. She'd been doing some paperwork – the table was littered with documents and loose sheets. As she stretched across it to turn off the lamp, she was struck by what she saw. Hundreds, literally hundreds, of newspaper cuttings. Julia looked over her shoulder. It was only four – she wouldn't be back for some time.

She recognised the girl on the top of the first pile – Clarissa Bowles. A quick flick through revealed 30 newspaper cuttings from the local and national press; most of them with the same photo of Clarissa in the playground, light shining through her skirt. The next pile was cuttings of Rebecca Morley, with more variation this time – her brother and family had thrown the family album at the press in a bid to find her. It saddened her, the desperate hope, as if more photos would somehow tip the balance of justice.

Julia heard a noise and walked back to the door to listen. Just wind rattling the kitchen blind. She returned to the papers, and took a photo of them to ensure they were in the right position when Diana returned. She should have done it before. Diana had a mania for detail.

Cuttings of objects made up another pile – blurred images in glass cases, as well as Rebecca's shoe and the conch. Diana had taken it upon herself to do an artist's drawing of Clarissa Bowles' ear with the conch, something the editors had clearly ruled out on the basis of taste and sensitivity.

The pile of paper closest to the window was yellowing. Julia tucked her hair behind her ears and sat down at the table. These looked interesting. The cuttings spanned the summer of 1996 – the original Sleeping Beauty Killings. It was a big pile. Naomi Foster, Esther Baker, Tania Beckingsdale and Lucy Ford. They were all there, in their '90s clothes – bought in boutiques, not online – a beauty pageant of young women cut down in their prime. She came across a bunch of cuttings held together with a bulldog clip. They were crime scene photos, most featuring the same guy. He was wearing casual clothes, as well as the ubiquitous CS gloves. The guy was young, and non-descript – looked like a scientist. But his zany red glasses marked him out. Diana had highlighted parts of the copy. They were all quotes by Al Chapman – 'Brains'. Julia was surprised he was given so much exposure – the forensics, at least these days, seemed to be the backroom boys. But, she could see, it really was a case for them. It was all about body parts and artefacts – the killer had circumvented the usual detective work – which was much harder back then, without CCTV, facial recognition technology and sophisticated DNA testing. Julia cupped her chin with her hands and read. It was fascinating stuff, so many experts and analysts giving their opinions. She could understand how Diana would be swept up in the mystery of it all, with her precise eye for detail. The thought pulled her up and she looked at her phone. It was 4.45. Time was getting on, but she wanted to pour over the material. She'd read and heard about most of the recent incidents. She snapped a close-up of the pile and then went through the papers, taking photos of them all, before putting them back in place.

'What are you doing?'

Julia started and spun round.

'Nothing. I just saw the light on. Nothing.'

Nick came over and took a look. 'Fuck, Di's a true crime junkie.'

Julia was shaking and rested a hand on her son's arm.

'You best get out of here fast, Mum. I just saw her car coming up the lane.'

'Yes.' Julia looked at her phone photos and back at the piles, scrutinising them for differences.

'For fuck's sake, Mum. You're the boss!'

'Mind your language. And manners. This is Diana's room.'

'But you're the one snooping in it!'

Julia tidied a pile and stood back satisfied. 'She notices if I put the mustard in the wrong side of the cupboard.'

'Talking of which – let's see what she keeps in her wardrobe. Broomsticks? Axes?'

'Nick!'

He went to open the wardrobe, but it was locked. He shrugged. 'The woman's paranoid.'

The kitchen door clicked open.

'Out of here now!' Julia hissed.

They could hear her bustling through the kitchen and heading for the stairs.

Julia shoved Nick out of the door and then remembered the keys and rushed back in for them. Damn. Which one? Which one! Julia fumbled with them.

Nick made for the stairs to stall her. 'Diana. How was your day?'

'Fine.' Julia could hear the suspicion in her voice. Nick wasn't one for pleasantries.

'We've run out of coffee, I think. Couldn't find any.'

Julia found the key and turned it. Pulling back her shoulders she joined Nick at the top of the stairs on the first floor landing.

'Nick. Don't bother Diana on her day off.'

Diana gave a small smile. 'Plenty of coffee in the larder.' She'd spotted the keys in Julia's hands.

'Jake's been in. He's fixed the water tank overflow. He left on the attic light.'

'That's funny,' Diana said, brushing past Julia as she walked towards her room. 'I left my desk light on too. I saw it from the garden, just before I went into Truro. But thought you wouldn't mind if I left it on, rather than going back to turn it off. I had a train to catch.'

Julia felt sick. And then brightened. She'd left it on. Thank God she'd left her light on while she looked at the articles.

'Absolutely. I hope you had a lovely day.'

Creature

July 31, 2019

He was standing outside the room. She could smell his aftershave, Lacoste Blanc, could see the black shapes stationed along the thin strip of light beneath the door. He'd been there for around twenty minutes. At one point she smelt the spicy, fishy aroma of his signature risotto. The 300 calories one. She was so hungry she would eat each and every one of those calories – and finish the plates of her dining companions. She hadn't eaten for two days – or so she believed, judging by the light and shadows. He'd pulled back her gag and given her water a few times. In stony silence. So this was the way it was to end? Like most relationships. A massive sulk after a perfectly reasonable – but seemingly offensive – action. She had a son. She had a life. Why wouldn't she try to escape? Any sane person would see that.

A key turned and the door opened – he was using his hip, holding a tray in both hands.

He didn't look at her and went straight to the dining table. The curtains remained open. She'd got to know her companions fairly well over the past few days – the contours of their bodies, their comparative decomposition, how some had more hair than others, more flesh, better stitching. The ones towards the far end of the table looked like they'd been worked on periodically – what stitching left was threadbare, bones poked through scraps of skin, dry as sacramental wafers. She was amazed at her dispassion, her acceptance of her fate. Something still stirred within, the survival instinct she was born with. But she was a realist and believed it would now – or probably (there lay the kernel of hope) – be impossible to regain his trust and her privilege within the household.

He was at the table serving the others, pouring them wine. Her stomach churned with hunger. This was torture. Kill me now. At least then I might get a plate of food.

He took a big slurp of wine and then another. Getting up abruptly, the chair legs scraping the parquet flouring, he marched over and stood before her.

'I can put yours in the microwave. Are you very hungry?'

She nodded and squeezed out a tear.

He looked distressed and then walked quickly out of the door, leaving it wide open. Well, nobody was going anywhere. She lifted her wrists, to test her theory. No. Her only hope of escape right now was to charm him. She could do it. Energy surged within. But she'd be careful this time – no mistakes.

He returned in minutes with a bowl of water, a flannel and the mirror. She would have to look presentable, she realised, before she could eat. He undid her gag.

'Thank you,' she said, her voice hoarse.

He immediately gave her some water and she did her best not to gulp it down. Everything now was about appearances. It had always been about appearances with him.

He put down the bottle, discreetly wiped her mouth with a hankie and stooped to unclamp her feet. She rotated her ankles to restore circulation. Then he unclamped her neck and, last, as usual, her hands. She remained motionless. Giving him total physical control.

'You can use the—' He motioned to the chemical toilet in the corner. The convenience of having an events toilet on site was thoughtful of him. He had manners, if not sanity.

She pressed the Open button and walked in. Pressed the Close button and sank onto the hard plastic seat. The release was immense. She hadn't been to the toilet since he'd dragged her back into the room. And she hadn't wet herself. He would have hated that. The last thing she needed was another reason for him to hate her. That's why she reluctantly got up and tidied herself before the mirror. She'd looked better, but pinched her cheeks to give herself a glow.

He was waiting outside, as she knew he would.

The bowl of water had rose petals in it and it made her sad. That small pointless gesture brought tears to her eyes.

A wash bag was by the side of the bowl and the hairbrush.

'I'll leave you,' he said, 'Get your supper.'

She turned to him and smiled weakly. 'Thank you.'

Ten minutes later she was trying not to gobble her risotto, eyeing the untouched dishes left by her dining companions.

How to phrase this? 'This has to be my favourite food. Delicious.' She gently pushed aside her empty plate – not one grain of rice remained.

He took a sip of wine. He'd had plenty. 'Would you like seconds?'

'If it's not too much trouble?'

'Of course not.' He got up and took her plate, pouring her half a glass of wine at the same time. It had been water at the start of the meal. He was softening.

She didn't rush for the wine. Allowed him to leave the room, heard him lock the door and took a long draft, topping it up with the red head's untouched goblet. She spilt a little, but hid the splash under a plate.

The wine and food acted like muscle relaxants – she felt heady and light. 'Cheers,' she said, raising her glass and looking around the table. 'We're going to get out of here. I will do everything within my power to get us all out of here.'

One of the flames flickered and leapt. But she didn't feel afraid. She felt companionship and empathy. These were her Band of Bodies. Spirit friends, their destinies entwined.

He returned with a piping hot dish of risotto – a little less on the plate this time – but, she noticed, there were small tubs of panna cotta with raspberry coulis.

She waited a beat before tucking in.

He was watching her: 'You've always had a healthy appetite. It's a delight to see. But be careful – those pounds can creep up on you.'

'Mmm,' she nodded, her head lowered, her mouth full of rice and haddock.

She'd have to slow down. Be more lady-like. It was hard in the circumstances, but she had to escape this hellhole. Console her son. Stop him killing. Lay these poor women to rest.

His face was flushed. He'd had too much to drink and she sensed an opening.

149

As always, he anticipated her. 'Shall we resume our tour of the gallery tomorrow?'

It was as if the last two days hadn't happened.

'That would be delightful. You said you wanted to show me a particularly important portrait.'

'I did,' he said, wiping the corner of his mouth with his napkin. 'And I will. Tomorrow. Then I will paint you.'

'In the bedroom?'

His face clouded. 'No. Not in the—' He hesitated and then stumbled over his next word. 'Bedroom.'

Not in that fucking chair.

'The studio. I have made up a bed for you in my studio.'

She took a sip of wine and studied him. Would he take her there tonight?

'Can I trust you?'

'Yes, of course. I was foolish. I didn't want to leave you. I wanted to see my son. Just briefly. I thought I could see him and return.'

He looked down and shook his head. 'I do understand. The bond between a mother and child – a son – is the strongest. There is no comparable love.'

He leapt up invigorated. 'You will sleep in the studio tonight. And you will, at some point, make contact with your son.'

'Thank you. Thank you so much for your understanding.'

He rested a hand near her on the table and she would have kissed it, if he hadn't snatched it away.

Brandon

July 7, 2019

A swing swayed and creaked on the porch. The wind was picking up and tumbleweed flew across the wide expanse of ground, with its dull mosaic of grit and stones. The door to the shack was off its hinges and banged open and shut. Looked like nobody was at home. But Brandon knew better than to jump to conclusions.

He pulled the gun from his holster and backed up against the wooden slatted side of the one storey build. From what he could see through the window, the place had been cleaned out. Cleaned out of anything of value. He edged towards the door and opened it. Silence, apart from the wind outside and the stuff it was flinging around.

Brandon moved slowly, arms together, stretched before him, the gun cocked and ready in his hands.

There was a small kitchenette to his right, a stinking pot of burnt vegetables and chicken on the stove, beer bottles and empty cartons of potato chips on the dirty surfaces.

He stood and listened. There was a sound coming from behind a door to the left – probably the bedroom. It was a low rhythmic moaning, like a mother soothing a baby. He edged across and felt the handle – locked. He glanced behind him, before kicking in the door.

Brandon wasn't prepared for the horror. He clutched his stomach and held a hand over his mouth to stop himself heaving. A young woman, or what remained of her, was sprawled on the floor, a dog at her side, nudging and pawing. The body was in rigor mortis, the blood still red from the many cuts to the torso, the legs, the face. A symbol was carved in her abdomen, innards spilling out over the thighs. Brandon shooed away the dog and went to close the bedroom door. Then something caught his eye through the window. Something just beyond the rise, in the copse of trees. Something twisting in the wind above the tumbleweed and grit – he rushed out of the door and ran towards her.

He woke sweating, heart racing, but relieved. It was a dream, another variation on the old one. He reached over for his phone to check the time. Suzanna Fitzgerald had sent a message. He turned on the sidelight and pulled himself up straight. The message was timed 11.30 – five minutes ago. She was working late.

'I've been thinking about the latest developments. Can we talk?'

He rubbed a hand across his chin, the other felt for his cigarettes and lighter on the side table. He lit up, the cigarette between his lips as he keyed a response. 'Good idea.'

His phone beeped. 'Now?'

'If that's good for you?' he wrote, the cigarette still between his lips, ash falling on his duvet cover.

He was brushing it off into the ashtray as his phone began to ring.

'Hi,' she said. The melodic tone of her voice calmed him. 'Working late?'

'No, just thinking.'

He took a drag and lounged back into his pillows.

'Never far from our minds is he?'

He could hear the smile in her voice. 'True. And I've known him longer than you.'

'That helps.' Brandon tapped some ash into the ash tray.

'I don't want to raise your expectations. I can only voice opinions. I'm not a clairvoyant.' She sounded defensive.

'We're all just working on hunches here. The more hunches the better.'

'The body part that turned up at your house.'

'Correction. Outside of my house. I wasn't going to let work infringe on my sanctuary. It didn't get past the door.

He heard her laugh. 'Absolutely. Maybe you are the clairvoyant, if you knew what was in your case.'

Brandon took a long drag before replying. 'I know the weight and shape of my Stentor. It was pretty obvious that it wasn't rattling around in a case that fits it like a glove. I'm a cop – you learn to be careful about what you handle.'

'I think he left it for you.'

Brandon sat up straight, reached over and stubbed out his cigarette.

'A copycat or Mr SBK?'

'The SBK. It was a fresh body part. Not old bones.'

'Yes.' Brandon was thinking of Al Chapman's assessment of the index toe, 'early stages of decomposition, clear cut through ligament'.

'And his delivery was clever.'

Brandon winced. 'Yes. But—'

'But?' He could hear her reach for something and the tinkle of glass. Lemonade? Wine?

'Well he's come in from the cold, hasn't he? He has to have been there that night. It was a bold move.'

'There were a lot of guests? Any ideas? Anyone who might look like a sophisticated, rich man with a penchant for beautiful women?'

Brandon lit himself another cigarette and took a quick drag. 'Quite a few. Julia has some well-connected, attractive friends.'

'Anyone that looks like Niki Lauda?'

Brandon laughed thinking about the identikit photo of the suspect in the Turk's Head garden. 'No. But we have a Swede.'

'Oh,' Suzanna said, taking a sip of whatever she was sipping.

'Yes, a financier called Axel Fleming – good looking, charming, in that Swedish way.'

Suzanna laughed. 'Björn from ABBA?'

'Brandon laughed too. 'No, he's better looking than that. Tall, blonde hair greying at the temples.'

'Swedish. Does he have an alibi?'

'Julia. He's her boyfriend.'

'Welded at the hip all night?'

'I wasn't watching their every move. No traces of his DNA on the body part or case. And he gave a good account of himself during questioning.'

'I'm sure.'

'Suzanna?'

'I'll check him out.'

'We have already.'

'And nothing untoward?'

'No. His background and movements all stack up.'

'I'll Google him anyway. Just to see what he looks like.'

Brandon smiled. 'Julia met him on the posh dating site BetterThanAllTheRest.'

Suzanna remained silent.

'You know it?'

'I know of it. Interesting. A man like that going on a dating site.'

'Jo thought the same. He has a plausible reason – couldn't meet the right woman in the old ways.'

He could hear her fussing around, maybe writing down some notes.

'Any other people of interest?'

'I didn't say he was one.' Brandon was smiling, but he had to be careful. Suzanna had a way of getting more information out of him than was strictly professional.

'I'll let you get some sleep now,' she said. Her voice didn't sound sleepy.

'Yeah. If I can.'

'Having trouble sleeping?'

'I had a bad dream.'

'Want to tell me about it?'

'I've forgotten it already,' he said, staring into the dark, waiting for her reaction.

'Goodnight, then.'

'Goodnight, Suzanna.'

He let her click off first and then reached for a cigarette. He lit up, the flame casting a shadow on the far wall. Sweden.

Brandon

July 8, 2019

They were going through The Hall's security CCTV. Well, Jo was. He trusted her to spot a lurking miscreant. So far they'd picked up no more than a few kids nicking bottles of wine from the fridge in the garden. Brandon smiled when he recognised the skinny hunched frame of Damian Kane, Chelsea's boyfriend. He returned to checking emails. It was taking forever for the Hatton Cross vintage specialists to come up with anything on the item of jewellery he'd sent them. No records.

He'd lean on them to check their overseas suppliers. God they were slow. He imagined some old timer poring over the earring with an eyeglass.

'Hmm.'

'Found something?' Brandon turned to Jo.

'Maybe.'

He clicked out of his inbox and came alongside her. She rewound to a reel of the back of a man walking fast and away from the gathering near the house. They lost him when he veered to the side. Jo rewound and froze him in the most revealing position, one that showed his frame and a slice of profile.

'Looks like he was heading towards Nayler's cottage.'

'But it's not Nayler?'

'I'd say not. The image isn't great, but this man's taller. Sleaker. Shame he's wearing a fucking cloak.'

Jo chuckled. 'Fancy dress isn't helping, is it?'

'Get a print out of the best images. We may recognise something or someone. Anyone looking suspicious around Gus's transit?'

Jo rewound some tape. 'His van was parked in the corner of the forecourt – not a great position for the cameras. I spotted a few people going to and from the area – the two valets, Gus, of course, and Diana, at one point.'

'The housekeeper?'

'Yes. Probably having a nose round. She doesn't exactly fit the profile.'

'Agreed. Keep looking.' He turned back to his iPad.

'Your fiddle hasn't turned up yet, Boss.'

Brandon shot her a look. 'Unlikely to. Arsehole. She was a beauty. Perfect pitch. A present from Jessica.'

Jo scrunched up her brow like she did when she didn't know what to say.

He could get another fiddle. Replace its smooth timber body, with its neck made for stroking, its belly of soul. It was just wood, he reminded himself. Just a piece of beautifully crafted wood. Beautifully crafted. Like the glass boxes. There was nothing like them on the web or being sold in the UK. Sweden? What had they got to lose, apart from precious time?

'Jo, could you chase Chapman on the analysis of the boxes – the composition of the glass and metal – and do some international research?'

'Sure,' she said, not looking up.

'It's a long shot, of course. But right now, with the body parts, the boxes are all we've got. And the jewellery.'

Jo usually liked doing detail stuff but she was looking underwhelmed.

'Bear with me, Jo. I could put Stew on this, but he'd have trouble sourcing a Big Mac carton. I've asked the Hatton Garden guys to check vintage jewellery overseas.' He paused. 'In Sweden, among other places. If you could look into the boxes?'

'Sweden?' Jo looked at him. 'Did you find anything on Fleming?'

Brandon wiped a hand across his mouth. 'No – his CV matches his LinkedIn profile – he was educated at The American International School in Johannesburg, before doing work experience for African charities in South Africa, Zambia and Namibia. Textbook, 'high achiever with heart' stuff. He returned to his birthplace of Stockholm when he'd just turned twenty, before starting an MSc in finance at the London Business School in 1994. His graduation photo is on LinkedIn.

He's got a tonne of alumni connections.'

'Where's he been working since?'

'Schroeders in London for ten years. Goldman Sachs, New York, before that.'

'Then why Sweden?'

'What have we got to lose?'

'Time.'

'Well get cracking then.'

Jo grimaced and returned to the CCTV.

Brandon watched her rewind the tape, let it run, and freeze it.

She made a small gasp, stretched out a hand and wiggled her fingers. 'The cloak – if you look really carefully—' her other hand was pointing at a triangle of black in the far corner of the frame. 'You can see it. The guy who's wearing it, is bending down round the back of the van.' She turned from the image to Brandon.

'Get Diana in. She might have noticed someone coming in wearing a cloak.'

They looked at each other.

'If the person came in wearing the cloak, that is.' Jo spoke his thoughts.

Creature

August 1, 2019

She looked magnificent. The fairest of them all; the Queen in Snow White, when the mirror was still telling her what she wanted to hear. He'd painted her in opulent green velvet, and she commanded the canvas. The backdrop was palatial: grand furnishings, ornate carvings, two plinths either side of her, one with a sculpture of Diana The Huntress, the other with Madonna and Child.

They were standing at the far end of the gallery, him a few feet behind her, his jacket rustling as he made small involuntary movements. The tics of someone in deep discomfort.

She swallowed before delivering her verdict. 'I don't know what to say. This is a remarkable portrait. Simply stunning. It breathes life into the work of the pre-Raphaelite movement. It's the beating heart of a Rossetti beauty.'

He made a long moaning sound – something between a sigh and gasp. Something that came from a dark place within. She stood still, her eyes on the woman before her, heard his feet move slightly towards her and then retract.

The woman in the painting had an aura that was hard to describe. She looked superficially serene – thick honey blonde hair brushed casually to one side, one arm draped over the back of her chair, the other resting in her lap – but there was something about the eyes. They were pale blue, like a layer of ice over a lake. A fragile veneer over unfathomable depth.

He coughed lightly to break her silence. 'You like the portrait?'

She turned to him, watched him struggle to disguise his pleading need for approval, and returned her gaze to the painting.

'I love it. The attention to detail is remarkable. The wall mirror reflects the back of her hair and the tucks and folds of her dress—' she paused, her mouth forming a small O. She turned round. 'I've just noticed the silver hand mirror on the pedestal table.'

He gave her a shy look and she instantly knew who the woman was.

'I'm so pleased you like the portrait. It is my best, I believe.'

'The others are of such a high standard and all with unique qualities, but—' and she hesitated before delivering her punchline, 'This is incomparable.'

He stretched out his arms towards her, his palms up and allowed her to take them, as she knew he would. 'Shall we go to the orangery, my love? I have prepared something delightful for lunch.'

The lunch had been delightful, if a little light – minted melon, feta and ham salad, with homemade lemon sorbet. Lemons from the orangery. An ice bucket of Chablis had rested by the side of the table, with its crisp, laundered white cloth. She wondered where he got his laundry done. Everywhere in the house was pristine. He either kept a dungeon of slaves to do all the work, or he managed it himself. There were dark pools under his eyes. Maybe he did do all the work.

She felt drowsy after lunch and was happy to recline on the chaise longue in his studio as he sketched her. In contrast, he was energised. She had suggested she posed nude – she was still hoping to seduce him. It had to be the easiest option for escape. But he'd dressed her in the same green velvet dress that the woman in the portrait was wearing. It smelt musky, infused with someone else's perfume and unique smell. He'd lifted the dress over her head, and buried his head in the folds of the skirt, his hands smoothing the material.

'Perfect,' he said, stepping back to admire her. 'A perfect fit.'

She must have dozed off. When she opened her eyes the studio was dark, the only light coming from a side window. He was gone. She moved on the chaise longue, checking for bonds, but there were none. It surprised her. But she would bide her time. This could be a trap.

He couldn't complain if she checked his work on the easel. The easel by the door. She slipped off the chaise longue and walked over, her dress brushing the wooden floorboards, making no effort to shush the sound. She was playing a part. The woman in green wouldn't sneak around a studio.

He'd made a good start on her portrait. The pose was a difficult one, but he'd captured it well. He hadn't worked on her face much – just a brief outline framed by a mist of hair. Not bad, she thought, looking around, picking up an apple from a bowl and taking a bite. She took every opportunity to eat and build her strength. An apple a day and I might get away. The thought made her laugh – a little too much – and she wondered if his mania was catching. Whether she did have the strength of mind and body to survive.

Moonlight streamed through the window and she dragged over a Van Gogh-style wooden chair and climbed on it to look outside. She knew where she was, of course. This was simply a chance to enjoy the view. Enjoy this new freedom that she had – which she had, apparently, earned.

There was a light in the orangery – maybe he was in there? Craning her neck, she could just see the outer wall of the garden, a few lights picking out the late roses. What she wouldn't do to walk through that scented garden again to freedom.

She stepped down from the chair, careful not to damage the dress or trip on it. She did a circuit of the room and returned to the easel. And the door. She was tempted to try the handle. But instinct told her not to. This could be a test. He may well be on the other side just waiting to catch her out. There was a snuffling sound – was he crying? There was no key in the door so she bent down to look through the hole. It went black. She leapt back and then edged closer, crouching to take a closer look. The dog's snout was nuzzling the keyhole, its body ramming the door, its paws clawing the tiled floor. She jerked her head back and it snarled. So she stood still, one eye on the keyhole, not daring to move until it backed off to sit in its guard position.

Julia

July 9, 2019

They were sitting on the patio, a bottle of wine on the table, the party fairy lights twinkling above them. It hadn't taken much to persuade Brandon to have a drink after finishing off the afternoon's heavy lifting. Most of his questions were formalities now. He seemed to accept that Jake wasn't the one and that her guests had credible alibis and no motives. She watched him ease into his chair, pour them both a glass of wine and smile for the first time that day.

'Have the forensics done with the fairy lights?' she asked, taking a sip of wine.

He looked up at them. 'Good point. Chapman and his beady eyes may have missed them.'

Julia laughed. 'You're not his greatest fan?'

Brandon rolled his eyes. 'He's good at his job, just not conversation.'

Brandon was drinking fast, so she topped up his glass.

'Maybe that's a little harsh. But I've been seeing rather too much of the man. Everything revolves around his analysis. There's little else to go on.'

She glanced down. 'Sorry I couldn't have been more helpful with the security CCTV. And Diana didn't recall the cloak. Which means she's unlikely to have taken it from anyone. She's an absolute stickler for detail.'

Brandon looked at her from below his fringe. It needed a trim. As did his beard. 'Diana's a character isn't she?'

Julia leaned forward. 'Shush. She's probably listening.'

'Brandon rocked back in his chair. 'You are kidding! Who's the boss around here?'

'She is.' Julia started to giggle.

His dark blue eyes were on her, a smile forming. 'I'm not buying that, Ms Trenowden.'

'Meaning?' Julia sat up straight.

'Meaning.' He took a sip of wine, his eyes still on her, 'You only give your staff so much rope. And you know when to tug it to keep them in line.'

'You got me sussed, Detective Inspector?'

'I doubt that.'

He held her gaze before turning to the bottle.

'Don't mind me. It's the booze talking and, possibly, my lessons in psycho-analysis.'

She gave him a searching look.

'I've been talking to a psychologist about the case. She's helping me build a profile of the killer. Fancy a top up?'

'I think you know the answer to that.'

He topped up her glass. 'Can't say I'm not enjoying these after-work drinks.'

'We bloody earned them. Cheers!' She clinked his glass. 'Cheers.'

'So, what's he like? Our SBK?'

Brandon hesitated before speaking.

'In a nutshell? I wouldn't want you to cross any professional lines.'

He raised an eyebrow. 'Smooth, considerate, refined, intelligent … attractive.'

'Do you have his number?' Julia said.

'Alas, no.' He smiled at her.

'I hasten to add. Damaged and dangerous.'

'I have been warned, Detective Inspector.'

A window closed upstairs and he looked up before turning to her. 'Diana?'

Julia leaned across the table and whispered conspiratorially. 'Yes. Right on cue.'

'God, I don't know how you put up with her, but—' he spread his arms and looked around. 'But I guess you have to. Running a place like this needs staff. Talking of which, is Jake still working for you?'

Julia averted her eyes. 'Yes. I couldn't let him go in the circumstances. It may be hard for him to get more work.'

'I doubt it.' Brandon was watching the upstairs window.

'Jake knows how to look after himself. But he doesn't fit our profile and his alibi is tight, so he's all yours.'

He was studying her. Had he guessed? The affair continued, but, like Jake, it was nothing more than handy.

She changed the subject. 'I found something odd in Diana's room.'

'Odd?'

'Piles of newspaper cuttings about the Sleeping Beauty Killings – dating back to the original cases in 1996.'

He flicked a look at the window. 'Wow. But hardly unreasonable. A lot of people get excited about true crime – and this case is a cut above – sorry, let me rephrase – is in a different league.'

'True. But sinister, all the same.'

'I agree. She gives me the creeps.'

Julia burst out laughing. 'I rather like Diana, but this does put a different complexion on our relationship.'

'How's your other relationship?' He was studying her again and she wanted to give him the correct response.

'Axel?'

'That would be him.'

'Still fine.'

'Fine?' He poured the rest of the bottle into her glass.

'Shall I get another?'

She didn't want him to make his excuses and leave.

'I'll get another bottle. Won't be a tick,' Julia said, getting up from the table and taking the empty one with her. Perfect timing. She didn't want him to go. And she didn't want to talk about Axel. She had two men in her life, both providing different needs, but the whole definitely wasn't greater than the sum of their parts.

'Julia,' Brandon called her from the table, his phone in his hand. 'Can we adjourn? Something's just come in. I need to get back to the station.'

She turned sharply. 'At this hour?'

'Yep. The cop's lot, I'm afraid. Doesn't make for a thriving social life.'

She walked back over and they stood facing each other and she wondered if she was managing to conceal her disappointment.

'Of course,' she said.

He gave her a thoughtful look. 'Put the wine on ice.'

'It's a red.'

'Then let it breathe.' He leaned over and kissed her on her cheek. 'Call me, if anything else odd happens. Or you need me.'

'Will do,' she said, briefly touching his face as he moved away.

Julia sat back down at the table and picked up her glass. She was far from reassured about Diana. But she didn't want to go through the hassle of finding another housekeeper just yet. And Diana was excellent – a little strange, at times, maybe. But better the devil worshipper you know. Besides, weren't they all obsessed with the SBK right now? She felt a chill and pulled her wrap around her. Brandon hadn't spelt it out, but his questions earlier in the afternoon made it fairly clear that he thought the killer had made an appearance at The Hall. So far, her guests were in the clear, but, and she glanced around the garden, someone had been lurking in the shadows. Someone hanging back, watching them all relaxed and having a good time, just waiting for his opportunity to drop off the hideous package. She looked into the dark recesses, wondered if the killer had left the glass case behind a plant, one of the ornamental urns, in the drinks fridge? The thought made her shudder and she got up, drained her glass and walked through the French windows into the downstairs salon. Nick must have gone to bed, so she locked up the doors and went through to the kitchen to turn on the security. As she climbed the stairs to her bedroom, she could see light from Diana's room on the wall before the staircase wound up to the second floor. She wondered what Diana's theories were and whether she wanted to share them.

It must have been past eleven when she heard feet on the staircase. Julia had been reading in bed, although her mind was wandering. She heard the kitchen door click shut. Julia slipped on her kimono and went to the window, as Diana was getting into her Polo VW and driving off.

God knows where she was going but, she figured, any trip would take at least ten minutes. Julia had the master house keys hidden away in the bottom drawer of her wardrobe under a pile of cashmere jumpers. Had it come to this? Yes. She took them and headed upstairs. Diana had locked the door and it took a few minutes to remember which one fitted the lock. She'd tag it.

The door whined open. The woman hadn't oiled the door hinges. Probably her creak alarm. Diana was on borrowed time.

That time had run out. Julia staggered back when she saw what was on the bed – heaps of clothing and underwear. Julia's clothing and underwear. Not neatly folded, or stacked, simply strewn on the bed – pairs of her shoes scattered on the floor. But it was the mirror – covered in photographs – that grabbed her. She walked over, expected them to be SBK victims. But no. There must have been fifty or more photos of Diana dressed in her clothes and shoes. She didn't know whether to laugh or cry.

Instead she screamed. For there, reflected in the mirror, was Diana herself, wearing Julia's clothes, shoes and scarf and somebody else's cloak.

Brandon

July 10, 2019

Al Chapman looked him straight in the eye. 'It's a fucking joke, isn't it?'

'You tell me,' Brandon said. The investigations table divided them like the River Jordan – at its centre was a tupperware box containing a pair of spectacles. They were the ubiquitous metal-rimmed ones men of a certain age and a certain profession wear. They were Chapman's.

'I wondered where my spare pair had gone,' Chapman said, with a smirk.

Brandon wasn't amused. He'd been dragged back to the station on what appeared to be a fool's errand. A stunt.

'Why would anyone – the SBK, copycat, joker – want to send us this message?'

'Good question,' Al said, shaking his head lightly and, for once, out of ideas and chat. Chapman had never been one to shun the limelight, but right now he was looking mighty coy.

'Is there any point you taking these back to the lab to verify ownership? Is it your tupperware too?' Brandon was trying to keep the smile off his face.

Al grinned up at him. 'I can't vouch for the tupperware. But, yes, the box and specs will be analysed at the lab – may pick up some DNA, other than my own.'

Brandon looked at his watch.

'I'd say we're done now.' Al was already packing the box in a container. He was keen to get on his way.

Brandon walked him to his car. 'Any thoughts as to why you may have been singled out?'

Al pinged open the boot and placed the container inside.

'Of course,' he said, walking over to the driver's door.

'Feel like sharing them?'

'It's getting late.' Al had glanced at his watch. 'Past midnight.'

Brandon didn't want to let him go. Give him time to fabricate some cock and ball story.

'You were high profile when the SBK was at his zenith. You're back on the scene now. That why he's playing you?'

Al turned and met his eye. 'Makes sense.'

'Of course,' Brandon added. 'It may not be the SBK.'

'Agreed.' Al had opened the car door.

'Have you annoyed anyone recently, Al?'

He shrugged. 'It's part of my DNA.'

Brandon had to laugh. 'Anyone in particular? Someone who would go to the trouble of nicking your spare glasses, packing them in an ironic box and sending them to the cops? Anyone that would have access to your home?'

'I'll give it some thought.' Al paused. 'Need a lift back?'

Brandon had his car out back. But he'd had a few drinks. Thought he might enjoy Al's company for a change. 'Thanks.'

Chapman hadn't been overly chatty in the car, but Brandon had found out one salient detail. He was, as they state on the dating sites, 'Just Plain Single'. And other than a cleaner, or lover – he didn't get that far with his informal questioning – who else would be able to get their hands on his specs? Al was a meticulous man. Not the type to lose them on the top of his head, or leave them in random places. It was a mystery and one, he felt, would be solved, if enough pressure was applied.

It was one in the morning, but he didn't feel tired. He would have picked up his Stentor, played something soothing, if it'd been around. He checked his phone. Chelsea had messaged to say she was in bed. He insisted she text on her way home from a night out – tonight she was in way before him.

There was another message. Julia. He hesitated before opening it, walked through to the kitchen, opened the drinks cupboard, and pulled out Jack. He didn't often look for his company. But tonight. Tonight. He felt there'd been developments, on a few fronts. He poured himself a large one and walked over to the French windows and went outside. It was a beautiful, balmy night – a clear sky, stars out, the moon centre stage, waves strumming the sea wall.

He sat down at the old wooden table, noted the flaking paint, made a mental note to give it a fresh coat, and got out his phone. His finger hovered over Julia's message – it was just below one from Suzanna Fitzgerald. He looked at Suzanna's first.

'Any developments? Love to talk. I'm free tomorrow and most of the week, Suzannax.' A kiss? Pretty much par for the course these days. But in a professional capacity? Brandon took a sip of whisky and moved onto Julia.

'Brandon. Something very odd has happened tonight. Call me when you get a chance. Jx.'

Brandon rocked forward on his chair and typed: 'Are you awake?'

'Yes.'

'Can you talk?'

'Yes.'

He dialled her. 'So, tell me what happened.'

July 10, 2019

'Why did you lie about the cloak?' Brandon was seated opposite Diana Chambers in the interview room. He'd called her in for questioning first thing in the morning.

'The cloak is mine.' Her expression was stony, like he was wasting her time, not the other way round.

'Okay, so it was you sneaking around the back of Gus Tyler's transit on the night of July 1?'

She pursed her lips. 'Sneaking? No, I was checking on supplies. Some bottles of wine had gone missing.'

'So you thought Gus may have stolen them and you decided to disguise yourself when you checked out his van?'

'Not disguise. It was late and I was getting cold. I wasn't fuelled up with alcohol like most of the guests.' She gave him a withering look.

'Why would you suspect Gus?'

'We didn't know him. Julia sourced him from the web. He seemed nice enough, but appearances can be deceptive.'

'You were checking up on Gus at 11pm?'

'We were running out of wine.'

'Really?' He couldn't imagine Julia allowing that to happen. However, Diana appeared to be in charge, so it was a possibility. God, the woman was cool. Had an answer for everything. Maybe not his next question, though.

'Why did you hoard Julia's clothes and shoes in your bedroom? And why did you dress up in them and take photographs of yourself wearing them.'

She delivered her answer. 'I was borrowing them. Ms Trenowden has a lot of clothes. She doesn't wear the ones I'd borrowed. She didn't miss them until she broke into my room to snoop on me.' Diana's face was flushed. It was the first time he'd seen her rattled.

'Ms Trenowden was in your room because you'd been acting suspiciously.'

'How?'

This was a tricky one. Julia had already seen the SBK cuttings – but mentioning the fact would incriminate Julia. He wouldn't put it past Diana Chambers to sue Julia for unfair dismissal and malpractice.

'Rushing out in the middle of the night. Turning off security to do so.'

'I'm an employee, not a slave. I have freedom of movement.' She shot him a killer look. 'Ms Trenowden shouldn't have been in my room, in my absence, without my permission. The door was locked. I believe the law would call that breaking and entering.'

'And stealing Ms Trenowden's clothes is called theft and abuse of your position, a dereliction of duty.'

The atmosphere was getting nasty. He glanced at Jo.

'What made you want to try on Ms Trenowden's clothes? Did you admire them? Do you admire her?'

Diana's head gave an involuntary jerk. 'Yes. She's a beautiful woman and has exquisite taste. I didn't think I was doing any harm. I would have returned the clothes, laundered and fresh.'

'I understand,' Jo said.

Diana cleared her throat. 'Julia means a lot to me as an employer and … friend. I would never do anything to hurt her or bring her into disrepute. I just wanted to walk in her shoes, be someone like her, for a little while. An innocent fantasy.'

'Fantasy or obsession?' Brandon asked.

Jo gave him a sharp look, but he wasn't convinced by Diana as fawning fan.

'An innocent fantasy.' She gave him a long, cool stare.

'You have a tendency to delve deep into your fantasies, don't you Ms Chambers? Act them out.'

She kept on staring.

'The collection of cuttings you have in your bedroom – they span twenty-three years. That's a long time to indulge an innocent fantasy.'

She glanced at the window and then back at him. 'I like true crime. It's a hobby of mine. Mine and many others.'

'But you don't share your interest with other people. There are plenty of chatrooms for like-minded amateur sleuths.' They'd done some rudimentary checks on her internet searches and activity. She was a lone operator.

'I'm happy to do my own research – come up with my own theories. I don't need to share my thoughts with others. Most of them are weirdos and losers.'

'What are your theories?'

She scoffed. 'Do your own investigative work, DI Hammett. Let's face it, the force has been lousy so far in these investigations.'

'Do you know Al Chapman?' Jo asked the question and Diana made a little croaking sound. Jo gave Brandon a quick look.

'Of course. He was on the case in '96 and he's on it now.'

'Do you know him personally?' Brandon was watching her carefully.

'No.'

'Is he someone you admire?' Jo said, leaning forward.

'He's good at his job.'

Brandon got up from the table and went to the metal cabinet at the back of the room. He pulled a photo of the tupperware box with Chapman's glasses.

He went back to the table and presented Diana with the photo. 'Do you recognise these?'

She knitted her brow. He could see she was intrigued – or, possibly, feigning interest.

'No.'

'Nothing familiar,' Jo said, leaning forward, Brandon by her side.

'Any theories?' he said.

She looked up. 'It looks like a wind up of some sort. A prank. Someone has mocked up SBK's style. Maybe someone – the SBK himself – is telling you how obtuse you are. That he's running rings around you and may still be, in another twenty-three years. Because you just can't see. You can't see the evidence in front of your eyes.'

He let her talk. There was no frog in her throat now. Her face was reddening, as she warmed to her subject, indulging another obsession.

'Whose glasses are they, by the way?' She looked him in the eye, daring him to slip his guard.

'You tell me, Ms Chambers.'

Julia

July 12, 2019

Diana handed over the clothes clean and pressed. It was excruciating.

'Thank you, Diana. You know that you are free to stay until you find somewhere else.'

'Thank you, madam, but I've found somewhere. I've called a taxi.'

Julia looked down and tugged at her sleeve. She couldn't offer to give her references – not in the circumstances. 'No hard feelings. You've been a marvel around here.'

Diana looked to the side. 'I'll be going then. Goodbye, madam.'

'Goodbye, Diana. I'm sorry it had to end like this.'

Diana nodded and walked away, leaving Julia the freedom to breathe an enormous sigh. She'd have to get all the locks changed. Update the security. Take the clothes to a charity shop.

The taxi arrived. The front door clicked open and Diana's sensible shoes could be heard on the gravel. Julia went to the window, careful to hide behind the curtain. Diana didn't look up, probably anticipated Julia's move.

Diana had been asked to be available for further questioning, so she wouldn't be going far. But right now, turning left at the end of the lane was good enough. Julia wanted to fumigate her room, exorcise its sordid secrets.

She threw back her shoulders, remembering Brandon's advice to 'always remember whose house this is', and climbed the stairs. The door was shut, but unlocked. It didn't even creak when she opened it. Diana's small smirk: 'I'll make it easy for you, Lady Muck.'

The room was spotless, surfaces cleared and clean, the bed stripped. Nothing under the bed, not even a fluff ball.

The wardrobe door had a key in it. Julia walked over and turned the handle – empty apart from hangers and a cardboard box. The package delivered the day Diana and Jake had arrived. She'd asked Diana to return it to Ann Summers – didn't think she'd need it. And here it was all the time, silently mocking her. Diana's last laugh. She hoped.

Brandon

July 12, 2019

Brandon looked up from the email he was reading on his phone as he waited for Jo to meet her date, a guy called George Nicholson. He'd spotted a man heading towards the Godolphin Arms in his peripheral vision. The fact that the man looked like any other, made him that much more suspicious. He put his phone in the glove compartment of his car and tilted his body to get a better look. The Skoda wasn't the only car parked on the main street of Marazion, but it was the only one with a person in it. Maybe that was what made the man stop at the entrance and reflect. He acted out some movements suggesting he'd forgotten something – his wallet, his phone – and then turned from the pub and walked swiftly away.

Brandon got out of the car and followed him as he headed down the road, past the galleries and cafés. It was seven in the evening and there were holidaymakers around, walking in fours, spilling out onto the streets, kids struggling with beach kit. He circumvented a family of five; the man was getting ahead of him.

Brandon watched him dart across the road, forcing the car at the head of a line of traffic to brake suddenly. He disappeared from view down a side street. Brandon zigzagged through the stationary cars and down the street, just as the man was turning the corner at the end. Brandon started to leg it, feeling for his taser. Too early to pull it now, but …

The guy was nowhere in sight when he reached the top of the road. A road lined with terraced houses and neat front gardens.

Brandon took the taser out of its holster. 'Show yourself. Come out, hands above your head.'

Silence. He had to be there, though. It was a long street.

Brandon searched the first garden on his left, his arms outstretched, the taser cocked and ready. No. He crossed the road to the garden opposite, prodded back the branches of a laburnum tree. No. A woman came out of her house a few doors up – he gestured for her to go back inside.

He traversed the street, checking the gardens and parked cars. He had to be there. There were four council recycling bins at the end of the road. Brandon edged towards them, arms outstretched. He kicked the first one. It swayed on its wheels, but betrayed nothing. The red one at the end was bigger, providing more cover.

'Come out, hands above your head,' Brandon said, rocking the bin with his shoe, rattling the bottles within

He was quick, that's for sure. And prepared. Brandon felt the bottle crack over the back of his head, making him fall forward, his hands reaching out to break his fall. The last thing he could remember was seeing the taser slide across the ground and land at his assailant's feet.

July 14, 2019

Brandon winced as Suzanna Fitzgerald applied ointment to his sprained wrist. It was the worse of several injuries sustained when the suspect cracked him over the head with a bottle two days ago.

They were sitting at her kitchen table – the bi-fold doors closed against relentless drizzle.

'What did he look like?'

Brandon grimaced. 'Beige.'

Suzanna applied some more ointment – circling the lotion into his swollen, bruised flesh with finger and thumb. It hurt a little, but was soothing all the same.

'His hair was light brown, or dark blonde. He was wearing a safari-style short-sleeved shirt, over cream chinos. Boat shoe slip-ons. And sunglasses, even though it wasn't sunny.'

'Camouflage.'

'Yes. Not too dissimilar to the identikit we have of the suspect in the Turk's Head. He was stooping as he walked, possibly to disguise his height. I'd say he was six foot two.'

'Jo was inside?' She was still kneading his wrist.

'Yes. I didn't have time to call her – otherwise she may well have caught him. She's a great sprinter.'

'There,' Suzanna said, freeing his hand and resting back into her chair. 'I would be surprised if he arranges any more dates – with Jo, at least. He must have been bristling with nerves to pick you up.'

'My thoughts, entirely. He was taking a hell of a risk. Or testing the water.'

'Did you pick up any DNA on the bottle?'

'No. He had the good sense to take it with him. He's clever.'

'We've established that.' Suzanna smiled at him.

He went to help himself to more lemonade – but winced with pain.

'Here, let me.' Suzanna poured some into his glass. 'You've really developed a liking for this.'

'Yes,' he said, taking a sip and wiping his right hand over his mouth. 'What do you make of the tupperware box and Al Chapman's spectacles?'

Suzanna narrowed her eyes. 'I've given it some thought. It is so out of character I would be surprised if the SBK dispatched it, unless he's losing it. Wanting to shake your cage, grab your attention.'

'He got my attention two nights ago.' He turned his wrist slowly, tried to make a fist of his left hand.

Suzanna smiled kindly. 'You have been in the wars. Did Al find any other DNA on the box and specs?'

'Apparently not.' Brandon rocked back on his chair, tried to lace his hands behind his head, before a shot of pain put paid to that.

'Odd.'

'We may have made some headway on the earring.'

Suzanna tilted her head towards him.

'Hatton Cross Vintage sourced some photos of the earrings – or a similar pair – in a private Zurich collection.'

'Interesting.' Suzanna leaned forward and went to pour him some more lemonade. But he waved away her hand.

'It appears the earrings were part of a stash of Nazi treasure, stored in Switzerland towards the end of the Second World War.'

Suzanna nodded. 'Go on?'

'I wish I could. The trail has gone cold, but Rami Abelson thinks he may be able to find out where they were sent on to. He's working on it. Very slowly.'

'Good news, all the same.' She'd cupped her hands around her face, which made her look uncharacteristically wistful.

'Yep, another piece in this mammoth puzzle.' Brandon picked up his phone, checked it briefly and put it in his pocket.

'Off already?'

He nodded.

'I can't tempt you to stay for supper?'

It was a temptation. To have someone cook for him, instead of struggling one-handed and end up calling for a takeaway.

'Thanks for the offer, but I best go.'

'Another time.' Suzanna rose from the table and showed him to the door.

There was more unsaid than said today. But you didn't always need words to confirm hunches. They'd largely agreed on the tupperware box and specs. A poorly executed meme designed to send them down a cul de sac. The earring showed more promise. It had taken twenty-three years to take it out of its box and hold it to the light. How much longer before they found its place in this macabre set-up? But now they had a lead, it was all about tracking the jewellery to its penultimate destination.

Brandon's phone buzzed. Jo had texted to say she was outside Suzanna's, waiting to give him a lift. He still couldn't use a gear stick.

'Has your fiddle turned up yet?' Suzanna was seeing him out, one hand on the open door.

'No. I wouldn't be able to play it right now, anyway.'

'Not right now,' she said. 'But, all things pass.'

The sooner, the better, he thought as he walked away, Jo turning on the ignition.

'You still having those dreams?' he heard her say as Jo opened the passenger door.

Of all the things left unspoken, she mentioned that.

August 1, 2019

The studio door opened and he came in bearing a tray of hot soup, toast and petit fours. The dog sat to attention outside like a stone ornament.

'You deserve this,' he said, resting the tray on a trestle table and arranging the bowls, plates and cutlery for two. 'Please join me.' He patted the back of the Van Gogh chair he'd pulled up for her, and searched around for a similar. 'This is the first time the studio has been used as a refectory.' He smiled and held the hem of her dress as she sat down at the table.

'Have a napkin.' He passed her one and tucked another into his shirt like a bib. She had become an expert in his visual clues. It wouldn't do to dribble soup down her frontage.

They sipped the thin broth in silence – she intent on getting through this awkward dining experience without spillages.

As always, the food was good, but light. She could taste thyme, parsley and saffron, with just a hint of garlic, seasoning the wild mushrooms and diced shallots. She'd learnt not to look up when eating – let him watch her, if it suited him – she'd developed the art of noiseless, dainty dining.

She went to take a second piece of toast, but he moved the plate away to make space for a pot of coffee. 'Black, my dear?'

'A dash of milk if you don't mind?'

His brow formed a small frown. 'I'll be back in a minute.'

He wiped his hands on his napkin, rose from his chair and strode purposely out of the door, leaving it open. The dog glanced up at him as he passed and then returned to its default position; front paws forward, back straight on sturdy haunches.

When she heard his feet on the turret steps she picked up one of the two remaining pieces of toast and tossed it to the dog. 'Good boy, good boy,' she coaxed as he fell onto all fours, sniffed the food and devoured it. He didn't leave a trace on the floor, so she tossed him the second piece. 'Good boy. What a good boy. What a good boy,' she said, watching him wolf down the toast, his tail wagging for more. Looking him in the eye, she hardened her tone. 'Sit boy. Sit.' He whimpered a little, but shuffled back into position as his master's feet sounded on the stairs.

Moving the plate to her side of the table, she trailed a finger in the buttery crumbs and put them to her lips, just as he entered the room.

He took in the dramatisation and smiled indulgently. 'I did have petit fours for pudding, but I see you are replete.'

She gave him a coy smile and stretched out a hand.

'Well, maybe one. How can I deny you?' He popped one on her plate.

Maybe, if I get the time, I'll let you know one fine day.

'Shall we?' he said, looking at the chaise longue.

'Of course. I took the liberty of checking your work earlier. A great start. I was thinking, however.'

His face clouded.

'That, possibly, we could use the dog in the portrait. Like you see in the old masters – it would be perfect for the image we're trying to create.' She'd started using the pronoun 'we'. He seemed to like it. Usually.

He raised a hand to his brow. She could see him flicking through mental archives of old masters. 'Darling, I don't think there were many portraits with dogs – not—' He clearly couldn't bring himself to say, ferocious looking guard dogs.

'Well, that makes it all the more—' She gave him her best simpering Scarlett O'Hara smile, without the dimples. 'Creative!'

'Wouldn't it worry you, having the dog in here with us?'

'Not with you here too.'

'Well, maybe we could try it this afternoon. See how he settles.'

'Do you think he would look better in repose – the tamed beast at his mistress's feet?'

He hesitated. 'Possibly. The masters often featured dogs as companions.'

'Perhaps we could try a variety of poses – see what works best.'

'You'll have him eating out of your hands, at this rate,' he said, a small smile on his face.

'Hardly. I don't even know his name.' The petit four was softening in her clenched fist.

He gave a sharp whistle and the dog fell onto all fours, ambled into the room to his master and rubbed his head against his leg. While he knelt to pat the dog, she stashed the petit four in her petticoats. The dog's ears pricked up.

'So,' he said, turning back to her. 'Let's start with you both in repose. Take a seat.' She went to the chaise longue, sat down and did her best to look relaxed. He walked over and adjusted the skirt of her dress so it fell in folds.

'Rest your head on your right palm.' He stood back and then crouched before her, sweeping her hair over one shoulder. 'Nearly there,' he said, feeling in the pocket of his trousers and pulling out a silk purse. He pulled open the tie strings and emptied its contents into the palm of his hand – a dazzling, art deco earring glittered with rubies and emeralds.

'Perfect,' he said, fixing it to her right ear.

July 15, 2019

Rain drops ricocheted off the top of the glass box, blurring the contents inside. Al Chapman had arrived just before Brandon, who was still having trouble doing the day-to-day, like tying his own laces.

'New day, new cove, new horror,' Al said, standing over the box as SOCOs rigged up the tape.

Brandon grimaced. 'What's in there?'

Al gave him a sideways glance. 'A braid of titian hair – that's a pleasant, rich shade of red—'

Brandon sighed. 'I know what titian is. Anything else in there?'

'A fancy hair clip. Very fancy, almost military. It has an eagle emblem. No script this time.'

Brandon stroked his chin with his good hand. 'A red head – worrying.'

'Why?' Al turned to face him.

'Keep up, Al. No red heads reported missing.' His body chilled as he said the words.

'Indeed,' Al said, bending down to re-examine the box. 'Very worrying.' He wiped away the rain with a cloth and beckoned Brandon to join him.

Another fine piece of vintage jewellery – not to his taste, he hated trinkets – but the Hatton Cross guys would be appreciative, that's for sure. The symbolism was stark – a snake in the claws of an eagle, the reptile's head back and ready to bite. Brandon took the cloth from Al, wiped over the lid and took a photo.

'I want to get this over to the experts, asap. They're very

slow. Unlike you, Al. How soon can you write up a report on this?'

'By the end of the day. Because, quite frankly, we are unlikely to find any traceable DNA. We could be lucky. But do we want to be lucky?'

'I think so, Al. Because if this braid belongs to a missing person on our radar, then at least he hasn't struck again.'

Al cocked his head and looked up at Brandon. 'The hair looks like it was washed this morning.'

It did. It had the luscious shine of health and life.

'Well, the sooner we can get some answers, the better. Call me any time.'

Brandon walked over to the cliff steps, winced as he took the first one – his right knee had taken a lot of the impact as he hit the ground. When he got to the top, he lit up and watched them doing their stuff below. The same old scene. How many more times before they put a stop to this horror show. He saw them go about their business, checking the area, taking notes, taking photos, part and parcel of their essential work. It had to stop. He had to make it stop. That was his job, one which would never be routine.

His phone beeped.

Jo: 'There's been another missing person report. Emily Paxton.'

'You thinking what I'm thinking?' Jo was looking at him over the photos of an attractive thirty-something red head that went missing two days ago. The day after Brandon was clobbered over the head with a bottle in Marazion.

'More than likely. We need to accelerate these investigations. Her sister, you say, reported her missing?'

Jo nodded.

'And she's fully cooperative?'

'Yes – when I visited she gave me loads of photos and items of clothing.'

'Excellent – I'll get the clothing over to Chapman. We should know within the day whether the braid in the box is hers.'

Brandon got up abruptly, winced when he knocked his leg and ran his right hand over his mouth. 'He's speeding up. And—'

'Yes,' Jo said, looking up from the table.

'The hair clip, or whatever it is. The symbolism – an eagle and a snake – represents wisdom and passion, morality and vengeance.'

'You are the font of all knowledge. You never cease to amaze me, Boss.' It was difficult to tell whether Jo was ribbing him, but she had certainly earned the privilege.

'Google, Jo. But the image did ring some bells.'

Jo smiled. 'Suzanna Fitzgerald is going to have a field day with this.'

Brandon smiled and nodded. 'Yep. But, Jo—'

'Yes?'

'You don't need a PhD in psychology to read this. Red hair, like your own. A strike straight after we almost caught him. This looks like vengeance.'

They looked at each other. Said nothing for a beat.

'I'll drive over Emily Paxton's things to Chapman right now.'

'Don't stop to pick up any strangers.' He wasn't smiling.

July 19, 2019

'Passport? Tickets? Currency? Cards? Phone? Charger?'

'Yes, Mum, you packed them last night, remember.' Nick was standing on the doorstep, a taxi behind him waiting to take him to Newquay Airport.

Julia gave a wistful smile and reached out a hand to draw him close. 'Be careful in New York, sweetheart. There are no go areas.'

'I'll be with Dad.'

Julia frowned. 'Exactly. Don't let him lead you astray. I've printed out all the danger zones and put them in the zip compartment of your suitcase.'

Nick drew back. 'Mum, you went through this on YouTube three weeks ago.'

'Just in case you've forgotten.'

'I'll text you when I get to New York.'

'Text me when you get to Dublin. And then when you get to New York.'

Nick gave a shy smile. 'Will do.'

'And every day, as well.'

'I'll be with Dad.'

Julia sighed. 'Every day.'

'Will do.' He glanced over his shoulder at the cab. 'Better go – plane leaves in less than two hours.'

'Yes,' she said, pulling him to her. 'Have a good journey. Love you.'

'Love you,' he said, pulling away and picking up his suitcase. The taxi driver rushed over and took it off him. He could smell the money.

She waved until the cab turned the corner at the end of the lane, and then heard the discreet displacement of gravel underfoot. Axel had come out of the house to join her.

'You okay,' he said, tilting her chin so he could examine her mood.

'It's always worrying when your child goes off into the unknown and you know you can't rush in to help as they're out of your orbit.'

He nodded sagely. 'I understand.' He looked like he did. It's what she liked about him – his consideration and maturity. He respected and understood her relationship with Nick – something Sam never had. There was no underlying jealously or tension – he always went out of his way to make Nick feel at ease. At one point, she'd wondered if he was gay, if he was attracted to Nick. But she soon dismissed that notion; he just had emotional intelligence and was aware of being perceived as an interloper. Maybe now Nick was away, he might feel more inclined to … inclined to what? Ravish her? She shook her head lightly – he was regarding her with his customary concern and indulgence.

'Let me fix you a cocktail.'

Julia raised an eyebrow. 'A cocktail?'

'A New Yorker. Let's join Nick in spirit.'

'You have the ingredients?'

'You betcha, ma'am,' he said, bowing lightly and ushering her back into the house.

She sat at the kitchen table watching him squeezing a fresh lemon and orange into the cocktail shaker, adding generous splashes of bourbon, claret and ice. It was picture perfect. Axel was a man of many talents, she was beginning to realise. Shame about that one area of deficiency.

'I was thinking,' he said, pouring the cocktails into two retro coupe glasses. He stood back and looked at his creations, before adding a touch more to one glass and flourishing each with orange rind.

'You were thinking?' she said as he placed the glasses on the table.

'That we could take a trip together.'

Julia took a sip – just the right amount of sugar. Cocktails could be syrupy.

'Good?'

'Lovely and refreshing.'

'Good.' He took a sip himself, put his glass down and rested his forearms on the table, like, she imagined, he'd done many times before in the board room. 'Have you ever been to Sweden?'

'No – I believe it's delightful.'

He smiled. 'Sweden gets a good press and rightly so. But, to be frank, we also have no go areas.' He must have overheard her conversation with Nick. 'But also some incredible must go areas. I'd love to take you to the mountains in Kebnekaise and Abisko – we could trek all day and night, if we like.'

'The midnight sun?'

'Yes – the light is quite spectacular well into early September.'

'Sounds fabulous.'

'I wouldn't walk you off your feet – plenty of glamping opportunities and, also, shopping in Östermalm.' She'd heard of Östermalm – any wealthy person would have. 'I have a place there.'

'You're just not selling it to me,' Julia said smiling.

'You'll love it – the place will wrap itself around you like an ermine coat.' He was watching for her reaction. 'Or was that a fur pas?'

'Maybe faux fur would be more appropriate? But, yes, I love the idea.'

She saw him slide a hand below the table. Air tickets? But he just brought out his phone.

He brought up a photo and passed his phone to her. 'Isn't it idyllic? Like walking with the gods.' A solitary figure stood by a lake, silhouetted against the blended pinks and purples of a setting sun.

'Is that you?'

'Maybe,' he said, taking back his phone. 'Looks a bit lonely, doesn't he? In need of a goddess?'

Julia smiled and picked up her glass.

'Do you know of any goddesses who might be free in the last week of July?'

'No.'

He laughed and took her free hand. 'Training comes free on the trail. Not that you'll need any – you will be in your element, darling.'

'Well, maybe in Östermalm.'

'Most definitely in Östermalm. Shall I book tickets?'

Nick wouldn't be back until August 16. It would be great to get away. 'Absolutely, darling.'

July 19, 2019

'Do you recognise this woman?' Jo handed him her phone.

'Can't say I do – although, something maybe about those piercing eyes?'

Jo took the phone back and enlarged the photo with her finger and thumb. 'Boss, how closely do you look at women? Really look at women?'

Brandon grimaced, shook his head gently and took the phone from her. 'Diana Chambers?' He twisted his neck to look at Jo, who nodded. 'She scrubs up well.'

'Could have had some work done – as well as the make-up. Photoshop maketh many people online.'

'Diana's on Huddle? I guess it makes sense. All sane women are leaving the site in droves and Ms Marple signs up.'

'Perhaps we should join forces? I think my cover has been blown.'

Brandon gave her an incredulous look.

'Joking, Boss!'

'Unless she's had a ton of cosmetic surgery done, I don't think she's going to lure the SKB.'

'Maybe the shot will be enough? Do you find her attractive?' Jo was scrolling through 'Natasha's' profile photos – all selfies. There was one of her in a long golden dress, her hair artfully arranged over one shoulder.

'No. She has a toxic aura. Freaks me out, frankly.'

'Maybe because you've encountered the real Diana.'

'Possibly. I'm sure she will appeal to some poor bastard out there.'

Jo burst out laughing. 'You are a bear with a sore head this morning.'

Brandon turned to her, stretched his lips into a thin line, an eyebrow attempted an arch. 'Add sore left wrist, aching right knee and open wound on my right palm. Regardless, Ms Chambers is not my idea of a sight for sore eyes.'

'Do you think she will appeal to the SBK?'

'A bit coarse. The man is a connoisseur. But I'm intrigued by her actions. Is she new to the site?'

'Yes – fresh blood.'

'Is she gay or bi?'

'She says she's interested in men. Otherwise I'd offer my services, Boss.'

Brandon smiled. 'Well, that makes sense. This is Diana's honey trap. I think we need to keep an eye on her. As much for her own safety as for any leads she might generate.'

'When do you want me to start, Boss?'

'I'll be in close contact, whatever happens. But tonight would be as good a time as any. You've got her address. Watch her movements. Buy a wig and get yourself a date for the night, to deflect attention if you need to follow her to a venue.'

'Stew?'

'The one and only. Sadly, Jo, we have a small pool of talent at the station.'

July 19, 2019

Three hours later, Suzanna Fitzgerald was standing on his doorstep brandishing a tupperware tub.

'I brought you some chicken soup. Am I allowed over the threshold with it?'

Brandon smiled and stroked his beard. 'If you can vouch for the contents?'

He moved aside and she glided into his hallway, her eyes, as ever, surveying and analysing.

'Would you like to come through to the garden room?' Brandon said, gesturing towards the small area by the French windows.

She smiled. 'I'll just put the soup in the fridge.' Well at least she wasn't going to boil it up on his hob. Suzanna had a calm, but commanding presence.

'Coffee?'

'Thanks, milk no—'

'I know.'

Brandon poured some hot coffee from the machine that took up far too much room on his small work surface, topped it up with milk and took it over to her.

'Any news on the other tupperware box?'

'No. Al Chapman couldn't find any DNA on it. It'd been sanitised. So just the great man's specs.'

Suzanna stirred her coffee with a spoon. 'And the SBK's delivery?'

Brandon shot her a look. 'So, we are in agreement – the second most definitely the work of the SBK. The tupperware – just a bad joke, or worse.'

'Or worse. It's quite sinister, isn't it? And it's marking Chapman out. How is he? Any theories on the titian braid and brooch?'

Brandon sighed. 'Chapman wouldn't be Chapman without a theory or five thousand. The hair has been identified as Emily Paxton's, the thirty-four-year old woman who went missing a week ago.'

'And the brooch?'

'As always, these artefacts take time to trace. Nothing on the web. I've passed a photo on to Hatton Cross Vintage. They've made some headway on the earring. This piece could well be from the same haul.'

'Oh yes?' Suzanna felt in her bag for reading glasses. 'Could I have a look, please?'

Brandon pulled out a photo from a file on the table and passed it to her.

Suzanna put on a pair of horn-rimmed glasses, which served to make her look even more intelligent. 'An exquisite piece of art deco jewellery. It looks very expensive.'

Brandon raised an eyebrow. 'No expense spared by our SBK.'

She returned the photo to Brandon and he studied it. 'The eagle and the serpent represent wisdom and passion, morality and vengeance.'

'I know,' Suzanna said, holding his gaze. 'I've never worked out which creature represents which element. They are both ruthless.'

Brandon looked away. 'Maybe that's it. Maybe our man is all of these things. Well he has to be. There is nothing more ruthless than abduction and murder.'

'True. And maybe, like all people, he is governed by one or more of these human conditions at any given time.'

'Vengence has to have taken top billing the other night.'

'The woman was a red head. He didn't take to you and Jo trying to catch him out.'

Brandon scoffed. 'This isn't the SBK Show. The cops have a job to do. Like stopping the arsehole.'

Brandon looked down and started fiddling with the dressing on his right hand.

'We'll get there, Brandon. I think you rattled him the other night. You almost caught him.'

'Well, if he thinks abducting another woman is going to deter me—'

'He wouldn't think that. He's just flexing his muscles. Letting you know who's running the show.'

Brandon ran a hand over his chin. 'I'll be there for the final curtain. The bastard won't get a standing ovation, believe me.'

Suzanna smiled and pushed aside her empty cup. 'Those dreams you've been having. Are they related to the case?'

Brandon shot her a look.

'You don't have to share them. But it may help.'

'There is a connection. I'm always transported to an armpit of a place in Alabama – the scene of some truly vile ritual killings ten years ago.' He paused.

Suzanna nodded. 'When you're ready.'

He shook his head. 'I'm never ready to relive that trauma, but, at least, the case was resolved. We nailed the killer and his accomplices after two long bloody months. But we, I, made mistakes on the way. They were thick. It made our job that much easier. But they also lacked any ounce of human decency, which made it that much harder. I wasn't prepared for the lengths a depraved person would go to. The visceral cunning to cover tracks.'

Suzanna remained silent, which, in interrogation mode meant, go on.

'The thing is, the killers couldn't be more different. Red necks, as opposed to some sort of gentleman with a god complex.'

Suzanna interrupted. 'Were the victims women?'

'Yes. Younger women. Some very young. The hillbillies weren't looking to save any one, unless they thought their human sacrifices would earn them a place at the Devil's top table.'

'But you stopped them.'

'Yes. Eventually, we stopped them.' Brandon steepled his hands. 'But—' He looked at Suzanna. 'There is always someone in the dream I can't save. Someone it's too late to save.'

Suzanna inhaled sharply and sat up straight.

'I run to her. I walk to her. I stumble upon her. But she is always out of reach.'

Suzanna leaned forward. 'Do you know this person?'

'Jessica, my wife.'

'I—'

'Jessica died five and a half years ago … of cancer. There

was nothing any of us could do. But it all gets mixed up in here sometimes.' He tapped his head lightly.

'Of course it does. There is no greater trauma than losing a loved one. Really.' She got up from the table and walked over to the fridge. 'Now, DI Hammett, you deserve a bit of mothering.'

He smiled. 'I do have a mother, Suzanna. A darn fine one as it happens.'

'Has she made you any chicken soup?'

'Can't say she has right at this minute.'

Suzanna touched him briefly on the shoulder. 'Where do you keep the bowls?'

August 1, 2019

'Don't be scared. You'll love this. I promise.' He was standing close behind her. So close she could feel his warm breath on the back of her neck. Her body was fighting fear; heart racing, fists flexing, her mouth dry as she swallowed hard.

'My treat. One which you deserve, my love.' He pulled something from his pocket and she flinched.

'I don't like games, really, I don't like games.'

'This isn't a game. Trust me. You do trust me?' he said placing a silk blindfold over her eyes and fastening it at the back of her head. It smelt of lilies.

'Please, please,' she said, 'I—'

'Darling, relax. You do trust me?'

She nodded, her lips unable to form words.

'Good,' he said, and started to turn her round slowly, and then a little faster so she lost balance and all sense of direction.

'Careful,' he said, catching her under the arm as she stumbled. 'Let me guide you.'

He placed an arm around her waist and helped her along the passageway which led from the orangery where they'd had lunch. She had no idea of the direction but was surprised when they didn't reach the turret stairs after a few steps. The realisation brought her up sharp – a new route. How much would she remember blindfold? And would it matter?

'There we go,' he said, as if reading her change of mood. He pulled her closer – closer than ever – and a pungent whiff of acid mingled with the cloying scent of lilies, reminding her of funeral parlours.

He turned her to face him. 'Put your arms around my

neck.' The breathless words brushed the light down of her cheek. She did as he said and he reached down, placing his arms under her legs to carry her. He was fit, but she could feel his body straining as he mounted the stairs. One, two, three, four, she counted as they circled upwards. The turret? She allowed one arm to relax a little and glance the wall, the cool stone confirming her theory. But they'd reached the top in ten steps, two less than usual. Another staircase, another wing? The thought terrified her.

He took five paces before he stopped. 'Let me carry you over the threshold,' he said.

He stood for a while, before placing her back on her feet and untying the blindfold.

'Now, can I trust you to behave yourself?' He was peering at her over his glasses, giving a mock disciplinarian look.

They were by the tapestry stand in the French bedroom. He'd allowed her back. She took a moment to collect herself before responding in kind. 'If you continue to spoil me in such a lavish manner, you can expect nothing but blind devotion.'

He gave a short laugh. 'So you like your new pastime?'

'Indeed, I do.' An antique wooden frame and sumptuous selection of cottons and silks was nothing less than daunting. But there was also a William Morris Cross Stitch Set for Beginners. She rapped the box to disguise her shaking fingers, and slow her heart beat.

'I can see you are eager to get going. Do you need more light?' The shutter slats were half closed, the evening sunlight fading.

'That would be excellent.' He knew, of course, that she had little to gain by a glimpse out of the window. She had been there, dragged back. But opening the aperture a fraction was another small victory in this war of attrition.

He walked over to the shutters and opened them wide, leaving the window locked. It wasn't stuffy in the room – he'd kept the door open and she could feel the cool breeze from one of the turret windows.

She started to assemble the contents of the cross stitch box on a side table, aware that she had an audience. He loved to watch her doing feminine things, so she indulged him. He was standing by the door when she sewed her first stitch, lifting the needle high to tighten the silk, before giving it a little jerk and plunging it into the canvas.

'You're a natural,' he said, one hand on the architrave. 'I could learn from you.'

She turned, smiled and watched him leave, the breeze reduced to a draught under the door. As she returned to her task, the needle pricked her finger and she put it to her mouth to stem the blood.

An hour or so later she tidied up her things and prepared for bed. The room had a small en suite. Its walls were covered in blue and white toile, depicting a young couple chasing through woodland. The paper looked new. She wondered if he'd refurbished it to her taste. Or to make a point.

There was a nightgown draped over a side chair. Not white like last time. She'd blotted that virgin sheet. This one was blue. At least it wasn't orange.

A book of poetry rested on the side table, but it was too dark to read. So she lay listening to the gulls yelling their good nights and the occasional shuffles of the dog outside the door.

He knocked lightly before entering, but it made her start and pull up the bed sheet.

'Just coming to clear away.' He walked over to the tapestry stand. 'A fine start, my love.'

She moved onto her side and stretched out an arm as if waking and then realised the futility of the action. He would have heard her movements – waited an appropriate time to come in and clear away what, she supposed, could be used as weaponry.

'Sleep tight, darling,' he said, casting his candelabra around, as if checking for errant needles, although he'd only allowed her the one. His steps sounded heavy on the wooden floor.

'Goodnight, darling,' she said in a sleepy voice, listening for the turn of the key. She sat up bolt straight, alerted to the sound of nothing. Nothing but the small whine of a dog bored of sitting and his heavy steps heading for the turret stairs.

When the footsteps faded, she swung out of bed and walked over to the small closet by the door. The green dress was hanging on a pink silk hanger, the petticoat neatly folded on the shelf above. She reached up and felt for the scraps of food she'd stashed from dinner. Some bread and one petit four. She gently lowered the door handle and pulled. The door was unlocked. She had to be quick. Didn't want the dog to howl an alarm. Heart hammering, the petit four melting in her palm, she opened the door a fraction more and tossed it. The dog pounced immediately, salivating with pleasure. Tearing up the piece of bread she tossed it out, bit by bit.

'Good boy, Good boy,' she coaxed, using the door as a shield. Now wasn't the time to test his loyalty.

Brandon

July 22, 2019

Brandon was sitting at home ostensibly watching a US Cop show with Chelsea. His daughter was trying to educate him on how to be a hard-arsed investigator. Brandon was having fun investigating the number of old actors in the episode, including Illya Kuryakin from the *Man from Uncle*. It was good to know that crime was supplementing their pensions. Mostly he was ruminating on his own case. An email had just come in from Abelman at Hatton Cross Vintage. The brooch, last valued at $22,000, had a similar backstory to the earring and had been, up until 1987, owned by a Swiss arts dealer by the name of Leon Schneider. Abelman had no further records on the piece. Brandon would hunt Schneider down via Interpol in the morning.

'Dad, what do you think?'

'Ask me in the morning,' Brandon said, getting up from his chair as his phone pinged.

'I guess you won't be going to bed right now then,' Chelsea said, as she clocked his expression.

Brandon raised a hand. 'Lock up after me, darlin. I've got to go out.'

'Now?'

'Yes.'

Brandon got into the Skoda, released the handbrake with his

good right hand, and headed off to meet Jo in The Mexican Inn car park in Long Rock. Jo had been following Diana for three nights. The woman was on a mission – each night a date with another loser or chancer. Stew was having a field day relating Diana's victims, who were all suitably packed off without the niceties after a preliminary coffee or glass of prosecco, if she was feeling generous or curious.

When he arrived there was only Jo's car parked. She walked over as he pulled up and opened the passenger door.

'Be my guest,' Brandon said gesturing for her to sit. 'Where's Stew?'

'He's following Diana, on foot.'

'So why am I here?'

'A hunch.' Jo stretched her lips into a thin line. 'Diana's date didn't show. And she waited a long time.'

Brandon flexed his left fist. It was becoming a habit.

'And then she left abruptly. After taking a call.'

'On foot?'

'Yes.'

Jo's phone rang and she put it on speaker.

'She's given me the slip. Or should I say, they've given me the slip.' Stew sounded pissed off.

'For fuck's sake how? Did she see you?' Brandon said.

'Not possible, I kept my distance. But she met someone – on the other side of the railway crossing, by the seafront – and I couldn't just belt over and join them. He had a car parked in the Long Rock carpark. Last thing I saw was them driving over the crossing in a white Mazda. I've got the reg.'

Brandon threw back his head. 'What direction?'

'Left towards the roundabout.'

'Okay. Stew, can you put out an alert on the Mazda. I know it's a big ask for the patrols, but in the circumstances understandable. And then pick up Jo's car. I'll leave the keys with the bartender.'

'Where you going, Boss?'

'To Diana's. Need to check whether she's been dropped off. Keep your phone charged and let us know if anything comes in.'

'You worried, Boss?'

'Darn right I am.'

The lights were off when they arrived at Diana's, a small cottage at the end of a four-house terrace which backed onto scrubby fields. Her Polo was parked at the side of her house.

Jo looked at him. 'Looks like no one's at home.'

'That's what it looks like.' Brandon eased up the handbrake with his right hand and undid his safety belt.'

'We're going over?'

'Yes. That hunch you had earlier, Jo. It's catching.'

The curtains were pulled, but there was a glimmer of light towards the back of the house. Brandon rang the bell and waited. Nothing.

'I'll just take a look out back. You wait here,' he said, walking around the side of the building, past the Polo, to the small back gate. He lent across it and jerked up the latch. The light was coming from a downlight section in the kitchen. He tried the back door and was surprised when it opened. Diana didn't seem the sort of person to be lapse on security.

The kitchen was predictably tidy and clean, although the freezer door was ajar. Brandon poked it open with his shoe; empty apart from some bags of frozen veg.

'Found anything?'

Brandon swung round. 'For chrissake, Jo!'

'Didn't mean to startle you.'

He sucked in a breath. 'A tense situation. What's that?'

There was a low moaning sound coming from above.

'Sounds human.' Jo looked as worried as he felt.

He put a hand on her arm. 'Let me take a look.'

She went to join him, but he barred her way. 'Watch the door.'

They both walked out into the hallway, Jo positioning herself by the door, Brandon taking the stairs.

He felt that familiar sickness born of anticipation and memories that can't be erased or rationalised. Finger on the trigger of his taser, he stepped up onto the landing and pushed open the first door with his foot. It was a cluttered small bedroom, some empty boxes on the floor and one on the bed.

He let the door ease shut and paused for a few seconds against the landing wall. The moaning had started again and was coming from the next room. He took a breath and pointed the taser before him in outstretched arms.

'Police. Coming in.'

Brandon kicked open the door, his injured left hand feeling for the light switch.

'Jesus!'

No amount of home visits could have prepared him for this. His left hand flew to his mouth, all thoughts of pain gone, as he took in the display of dismembered body parts on the floor. A hand, a foot, an ear, what looked like a nose, spewed out on a bedroom rug.

Diana was watching him from a chair by the bed, her hands and feet bound, a gag tied fast around her mouth.

A piece of paper was by her foot, 'Cheap Copy' scrawled on it.

He skirted the sea of flesh and bones and untied the gag.

'I can explain,' she said, wide eyes locked onto his. 'I can explain everything.'

'Where is he?' Brandon went to a wardrobe and flung open the door. 'Where the hell is he?'

July 22, 2019

'Those body parts – they belong to a vagrant, a woman, who died years ago. No one claimed the body. I didn't murder anyone.' Diana volunteered the information as they sat at her kitchen table waiting for the CSI team.

Brandon blew out. 'We'll be the judge of that.'

'I'll be proved right.' Diana was defiant as ever, despite being caught dead-handed.

Time to get official. 'Ms Chambers, you do not have to say anything. But it may harm your defence if you do not mention when questioned something that you later rely on in court. Anything you do say may be given in evidence."

Diana was bristling. 'You're charging me?'

'Ms Chambers, you have an awful lot of explaining to do. How come the body parts of a dead woman happen to be scattered all over your bedroom? You can't wave this aside as if it's a bad smell.'

'A friend gave me access to them.'

Brandon shook his head. 'Count Dracula?'

Diana pursed her lips and glanced up at the line of people at the front door. 'I'll let him explain for himself.'

Him was at the back of a queue of SOCOs making their way along the hallway and into the kitchen.

Brandon got up to greet them. 'The crime scene is upstairs, second bedroom.'

As they turned to go, Brandon called back Al Chapman. 'Al.'

He turned slowly, studiously avoiding Diana who was sitting, arms folded, eyes boring through him. 'Yes?'

Brandon went to say something but paused. 'I'll come up with you.' He glanced at Jo, although she didn't need to be warned to watch Diana.

When they got to the bedroom, the SOCOs stood stock still like pillars of salt.

Nadia McGowan broke the line. 'What the fuck,' she said, twisting round to Al.

'Just do your job, Nadia,' he said, his glasses steaming up above his mask. He'd come in civvies.

'What do you reckon?' Brandon was watching him carefully. Al wasn't one to give too much away, but he had yet to look Brandon in the eye, which said it all.

'Diana is a loose cannon.' He was still looking away.

'You know her?'

Al turned to him. 'Yes. Or, rather, we knew each other.'

Brandon gestured for Al to follow him out onto the landing. 'That sounds ominous.' To be honest, everything about Diana Chambers was ominous.

Al rubbed the back of his neck. 'She's a bit bonkers. Too hot to handle, that's for sure.'

'Meaning?'

'She got in touch with me a few years back about the original Sleeping Beauty Killings. She was a true crime obsessive – she wasn't the first, or last of that kind to contact me – but she was persistent and, also, displayed a certain level of intelligence.' Al gave Brandon a quick look. 'And she was reasonably fit.' He met Brandon's steady gaze. 'Believe me, the majority of these fruit cakes are chubby, sweaty men living in their mothers' basements.'

Brandon suppressed a smile. The whole scene was getting surreal and it was knocking on midnight. Maybe Count Dracula might join the party after all.

'She also said she was studying criminology. We regularly do mortuary tours for students.'

'Did she come carrying a bag? A cool box, perhaps?'

Al gave him a look. 'We don't do bag searches at the door, so maybe. But she came a few times.'

'Did you check her credentials? Her Uni?'

Al looked away. 'No. I took her word for it. She may well be a student – have got her degree. I don't know. We lost contact.'

'Why?'

Al looked him in the eye. 'Why do you think?'

Brandon held his gaze. 'It's not what I think, it's what you can tell me. Now. Why didn't you mention your … relationship, connection before?' He paused and looked to the ceiling. 'The specs in the tupperware box? Was this her work? You must have suspected?'

Al looked to the side. 'Possibly. I thought it was a harmless dig. That she was getting back at me for dumping her. I didn't want to … respond. Get involved again.'

Brandon gave him a long cold stare. 'You have crossed the line in so many ways, Al. You really need to say something plausible to drag yourself out of this hole.'

'Diana was just too much. Too controlling. Too obsessional. Frankly, too dangerous. I didn't know she'd stolen the body parts. I mean, if she did steal them from the morgue. Honest to God. But she was never satisfied with how the case was shelved and the killer left free to roam. Maybe—' Al looked down and then back up at Brandon. 'Diana used the parts as bait to lure the SBK out of retirement?'

Brandon bit down hard on his bottom lip. 'You're saying Diana Chambers rattled the SBK's cage with old bones and didn't think that, possibly, she'd send him off on another killing spree?'

Al nodded. 'Could be. I hadn't given it much thought, until now.' He waved a hand towards the room. 'But isn't that what this looks like?'

Brandon shook his head lightly. 'Perhaps you should have asked yourself these questions earlier? Or at least shared any suspicions.' He paused before continuing. 'You didn't notice body parts going missing?'

'I'm not a lab technician. Things get tagged and logged but mistakes can happen. Things go missing. Particularly—' Al looked to one side. 'Particularly when no one is bothered about the deceased.'

'Al, I'm going to have to take you off the case until we've cleared all this up.'

Al went to protest, but Brandon had turned to Nadia. 'Can you take over tonight, please?'

Nadia gave him a searching look.

'A complication.'

Al nodded and gave Nadia a quick look. 'You know the drill. Finish up here and get the body parts to the lab.'

Nadia went to speak, but Al cut in. 'Just do it, okay.'

He turned to Brandon, a bead of sweat slowly making its way down his forehead towards his nose.

'Whatever the outcome, this is just part of the story, isn't it?' Al's eyes were shining behind his spectacles. 'Diana didn't gag and tie herself up.' Al raised his palms in defence. 'And, before you pull me in for questioning, not guilty.'

Brandon ran a finger over his top lip. 'No more questions for tonight, Al, but keep your phone on. Goes without saying you won't be leaving town.'

Al grimaced. 'I wouldn't miss the grand finale of this grim fairy tale for the world.'

'It's been a long-running saga, Al, and you've clearly had your part to play. That won't go unnoticed.'

Al ran a hand through his thinning hair. 'I was unprofessional. But in over thirty years of good service, maybe I'll get off with a firm slap on the wrist.' He glanced at Brandon's neoprene wrist support.

'Maybe.' Brandon watched him walk swiftly along the landing and down the stairs and thought he did have a point. Al was good at his job. Very good. But that one time he allowed himself to be flattered and then went on to turn a blind eye could cost him.

July 23, 2019

Jo came into the interview room and drew up a chair next to Brandon and opposite Diana Chambers.

Brandon glanced at Jo. 'Shall we start?'

Jo switched on the recorder. '1am, July 23, 2019.'

'Ms Chambers, when we rescued you from your house, your first words were, I can explain. Please do.'

Diana glanced at her legal aid lawyer, Jimmy Shafter, who'd been called out of bed to represent her. He looked his usual dishevelled self. Brandon wondered, briefly, why he was so keen for the work.

'You don't have to answer the question.' Jimmy rolled off the usual spiel.

'Yes, I do,' Diana replied. 'Although, first of all, I have a question for DI Hammett and DS Menhenrick.'

Brandon stifled a yawn and nodded.

'You say you rescued me. In fact, you broke into my house and came upon me. Is that standard police practice?'

'Ms Chambers, you are a person of interest in these investigations. As such you have been under surveillance. You were seen getting into the car of a stranger you most likely met on Huddle. Two young women have gone missing, their body parts found, after meeting up with a man/men on the dating app. We were safeguarding you. When we tried your back door it was open – suspicious in its own right – and then we heard you moaning.' Brandon paused. 'Now, shall we get on? This only needs to be as long as you want to make it.'

Diana readjusted her seat. 'First of all, I want to make it clear that I didn't steal the body parts. CSI Al Chapman gave them to me to look after for him.'

Brandon widened his eyes and gave Jo a quick glance. 'Why would he do that?'

'Because he is the SBK copycat.'

'And he sent a pair of his own spectacles to the station in a tupperware box to let us in on the secret?' Brandon's eyes were ranged on her.

'To tease and test you.'

Brandon's eyes flicked up at the clock. 'I really hope you're not wasting police time with false allegations, Ms Chambers, because you are up to your neck in this charade. Just to save you some spinning time – Al Chapman was at his mother's when you were tied up in your bedroom. Nadia McGowan picked him up and drove him to your place. We will check the timings of your visits to the morgue, as a guest of Mr Chapman, and what was in the fridges at the time. Need I go on?'

Diana's face hardened. 'He was a party to all of this. He's no fan of police failure either.'

Brandon looked her in the eye. 'By taking the law into your own hands, you may well be responsible for the mutilation and death of three women. Your actions, wittingly or otherwise, unleashed a dormant devil.'

Diana sat up straight. 'Tortured soul.'

'Is that what you think? Is that why you've been trying to date him on Huddle?'

Diana looked over his head at the clock. 'No and yes. I want to see him brought to justice more than anyone. Why would he cut down those beautiful women just as they were entering their prime? It's the why that interests me. I need to know.'

'So much so that you endangered the lives of other women?'

'You're jumping to conclusions, DI Hammett,' Jimmy cut in.

Brandon nodded. 'Ms Chambers, shall we cut to the quick. What did the killer look like?'

Diana's sharp eyes were tearing into him. 'Aren't you going to ask why he didn't abduct me too?'

Brandon looked to one side and then back at her. 'I'm more interested in what he looks like right now. But yes, I'd also like to know why he didn't take you, although the note he left – Cheap Copy – gives me a darn good idea.'

Diana sniffed. 'He can talk. Everything about his voice last night, everything about him, was false. I wasn't falling for it.'

Brandon nodded. 'He didn't seem real?'

'No. I'd say he was in disguise. A good one, but there was something rubbery about his face and his hair looked like a wig.'

'What colour hair?'

'Auburn.'

'Not the dark blonde of the suspect seen at The Turk's Head.'

Diana shook her head. 'No. And he was a little stout.'

'Could have used body padding.'

'My thoughts.'

Brandon could see what Al and Julia had meant about her intelligence and attention to detail. But it didn't detract from the fact that the woman was a loose cannon who could have triggered this whole killing spree.

'Describe him to me, regardless.'

'Six foot two, short, thick auburn hair, parted on the side, light blue or grey eyes, behind heavy-rimmed glasses, full-face, wide, slightly bulbous nose, lightweight blue jumper over slight paunch, navy blue chinos, brown brogues. No body art, on show. Or jewellery. He had a Cornish accent. But it seemed put on.'

'We'll get an identikit out. Someone may be able to help with his movements prior to and after he left you.'

'Has the Mazda turned up yet?' Diana said.

'No.'

'Probably stolen.'

'Any particular reason for thinking that?'

'Kids clothes in the back. Empty sweet wrappers on the floor.'

Brandon glanced at Jo. It would make sense. The man wasn't going to make it easy for them by driving his own car. If he had one.

'No further questions now. But I'm going to have to ask you to come back to the station later, Ms Chambers,' Brandon said, easing himself out of his chair.

'On what charge?'

'No charge. But we need answers concerning those body parts. The forensics will do their report, but the sooner you can fill us in with the details, best for everyone. This is not a good time to waste valuable police time.'

Diana got up from the table and went to say something, but stopped. He'd appealed to her sense of justice, but Diana's was evidently skewed.

'What time do you want me in the morning?'

'Eleven.' Give the forensics time to do their report. They'd finished at Diana's.

'Are you okay about going back to the house?'

Diana's face softened, before tightening again. 'It's not the dead that can hurt you Detective Inspector. And I'm not the SBK's type. I'll be fine.'

'I'll get you a lift,' Brandon said, steering her to the door, Jimmy already ahead of them, Jo waiting behind to switch off the lights.'

August 2, 2019

She woke to hear the dog snuffling outside. It began to whimper and bang against the door. Something was troubling him. She got out of bed and walked to the door, opening it a crack.

'What is it boy? What's the matter?'

He pushed his snout through the gap and she caught a look in his eyes, which could have been sadness, or fear, or both.

She crouched and he pushed into the room to nuzzle against her knees, knocking her off balance.

'Good boy, good boy,' she said, stroking his head, as he circled a patch on the floor. 'What is it boy? What's the matter?'

As she spoke she could hear what was worrying him. A low howling was coming from the bowels of the house. The dog was panting with fear and pawing the skirt of her nightdress as she knelt to comfort him.

'Let's go see, shall we?' she said, getting to her feet, the dog looking up at her. 'Come on boy, you lead me. Come on, let's find him.' The dog trotted beside her as she left the room, looking up at her for guidance, his tail wagging. 'Go boy,' she said, encouraging him to take the lead, 'Go.' He sprinted off along the landing and down the stairs, pausing, from time to time, to look back and allow her to catch up.

The howling came in bursts; terrible sobs, each one dredged

from some vast vat of despair. They were on the ground floor now, in the hallway that led to the dining room and she stood rooted to the spot, the dog looking back at her, cowering, his tail tucked between his legs.

It positioned himself at the door. Would he cross that line? Could she?

The sobbing had become low and rasping, the death throes of anguish. She edged towards the door, leaning to stroke the dog's head, slowly raising her own to look in. He was slumped at the dining table, his head in his hands, surrounded by bottles and what looked like a medical kit. There was no disguising the acidic stench of formaldehyde and she put an arm to her face.

He started to mutter and drew himself upright. She pulled back from the door and watched him begin to fuss with the things around him. Pulling something heavy across his lap he wiped and dabbed it with a cloth, before reaching for a satin quilted box on the table. It looked like a sewing box – one her mother used to have, and what she still used herself from time-to-time. He sniffed, took off his glasses to give them a quick clean, and replaced them before opening the box. She took a step back, preparing to leave, just catching the sheen of a long thread caught in the candlelight and a flash of metal.

She crept away, confident that he wouldn't notice, so intent was he on his task. The dog pattered softly behind, before brushing against her leg and looking up. She stroked his head and they made their way to the turret stairs, stopping at the locked garden door, its key absent, dangling, as always, from the chain he clanked around with him. In a way it was a relief. So much ground covered today. Such a revelation to see him slumped at that table, a figure of torment and exhaustion, toiling away at a thankless task. Trying to fix the unfixable. She imagined him tutting and fretting over her own decaying body, as his aged too. His stitches increasingly big and clumsy, hastily sewn in rheumatic hands, leaking formaldehyde forming splodges.

She parted company with the dog at her door, giving him a last piece of bread before shutting it.

Slipping under the bed sheets she gazed at the walls, counted the strips of moonlight cast through the blind. Like him, she was tired – but possibly more determined. She had a life outside these walls. He had nothing. His idea of creating some kind of heaven was a hell of his own making. Eternal strife.

She'd bide her time, wear him down, conserve her own strength, watch his drain away.

August 2, 2019

He was sitting in the chair by the tapestry stand when she woke.

'Morning, sleepy head,' he said, smiling gently.

He looked fresh. Maybe he was Count Dracula and had downed a pint of recuperative blood?

'Morning, darling.'

'It's a glorious sunny day.' He got up, went to the window, and flung open the shutters, a light breeze making shadows dance on the bed sheets.

She stretched and sat up, pulling her knees to her chest. 'It would be lovely to go down to the sea.'

His brow clouded. 'We can't do that, darling. But I have a little treat for you in the garden.'

'A paddling pool?'

'Darling! But maybe, just maybe, you will like my little treat.'

A helicopter? She had to bite her tongue. Her playful manner would only be tolerated so far.

'Are you hungry, darling?'

As a matter of fact, she was. She was always hungry, but even more so at that very moment. 'What time is it?' she asked, looking out of the window, seeing the sun high above the trees.

'Noon. I let you sleep.'

Or made her sleep. She rarely slept past 6.30, whatever time she went to bed.

'I'll let you get ready and then we can go down for lunch,' he said, rising from his chair.

She took her time to get ready, remembering her plan to

wear him down. He had so much to get on with, the delay would gnaw at him.

She was right. Twenty minutes later she heard him rap tersely at her door and opened it to see his taut face struggling to form a smile. The dog wasn't there, but she didn't mention it.

'You look lovely, darling,' he said, admiring her in a floaty summer dress, one of a collection he had selected for her. It matched a straw hat which hung at her back, its yellow ribbons caught at her neck in a bow. She let him lead her down the turret stairs to the ground floor hall and the garden door. He used a small key, a replica of the one she'd found in the flower pot, and opened the door onto the garden. The table was laid for lunch – a net over a plate of cheeses and hams and slices of bread; a butter dish and bowl of cherries to the side.

'I made the bread,' he said, his hands clasped together. 'Someone will be joining us for lunch.'

Her mouth fell open and her heart sank, as if yanked down by that damn key chain. She composed her face and met his eye, all the while spying from the corner of hers.

'Don't you want to meet our new house guest?'

'Of course,' she said, taking his outstretched hand.

'Come, on then. The perfect female companion for you.' His step had livened, and she scurried to keep up with him as he hurried to the bottom of the garden, past late runner beans and forlorn sunflowers, to a hut in the corner.

'This is new?' she said, turning to him.

'You are observant. But, yes, it is new and so is—' He lifted the latch and the door opened a bit and then a bit more, as a bundle of white fur pushed its way out, tail wagging, brown eyes shining.

'Oh my God! Oh my God!' It was the cutest Shih Tzu puppy and her heart immediately went out to it.

'Do you like her?'

'I love her,' she said, swooping down to pick her up and rub noses. 'She's delightful. What's her name?'

'That's for you to decide,' he said smiling at her. 'She's all yours.' He paused. 'You are so well-matched. I thought she would be much better suited to you in the portrait.'

She looked him in the eye, caught that glint of steel, and chose to say nothing.

'You'll take good care of her, won't you?' he said.

'Of course.'

'Only—' he'd turned to his left and started to walk towards the iron gate. 'Only, the little gate managed to work its way open last night.'

How? She creased her brow. 'How extraordinary.'

'It's old and the metal erodes and weakens under stress.' He pushed it open and walked through, beckoning her to follow him down the slope to the cliff edge, the puppy squirming in her arms. If those arms had been empty, she would have used them to push him over. Instead, she joined him on the edge and looked down into the cove. Saw the broken body, the clumps of blood-matted fur, the sandy paws outstretched as if clawing their way back, the hind legs half submerged in the incoming tide.

The puppy yelped and struggled to be free, but she pulled it close, burying her face in its fur to mask her tears.

'You need to be very careful, my dear,' he said, steering her back up the slope to the garden. 'Very careful.'

Brandon

July 23, 2019

The body parts that Diana Chambers had kept in her freezer couldn't be identified. There'd been no dead vagrant stored at the morgue around the time of Diana's visits and so, on the face of it, Al Chapman was largely off the hook. Chambers had been bailed and made available for further questioning, when, Brandon hoped, she'd come completely clean. But right now he was more interested in nailing the real SBK. Jo was searching through CCTV footage around Marazion and its surrounds to see if anyone fitting Diana's detailed description cropped up. The forensics were pawing over the upholstery in the Mazda for clues. Diana had been right about the car being stolen. It'd been found dumped in the small village of Gulvar, on the outskirts of Penzance. Stew was making door-to-door calls to see if anyone had noticed another vehicle parked around that area.

'Rami Abelson for you.' PC McNabb was on the station landline transferring a call to the incident room.

'We may well have located your pieces.' Abelman sounded pleased with himself.

Brandon sat up straight. 'Okay.'

'Leon Schneider's son got back to me. Those pieces have been round the block and back a few times. Both limited editions made by top French jeweller Bijoux Chérir. A Polish Contessa got her hands on the earrings and brooch just before the war and, the story goes, she lost them in a game of poker with a Nazi commander in Wroclaw, days after the tanks rolled in. He smuggled them into Switzerland as a nice post war insurance policy. The guy never collected them and Schneider senior bought them at auction in 1987.'

'Who did he sell them to?'

'An American based in Zug. Marty Green. He's since moved to Mexico. I have an address, if you want to follow this up.'

'You say the pieces were limited edition?'

'Yes. But Bijoux Chérir went out of business twenty years or so ago. The only way of tracing the pieces today is via the dealers. Schneider's the best we have at the moment. The other pieces are, most likely, family heirlooms, which may never have re-emerged on the open market.'

'Thanks, Rami. Could you give me Green and Schneider's contact details, please?'

'I'll email them.'

'I can wait while you get them,' Brandon said, rocking back in his chair. This had to be the best lead he'd had to-date.

August 2, 2019

The dog was playing at her feet as she buttered bread and smeared it with cheese and ham. Every so often she'd throw a morsel to the dog, who squealed with delight and wagged her tail for more.

'You'll make her sick.' He was observing her over his glasses, watching her consume each dainty mouthful and now the mouthfuls she was feeding her dog. For the first time, he had a folded newspaper on the table, although he didn't open it. August 2. She'd been captive for eight long days. She wondered if she – or any of the others – were on the front page. All she could see was an arts spread about a new exhibition at Tate St Ives.

'Will you feed her then?'

'Yes. She is yours for pleasure not work.' He was rapping his fingers on the table, clearly itching to get back to business. He couldn't relax, which wasn't surprising in the circumstances. She was taking an age to eat the food. He'd finished long ago and now made a play of opening out the paper and reading it. She took another dainty mouthful, before leaning down to pick up the dog.

He frowned as the dog sniffed and salivated at the food and scrambled to get onto the table.

'Darling, she has a full bowl in her hut. Don't encourage her.' He paused and refolded his paper. 'She needs to be trained – and then she will be as good as gold.'

'You've had one before?' She cut three thick slices of bread and smeared them with butter and chunks of melting Cornish camembert.

His eyes were on her as she picked up one piece and shoved it in her mouth.

'Er, yes. We had one when I was little.'

'Your mother's?' she said, her mouth full.

'Why, yes. But—' He watched her chewing. She could feel a drop of cheese at the side of her mouth, but left it there.

'But?' she said, picking up another piece and ramming it in her mouth. 'She became your companion?'

'Darling, I wouldn't say that …' He picked up a napkin and dabbed at the side of his mouth, his head nodding slightly, suggesting she do the same.

She ignored him. 'What happened to the dog?' Her mouth was full, but she took the last piece and went to put it to her mouth.

'Darling, you have a little bit of cheese on the side of your face. Here, let me.' He leant over to wipe it off and, as he moved back, she shoved the last piece of bread and cheese in her mouth.

'What was the dog called?' She was masticating exaggeratedly as she spoke, like an arrogant crime lord, the dog at her side, trying to clamber up on her lap.

He ran a palm over his brow and looked down. 'I'm not sure I recall. It was a long time ago. She was my mother's dog. Her beloved dog. Darling, shall we retire to the gallery. I so want to paint you both.'

Taking the napkin, she dabbed the sides of her mouth and watched him visibly relax.

'What was your mother called?' She looked at him steadily, even the dog stopped its frantic fussing and watched him from her lap.

'Greta.'

Stroking the silky head of her new companion, she smiled. 'Then that is what I choose to call my darling doggie. What a lovely name Greta is. Change one letter and it's Great.'

'How clever of you, darling. How very clever.'

Julia

July 23, 2019

Brandon was standing in the garden at The Hall. The forensics, led by Nadia McGowan, were doing fingertip searches. There was another team inside going through the freezer and larder.

'It might be an idea to have a look in the summerhouse. We keep a freezer in there,' Julia said as she watched them work.

Brandon gave her an appreciative look. 'Thanks, Julia. I'm so sorry to have to put you through all this again. I think the SOCOs are already in there.'

'It really isn't a problem.' For much longer. But the gift of Diana Chambers kept on giving. Not only had she soiled her clothes and spare room, she'd left scraps of dead people's DNA, and god knows what else, in one – or all! – of her freezers.

Diana had been charged with wasting police time, creating a climate of fear in the local community, and inciting the abduction, mutilation and possible murder of three local woman.

'I think we have something.' A SOCO was walking across the lawn from the summerhouse towards Brandon, a plastic bag, inside a plastic bag, held in front of him.

Brandon said a few words before the SOCO sauntered off to join his colleagues.

'I would say that's a wrap,' Brandon said, strolling over to Julia.

'You found what you were looking for?'

'Enough. It's over to the lab now.'

'Oh, Diana!'

'Some broad.'

'But she didn't kill anyone?'

Brandon grimaced. 'It's not looking likely.'

'Where? Where on earth did she get the ... body parts?' Julia was having trouble fathoming it.

Brandon lowered his voice. 'The dark web, possibly. Or maybe Diana broke into a medical hospital. I wouldn't put it past her. It's in her best interest to come clean with us.'

'Is she likely to go to prison?'

'Depends on the jury, the judge and how cooperative she is. But she could get a suspended sentence.'

Julia frowned. 'Knowing Diana, she would consider a short spell in prison as useful research. Campaign to become top dog!'

Brandon burst out laughing. 'Indeed.' He paused, before saying: 'Everything okay around here, otherwise?' He glanced across the lawn at Axel Fleming, who was chatting to a few of the forensics.

'Nothing dramatic – thankfully. Nick's off on his holidays in New York.'

Brandon smiled. 'Chelsea's booked a few days at a festival for when St. Piran's breaks up. Yourself?'

Julia paused. Right now, the way he was looking at her, she didn't want to mention her Sweden jaunt. She didn't have to. Axel bounded over to join them, a big smile on his face, his hand feeling for hers.

'All sorted?' He looked at Brandon, before giving Julia a loving smile.

'No.' Brandon eyed him warily. 'There are lots of pieces to this puzzle. Many, if not most, are not falling into place. But they will.'

'That's the spirit, Detective Inspector. Any leads on the identikit suspect – Diana's date?'

Julia crinkled up her nose in disapproval.

'Some sightings, yes. The car's been found.'

'Where?'

'Out of town, as would be expected. Where were you on July 22?' Brandon paused. 'Between 9 and 10pm?'

'Am I a suspect?' Axel's face hardened.

'No more than anyone else who was at Julia's party. We've ascertained that the killer was there, either as a guest, worker, or lurking.'

'I was here. Julia cooked supper and then we retired to bed.' He squeezed Julia's hand.

Brandon was looking at her, and she felt she owed him some sort of response.

'Axel was here for most of the day. We played tennis, I cooked and Axel stayed over.'

Brandon shook his left wrist, subconsciously exercising it, and nodded. 'Okay. Thanks. Look, we're all finished here now. Let's hope this is the last time I have to make an unannounced call.'

'You're always welcome, Brandon. You know that,' Julia said, smiling warmly.

He smiled back and turned to go, Axel watching him steadily, still holding Julia's hand.

Julia freed her hand and looked at her watch. 'Only one? I feel like I've been up for hours.'

'It's been a busy morning.'

Julia frowned. 'It's endless, isn't it? All these searches and questions and no answers?'

'Poor love,' he took her in his arms and kissed her lightly on the forehead. 'What you need is a holiday.'

'Don't I just.' She snuggled up to him, felt his warmth. He'd been loving last night, but nothing had happened. He'd made some excuse about checking flights and lodge reservations and left the room after a respectable time, not returning until later when he thought she was asleep. He was up before her in the morning – leaving some brochures on the bed, printed out the night before, as well as a small vase of flowers picked from the garden.

'Not long now and we can forget all this trouble and strife.'

'I can't wait.' She imagined herself diving into the clear waters of a fjord under the midnight sun, strolling back to an ice hotel, artificial flames licking the walls, Axel melting into her arms.

He smiled and gave her two quick kisses on her mouth. Progress. Her heart, if not his, was melting.

Brandon

July 24, 2019

The Mazda had traces of Jake Nayler's DNA on the driving wheel and seat. Brandon sighed deeply. He was the last person he expected, or wanted, to pick up. It just didn't make sense. But, of course, he'd go through the motions – was already going through the motions. Stew was at Nayler's cottage in Heamoor right now calling him in for questioning. He cringed thinking how Diana would react to this development – there is no way, he reckoned, Nayler would be able to pull the wool over Diana's eyes, with a wig, a rubber mask and phoney Cornish accent. But she might enjoy making him squirm. If only it was possible to set up a boxing ring at the station and let them slug it out. And now he had to phone Julia again with the news. It was always swell to hear her voice and listen to her calm reasoning, but he had so many things to get on with, not least the call to Marty Green in Baja, California. It made his pulse race thinking about it.

It was still pretty early in Mexico. The call could wait.

He caught the smallest twitch of a smile on Diana's lips as she sat in the interview room. She was taking forever to answer the simple question he'd put to her.

Eventually her thin lips parted. 'And you accuse me of wasting police time?'

Brandon's eyebrows hit a new high. 'The question had to

be asked, Diana. Just give me a straight answer. Was Jake Nayler the man you met in Long Rock and who drove you home, tied you up and emptied the contents of your freezer on your bedroom floor?'

Diana placed a finger to her mouth and looked him in the eye. 'Do you think I couldn't smell that rat from 20 paces?'

Brandon gave her an imploring look. 'So not Nayler?'

'You nailed it DI Hammett. Not Jake Nayler. Nayler messes with women in a different, less creative, way.'

'Still holding a torch for our SBK then, Ms Chambers?'

'Just holding a torch up to the evidence so we can draw him out and into the light.'

'Anything else to add? Any more pieces of evidence that you feel might be useful to our investigations? Like where you got those body parts.'

Diana sighed.

'We're going to keep asking that same question until you answer it satisfactorily. And honestly.'

'It's not holding up your investigations.'

'Random body parts, found on my beat, have a tendency to niggle with me. I like to tie up loose ends, Ms Chambers. Free up my mind for more important lines of inquiry. Let Al Chambers get back to his important work. Few can do it better. You don't strike me as being a vindictive person. You admired his work yourself. Don't drag him down with you. And, of course, this will help you in the long run as far as sentencing is concerned. Stealing body parts from a mortuary or hospital is serious theft.'

'The dark web. Satisfied? I'd give you the receipts but, you know, they didn't issue them.'

Brandon leaned back in his chair and glanced at Jimmy Shafter. 'Thanks, Ms Chambers. This has gone so much better than it could have. No further questions. Interview over.'

Diana started to get her things together, the others standing around, providing an audience for someone who had stepped into the limelight herself. Brandon didn't expect this would be her last performance.

He watched them leave the room. As soon as the door closed, he put a call through on the landline. It took a while to make a connection and then start ringing into the hollow distance. He could imagine the scene, Marty Green sitting on the patio of his hacienda, a servant padding across the tiled floor into the house to pick up the phone.

He was wrong. Two minutes later an adult male voice picked up. 'Yeah.'

'Marty Green?'

'Who wants him?'

'DI Hammett, Penzance Police, the UK.'

'Not here,' said the voice, before the line went dead.

Julia

July 24, 2019

'Julia, he's got to go.' Axel was looking out of her bedroom window.

'Why? He's done nothing wrong.' Julia had joined Axel and was looking down at Jake unloading tools from the back of his van.

'No smoke without fire. Isn't that one of your English idioms?'

'There wasn't sufficient evidence to charge him. His DNA could have come from Diana, for example. And Diana didn't identify him as her abductor.'

'You know that?' Axel was studying her.

'I'm not privy to the investigations, but it's obvious. Jake wouldn't be here if they'd found anything to incriminate him. Diana would have identified him instantly. Disguise or not.'

'Fair point. You're becoming quite the expert on police matters.'

Julia glanced at him before turning away from the window. 'I'm learning on the job. The immersive theatre of my life.'

'Darling, it's been such a struggle for you. But not long now. I'm going to take you away from all this. Now, do you want me to get in one of my builders? So you can draw a line under this episode, at least?'

'He's only going to plane the kitchen door, darling.' She took his hands, 'But thank you for the kind offer.'

'I just want to make you happy. You know that,' he said, smiling softly and stroking the side of her face.

But you're not, she thought, as she slipped her arms around him and felt him stiffen. The trip to Sweden would be make or break. She felt a little guilty about letting him go to all the expense and trouble, but he was right. She did need a break. She did need to be spoilt. She needed a holiday and a new place to explore. And, if she was honest, she wanted to surprise folk. Julia Trenowden, tragic widow, casting off her responsibilities and doing Scandinavia with a handsome, rich, charming Swede. It was a boost and a boast.

She moved back, but he held onto her, before pulling her back and kissing her lightly. 'I adore you, you know.'

She smiled up at him, letting him indulge the fantasy.

'Now, what have you got on today?' he said, drawing away.

'The gallery. We're just getting started on the Miller exhibition.'

'Miller?'

'A new local talent. You'd like him.'

He smiled. 'You're the expert. I'll leave you to it – I've got some numbers to crunch, so I'll get back to St Ives. I've also got my own army of builders to contend with.' He frowned, but she sensed he was happy to get away for a while. She'd yet to see his place in St Ives, but she'd seen his plans and it was going to be an amazing – bright, light and manageable. Perfect for a man like Axel Fleming.

Jake was finishing off the door when Julia went through to the kitchen.

'That's it then,' he said, turning to her, wiping his hands down his jeans.

It was a loaded remark. She wasn't sure if that was it, but the writing was on the door. She walked over and ran her hand down the architrave's sleek new edge. He moved closer, as she knew he would.

'Any other jobs you need doing … today?' That small pause said it all. Today. One for the road. A cheeky fond farewell.

She turned slowly – he was just inches away, his mouth hard, his eyes cold, all his rough edges bristling.

'No. Everything's good,'

He reached an arm over her head and rested one hand on

240

the architrave. 'Are you sure?' His other hand felt for her. 'Are you completely sure?'

She could smell his sweat, feel his heat, and she slipped away just as he pressed forward.

'So that's how it is?' he said, leaning against the door.

'Yes. I thought you understood?'

'Yeah, I did. I do. But why the sudden—' he looked her in the eye. 'Dismissal. Is it all this shit about the SBK? You can't believe I'm a killer. For fuck's sake, Julia.'

She looked at him and saw Jake again. Not the sexed up, angry brute of a few seconds ago.

'My opinion of you hasn't changed. I don't believe you are the killer but things have moved on with Axel. It wouldn't be fair to you or him, if I don't stop this now.'

'He stayed over the other night? I saw him around in the morning.'

'Yes.'

'So that's it.'

'I'm sorry, Jake.'

'No need,' he said, leaning down to pick up his things. 'All good things come to an end, don't they? And bad ones too.'

'Goodbye, Jake.'

She watched him walk out, leaving the door wide open.

Julia

July 26, 2019

Julia cast a look around. She couldn't quite believe she was getting out of Hartington Hall. Getting on a plane and getting out of Penzance. She needed a break – and somewhere as fresh and wholesome as Sweden was perfect.

Axel had suggested she pack light, and she'd mostly followed his advice. She'd picked up some outdoor gear for the hikes around the fjords and her suitcase had plenty of room for purchases in the shopping malls of Östermalm.

It had all been relatively effortless. Axel had organised the tickets and accommodation and she just had to wait for him to arrive in the taxi. She looked at her watch. In ten minutes.

The Hall felt strangely quiet. She'd given Elena, the cleaner, a week off and Nick was still away. The undercurrent of antagonism and action that Diana and Jake had generated was gone, and in its place weighed a pregnant silence. She checked her watch again. No time to check the electric sockets and back door again.

She jumped when her phone began to ring. 'Nick, hi!'

'Just calling to wish you a good time. I hope it's cooler in Sweden than here in New York.'

Julia frowned. 'Is it too hot for you, sweetheart?'

'No,' he replied. 'But Dad is forever whinging about the air conditioning!'

Julia laughed. 'I can imagine. Everything else, okay?'

'Yes. We've been to a ball game and a comedy show, which were awesome. And MoMA. Yawn.'

'Philistine!'

'I'm proud to be one. Despite yours and Dad's best intentions. He's taking me to an arty party tonight.'

'Well, keep off the wacky baccy.'

'Fear not, Mum.'

'Have you been to Central Park?'

'Yes. And Dad's shown me the brownstone apartments where *Friends* is based.'

'Did you see the Smelly Cat?'

'Cheesy, Mum. Gotta go. We're off out for a pastrami bagel.'

'Your Dad is pushing the boat out. Enjoy and take care.'

'And you Mum. Love you.'

'Love you, sweetheart.'

She could hear the sound of the cab drawing up on the drive. 'See you soon.'

Julia walked to the door and opened it before Axel had time to knock.

'Excited?' he said, looking her up and down. 'You look stunning, as always. The intrepid explorer.'

'I clean forgot to pack my pith helmet,' she said, bending over to kiss him on the cheek. He smelt exquisite. Of mountain flowers and icy lakes, or so she imagined.

'Now, have you got everything? Turned off the coffee maker? Locked the back door? Turned on security?'

'All present and correct,' she replied. His condescending concern was charming, but, she could imagine, would become grating. Hell, she was going on holiday and nothing was going to spoil her mood.

He presented his arm for her to hold and they walked to the car.

'Oh, you didn't book a cab?' she said, noting the driverless Volvo on the forecourt.

'No,' he said, smiling gently. 'I'll just get your luggage.'

July 26, 2019

'What is it?' Jo was standing before him with a tray of coffee and a plate of biscuits.

'Marty Fucking Green.'

'Oh,' said Jo, placing the tray on the incident room table. 'Still not picking up?'

'No. Well, yes, a few times, but he just slams down the receiver.' Brandon was sitting at the table, his elbows boring into it.

'I've tried the local police, but they're not interested. Said they have a lot on. Crime rate is crazy. May find time to send someone round "shortly". I could apply more pressure, but hey, we're talking manana time here.' Brandon was rapping the good fingers of his right hand on the table.

'Have a coffee.' Jo picked up a cup and plonked it in front of him. 'And a muffin. Blueberry. I did us both a favour and gave Stew's café a miss and went out.'

'Jo, what would I do without you?' He smiled at her before picking up a muffin and taking a bite. 'Very nice. And enticing.'

'Muffins have that effect on you?'

Brandon rocked back on his chair. 'They can have. I've been mulling over a few things.'

'No really?'

Brandon rolled his eyes. 'I think I'm going to have to book an air ticket.'

'To Mexico?'

'Well, not the Isle of Scilly.' He fiddled with the muffin wrapper. 'I've got to speak to Green. If only to eliminate him from the inquiries. He holds the key. Or, more specifically, he holds – or did hold – the two pieces of jewellery that could move this sad story to a conclusion.'

'I agree,' Jo said, taking the seat opposite.

'You not having a muffin?'

'No, I'm watching my weight.'

Brandon grimaced. 'Jo, you have no weight.'

'I've gained a little.'

'It doesn't show. I hope you're not taking this dating thing too seriously?'

'Of course not.' She looked down and reached for her black coffee.

'And the undercover work is wrapped up. He would be a fool to chance a dating app again.'

'I agree.'

They looked at each other and Brandon let it go. Going on dates, clearly, wasn't all work, no play.

'So,' Brandon shook his head lightly, 'Just what is it that we are agreed on?'

'You going to Mexico. Want me to book the flights?'

'Will you be okay here?'

'Stew's around. We have Max in Newquay – and the whole of MCIT are primed.'

'I do worry, though. About you living alone. Can you go and stay with your mom?'

'My place is like Fort Knox, Brandon. I sleep with my taser under my pillow and one eye open.'

'Your good eye?'

She raised an eyebrow. 'Yes, the bionic one that fires daggers.'

Brandon smiled and took another bite of muffin. 'Forty-eight hours. That's all I need. Get me an open return flight to Los Angeles and a hire car. I'll drive to Puerto Nuevo.

'Not stopping off in Louisiana to see family?'

'No.' He finished the muffin and scrunched the wrapper in his right hand. 'But, when this is all over, Jo, I'm going to take a holiday. One hell of a holiday. Hang on—'

Brandon reached over and picked up his vibrating phone. 'Nadia?' He looked at Jo, and put the phone on speaker.

'Just been doing some analysis on the copycat boxes. The ones Diana Chambers is assumed to have used.'

'Go on.'

'They look like the ones the SBK uses, but they're not the same. Diana – can I say Diana?'

'The suspect,' Brandon corrected.

'The suspect did a good job, but the parts can be bought online and in UK stockists. Unlike the originals, which we still can't trace. I just thought you might find that useful, as Di – the suspect did a good job.'

'Thanks, Nadia. You have been helpful.'

Brandon clicked off and looked at Jo. 'Let's hope the jewellery provides more clues. Maybe the boxes will turn up too. But first I've just got to hope that Green turns out to be worth the time and airfare.'

August 2, 2019

This was her fifth sitting. He was taking his time to produce what he hoped would be a portrait to rival, but not surpass, the original Woman In Green. The elegant beauty in the room they didn't refer to. His mother, Greta. Assumed dead. There was a small shrine to her under a lemon tree in the orangery. She had been a beauty and he'd captured that on canvas.

Little Greta, her darling Shih Tzu, was very much alive and peeing on the floor by her foot at that very moment.

'Naughty Greta,' she said, kicking out her shiny shoes.

'Very naughty,' he said, frowning, before an indulgent smile snuck onto his face. He ripped off two sheets of art room blue paper and strode across to mop up the mess. Greta immediately snuggled up to him, wagging her tail and butting him with her silky blond head.

'Why don't we take a break? Walk Greta around the garden?'

'Well—' He looked conflicted and ran a hand through his hair.

'I could do with a break too. Stretch my legs.' She hitched up the dress a little and wiggled them out in front of her, all the while watching for the male gaze. Sometimes she imagined she saw it. How could he suppress it?

'Okay, okay. But no peeking at the portrait while you pass.'

She pouted. 'It's been five days. I'd love to see how it's developing.'

'You know how I love to indulge you. But you must wait! It must be perfect.'

'It will be perfect.'

'Yes. Yes,' he muttered.

'Can I just change? I would hate to dirty the dress ... again.' She'd let it trail through the dirt and grass on their last outing. He'd tried so hard not to be annoyed – at the time and after an hour of cleaning it. She'd pushed him to the brink that day.

He looked around for something appropriate for her to change into. There was nothing but a vintage artist's smock.

'It will do,' she said, adding, 'Or we could go to my room and I could find something else.' And waste more time.

He creased his brow. 'As you will, my dear. The smock will look charming on you.'

She smiled and slipped off the chaise longue, Greta at her feet.

'Could you help me with the buttons?' The dress had twenty of them snaking down the back and she didn't know whether he sighed with anguish or pleasure as he worked his way along them.

'All done,' he said, his brow briefly touching the skin on her back.

She let the dress fall to the floor and stepped out of it.

'Here,' he said, thrusting the smock at her as she stood in her corset. 'I'll get Gigi's lead.'

She took her time to dress in front of the free-standing mirror, conscious of his attention. The smock rested above her knees, and she looked as cute as a Mary Quant model from the '60s. Greta was pulling at her lead trying to get to her.

'You have a fan,' he said, letting go of the lead and letting Greta rush to her. 'Now, I suggest we get on, before little Gigi does another PP.'

That was possibly the first joke she'd heard him crack and she forced a laugh.

'Come on, you two rascals.'

The three of them practically skipped down the stairs, Greta in the middle, her head oscillating between them. It would have been easy to forget their situation. How this was all expected to pan out. But she thrilled to this new freedom and wondered if it could lead somewhere other than the ... She was thinking gallows. But it wouldn't end like that. It would be short, swift and clean. A psychotic euthanasia.

She let Greta off the lead when they entered the garden

and she sped off into the long grass in his cultivated meadow, her tail wagging among the yellow and white flower heads.

'I'm worried she may pick up a tick,' he said, his brow creased, thumb supporting his chin.

'Did that happen with your mother's dog?'

He turned to her quickly. 'Yes,' he said, walking towards the meadow. 'It's not uncommon. Gigi, come here, girl. Gigi.'

He knelt to greet her as she scurried out of the meadow. Her brown eyes shone but looked over his shoulder.

'Go to your mistress,' he said, getting up and turning, a small smile on his face as if, on some level, this new relationship filled a void.

'Shall we go back to the studio?' she said after a time. The light was fading, a pale moon rising above the turret.

'Not this evening.' He was sitting at the table, watching Greta play. 'It's perfect out here, isn't it? Shall we dine here tonight?'

'That would be lovely.' Anything but the room. Last night it had stunk of blood and formaldehyde, and she'd gobbled her food to get it over with, as much as to annoy him. The dog hadn't been allowed in. She wondered what Greta would have made of it. Whether the stench of death would have killed her puppy enthusiasm.

'I'll bring out a burner heater. So, we don't all catch cold.' Was he kidding? But there was something sad in his preoccupations – his desire to please and to make it all right.

'We'll finish off the painting tomorrow,' he said, catching her eye, his lips turned down at the edges. 'I hope you like it. I will know if you don't. You can hide nothing from me. Not now.'

Clouds were gathering. The heater would be needed.

'Can I write to my son tomorrow?'

'Yes.'

Brandon

July 28, 2019

He drove the Chevrolet across the border and into Tijuana no problem. It had been the easiest link in a journey that had taken him from Newquay, via Heathrow, to Los Angeles. After a carousel of departure lounges, travelators and economy crush, it was good to be on the open road, the automatic resting his left wrist, the air conditioning cooling his brow. Tijuana, billed the most violent city in the world that year, hadn't changed much since he last passed through. Shadows flitted between the high rises and shanties and snatches of old Spanish splendour, as he headed out of town to the beach resort of Puerto Nuevo. Marty Green was a Vietnam vet and retired realtor, not a drugs or people trafficker as far as he was aware. All the same, he'd packed his taser. He didn't seem the most obliging of old men.

His villa was in the Spanish hacienda style in a sheltered spot on the hills above Rosarito Beach. Nice spot and in spitting distance of the golf clubs, casinos and bars vying for his bucks below. The Chevrolet circled the spiralling road with ease and Brandon would have enjoyed the view, if he hadn't been preoccupied with what lay ahead. He was staking a lot on what resided behind that gated villa up front. He parked the car, got out and pressed the buzzer. It took a while before he heard a crackle and a voice.

'Who is it?'

'DI Hammett, Penzance, UK, Major Crime Dept.' He added the American tag for context.

The line went quiet. It was a minute, maybe two, before the gates eased open and he got back into the Chevrolet and drove in.

The opulent front door opened as he got out of the car.

A woman, late fifties, dyed blonde hair and caked on make-up, stood in the doorway, her arms at her side, bracelets jangling.

'To what do we owe the pleasure?' She was American, with a southern twang, not the Mexican he'd heard a few times when he'd called.

Brandon showed his badge. 'I've got a few questions for Mr Green. Nothing to be alarmed about.'

'Come in,' she said, looking him over. 'Can I get you a drink? You've come a long way, honey.'

'A glass of water, please.' The place was empty apart from a maid sweeping away leaves below an arch leading to the terrace.

The blond followed his gaze. 'I'll ask Juanita to bring a jug out onto the veranda. This way.' She led him out onto a large patio.

'Please,' she said, as Brandon hovered by a wicker table and matching chairs.

As he went to sit down she stretched out a weathered, bejewelled hand. 'My name is Selma Green. Sure pleased to meet you, DI Hammett. I do hope you haven't had a wasted journey.'

Brandon shook her hand lightly and perched on the edge of his chair, looking up when he heard footsteps. The maid was making her way through the extravagantly furnished living room towards the open French windows with a heavy tray. She placed it on the table and arranged two tumblers, before topping them both up with iced water and lemon slices.

Brandon waited for her to leave before speaking. 'Is Mr Green in?'

Selma thought hard before answering. 'No.'

'When will he be back?'

'Hard to say.'

'Where can I find him, Mrs Green?'

Neither of them had touched the water. Until then. Selma reached for hers and stirred it slowly, the clinking ice cubes breaking the silence.

'He's at La Fonda. You know the joint?'

Brandon knew it. The hotel resort had quite a reputation, earned in its glory days, when the Hollywood greats and wannabes crossed the border for rest and recreation.

'Reckon I do. Would you like to call ahead and say we're coming?'

She smiled and jangled the ice in her glass. 'Oh, I've already done that, DI Hammett. He's expecting you.'

He followed her soft top Merc back down the road to the waterfront, before turning north to La Mission. She'd insisted on taking her own car so she could 'peel Marty off the bar' and get him home.

So Marty was an uncooperative drunk? Best way to handle him was to get a round in.

He was sitting at a table on the terrace when they arrived, chatting to a couple of backpackers who may have been trying to fleece him, or may have been making polite conversation. They looked happy enough to say their goodbyes when Selma strode over.

'DI Hammett, meet Marty Green, my godforsaken husband.'

He didn't get up.

'Can I get you a drink, Mr Green?'

His rheumy green eyes washed over Brandon before responding. 'It would be impolite to say no.' He nodded at the empty chair opposite and Brandon sat down.

Brandon glanced at the centimetre of golden liquid in Marty's glass. 'Same again?'

'Jameson. Make it a large one. Selma will have a margarita'

'I'm drivin, Mart!'

He shrugged. 'When's that ever stopped you?'

'Well, just the one.'

Marty looked more like a retired realtor than a Vietnam vet. There were no hard edges. Or maybe the booze had washed them away over the years. He was dressed down in a safari style short sleeved shirt, over a white vest and cream chino shorts. Two massive bunions pressed up against one of his Birkenstocks. No wonder he was sore.

Marty picked up his glass and swirled the contents as a waiter took Brandon's order. Brandon broke protocol and got himself a double Jameson too. He'd check in for the night; it was as good a place as any to rest up.

'Now what's so important that's got you chasing across the pond to speak to Marty Green, Detective Inspector?'

'A missing persons' case that needs resolution.'

'You sayin this missing person—'

'Persons.'

'Persons, are hiding out in Baja California?'

Brandon shook his head lightly. 'Some artefacts, found on the body parts of the missing women, are from the same limited editions that you bought from Leon Schneider in 1987.'

Marty nodded. 'The Bijoux Chérir earrings and Mexican flag brooch?'

'Yes.'

'Well, why didn't you just say so? I have those in my safe back at the hacienda.'

'Can I see them?'

'Sure. Tonight. Tomorrow morning. I can get Juanita to take a photo of them right now, if you want.'

Brandon's shoulders slumped and he remained silent when the waiter set out the drinks. Selma was the first to reach for her glass.

'Honey, you look disappointed.'

Brandon grimaced and looked up at her. 'Could say that. I'll need to check the pieces myself, if that's okay?'

Selma handed him his drink. 'Least we can do, honey. They are to die for. Real gems. Only a few made and you can't get them on the market. I've looked.'

'Yeah, she's always checking out their value,' Marty said, picking up a handful of cashews and popping them in his mouth.

'The Swedish Royal family have the exact same pieces. Bought direct from the jewellers.'

Brandon put down his glass. 'No kidding. Tell me more?'

Marty chuckled and beckoned over the waiter. 'Another round.'

'Go on.' Brandon dispensed with the platitudes.

'They rattled around in the Östberg treasure trove for years, last seen out in public on the beautiful body of Greta Östberg, the wife of Rolf Östberg, a notorious rogue and womaniser,' Marty butted in.

Selma wasn't to be silenced. 'The Östbergs were a power couple back in the '80s – she was besting Grace Kelly as Europe's glossy princess. All over the news and Hello! magazine. Until she did a Princess Di and died early.'

Brandon shifted in his seat. 'What of?'

'Suicide. Hung herself.'

Selma pulled an olive off her cocktail stick with her teeth and chewed on it. 'Real tragic.'

Brandon was leaning forward, his whiskey untouched. 'You say the jewellery never re-emerged on the markets?'

'Nah,' Selma said, fiddling with her cocktail stick. 'Well not that I've noticed.'

'And she notices everything,' Marty cut in.

Brandon sat back as the waiter came over with a fresh round. 'The husband, Rolf Östberg, what happened to him?'

'No idea,' Selma said, reaching for the new margarita. 'There were a few items on him with other women – all much younger. And then nothing.'

'As is the way,' Marty said. 'Their luck runs out. My luck ran out the day I ran into Selma.'

'Get over yourself, you ol' fool. I saved you from yourself.' Selma rolled her eyes and took a slug of margarita.

'And everyone else,' he hissed.

Brandon could see the way this was heading. 'You know, y'all may have saved my hide.'

'We've been helpful, honey?'

'Mighty so.'

'I reckon that calls for another round,' Marty said lurching forward.

'Smuck, has no manners,' Selma said, leaning towards Brandon.

'Why don't I get y'all a taxi back? I can drive down in the morning, check the jewellery, strictly for procedural purposes, and then drive you back here to pick up your car.'

'You are a man with a plan,' Selma said, reaching out to stroke his cheek.

'You could save yourself some time and money and drive us back now. Stay over,' Marty said.

'You've hardly touched your drink, honey. Makes sense.'

'I need an early night – long journey tomorrow.'

'All the more reason to stay with us. This joint will be jumping 'til dawn. I'll be asleep before the cab gets to the top of the hill. If you can fend off Selma, you should get plenty of shut eye.'

Selma lent over and slapped him playfully. 'Don't you believe a word he says.'

Brandon smiled and picked up his glass. There was a certain logic in it. In all honesty, he doubted whether he would get any sleep. Too much to mull over.

'When you're ready then,' Brandon said easing back into his chair.

An hour later, they were decanting Marty out of the cab – Selma under one shoulder, Brandon the other. It had been the proverbial hard day's night, but the end was in sight. Brandon spotted Juanita through the arch of the terrace, clean towels folded over her arm. He longed to get in the shower and wash off the day.

They carted Marty up the stairs and onto his king size. Brandon left Selma to pull off his Birkenstocks and pants.

'Help yourself to a drink from the tray, hon,' she yelled, as he made his way down the tiled stairs. Why not? They'd done talking – he hoped – and so he poured a stiff one, took it outside to the veranda and stretched out in a wicker chair to admire the view. The hills glowed with lights and way down he could see the neon of the waterfront and white foam against a navy sea. It was still warm at midnight, but the air was clean and his world felt expansive. He'd become boxed in in Penzance – as if his head was in one of those fancy glass cases. It didn't surprise him that it took this distance to get things into perspective. Coming here could have been a fool's errand. But it was the only avenue left to him and he felt he was on sure footing now. He took a sip of whisky and watched the night. It was eight in the morning in Penzance – he'd call Jo before he went to bed. Get it all in motion before he drove to Los Angeles. The Swedish royal family. Maybe Axel Fleming could help out there? He wasn't exactly royalty, but he'd have connections. Brandon rubbed his beard – it was getting tatty, time to go. Fleming. The man had come through all the checks so far blameless. But he was around, right now, when women were going missing. And he was Swedish. Two and two might not add up to him being the one. But, then again ...

'Tada!'

Brandon turned to see Selma grinning widely and wearing the Bijoux Chérir earrings and brooch.

'Do they suit me, Sir?'

'Darn right they do,' Brandon said, raising his glass appreciatively.

'Wanna photograph them?' Selma was swaying unsteadily on her high heels.

'Let me help you.' Brandon got up and steered her to her seat.

'I guess you want to photograph them … without my ugly mug involved?'

Brandon smiled. 'You look a million dollars in those gems, ma'am. But, for protocol's sake, I best photograph them on the table.'

'You are the charmer, Detective Inspector. Why don't you come and work back here in the States? You being from round here and all.'

'Family … and friends.' He paused. 'But I've got them over here too, and I'll be back for one hell of a holiday when this is all over.'

He got up to take a photo and stood there, looking out over the hills.

'When you're next in town, be sure to look us up, DI Hammett.'

He turned round and smiled warmly. 'I will.'

'I guess you'll be up early morn,' she added.

'Six thirty.'

'I'll ensure Juanita leaves some breakfast out for you, honey.'

'If it's no trouble?'

'Our pleasure. But there is a condition.'

Brandon looked at her.

'You tell me how it all pans out. Send me a postcard from Penzance.'

'I sure will, Selma. That's a promise.'

July 29, 2019

'Rolf Östberg was a minor Swedish Royal. He died from complications related to alcoholism in 2002,' Jo said.

Brandon was impressed by the speed of her intelligence. She'd come back with vital information before he'd checked in at Los Angeles airport. His eyes flitted up to the departure board. An hour before boarding.

'Any kids?'

'Yes. Twins. A boy, Alex, and a girl, Anja. They'd be in their mid-forties now.'

'Where are they?'

'That I haven't been able to find out. This is a minor schism of the Swedish royal family, so I will need a bit of time to trace them.'

'They'd have been around twelve when their mother died?'

'Yes. So sad.'

Their conversation was interrupted by a boarding announcement. He waited a beat. 'And the jewellery?'

'Working on it, Boss. Is that your flight they're calling?'

'No. But I'll let you get on.'

'Glad you made the effort?'

'Time will tell,' Brandon said, regarding the check-in queue. 'I best get in line. Keep up the good work and keep me informed.'

Brandon

July 30, 2019

Brandon strode into the incident room, peeling off his jacket, his mobile pressed against his ear.

'Good morning, Boss,' Jo said, watching him approach. 'Am I your first port of call?'

'Good morning, DS Menhenrick. Yes, just phoning family to let them know I landed safely and I'm back.'

'You look shattered. Have you had breakfast?'

'On the plane. But I could do with a coffee.'

Jo called through to the office.

'Right, what have you got for me?' Brandon sat across from Jo, rain dripping from his hair onto the table.

'A Zoom meeting with Anja Östberg at 10.45 tomorrow.'

'Brilliant, Jo. I don't have time for another excursion. And Alex Östberg?'

'He's dead.'

'Dead?' Brandon looked at her in disbelief.

'Yes. A boating accident.'

He shook his head lightly and rubbed his beard.

'Any details?'

'No. I didn't want to push it after managing to get this interview with Anja.'

'Yes, of course. Difficult?'

Jo wobbled her hand. 'Not easy. She is very withdrawn. Which, I guess, is understandable having lost all of her immediate family.'

Brandon nodded. 'What does she do?'

'Runs an eco lodge with her partner. Somewhere in the wilds of Sweden.'

'Interesting.'

'She speaks English, I assume?'

'Fluently. She's clearly educated.'

'Well done, Jo. This could be a major break.'

'Thank you, Boss.'

The door opened and PC McNabb came through with a tray. Brandon let him go, before turning back to Jo.

'Any other developments? Did the "Red Devil" turn up on any more CCTV?'

'No. He was so careful. The man is clever. I couldn't even trace where he bought the wig. Assuming it is a wig.'

Brandon picked up a custard cream from the dish in front of him. He observed it, took a bite, and put it down. 'I think I'll invite Suzanna Fitzgerald along to the Zoom. She may pick something up which we miss.'

'Good idea,' Jo said, taking a sip of coffee. 'This meeting's important, isn't it?'

'I'd say so. I'll make the call. And, also, call Julia.'

Jo gave him a questioning look, which he answered. 'She's dating a Swede. Axel Fleming remains a person of interest. As much as anything else, he might have some more gen on the Swedish Royals.'

'He bothers you, doesn't he?'

Brandon picked up the biscuit and turned it in his hand. 'Yes.'

July 31, 2019

Suzanna Fitzgerald arrived just after 10.30. Brandon briefed her and settled her in the interview room ante-chamber so she could watch the interview with Anja Östberg.

'I haven't felt this excited in years,' she said, smiling up at Brandon.

'I don't want to build your hopes up.'

'With that look on your face, Detective Inspector, I would say you've already failed.'

He gave a short laugh and ran a hand over his mouth. 'That obvious is it?'

'Yes.'

'If anything strikes you during the interview, text me. We can take a break if need be. I just hope this doesn't lead us down another blind alley.'

'Good luck, Brandon. You deserve a breakthrough.'

'That we all do.'

He walked through to the interview room to join Jo who had set up the meeting.

Two minutes to go. He looked at his phone; a text from Chelsea and one from his mom.

Jo glanced at him. 'Everything okay?'

He frowned. 'Julia's not picking up.'

'Is that unusual?'

'Well, I'm not in the habit of calling her every day, but …' His eyes flicked to the computer screen and the time on the bottom right. 10.38. 'I'll just give Rachel Matthews a quick call.'

Jo jerked her head up. 'Now?'

'Yes. One second.'

The phone rang and rang before Rachel picked up. 'Hi, Rachel. Hope I didn't drag you away from anything. Just a quick question. Julia? Is she away at the moment? She's not picking up her phone.'

Jo was staring at him and he waved a hand to calm her.

'She's probably trekking around a fjord in Sweden. She's taking a holiday with Axel – shopping in Östermalm and hiking in the wilderness.'

'Thanks, Rachel. That could explain it. Can't talk right now. Take care, hon.'

'Right. Zoom me up, Jo,' he said, clicking off his phone and twisting round to the screen.

It took a while before Anja picked up and they heard her quiet, lightly-accented voice.

'Good morning Ms Östberg,' Brandon said, looking at the dark box next to his and Jo's where Anja should have appeared. 'Can you see us okay?'

'Yes. Good morning, Detective Inspector Hammett and Detective Sergeant Menhenrick.'

'If you wouldn't mind clicking on the video icon,' Jo said, helpfully. 'It's to your left at the bottom of the screen.'

'Of course,' she replied, her face emerging in pixelating blocks. There was nothing about her mousey demeanour that suggested privilege. Her greying hair hung limp either side of a face etched in lines and devoid of artifice. She wasn't wearing a scrap of make-up, or jewellery and, from what he could see, was dressed in a plain cotton top and ill-fitting cardigan.

'Thank you for your time,' Brandon said.

'How can I help you?' The camera zoomed in, revealing ice blue irises; a touch of colour on a dull palette.

Brandon paused before speaking and Jo stepped in. 'If you could explain a little bit more about the jewellery we corresponded about. The origins and where they are now.'

Anja looked to the side as if trying to recollect. 'They were my mother's. But, after she died, they were displayed in the family museum in our house in Östermalm, with other family artefacts.'

'Are they still there?' Brandon said, regarding her closely.

'As far as I'm aware. I haven't been back to the house for many years.'

'Who lives there now?' Brandon said.

'An elderly cousin. I believe she rents out apartments.'

'And the museum? Is it still open?'

'Occasionally,' Anja replied. 'It was one of the conditions when I ... we ... allowed Cousin Freya's family to move in.'

'Do you think the jewellery and artefacts are safe in these conditions?' Brandon was amazed at her passivity. Few people would walk away from the family jewels.

'The museum is well run. The curator and his family have apartments in the house and are to be trusted. Implicitly.'

'Been with the family a long time?'

'Yes. Before we were born.'

Brandon glanced down at his phone.

Suzanna had texted. 'Good time to ask her about her brother.' He smiled to himself. Just getting to that.

'If it's not too distressing for you, can you talk a little about your brother? Did he stay at the house after you left?'

'No.' She looked down, before continuing. 'He left before me. It was decided that we should both go to boarding school after ... what happened. I objected, for a while, wanted to stay with Papa. But Alex couldn't wait to leave.'

'Why?' Jo asked the question on his lips, but he was grateful for her feminine intervention.

'After what happened. You don't know?' Anja's eyes widened.

'Brandon frowned and nodded his head gently. 'No. If you don't mind—'

'Alex found Mama. He found her hanging from a beam in the orangery. He tried to get her down. He tried to save her, but it was far too late—' She inhaled deeply before continuing. 'They found him, hours afterwards, clinging to her body. He'd managed to cut her down with gardening tools, and they found him cradling her in his arms and weeping.' Her eyes misted over. 'I never saw him cry again. He loved Mama, more than any of us. More than me, more than Papa. I think he thought it was a personal failure that he couldn't save her then, and save her before, by just ... loving her.' She shook her head and let the drab flaps of hair fall across her face. 'He worshipped her. And we all thought she felt the same and yet.'

Someone had moved into the frame and rested a hand on her shoulder. She looked up at him and placed her hand over his, before turning back to the screen.

'I'm sorry,' she said.

'No need to be. Perfectly understandable. Shall we take a

short break?' Jo said. Brandon shot her a look. He really didn't want to lose the thread now.

He watched as Anja exchanged a few words with the man at her side.

'Give me a minute. I'll be fine. Just fine.'

Brandon and Jo joined Suzanna in the antechamber.

'Are you thinking what I'm thinking?' Brandon said, looking at Suzanna.

'The boy fits the profile. Traumatised at the age of twelve.'

'Dead at … actually we don't know exactly when he died,' Jo cut in. 'I did a search and couldn't get any details online. They must have kept it out of the papers.'

'Surprising? But we need to find out,' Brandon said, 'And we need to have a word with the museum curator. See if those heirlooms are still on show.'

'Agreed.' Suzanna was looking through the one-way glass at the screen. 'And ask for photographs of Alex. I realise this may seem intrusive. But it could be invaluable.' She paused. 'She's back on screen.'

'Okay. Thanks, Suzanna,' he said.

Brandon and Jo walked back into the room and he tapped the mute button.

'Ms Östberg, as you know, the jewellery is important to our investigations. I would like to speak to the museum curator. Could you give me his name and number, please?' Brandon started with the easiest request.

'Of course. Arvid Larsson. You can get his details on the Östberg Museum website.'

'Thank you. And Alex, your brother. When did he pass?'

Anja didn't hesitate. 'In 1995. He was staying with us, here at the lodge. He just went out one morning alone and didn't return. The boat was found on the other side of the lake. We never found Alex's body.' She paused; seemed to read his thoughts. 'The lake is very deep and wide and is a tributary for others. It isn't so unusual for people to drown and not be recovered.'

'I see,' Brandon said. 'Was there coverage in the papers?'

'Just one small item in the local news. We tried to keep it as private as possible. Alex would have wanted it that way. Media exposure was a factor in Mama's demise.'

Brandon held her gaze. 'In what way?'

'Mama was feted for her looks. She became obsessed with them and, sadly, she believed she was losing them. She began to shun the press. Which made them even more interested in her. When she died it was all over the news. Like her beauty, the story blazed and faded. We didn't want to stoke the fires, Detective Inspector. You understand?'

Brandon nodded. 'Alex was your twin. Were you close?'

'Up until Mama died. But he closed off. I couldn't reach him. Not like I used to.'

'But he came to stay with you. So you didn't give up trying?' Jo said, nodding her head lightly.

'Of course. We were always there for him.'

'We,' Brandon said.

'My partner Erik and I. Alex was estranged from Papa.'

'Do you have any photographs of Alex?'

'No. He didn't like having his photograph taken.' A hand appeared on her shoulder and she looked up. 'If there's nothing else, Detective Inspector?'

'No. Not at the moment. You have been very helpful. But if you could take a look for any photos. School ones, IDs, family gatherings and forward them to my mobile. That would be appreciated. Thank you Ms Östberg.'

She gave a brief nod before disappearing.

'Do you think she's covering for him?' Brandon asked Suzanna.

'Maybe, on some level. She seems sincere.'

Jo was on her iPad. 'I've got the number,' she said, passing Brandon the device with the Östberg Museum website on it.

'Thanks, Jo.' Brandon immediately tapped Arvid Larsson's number into his mobile.

'Detective Inspector Hammett,' Brandon said, grimacing, 'Please return my call when you get this message.'

Jo hit her forehead with her palm. 'Typical.'

'I shouldn't imagine Arvid gets much traffic at the museum. Let's hope he checks his messages more than twice a year.' Brandon glanced at his phone. Still no response from Julia.

'Julia's probably shopping the Östermalm malls right now,' he said, answering Jo's look.

'She's in Sweden?' Suzanna said, 'With Axel Fleming?'

'Apparently so. At least that's what she told her best friend. She could look in at the museum for me. Save me a flight.'

Brandon gave Suzanna an ironic look just as his mobile started to ring.

'DI Hammett.'

'Arvid Larsson. You wanted to speak to me?'

Brandon gave a thumbs up to Jo and Suzanna. 'Yes. Have you got a minute?'

He put his phone on speaker and the two women huddled around. 'I'm interested in two pieces of jewellery which I believe belonged to the late Greta Östberg. A pair of art déco earrings and a brooch with an Eagle and Serpent emblem. Both from Bijoux Chérir. Are they on display?'

Arvid took a while to reply. 'No. They haven't been part of our exhibition for over twenty-five years.'

Brandon's eyes widened. 'Are they in storage?'

'Signed out.'

'By who?'

'Rolf Östberg.'

'And he didn't return them?'

'No.'

'And you didn't question this?'

'They were his to do with what he pleased.'

'They didn't re-emerge after his death?'

'No.' Arvid coughed. 'We assume he gave them to a lady friend, or possibly sold them or gambled them.'

Brandon glanced at the others. 'Was there a funeral for Rolf Östberg?'

'A small affair. His daughter and her partner, his cousins and a few of his "friends".'

'Was his son, Alex, there?'

'Perhaps, in spirit. Alexander died many years ago.'

'Do you have any family photographs? Of the family in happier times? Of Alexander Östberg?'

Arvid went silent again. 'I have a small selection of the family in happier times. And others at the family cemetery, in the grounds. Would you like me to fetch them for you?'

Suzanna put her hands together in prayer.

'Yes, please,' Brandon said, smiling widely.

'I will be a little while,' Arvid said, and they heard the crackle of the connection as he placed the receiver on a table.

Brandon tapped off the speaker and rested back in his chair. Suzanna leaned against the table, as if overcome by expectation and the weight of time.

Jo threw back her head. 'Come on.'

'It's not like you to be impatient?' Brandon observed.

'It's like I can hear his every shaky footstep as he creaks to the family vault and back.'

Brandon smiled. 'Let's hope he doesn't fall down the stairs. A lot's riding on this.'

'I've got them,' Arvid said in a breathless voice ten minutes later.

'Excellent,' Brandon said. 'Could you take some photos on your phone and send them over?'

'I don't have a smart phone.'

Brandon let out a massive sigh.

'I can show you on Zoom. You have an account?'

Brandon smiled. 'Absolutely.'

Fifteen minutes later Arvid's gaunt, pale face appeared on their laptop.

'Hello,' he said, smiling politely. In the background Brandon could see plinths and glass boxes. He gave Jo a look and discreetly pointed at the display cases, just as they disappeared from sight and two framed photographs came into view.

'Could you put the frames closer to your screen, please, so we can get a better look,' Jo said, peering in.

A line of people drew closer. Two adults at the centre – a mother, holding the hand of a boy of around seven or eight and the father with his arm around a girl, who must have been Anja. They were a beautiful looking family. The kind of idealised image you'd see in an advertising shot. Brandon focused on the boy. Blond, light blue eyes, like his sister, slim build, a sensitivity around the mouth. Arvid propped up another photograph of the twins, maybe a year or so older. They were messing around on a boat on a lake. The boy was smiling right into the camera.

'There's something about the boy. He looks familiar,' Jo said.

'Do you have any more photos?' Brandon asked. She was right. The boy looked familiar. But it could be that he just radiated the innocence and freshness familiar in youths.

'Only ones of the funerals.' Arvid's head disappeared from view and they could hear him sorting through a box of frames.

There was a short interval before a photo of what must have been Greta Östberg's funeral appeared on the screen. It was a grand affair, teeming with people, but the twins caught Brandon's eye. They were at the graveside – the boy's face turned down and in profile. He would have been twelve then and his features looked more formed, his cheekbones curving below tidy blond hair.

The photo disappeared from the screen and was replaced with another. This time the boy was looking back and glaring into the lens.

Jo nudged him. 'It looks so much like—'

Before she got a chance to finish another photograph appeared on the screen. Rolf Östberg's funeral. It was a small gathering and he could easily recognise Anja Östberg and her partner Erik. There were a few others around the grave. Some looked like family members, some like members of staff. Arvid was there, head lowered, hands clasped together. Standing back were a few glamourous women, who, Brandon assumed, were the lady friends referred to. To their left, standing a good few feet away, was a man. His head was bowed in a similar fashion to the young Alex. Except Alex Östberg was dead. And Axel Fleming was standing there in his place.

August 3, 2019

She'd been sitting for him for two hours, Greta fussing at her feet and sleeping in turn. It was the longest session yet and he seemed set on finishing the portrait. What was left for her after this? A permanent seat at the dining table? Her foot twitched and sent Greta scurrying to his side.

'Sorry, Gigi,' she said, using the dog's pet name.

He smiled. 'Are you getting stiff?'

Not yet, she thought. Not for a very long time, if I have my way.

'I would love to take a break.'

He looked at her over his glasses. 'How can I deny you?' He leant down and stroked Greta's head. 'Shall we go and pick some beans for lunch?'

'Good idea,' she said, sliding off the chaise longue and turning her back to him. He came over obligingly and began to undo the buttons.

'I'll miss this,' he said, his breath making the hairs on her back stand up.

'Miss what?' She held her breath waiting for his reply. Miss the blood cursing through her veins? Skin that responded to touch? A voice other than his own?

'Getting to know you. And …' he let his arms fall to his side.

'And?' she said, turning to face him.

'And protecting your essence.'

'My essence?'

'Your intrinsic beauty.'

'Can I see the portrait?'

'I just have a little more work to do.'

'Please?'

'After lunch.'

She changed into the smock but the gaiety of the previous day had gone. The garment felt more like the chemise Marie Antoinette had worn in the tumbril to the guillotine. They picked the last of the runner beans in silence, tossing the straggly ones to one side for Greta to play with.

She followed him into the orangery and the small kitchen he'd set up, and watched him boil the beans and prepare the salad nicoise, Greta chasing a butterfly around the lemon trees. It felt like the end of term, with all its conflicting emotions. But it wasn't. It most definitely wasn't.

He handed her the bowl of salad and followed her out into the garden, carrying a tray with plates and cutlery and a bottle of wine. He didn't always serve wine for lunch. Maybe, tired as he seemed, he'd dose off and she could bottle him. The thought cheered her. His unconscious state was her only chance for escape. He must have her under some sort of surveillance – god knows she'd tried to find cameras and bugs.

They ate in silence. She didn't bother to irritate him. Her attempts to wear him down had been futile. A nervous, determined energy was keeping him on top of things. If anything, he seemed stronger today, detached, pleased that he had just about finished his portrait, looking beyond it.

Greta started to make a fuss under the table, growling and tossing something between her paws and mouth.

'What is it girl?' she said, leaning down to one side to see.

'A mouse?' he said, stabbing his folk into a slice of egg yolk and tuna.

She took a look, hitting her head on the bottom of the table as it shot up in shock. Greta had picked up a rotting finger from somewhere, the flesh flaking from the bone.

'A dead mouse,' she said, when she settled back into her chair.

He gave a brief nod, his eyes on some faraway place. And so she kicked the thing away, let Greta chase it and carry it off into the meadow, before putting down her fork to follow her.

'Greta, naughty girl. Let it alone, girl,' she said, kicking away some earth and pushing the severed finger deep into a shallow grave. 'Good girl, good girl,' she said kneeling down and patting the earth over it. 'Rest in peace,' she murmured, scooping Greta up into her arms and taking her back to the table.

He smiled absentmindedly when she stood in front of him, Greta in her arms.

'Shall we go back in now?' she said.

'As you will,' he said, 'As you will.'

She changed back into the dress and adopted her pose. He adopted his: brow creased, paintbrush making small, intermittent strokes, a step back, thumb under chin, glance her way, repeat. Greta was playing with a paintbrush on the floor, tossing it in the air and pouncing on it. She thought of the finger and whether he'd missed it yet.

'Finished,' he said, standing back and folding his arms across his chest. 'Want to come and look?'

'Okay,' she said, slowly levering herself up.

He was staring at the portrait, his thumb beneath his chin, fingers curled over his lip.

She walked over, stood alongside him and said nothing. It was an arresting piece. He said he knew her, and, judging by the expression he'd painted on her face, he did. Her eyes were piercing, appraising, calculating, defiant. There was no sign of the teasing minx, the lady of the manor, the obedient companion. Just Julia. A woman living on her wits, not her beauty, which had always been just one of the currencies at her disposal.

She stroked her top lip and took a step forward. 'I thought you were going to deal with those fine lines between my eyebrows,' she said, smiling ruefully.

'I was. But I've grown to like them. Very much. Do you like your portrait, Julia?'

'Yes. But will I get to enjoy it?'

She turned to face him.

He was looking at his hands. 'I'm conflicted, my love. I wish I'd never met you. You don't need me.'

'No,' she said, tossing back her hair. 'I'm not your mother. But I am a mother and my son needs me.'

He sucked on his top lip. 'Yes.' He spread out his hands. 'But how. How?'

275

'You'll need to give yourself up, Axel.'

'I can't do that. My life's work is here. These women need me. You might not, but they do.'

'They need to be laid to rest. Their families given closure. You have the portraits. You have immortalised them. Each one such a unique beauty. But this can't go on. I think you know that.'

'I don't. Maybe I can make you understand? In time.' Julia looked back at her portrait. 'Or maybe I can persuade you.'

'You have courage. Guile. Confidence. Beauty – physical and spiritual. My mother had just one of those attributes. And it killed her.'

'That was tragic. But it doesn't have to end like that for me and Nick. You can let me go. Let me send Nick a letter. By the time he gets it you can be long gone.'

He shook his head and ran a hand through his hair. 'I will never leave. I don't want to. I have to stay here, with my beauties. That is my promise to them. I will never let them down. Never leave them.'

Julia sighed and let her shoulders droop, her arms swinging gently at her side. 'So what happens now? You kill me and look after me forever? I don't need looking after, Axel. You know that. You know me.'

He stretched his lips into a thin line. 'Yes. You have surprised me. You've grown in so many ways since I first met you.'

'I've grown a few more grey hairs,' she said, raising an eyebrow.

He reached over and brushed a strand from her forehead. 'No, you haven't, my love.'

They looked at each other for a while.

'Look, I have a few things to do right now,' he said, feeling in his pocket.

'Anything I can help you with?'

He sniffed. 'I've mislaid something important.'

Her heart stilled and she glanced at Greta who was growling playfully, and chewing the paint brush.

'What is it?'

'Nothing to concern yourself with, my dear. Stay here, enjoy the portrait. I won't be long.'

He strode to the door, jangling its key. She went straight to

Greta, pulled the paintbrush away from her jaws and tossed it to the other side of the room. 'Fetch,' she said.

Greta rushed back, tail wagging with it in her mouth. If only it would be as easy to fetch that finger. She could see there would be no peace until it was back in his murderous hands.

She moved to the window, dragged over a chair and looked down into the orangery. He was there, pacing up and down, running his hands through his hair, pushing aside plant pots, looking under the tables and urns.

How to turn this to her advantage?

Brandon

July 31, 2019

Brandon was outside The Hall banging on the front door. He'd rushed there after the Zoom with Arvid Larsson – it had become clear that Axel Fleming was now prime suspect.

'Julia!' he yelled up at her bedroom window. It was pointless, he knew, but yelling his lungs out was a release of sorts.

He rushed round to the back door and tried the handle. Locked. The whole place was bordered up, shutters closed, lights off, the Mercedes parked on the forecourt, alarm pulsing red.

'Jo, check the airport. See if Julia Trenowden and Axel Fleming have taken a flight out of Newquay in the past two days. Check the car rentals to see if they hired a car.' Brandon was pacing up and down, treading the gravel into the forecourt, his mobile clamped against his ear.

'Will do, Boss. Are you coming back to the office now?'

'Yes. Need to organise some things. Axel Fleming being the main one.' Brandon clicked off, pinged open the Skoda, got in and put his foot down, the tyres screeching as he sped off.

He slammed on the brakes when he got to the end of the lane just as a cyclist peddled past. He needed to cool down. But this had just got personal. He cursed himself for not keeping a closer eye on Fleming. For believing his smooth patter. But Julia had given him an alibi the night Diana Chambers was abducted. His gut had been right, but instinct can't always be trusted. He reached for a cigarette, lit up, took a drag, released the handbrake with his left hand – it didn't hurt so much, small mercies – and shifted into first gear and out onto the road.

'Julia Trenowden and Axel Fleming have not flown out of Newquay in the past week,' Jo said, over the car coms. 'No car rentals in their names either.'

'Okay,' Brandon, slowed down as he took a bend. 'I'll be with you in five minutes. Could you search Alex Östberg and Axel Fleming? Find out when the change occurred. Anja said he died in 1995 – a year before the disappearances.' He paused. 'It might be an idea if we got hold of Anja Östberg again. It could save some legwork.'

'On Zoom?'

'First step. If either one of us has to go over there, so be it. But I don't want to waste valuable time. Let's see what she can give us without going to the trouble.'

Jo was at the main desk when he strode into the station. He gave her a nod and she followed him into the incident room.

'I was just getting Stew to check out Fleming's back story. The Africa years!'

'Nice piece of delegation, Jo. I'm guessing he greased a few palms to get that on his C.V.; let's see if Stew can use his charm to prise out the finer details.'

'I managed to get hold of Erik Anderson. That's his surname,' Jo said, standing by the incident room table. Both of them were too wired to sit down.

'What did he have to say?'

'He said Anja was resting. That she often rests in the afternoon, but he would take her some tea and explain the importance of speaking to us.'

Brandon thumped the table. 'Importance doesn't come close. I'll fly over and paddle down the fjords to speak to them in person if Anja doesn't give me some answers right this minute.'

'Steady on, Boss.'

'I'm trying, Jo. I'm trying very hard. But pardon me if I don't have the Swede's sang froid.'

'Well, try a bit harder. Please. I need to tell you that Nick Trenowden called the station, around fifteen minutes ago. He has been trying to get hold of his mum for some time. She's not taking calls or messages. He last spoke to her on July 26, 8am, UK time.'

Brandon gasped and stooped over the table, stretching out both his arms and rested there a while. And then he lifted his bowed head, picked up his phone and tapped in Anja's number.

'Yes,' said her tired voice.

'Detective Inspector Hammett. It's very important that we speak to you now about your brother Alex.'

'Okay,' she said, 'On Zoom?'

Brandon hesitated. He wanted instant answers but he also wanted to read her expression, difficult as that was. 'If you can set up a meeting in the next five minutes.'

'I can.'

Anja was as good as her word. Her tired grey face appeared on the laptop in four minutes and forty-five seconds. Brandon had been counting.

'Ms Östberg, thank you so much for your time,' he said, remembering his manners.

She nodded.

'I have to ask you some important questions about Alex. Please answer them to the best of your knowledge.'

'Okay. Can you explain why?'

'We believe your brother is alive and using the name Axel Fleming.'

Anja blanched. 'He's alive?'

'He was at your father's funeral, Ms Östberg, 17 years ago. We saw the photograph.'

She looked down and nodded gently. 'Yes. He did come. He kept back – well away from the family. But he was there.'

'Why didn't you say?' Brandon was staring into those reservoirs of blue. 'Why did you lie about the boating accident? This could be serious, Ms Östberg, I can't deny that. Aiding and abetting a prime suspect in a missing persons' investigation.'

Anja hesitated before answering. 'I had no idea of the gravity of the situation. He asked me to go along with the disappearance. To not make a fuss. That he needed to reset his life. Be someone else other than Alex Östberg.'

'Did he tell you who his new persona was?'

'No.'

'What did he tell you? Did he tell you that he'd been on a killing spree in the United Kingdom?'

Anja's jaw dropped. 'No. No. Why would you say that? Why would he?'

'Because, Ms Östberg, your brother, Alex Östberg, now known as Axel Fleming, is suspected of abducting and possibly murdering seven young women.'

'No. No.' Anja was shaking her head and Erik's face appeared on the screen.

'Please,' he said, 'Please. Anja can't cope with this sort of pressure. She is very fragile.'

'I'm sorry. But I need to ask Anja a few more questions. Her brother is prime suspect in a missing persons' case. Four women have gone missing in Penwith, Cornwall, over the past two months. Her help now is vital and could save lives.'

Anja touched Erik's hand and looked up at him. He moved back, but left his hand on her shoulder for her to hold.

'I will help you as best I can. But, believe me, Alex is not a bad person. What he has done, if he is guilty of these crimes, he has done because of some compulsion. He has suffered.'

Brandon nodded. 'I understand, but please, Anja, help me find him and get him the treatment he needs. And, I can't stress this enough, help us find the women he is holding captive before it's too late for them.'

Anja fixed him with her pale eyes. 'What do you need to know?'

'When was the last time you spoke to Alex?"

'June 2002. He stayed at the lodge for a few days after Papa's funeral.'

'What had he been doing up until then?'

'He'd been travelling. Africa, I believe.'

'So he has spent time in Africa?'

'Yes. He went there after school – saw it as a way to cleanse his soul, he said.'

'Did he go into finance?'

'Yes. It was Papa's idea. Alex was very clever. Brilliant with numbers and technology. But it wasn't his passion.'

Brandon stopped to think. So far Alex and Axel had the same career path. And somewhere along the line he changed his name. He figured it had to have been before his stint at the London Business School in 1994.

'Where did he work?

'Credit Suisse in Zurich and New York.'

'You have evidence of that?'

'Only his word. He didn't speak of his work. He considered it a dull subject.'

'What did you talk about?' Jo asked.

'The lodge, our environmental work. Family matters.'

'Did you talk about your parents?' Brandon asked.

'No. Never.'

Brandon held her gaze.

'It wasn't a subject either of us felt comfortable with.' Anja squeezed Erik's hand.

'Did Alex ever refer to himself as Axel Fleming in your company?'

Anja shook her head. 'No. It is the first I've heard of this other person.'

Brandon leaned forward. 'Anja, think very carefully. What was Alex doing in 1995 and 1996? The period after he stayed at the lodge?'

Anja looked up at Erik. Brandon could see his goatee nodding.

'He was in the UK.'

Brandon blew out. 'Where in the UK?'

'Art School. Falmouth.'

Jo turned her head sharply towards Brandon. Suzanna beeped him a text. Brandon raised his dark blue eyes to meet Anja's ice blue ones. 'Art was his passion?'

'Yes,' she said. 'The pursuit of perfection. Something he inherited from Mama. He had a reservoir of untapped talent.'

Brandon glanced at Jo. 'I see.'

'Is there any way you can contact him? Do you have an address – addresses – for him in the UK?'

'No. If I did I would gladly give them to you. Alex – my twin, the brother who shared everything with me – hasn't confided in me since the day Mama died.'

Brandon

July 31, 2019

'Open up, police!' The Newquay firearms squad were at the door of Axel Fleming's spacious pad in St Ives. Two hundred and eighty-five miles east, the Met were bashing open the door of his Hoxton penthouse.

Brandon followed the Newquay team in, treading carefully up the half-decorated staircase, to an expansive first floor. The place was covered in dustsheets and pots of paints; patches of brickwork open wounds in the plaster.

A spiral staircase led to a mezzanine level. Brandon felt his way up to what looked like Fleming's office cum bedroom. He was surprised to see formal portraits on the wall, rather than the ubiquitous abstracts found in loft apartments.

He heard Al Chapman before he turned to see him winding up the staircase.

'You can't keep a good guy down,' Brandon said, looking surprised.

'Believe me, they did try,' Al said, a tight smile slashing his face. 'But I'm back, reporting for duty, Detective Inspector.'

'Can't say I'm not relieved.' Brandon was surveying the anodyne contents of the room. 'You'll have your work cut out finding anything incriminating here.'

Al stretched open a blue glove and pulled it on his left hand. 'It you don't know me by now.'

Brandon grinned. 'I'll leave you to it.'

He turned to leave and then stopped. 'By the way. I'm expecting a delivery of another box.'

'Tupperware or glass?' Al said, pulling on the other glove.

'Glass. Antique glass and metal.'

'Oh yes?' Al said, cocking his head.

'I'm hoping you'll be able to match the display cases in the Östberg Museum in Stockholm with the ones used by our SBK.'

Al stood there taking it in, before saying: 'Nice work, Brandon.'

'We'll see, eh,' Brandon said as he walked over to the staircase, his phone ringing.

Julia

August 3, 2019

He was getting increasingly frantic, rushing from platform to plant, overturning pots, tipping up bags of compost, crawling on his hands and knees searching.

She watched him leap up onto a metal chair and scan the orangery, as if trying to get a new perspective on things. His chin shot up and she ducked down. When she looked again he was staring up at the window. Julia climbed down from the chair and walked over to the chaise longue. He was at the door in minutes, breathing heavy, his hair messy, eyes blazing.

'What have you done with it?'

'Done with what?'

'Where have you put it?'

'What?'

'Don't try to fool me. You forget, you can't lie to me. I know you.'

'Don't be ridiculous,' she said. But he was frightening her. She had become a problem. How simple and convenient it would be to dispose of a problem.

He was up close now. Like that first time. She could smell his breath – the food on it. Some sort of lemon-based dressing. Something acidic. He took hold of her wrist, clenching it hard.

'Where is it?'

Greta was whimpering by a pile of material on the floor to their right. 'Shut up!' he shouted, making her whimper more.

'If you mean the … object Greta was playing with this morning?'

His face was right up against hers. 'Of course. Of course.'

'It's in the garden. Where she left it.'

'You left it. Don't blame your ... your despicable behaviour on an animal.'

He still had hold of her wrist and was pulling her closer.

'I'm not. Greta is innocent. Like any animal. I just placed it out of her reach.'

'Why didn't you tell me?' He moved back to watch her reaction, loosening his grip a little.

'Because I didn't know how to. What was I meant to say? Even now I can't frame the words.' She slumped onto the chaise longue, all strength gone.

'Take me to it.'

She couldn't move, her mind was racing, but her limbs were leaden.

He yanked her arm, dragging her up onto her feet. 'Come on. Take me to it. Before it's too late. You understand. Do you understand?'

He was shouting now and she did understand. Or thought she understood his warped reasoning. A bird could have found the finger. Or a fox. Or some industrious worm. She felt sick. How much more of this did she have to stomach? She wanted to curl up in the meadow herself and let nature take its course.

'Okay,' she sighed. 'You best get a torch.'

He thought for a second before racing over to a closet on the far side of the studio and rummaging inside.

'Not here. You're going to have use what natural light we have left. Come on, we have little time.'

He grabbed hold of her arm and marched her out of the studio, along the landing and down the stairs, the green dress catching between her legs and making her stumble. When he got to the garden door, he let her go and felt for the key, patting a pocket and thrusting one hand in deep. It wasn't there. He started to swivel his head, thinking and looking before stretching up to the plant pot and feeling. She heard the sound of metal against ceramic and a sigh as he brought his hand back down and placed the key in the lock. She was surprised he'd used the same hiding place. She wouldn't have.

He opened the door and pushed her out. 'Find it.'

It was a cloudy, starless night, but she calmed herself and tried to remember the coordinates. She'd been sitting facing the iron gate, the meadow fanning out before her. She'd only let Greta go a few feet or so before grabbing her by the collar and making her give up the finger. She walked over to the spot where she thought it might be.

'Get down. On all fours. Get down and search.' He pushed her to the ground and she brushed aside the grass, clawing back the earth with her hands. She crawled on her knees, scraping and digging, tears stinging her eyes, making it hard to see.

'Keep looking. Look until you find it.' She turned her head to see him standing there, his face a picture of pain and fury.

He knelt down beside her. 'Find it,' he said, pushing her face into the ground. 'Find it.' She clamped her mouth shut and closed her eyes as his hand tightened on the back of her neck, forcing earth into her nostrils, forcing the life out of her.

'Is this what you want?' he said, releasing his grip. 'To be buried? Left in the dark? Patted down and forgotten? Left to rot unattended?'

She gasped and scrambled back onto all fours, shaking the dirt from her hair and using an arm to wipe it off her face. And then she continued her search, her hands sweeping through the undergrowth, feeling and patting, scraping and digging. He followed her, at a short distance, for what must have been half an hour, as she combed the area in silence, tossing aside lumps of soil, stones and sticks, until she felt the brittle curve of a nail.

He stooped down as soon as he saw the tip of the finger piercing the earth and carefully removed it in gloved hands. After examining it and dusting off the residual earth, he slipped the finger into a plastic bag and stood up.

Julia remained on the ground, waiting for his word.

He turned towards the house. 'Get up.'

Julia patted down her dress and followed him past the forlorn vegetable patches and drooping sunflowers to the back of the orangery. He was holding the plastic bag in front of him, and, every so often, it lit up like a lantern as the moon peeped out from behind the clouds.

There was a brick building at the back of the orangery that Julia hadn't noticed before, even when she had the aerial view from the studio. She assumed it was a powerhouse for the small kitchen he had constructed in the orangery and, possibly, for his gardening appliances.

His left hand was fumbling in his pocket as he approached the small wooden door. Julia stopped a metre or two behind him and let him unlock it. An owl hooted as it flew above and he watched until it disappeared into the night.

'After you,' he said, turning to Julia. She walked slowly, calming herself. She had become accustomed to these nerve-wracking excursions. They varied in their degrees of shock and awe and, she argued, she was becoming desensitised. But her heart thumped and her words shook as she whispered, 'Thank you'.

It was pitch black in the room – until it burst into white light. The sudden change blinded her, making her stagger back against him. He pushed her away, forcing her to confront the scene.

A pale body lay prone on a marble slab, long red hair draped over the shoulders. The skin was flawless with the luminosity of a pre-Raphaelite beauty, the arms raised like Millais' Ophelia. The right hand held a posy of wild flowers; the left was empty and minus the middle finger.

'See,' he said, registering her shock. 'See, how important my work is. How important each and every detail is. You can't bury things that you don't like. That disturb you. Everything has its place.'

Julia looked at him. Why did he remove the finger?

As always, he read her mind. 'The bereaved must have tokens for their earthly rituals.' He waved a hand. 'I return them, beautifully presented. It is not for you to act on their behalf.' He frowned at her. 'I am concerned with the immortalisation and preservation of beauty, not the ugly machine of life that produces, reduces and destroys. And moves on. I will never do that.'

Julia nodded. She wasn't prepared to get into a metaphysical debate with a madman. Her own skin was very much alive, bristling with fear and spidery sensations. The body on the slab was prone, but its presence filled the room.

A physician's table ran alongside the slab. There was a medical box at one end, with some utensils and bottles.

'Your despicable act,' he said, walking towards the table, 'cost me a lot of time today. Time I need to make up.'

Julia froze. Then lurched for the door; but he rushed to it and forced it shut with his back.

'Don't worry,' he said, 'I wouldn't trust you to assist me.' He shook his head in disbelief. 'Is that what you thought?' He bent his neck so his face was right up against hers. His anger burned off it, setting her own cheeks alight as the blood rushed to her head. She felt sick, she felt faint, and her legs buckled and collapsed beneath her.

'Get up.'

When she couldn't, he dragged her onto her feet and she fell back against the door for support. He reached behind her and locked it, giving her a hard stare before pocketing the key and walking to a small sink in the corner. He washed his hands, dried them on a freshly laundered towel, and pulled a new pair of surgical gloves from a plastic container beneath the sink. He snapped them open and pulled them on.

'Look and learn. I'm studying myself – the plastination process. Applied well, it can preserve flesh for eternity,' he said, as he walked over to the table and poured liquid into a beaker. 'My last assistant was a poor student and had to go. Such a shame. We were close.'

Brandon

August 2, 2019

'The box is of the same style and composition as the original cases used in the 1996 killings,' Al Chapman confirmed over the phone while Brandon was driving to Truro.

'Good work, Al,' Brandon said.

'Any news on the other investigations?'

'Well, apart from Fleming's DNA – which you also found in St Ives – the Met didn't uncover anything helpful. Just work files. Fleming was a financier – I guess he needed the money to fund his hobby. And also, I'm guessing, his third residence.'

'Makes sense,' Al said, 'He has to have somewhere in the Penwith area where he can operate from with impunity.'

'It's just a case of finding it,' Brandon said, taking the third turning off the roundabout.

'Tricky.'

'The net's closing in. He'll be aware of the raids. Let's see if these new developments shake his nerve or strengthen it.'

'Any news on Julia Trenowden?'

Brandon ran a hand across his cleanly shaven chin. 'No. I'm hoping that, because she knows him, she can manipulate him. Julia is an incredible woman. But —' Brandon threw back his head and thumped the steering wheel with his good hand. 'But God knows this man is dangerous. He has his own set of beliefs – death being just one step to his divine justice. I just hope we can reach her before it's too late.'

'Brandon, call me anytime if I can be of help. Anytime.'

'Thanks, Al. That's sure good to hear.'

Suzanna Fitzgerald was at the open door of her town house when Brandon drew up outside. He manoeuvred into a tight spot and got out of the car.

Suzanna didn't say anything. She didn't have to. He followed her into the house, down the tasteful hallway, and into the garden room. The table was set with coffee cups, a cafetière and a plate of homemade cookies. Brandon wished she hadn't bothered. He wasn't hungry. There were too many things gnawing at him.

'So, we know who the killer is and why he kills. How do we find him? Trap him? Stop him?' Brandon was fiddling with the teaspoon in his saucer.

Suzanna inhaled deeply. 'Would you like a revelation with your coffee?' she said, smiling, and picking up the cafetière to pour.

'That would be nice,' he said, smiling back.

'Shall we call him Alex?' Suzanna said, offering Brandon the plate of biscuits.

He waved them away politely. 'Thanks, Suzanna. But I'm not hungry today. But, yes, let's call him Alex. Anything to get into his mindset.'

'Okay,' she said, putting the plate to one side. 'Alex is in a tight corner right now. His two bolt holes – three, if you include The Hall – have been closed off. He is now stuck in his hidey hole, wherever that may be. Do we think he's in a happy place?'

Brandon shook his head. 'You'd like to think not.'

'He's surrounded by death.'

Brandon's head shot up. 'We don't know that.'

'No, but it would be wise to consider this scenario. Four women have gone missing in two months, body parts turning up, it would be difficult to keep this under wraps if they were all alive.'

'Not necessarily,' Brandon cut in. 'With planning and finance. The man is clever and resourceful.'

'True,' Suzanna conceded, 'but his latest captive has thrown him off kilter.'

Brandon narrowed his eyes.

'Julia Trenowden is different in so many ways to his other victims. She's a mother. She's rich and successful. She knows him,' Suzanna said.

'Does that make her any more safe?'

'It could make him more wary, or considerate. It will depend, of course, on how Julia handles the situation.'

'Yes,' Brandon agreed, 'But I would wager she's handling it as well as can be expected … in the circumstances. She is a strong, intelligent person.'

'That puts her at odds with the other major influence in his life.'

'His mother?'

'Yes. Maybe he saw something in Julia that resembled Greta Östberg?'

'But isn't that what he was seeking in all of his victims – a vulnerability he could protect. A beauty he could preserve?'

'I would say so. But, by now, he may be realising he underestimated Julia. And, possibly, his other victims.'

'Either way she's in a precarious position.'

'Exactly,' Suzanna said, reaching for a biscuit. 'And so is he. He must be conflicted. Torturing himself. Knowing, or denying, that Julia doesn't need saving from herself and society. Just him. I wish I could say I knew which way he would turn. But I don't.' Suzanna bit into the biscuit.

'He has demonstrated bouts of temperament and rage. The estrangement with his father, the attack on me.' Brandon waved his left wrist. 'The spiteful abduction of red-haired Emily Paxton the day after Jo almost trapped him, his treatment of Diana Chambers. He can be Old Testament God as well as New.'

Suzanna looked at him. 'I'm impressed with your analysis, Detective Inspector.'

He smiled. 'I look and listen.' He paused and reached for a biscuit.

'Is your appetite back?'

'It never goes too far away, Suzanna.' He took a bite and got up from the table. 'Thank you for going through things with me. Even though your thoughts confirm my worst fears.'

'He's a caged and damaged man, Brandon. A very

dangerous one. I don't think I need to tell you to tread carefully.'

'Carefully and swiftly. We'll be watching the roads. Watching for unusual behaviour and purchases. His days are numbered. The only protection he's going to get soon is in a high security cell.'

'Watch your back, Brandon,' Suzanna said, folding three biscuits into a napkin for him.

He took the biscuits, lent down and kissed her lightly on the cheek. 'I can't begin to tell you how helpful you've been, on so many levels.'

'Don't get crumbs in the car,' she said, laughing lightly, getting up to show him the door.

Julia

August 3, 2019

Julia was sitting opposite him at the dining table, a brunette in her first flush of decomposition to her right, and a bottle blonde who'd seen much better days on her left. It was hard to keep the contempt off her face. He had a sulking scowl on his.

Supper was a smorgasbord of cold meat, which made her skin creep. But she was hungry so helped herself to the sour breads, salamis and hams and also to the wine.

He'd only given her a miniscule amount, so she downed it in one. He declined to top her up, instead pouring more into his own glass.

Julia turned to Bottle Blonde. 'Can we not tempt you to a glass of Medoc this evening?' She nodded and pursed her lips. 'I see. Watching your weight. Well, if you're sure?' Julia picked up her companion's glass and raised it to her lips, watching him all the while.

He had his eyes on her. 'You only have to ask if you want more wine. Here.' He stood up and poured wine into her empty glass, filling it to the brim.

'Most kind,' she said as he sat back down.

He reached behind his chair to a food trolley and picked up a plate. 'Pate?' he said as he placed it on the table.

It was foie gras and wobbled, like a liver, in a burgundy sauce.

'Watching my waistline.'

'I'd say you were losing weight. Here, give me your plate. This really is delicious.' He picked up her plate, cut into the foie gras, and served her a slice.

'I don't like foie gras,' she said, pushing the plate away.

He held her gaze for a while before serving himself and forking a slice into his mouth.

Julia turned away and reached for her glass. They sat in silence. He helping himself to the meats and pate, and she slugging back the wine.

He placed his knife and fork at 10 and 4 o'clock on his plate and pushed it aside. Julia pounced on the gesture as an excuse to get up from the table.

'Sit down,' he said, folding his napkin.

'We've finished.'

'There will be pudding. I'll just clear away.'

Julia sat back down and stared ahead in stony silence. Her feet were kicking out under the table as she watched him tidying away like a fussy old butler.

'Can I help you?'

'If you would just pass me your companions' wine glasses,' he said. To ensure she didn't drain them? But she'd already had quite enough on an empty and bilious stomach. She stretched over for the brunette's glass, knocking her off her chair as she did so.

'I'm so sorry. So sorry,' she babbled, pushing her chair back to get up and help.

'Leave her,' he said. 'No one's fault. Let me.' He was at their side in moments, helping the body back into the chair like a solicitous gentleman. 'No harm done,' he said, picking up the wine glass and putting it on the trolley with the others.

She watched him clear away the rest and stoop down to a chilled section in the trolley.

He brought out a coupe glass with two white orbs. 'You like sorbet?'

'Sometimes,' she said, as he placed the glass in front of her.

'And,' he said, a flicker of a smile on his lips, 'dessert wine? Chateau d'Yquem?'

She nodded and watched him pour, the sorbet melting in the glass.

His eyes were on her as she dipped her spoon into the iced lychee.

'I'm sorry I had to scold you earlier,' he said, making her splutter.

He quickly filled her tumbler with water and she took a gulp.

'I should have realised how important this all is to you. I apologise.'

He sighed. 'I thought you understood. Perhaps I hadn't made myself clear.'

She looked at him. Saw the sad desperation in his eyes. His need to be understood and ... forgiven? Had it come to that?

'Maybe I didn't fully understand before, but I do now.'

'Drink your wine.' He poured her more, 'And may I just add that you look delightful this evening. As always. But your choice of dress – the touch of autumnal gold in the stitching, is exemplary.' You picked it, she thought, but didn't say.

Instead, she looked at him, tears rolling down her face, her food and wine untouched.

He left her a while, fussed around the trolley a little more, before coming round to her side of the table.

Stroking the side of her face, he said. 'Shall we take our drinks outside? See Gigi?'

She bit her top lip and nodded.

'Take my arm.' He led her out of the room, and along the familiar passage to the garden.

There was a chill in the air, and he turned on the heater and gave her a rug for her lap. Greta immediately tried to scramble up onto it.

'Better now?'

She looked him in the eye as he stood in front of her; a bottle of Medoc in his hand, that concerned expression on his face. It was never far away.

'You said I could write to Nick. I think it's time, don't you?'

'Is it time?'

'Of course it is. This can't go on. It's purgatory, for Nick, for me, for you.'

He put his hands on his hips and shook his head. 'I don't have the writing materials right now. Can we leave it until the morning?'

'Yes.' Her eyes felt heavy and she took the wine he was offering without looking at him. She relaxed her legs and Greta slid off her lap and padded over to him. He leant down and patted the dog's head.

'You're tired, of course.'

'What time tomorrow?'

He frowned. 'Tomorrow?'

'When I write to Nick?'

He took a sip of wine before resting his glass on the table and leaning back in his chair, his hands clasped behind his head.

'Why don't we go one better?'

'Hmm?'

He was staring into the night sky. 'I have been thinking about arranging a meeting with the police. With DS Menhenrick. I believe you know her?'

'Jo, yes. You met her too – at the party.' Julia shifted to the edge of her seat.

'I can't be totally upfront with her, as you will understand. But if we can arrange for DS Menhenrick – Jo – to meet at a rendezvous of my choosing, then we can start a conversation. You can also use the opportunity to give her a letter for Nick.'

'That sounds like a brilliant plan. When were you thinking of setting up the meeting?'

'Tomorrow. If that suits?'

'Well, yes,' she said, watching him top up his wine. She picked up her glass, before he could refill it. She'd need her wits about her in the morning.

August 4, 2019

There was a fine drizzle in the air, so they had breakfast in the orangery. He'd prepared some scrambled eggs, which were placed under a dome on the trolley. Greta looked up appealingly as he ladled portions onto their plates.

'Be patient, Gigi,' he said, scolding the dog, 'You will get your share.'

They ate in silence, listening to the sound of rain on glass.

He finished quickly, spooned a helping of egg into a bowl and placed it on the floor for Gigi. The dog rushed to it, wagging her tail.

'How simple it is to make her happy,' he said smiling at Gigi indulgently.

And me, screamed Julia's expression. Just let me walk away.

She started to clear away the breakfast things until he got up and raised a palm.

'Leave that, darling. It can wait. If you're ready, why don't we make a start on … our correspondence.'

She followed his eyes to an area at the far end of the orangery.

'Why not?' she said, getting up and walking with him to a trestle table with a box and a book of writing paper on it.

He pulled out one of two chairs for her to sit on.

Julia opened the box, fully expecting to see a quill pen and inks inside. But there was a selection of good quality pens in different inks. She picked up a few Mont Blanc ballpoints. He watched her scribble some lines on a sheet of paper to test the ink until she found blue.

'You don't want black?'

'No,' she replied.

Hunching over the writing paper book, she cradled it between her arms like a school girl doing an exam.

'I'll leave you for a while. Give you some peace.'

She turned back and gave a weak smile, and he walked back to the breakfast table and started to clear away. She briefly thought that, in different circumstances, he would have made a perfect partner for someone.

The drizzle had turned to driving rain and sounded against the ceiling and walls. She was happy to have it join the conversation and obscure his background tinkering.

'Dear, Nick, my darling son,' she wrote. That was the easy part. How best to continue and strike the right tone?

Write it straight, she decided. 'I miss you so much and hope to see you very soon.' She put aside her pen and wiped away the tears streaming down her face with her sleeve.

'I know this separation must be so hard for you,' she continued, swallowing down her grief. 'Harder than it is for me, as at least I have the knowledge that you are safe, with family and friends and that you have the strength of character to withstand this ...' she hesitated over the word 'torment' and added 'uncertainty'.

'I will, therefore, assure you that I am being treated well. I have good food, exercise and am not being hurt physically.' She rested her pen and took a deep breath.

'But I long to be with you again. For us to return to normality,' she continued, writing fast, like she did in those last minutes of exam time. 'To see how much you've grown since coming back from the States. Another inch? Two? To hear stories of your great adventure and, when term starts, to bully you about schoolwork. MAKE SURE YOU DO IT!'

'I know it will be difficult for you to concentrate. But please try. For me. Keep your spirits up, as I am doing. Be assured that I am well but missing you terribly. I can't wait to see you again.' She stopped briefly when she heard Axel walking across the room towards her.

Curling around the book, she continued. 'Whatever happens, please be aware of my love and how much you meant to me in the time we had. You were/are my rock. My one and only. The best son in the world. ☺ Give my love to Grandma and Grandad, Rachel, Brandon and Chelsea and all our friends. But, more than anything, receive my undying love.

Yours, forever,
Love You
Mum xxx.'

Axel was standing over her reading. 'Beautiful, my love. He is a lucky boy.'

She presented him a face wet with tears. 'Lucky?'

'To have a loving mother. Like I did.'

Julia returned to the book, carefully tearing the sheet of paper along its perforated line. 'What next?' she said handing it to him.

'I will need you to make a phone call. I'll tell you what to say.'

August 4, 2019

Brandon was at Penzance Station preparing for a 9am press conference. He placed his mobile on the incident room table and looked at Jo. 'I'm going to be in Newquay later this morning to discuss the next steps.'

'Okay,' Jo said, folding her arms and looking at him.

'I want to persuade them to do a major man hunt. Door-to-door, in some areas, if the media appeal triggers leads.' Brandon was pacing the room. 'With this extra information we should be able to flush him out. Östberg's face is going to be all over Penwith, the UK, Sweden and beyond. Unless he's managed to hide himself away in a bunker in the Swiss Alps, he's going to have to surface at some point. Someone will have spotted him. I just hope it isn't too late.'

'For Julia?'

He gave Jo a sideways look. 'Yes. And for all those other poor women. Dear God, he's a fucking crazy.'

Brandon had the mic unclipped as soon as the cameras stopped rolling and the last of the reporters had finished questioning him. He brushed them aside as he walked away from the station steps.

'I've got you a coffee,' Jo said, joining him as he walked and offering him a paper cup.

'Thanks,' he said, stopping by his car parked out front. 'My nerves are jangling. Not sure the caffeine is a good idea.'

'It's nice and milky,' Jo said, smiling up at him.

'Jo, you think of everything. Keep your mobile close. I'll phone you with developments. Let me know if the press conference generates any leads. It certainly should.'

'Will do, Boss.'

Brandon

August 4, 2019

They'd had a few calls into the station since the press conference, but nothing to grasp hold of. Brandon was taking a cigarette break outside Newquay Police Station waiting for one of the MCIT team to turn up so they could agree strategies, other than getting the uniforms sweeping the coves and responding to local intelligence. Brandon glanced at a text that had just come through from Jo.

'Julian Crowthers, a farmer in the Zennor area, says he found a piece of female clothing hanging from the door of one of his barns. He discovered it a few days back but wrote it off as "hanky panky" in the field. Shall I pass it to Chapman?'

Brandon texted back. 'Absolutely. Get Chapman on it ASAP.'

'How's it going?'

Brandon sent a rolled eyes emoji. 'I'm glad I'm here – I want to ensure we act swiftly and comprehensively, but we don't force Fleming, I mean Östberg, on the attack. We've seen how nasty he can get when provoked.'

'Agreed.'

'Speak later,' Brandon said, taking a last drag and stubbing his cigarette out against the wall. He dropped the stub in an empty packet and put it in his pocket. 'I'll let you know when I'm on my way back.'

Zennor. Brandon knew the location well. There were fields and coves; plenty of houses for Östberg to hide away in. He was in two minds as whether to ask the MCIT guys to do some searches now or wait for Chapman's analysis on the clothing. He was tempted to push his luck. It'd been running in his favour of late.

Julia

August 4, 2019

They were sitting at the table in the dining room. Axel was staring at his phone. He'd been doing that a lot this morning. He had his earphones in so she couldn't hear what he was listening to, but he wasn't talking. His brows were knitted in concentration. The news?

Something was brewing. She assumed he'd picked the dining room to make the call he'd spoken about for security reasons. He'd mentioned airplane mode when he'd allowed her to read texts on her own phone that first day in the room. Maybe the basement gave another layer of protection? Whatever, the setting seemed appropriate. As if the others were also privy to an important development, like directors at a board table or generals in a war room. The beauty she had knocked off her seat had a tilted head, as if straining to hear.

He let his screen go black and turned to Julia. 'We're going to call DS Menhenrick at Penzance Station now.'

'Listen carefully. Everything depends up on how you conduct yourself in this conversation. Do not announce yourself. You call yourself Sadie Williams. Do you understand?'

'Sadie Williams,' she parroted.

'You say you saw DI Hammett on the TV this morning asking for information about the … disappearances.'

Julia gasped involuntarily.

He gave her a look. 'You say you saw DI Hammett on TV this morning asking for information about the disappearances and you may have something interesting.' He stopped to see whether she was taking it all in.

'I saw DI Hammett on TV asking for information about the disappearances and I have something which may be of interest.'

He paused, his eyes looking past her. 'Yes, that will do. Better in some respects than my version. You say you saw a case, identical to the ones used by the —' He couldn't bring himself to say the words.

'Sleeping Beauty Killer,' Julia added.

He nodded. 'In the car park of the Farmer's Arms in Porthmeor.'

Why the pub carpark? And not a cove?

He was staring at her over the rims of his glasses. 'Are you with me?'

'Yes. I saw a case, identical to the ones used by the SBK in the Farmer's Head pub carpark. In Porthmeor.'

'Okay. I'll put through the call to the station and hand it over to you. Don't try and be clever. The whole deal is off if you betray me.'

'Will you place the letter in the case?'

'Of course,' he replied, picking up the mobile.

It took a while for Jo to come to the phone. Axel was rapping his fingers on the dining room table and glaring at Julia, as if it were her fault. The act of petulance stiffened her resolve and steadied her nerves.

'Detective Sergeant Menhenrick.' It was so good to hear Jo's voice.

'Thank you for taking my call,' Julia said, ignoring his disapproving stare.

'No problem and your name?'

She thought about stuttering over a J, but decided not to risk it. 'Sadie Williams.'

'Address, please?'

Axel looked mortified and started to scribble something on a piece of paper. 'London. I'm a holidaymaker.'

Good call, she thought, before repeating his words.

'Okay, Ms Williams, what did you want to tell me?'

He was holding onto her wrist. 'I saw a glass case, identical to the ones used by the SBK, in the Farmer's Arms pub carpark in Porthmeor.'

'I see,' Jo said. 'Is it still there?'

'Yes.'

'Can you send a photo?'

He was shaking his head and palm.

'No. I – I haven't got a smart phone.'

'Is there anyone else with you?'

Axel looked put out, as if affronted by these extra questions. He scribbled 'No' on the piece of paper.

'No.'

'Stay there, I'll get someone along as soon as possible.'

He was looking incensed. 'Will it be you?' he wrote.

'I'd feel safer if it were you.'

Axel smiled at her ingenuity. A lone woman may well prefer a female, in the present climate.

'I'll be there shortly.' Julia detected a peevish tone to Jo's reply before she ended the call.

'Let's go.' Axel sprung to his feet.

'Both of us?'

'Yes. Any objections?'

'None whatsoever,' Julia said, casting her eyes around the table and her dining companions for what she hoped would be the last time. She couldn't understand why he wanted her there. To release her? Unlikely. It was a risky manoeuvre, but it offered her a chance of escape.

Julia

August 4, 2019

He was hurtling down the country lanes at 70mph. Am I going to die in a car accident after all this? Julia couldn't help thinking as she slid from side to side, her hands and feet bound tight. Escape? She'd have to be Houdini. His eyes kept flitting to the rear view mirror to check on the glass box, which he'd wedged between two cushions.

He slowed down as the Farmer's Arms came into view; the carpark empty apart from a beaten up old Honda. It was ten in the morning and as lonely as a down-at-heel pub could be. He glided the car into a spot away from the entrance and turned off the engine. Reaching over to the back seat, he picked up the box with one gloved hand. It contained the letter and nothing else. He wound down the windows before opening the car door and going across to the low wall that ran alongside the road. Glancing up as he heard the sound of a car engine, he placed the box on the wall and walked back to the car and crouched behind it.

'Don't speak until I say so,' he said, prodding the barrel of a gun through the passenger door window. 'I'll use this on you and Jo, if I have to.'

A police car pulled up outside and blocked the carpark entrance.

Axel popped his head up and sucked in a breath. It was a clever move.

'Don't say a word,' he hissed.

Jo was out of the car and looking around. She'd spotted Julia in the Volvo and also the box on the wall, which she was examining.

'Call her over,' he said.

Jo was taking pictures of the box when Julia shouted. 'Over here.'

Jo turned to the car and took a photo, moving to the right, so she could take one of the reg.

'Get out of the car. Hands above your head,' Jo said, walking towards the Volvo. She had a taser in its holster, one hand hovering above it.

'Don't move, Julia.' Axel remained hidden by the rear door.

Jo stopped a short distance from the Volvo and tapped on her phone. 'Out of the car now, hands above your head,' she said putting away her phone and drawing the taser.

She was a metre away from the Volvo when Axel sprung up and shot her, Julia screaming as Jo staggered back before hitting the ground hard.

'Shut up,' he said, his head oscillating, checking for onlookers.

'You've shot Jo. You've killed Jo!'

'Keep calm, I said. Stay still.' He grabbed a bag from behind the driver's seat, took hold of Jo's limp body, pulled it up over his shoulder in a fireman's carry and walked to the police car. It was unlocked and Julia could see keys in the ignition. He put Jo in the boot, returned to the front and took something out of the bag. He fussed with it for a minute or so, before going to the wall and placing it by the glass case.

Julia was crying when he returned to the Volvo. 'What have you done? What have you done? What was the point in coming here? Bringing me here? To trap Jo? To kill one more woman?'

He pulled a gag out of his pocket and fixed it around Julia's mouth. Jerking her tied wrists over his head, he heaved her into his arms and carried her struggling body across the carpark to the police car. Opening the passenger door, he dumped her onto the seat.

Scanning the dashboard and shifting the gear stick into first, he drove out of the carpark and down the road.

'Skoda,' he said, shaking his head lightly, the faint sound of police sirens just audible in the distance.

August 4, 2019

Brandon was looking at the photos Jo had sent over as one of the MCIT team strolled into the room and took control of the meeting. Detective Chief Inspector Jackson Truman was notoriously tight-fisted with his budget.

'We need to use our resources wisely. Just because Julia Trenowden is a—' Posh bitch, he might well have said, if he hadn't been interrupted by a big thump on the door.

Al Chapman was standing in the doorway waving a piece of a paper.

Truman didn't look best pleased. 'Yes?'

'The piece of clothing found on the barn door at Crowther's Farm in Zennor has traces of Julia Trenowden's DNA.'

There was an audible intake of breath in the Newquay incident room.

Brandon got up. 'I guess those resources might be employed now we have credible evidence that the missing person, Julia Trenowden, has been in the area recently. I doubt very much she'd been strawberry picking.'

Truman's face fell, and perhaps Brandon shouldn't have made the dig, but it felt good. Now they would have to exercise all the manpower they had at their disposal.

'Meeting adjourned,' Truman said, going over to Al.

Brandon gave them a moment and checked his phone. Two photos from Jo. One of another glass case and one of a Volvo with the registration GP68 UCF.

He scrolled to her message. 'I'm at The Farmer's Inn in Porthmeor. I was called here by a female called Sadie Williams

– holidaymaker from London. I didn't have time to verify the identity.' Brandon exhaled sharply. 'She sighted a glass case on the wall of the pub carpark. She was sitting in the passenger seat of the car when I pulled up. Alone. Just going over now.'

The text was timed 10.10am. It was 10.30 now. Brandon went back to the photo of the car and enlarged the image so he could see the face at the window. It wasn't a great shot but, and he sighed deeply, the female looked very much like Julia. He enlarged the image further. It was Julia.

'Truman,' he yelled across the room. 'A development.'

August 4, 2019

There were two glass boxes on the low wall of the Farmer's Arms carpark. Brandon was studying them when Al Chapman's Toyota Prius screeched to a halt outside. Al leapt out of his car and rushed over.

The contents of the boxes needed little explanation. One contained an envelope address to Nick Trenowden. The other displayed a lock of red hair and a police badge.

'Jo's?' Al said.

'Yes,' he replied, his right hand a tight fist. 'Yes.'

'Nothing I can do for you here, Brandon. Apart from taking the items away for validation. What next?'

'MCIT are searching the area, door-to-door, on the basis of the piece of clothing found at Crowther's Farm. Thanks, Al, for getting that to us so quickly.'

Al nodded.

Brandon jerked a thumb at the Volvo. 'A check's being made on the vehicle right now.'

'A lot hanging on that?'

Brandon nodded. 'I'm going to wait here a while. He's around here somewhere. I can smell him.' The remark was figurative, but Östberg's scent was all over the Volvo.

'Good luck, Brandon,' Al said, touching him on the shoulder as he walked away with the cases in a plastic container.

'Yeah,' he replied, sitting down on the wall, his mobile in his hand.

Julia

August 4, 2019

He'd taken Julia straight to her bedroom, untied her wrists and
ankles and left her. Hadn't spoken a word since they sped out
of the carpark. She'd heard him thudding down the turret
stairs and tried the door. He'd locked it. She held her head in
her hands and sobbed. She'd tried everything. God knows
she'd tried to escape. But he'd won. And locked them both into
a lose-lose situation. It was only a matter of time now before
the police found them. He'd seen Jo send the photos. Heard
the sirens as the police headed for the pub. Any sane man
would give himself up now.

The light was fading when she heard Gigi scratching at the
door, and then his steps on the stairs and the landing. She
heard him pause outside her door, Gigi giving a welcoming
woof before he continued on into the studio next door.

She could hear him fussing over Gigi, maybe giving her
some food, before he started to talk. At first she thought he
was talking to himself, as he often did, but the pausing rise and
fall of his voice suggested a phone call. Julia went to the wall
and pressed her ear against it

His voice was getting louder. 'I thought I could trust you.
You more than anyone know the value of what I'm doing. The
legacy I'm building. And now what?'

He didn't speak for a while and she could hear him pacing;
Gigi whimpering and vying for attention.

'I'll never do that. You can't ask me to do that.'

Silence. A silence so long and loud it deafened her.

'No. Don't visit me. We have nothing to say to each other.
We haven't had anything to say since that day. You could have

319

warned me then. But you didn't. You could have warned me now. Goodbye, Anja.'

Julia walked back to her bed to wait for him.

It was five minutes before she heard the gentle knock on the door and the turn of the key. She couldn't look at him. Any residual pity she had went the moment he pulled the trigger.

'Let me explain.'

He walked towards her. 'At least forgive me.'

She turned her head away.

'I haven't killed her.'

He was standing over Julia and she raised her eyes to his. 'Maybe you should explain.'

'I stunned DS Menhenrick – Jo – with a taser. She's alive and ... well.'

'Hardly well.'

He sat down beside her on the bed. 'She's ruined my life. Can't you see that? She contacted my sister. Named me. Triggered a manhunt for me.'

'Jo was just part of a police investigation. You can't single her out. It's her job to find killers like you.'

He bristled.

'You can dress it up anyway you like, Axel, but you're a killer. And I'm your next victim.'

They were both looking at the door. He took her hand and squeezed it.

'I'm letting you go, Julia. I probably would have done this morning, if Jo hadn't blocked in my car and come over with the weapon.'

She turned to him, her hand still in his. 'You expect me to believe that?'

'No,' he said. 'But it's true.'

'And Jo. What have you got in mind for her?'

'I haven't decided. Whatever you say, she is the architect of my downfall. She tried to entrap me once before. But failed.' Julia remembered when Brandon got clobbered.

'But she succeeded this time. She's dragged my sister into this too. Dragged my family name through the mud.'

Julia thought about the green dress and how he'd painstakingly cleaned it, brushing off the mud, combing through the velvet, buffing the pile. This was torture for him. Something he couldn't fix. Or control.

'Can you hold me? One last time? I want to hold you before you go.'

She looked at him and saw the tears streaming down his face. She wondered whether he was seeing her, or someone else.

She allowed him to pull her close and bury his head in the folds of her dress and stroked his hair until the sobbing stopped.

When he pulled away, he gave her a look of such unadulterated gratitude and trust that it made her think that this was, quite possibly, the catalyst for his undoing. And always had been.

'Can I dine with you and your beauties one more time?' Julia said, as they sat holding hands, Greta playing at their feet.

'If you wish, my love.'

'I do,' she said, reaching down, scooping up Greta and plonking her on the bed. 'I'll dress for dinner.'

Brandon

August 4, 2019

The Volvo belonged to George Nicholson of 12 Old Street, London EC1. The name immediately rang bells. George Nicholson, Brandon didn't have to try too hard to recollect, was Jo's date the night he was clunked over the head with an empty bottle of burgundy. The car was only a few years old, so it was a real possibility Östberg had used the alias to buy or rent his hideaway in Penwith.

Brandon put a call through to Stew. 'Check the property registries for any Cornish purchases made by a George Nicholson in the past twenty-five years. And also rentals. Nicholson is an Östberg alias.'

'Run checks on his other names too?'

'Those have been done.' Brandon paused. 'Check on Anja Östberg, she may have used a married name. Her partner, Erik Anderson and Arvid Larsson.'

Stew whistled. 'No Swede unturned, Boss.'

'You got it.'

It was just before five in the afternoon. Brandon was sitting in the bar of the Farmer's Arms. He'd questioned the staff and a guest about the Volvo and abduction. A cleaner had heard a bang that sounded like a gunshot and seen the police car leave the entrance. The SOCOs were sweeping the area outside, looking for bullet shells and gunshot residue. It was fucking worrying. Jo would have had her taser. The bastard must have surprised her, been lurking behind the car.

'Can I get you another?' Suzanna Fitzgerald had come into the bar and was untying the scarf at her neck.

'I'm good,' he said looking up. 'My round, I'd say. What would you like?'

'I suppose I should say a Coke, like your good self.' She was looking at his half pint mug, 'But I'd love a glass of Sauvignon Blanc.'

So would I, thought Brandon, as he went to the bar.

'So,' she said, as he set the large glass of white before her. 'What can we expect of Alex Östberg now?'

'I was rather hoping you might tell me,' Brandon said.

'He's cornered. And he's hurting. And that makes him unpredictable. A difficult position for a man who likes to be in control.'

'I can see that.' Brandon gave her a sideways look. 'Why do you think he lured Jo to the carpark?'

'Hard to say? She is a very attractive woman, but she's short of being beautiful.' Brandon gave her a disapproving look. 'And she's not vulnerable. In a nutshell, she's not his usual type, although she shares some of the characteristics – at the low end of his 30-35 age range, beautiful red hair – but her physique is athletic rather than slim or hourglass.'

'I get the point, Suzanna,' Brandon said. 'So why did he abduct Jo?'

'He may have killed her.'

Brandon reeled. 'I don't believe that. There are no traces of bullet shots. No blood. My guess is he took her by surprise and stunned or drugged her.'

'Sorry, Brandon. I should have been more tactful. This is the first time that we have a witness to the abduction and that witness could only speculate that she heard a gunshot. We have no idea if and when he kills his victims.'

Brandon settled back in his chair. 'She's not his type. This is looking more like revenge. Or a hostage situation. Not good, either way.'

He finished his Coke, pushed the mug away, and got up. 'I'm sorry, Suzanna, I can't see the point of going over all this now. I need to go for a walk, clear my head.'

Suzanna got up too. 'You're right. We know who we're dealing with, but we can't second guess his actions now.'

Brandon tilted his head to the side, his fringe sweeping his eyes. 'It's a waiting game. Hell, maybe it's not. Maybe I'll take the car out and see if I can't spot a Skoda skulking in the undergrowth.'

Julia

August 4, 2019

Julia was going through the rack of polythene-bagged clothes in her wardrobe. She wanted something symbolic. And practical. A light mustard dress with a green and red leaves pattern caught her eye. It had that late summer look and, more importantly, although elegant, with its 1950s shirt neck and pinched waist, it had a loose flowing skirt. A pair of low-heeled pumps were in an open box below.

Ten minutes later, he was standing by the door wearing a cream linen jacket, cream chinos and a pale blue shirt.

'You look beautiful, Julia,' he said, before presenting his arm.

It felt strange to walk down that corridor for what would likely be the last time. It reminded her of the walk along her own landing before they went down to greet guests at her party. That evening seemed a lifetime ago. Belonged to a different time. A different person.

'Can I just have a look in the gallery?' she said as they came to the double doors on the landing below.

He looked pleased she'd asked. Why wouldn't he? All that effort for such a limited and specific audience.

'Yes. Of course,' he said, opening the doors.

The early evening sun streamed through a skylight, the only window in the airless room. He turned on a light and stood back and watched as Julia walked up to the first portrait and made her way down the line to her own one. It was rubbing shoulders with the matriarch in the room, Greta Östberg, and looked pissed off at playing second fiddle. Julia smiled.

Alex came alongside her. 'Are you happy with your portrait?'

'Immensely,' she said, drawing the fine lines between her brows together. 'You have captured me perfectly.'

'If you say so,' he said, smiling, and she took his arm and they walked back past those watchful eyes and out of the room.

Brandon & Julia

August 4, 2019

Brandon was on the B3306 coast road approaching The Gurnard's Head pub when the call came in.

'If you're driving, Boss, I suggest you pull over,' Stew said over the car coms.

Brandon took a left into the pub carpark and turned off the ignition. 'I'm listening.'

'Anja Anderson bought Highcliff House in 1996. It's a Victorian pile, perched on the cliff overlooking Puffin Cove. You can see it from the coastal path that takes you past the Gurnard's Head promontory.'

Brandon fell back in his seat and exhaled. 'I know it well. Jeez. Anja bought it in her partner's name? It used to be a guest house when I was a kid.'

'What next?'

Brandon shifted the gearstick into reverse and then first. 'I'm heading out there now. Get onto MCIT. Firearms squad. Cars. Warrant. Although I may gate crash the darn place before you get one.' He switched on the Sat Nav, not convinced it would find the dirt track that headed up to the house. But he'd drive the car over the fields to get to it, if need be.

His gut told him to turn back on himself and take a left down one of the country lanes. The SatNav made an indignant warble as it reset and then reluctantly agreed with him, sending him off down spindly Postman's Walk. He put his foot down, slamming the horn as he took the bends, praying the postman had done his rounds.

The SatNav lady was losing it as the road narrowed, telling him to take a left, through a field and, as far as he could make out, off a cliff. So, he turned her off and pushed on, the Skoda shoving back hedges, and clearing a path, he hoped, for reinforcements.

'Stew, see if you can get a helicopter,' Brandon, said over the coms. 'I'm having to plough my way through.' It made him wonder how often Östberg took out the Volvo. And where the hell he'd dumped Jo's car.

Julia caught her breath as they stood outside the dining room door. She could hear Jo moving. Knew the familiar sound of chain against metal.

'Shall we go in?' he said, opening the door for her.

She nodded, pleased to enter first. Her eyes went straight to Jo and she tried to convey solidarity in them. He went to walk past, but Julia stopped and took one of Jo's manacled hands.

'What the hell do you think you're doing?' he said, spinning round and grabbing her by the arm.

'How can you expect me to dine with you when Jo is manacled to a chair, hurt, scared and hungry? I can't.'

'You can,' he said, pushing her forward. 'Be grateful you have the freedom to empathise with those less fortunate.'

Julia's mouth fell open. He was pushing her. He'd pushed her to the brink over the past two days. He'd used the term freedom. Something he'd promised. But on what terms?

Gigi padded over as he opened a lid on the trolley, a nauseous smell of stew wafting out.

He lit seven candles on one of the two candelabras, and gestured for her to sit at the bottom of the table by the red head he'd just embalmed. A white glove covered the hand with the missing finger. One side of her face was collapsing. He'd done a sloppy job.

He ladled some beef stew and rice onto a plate and passed it to her. Julia pushed it away.

'Eat up,' he said, jauntily. 'This is a big night for you, my love.'

She picked up a fork. Then let it drop on the table. She couldn't see Jo but could hear her struggling. Not much, because the chains had little give, but enough to make herself heard.

'Is she annoying you?' he said, scrunching up his napkin and letting it fall on the table. 'I'll have a word.'

Julia twisted round as he got up. 'No. No. I just can't eat while she's hungry and uncomfortable. Can't you ask her to join us?'

'No!' he shouted, as he pushed back his chair and got up. 'She is not my guest. Never will be. You, my dear, need to learn what side your bread is buttered.'

He strode across the room and stood over Jo.

'Those chains are clearly a little loose. You keep rattling them. Bad manners, DS Menhenrick. Let me tighten them for you.'

A turret soared into view as Brandon took the next bend. There had to be a drive soon. He was right. There was a lonely looking lane, not much wider than the one he was on, which wound down to a gate. Trees lined it; gnarled and twisted branches formed an arch to the evil kingdom.

As if placed there by the devil's own hand, a cow, and then another, sauntered out of a gate on the left, their haunches swaying, their large eyes facing him down.

Brandon slammed on his horn. They didn't budge.

'Get out of the fucking way!' Brandon shouted, jumping out of the car, pushing past them looking for a farmer, finding more cows.

He rushed back to the car, got in and started to drive, nudging them gently back until he got to the gate, where they stood their ground. All five of them. They clearly had an appointment in the next field.

'Fuck it,' Brandon said, spinning the steering wheel and car off the lane, through the gate and across the field.

Jo continued to rattle the chains as Alex stood over her, his clenched fists within inches of her face.

329

'Shut up, do you hear me, shut up!' he said, pushing Jo's head back against the chair rest, so the choker cut into her neck.

Julia rose quietly from her chair. She stood still, watched as he let Jo's head fall forward. Watched as he felt for his keys and became engrossed in his brutal task. Then she picked up the unlit candelabra and crept up behind him as he knelt on the floor, tightening the metal band around Jo's foot. Jo started rattling the chains again, louder this time, all the while looking at Axel, rather than Julia. As such, he didn't notice Julia until she was standing behind him. He turned around at the exact moment Julia smashed the candelabra down on his head.

His eyes were wide with disbelief as she hit him again and again. 'Julia, no, no. No. Stop now. I'm going to free you. No.'

Julia took another swing, heard his skull crack, saw the blood pouring from the wound. He fell to the floor, but struggled on, crawling on all fours as she backed away towards the table. 'Help me. All I wanted to do was help you. To help all of you. '

Julia kicked him in the head.

'I wanted nothing from you. I gave you my all. I gave you immortality. I gave you love.'

She kicked him again and again as he dragged himself towards the table, that furious energy keeping him going, keeping him alive. When he got to the curtains, he grabbed hold of them to pull himself up. But the rail was weak and the curtains heavy – the whole lot came crashing down, onto the floor, onto the table, knocking the red head over, her extended left arm toppling the lit candelabra. The antique curtains burst into flame.

'What have you done, what have you done!' Axel yelled at Julia.

Julia poured a jug of water and two bottles of wine onto the velvet, but it made little difference. The fire was spreading to the wooden table and was eating into the parquet floor. Axel was still on the ground and Julia fell on him wrestling the keys from his pocket, leaving him crawling towards his beauties.

She rushed to Jo and untied the gag. 'I know these keys. I'll have you unlocked in no time.'

'I'll watch him,' Jo said.

Brandon dumped the car at the far end of the field by a six foot hedge. He was six foot two and could see the house two fields over. It'd been raining in the morning and his shoes were weighed down in mud, but he lifted them up, grabbed hold of some hedge and vaulted into the next field. Head down, he sprinted across it, hugging the roadside. When he raised his head he could see smoke coming from the house. It'd been raining, but it was still warm, no need for fires. He looked around, saw a wooden stile in the far right hand corner and made for it. When he mounted the stile he could see flames and smoke billowing from the west wing of the house.

Brandon took out his phone and tapped Stew's number. 'We need a fire engine and get an air ambulance if you can. The place is on fire.'

He leapt down and ran at full pelt to the other side of the field, through the muddy tracks, jumping the stumps of harvested corn, to a small clearing and the drive.

Julia flicked through the bundle of keys, found the smallest and fitted it into the ankle manacle he'd been working on. She snapped it open and went on to the next, freeing both of Jo's feet.

She glanced up at Jo and saw fear. She didn't need to turn to know what had triggered it. The place was getting hotter, smoke swirled around them, choking them, making them cough, making it hard to see.

'Hurry, Julia. Hurry,' Jo said. 'He's on his feet.'

Julia looked over her shoulder. 'Okay,' she said, fumbling with an old bronze key. She put it in the left wrist manacle but struggled to turn it. The key had given Axel problems. She felt Jo tense.

Jo jerked her head. 'He's coming over.'

Julia swung round to see Axel staggering towards them. She left the keys hanging from the manacle and went up to him, pushing him hard. So hard he fell onto his back. His arm shot out and grabbed her foot, bringing her thumping down next to him.

He had her by the shoulders, pinning her down, his face up against hers.

'Julia,' he was crying, 'Julia. Forgive me. Forgive me.'

'You're on fire,' she said, snatching her fingers away from flames on the back of his jacket.

As he rolled over to extinguish them, she sprung up and rushed to Jo, her hands back on the wrist manacle, wiggling the key, sweat running into her eyes.

'Go. This place will be an inferno in a few minutes,' Jo said, lifting her wrist to try and help.

Julia kept her head down, pushing and turning the key until it clicked in the lock. Then she moved on to Jo's other wrist, all the while listening for him.

'What's he doing?' She looked up at Jo as the right wrist manacle sprung open.

'He's moving the bodies away from the table,' Jo said, undoing the thick leather belt around her waist with her free hands, her head still pinned to the back of the chair.

'Now he's coming over. He's coming back.'

Brandon belted down the drive and up to the front door, noting the boot of Jo's car poking out of an open garage. Nowhere to hide now, he thought, looking up at the house. Back-up was on its way, but Brandon wasn't waiting. He was sick with worry. But, more than anything, he was angry. Blood and adrenalin coursed through hm.

Julia rushed to Alex and shoved him back down, stamping on his hands as he tried to get onto his feet. Her dress was drenched in sweat. She wiped one clammy hand down it, the other feeling for the neck brace key.

'Just one more now, Jo. Nearly there,' she said, returning to her.

There was a sudden thud at the door.

Julia started, the keys flying from her hands.

'Open up, Police!'

It was Brandon. Thank God.

'We're in here, Brandon. We're alive. But the fire is out of control,' Julia shouted, stamping on a line of flames that had chased across the parquet.

Brandon was kicking in the door, as she fell to her knees, frantically searching the floor for the keys.

'They're to your left,' Jo shouted, 'by the side table.' Julia picked up the leather belt and swung it at the keys, nudging them away from the burning table. She stretched over and grabbed them, her fingers searching for the long slim one. She was turning it in the lock as Brandon crashed through the door.

He had one arm across his mouth, fending off the smoke, the other waving them out of the door, Julia's arm around Jo.

'Brandon. Get out! The ceiling's going to cave in,' Julia shouted over the roar of fire.

'Are you both okay?'

'Yes, we're fine,' Julia said, nodding frantically.

'Yep. Go!' Jo urged.

'There's someone at the back?' Brandon had moved further into the room, stooping below the smoke.

'It's Axel.'

'I can see him. There's someone else on the floor. A child?'

'Gigi!' Julia hollered. 'A dog. She'll be terrified.'

'And the table, are there people at the table?'

'Dead. I'll explain later. Get out, Brandon. For godsake. Get out while you can.'

Brandon threw Julia his phone. 'Make any calls you need to. Code 1985. Leave now both of you. Please.'

'Save the paintings, Julia. Save my beauties. Save yourself, my love. I tried. I failed. Forgive me. Please forgive me.' She heard Axel's voice, just audible above the crackling flames, and the intermittent thuds of timber hitting the ground.

'Call her. Call Gigi. Call her,' Östberg was yelling from the far end of the room. He was partly obscured by a flaming curtain hanging from a broken rail, and, to its right, a burning heap on the ground, which was probably the matching one. Brandon could see him struggling to lift a body off a chair, all the time patting down flames with a cloth.

'Call Gigi, the dog,' he shouted over his shoulder, dragging the body across the floor towards the gap between the curtains.

Brandon dashed to the curtains, his arm over his face, and bent down to look for the dog.

'Gigi. Come here, girl. Come here, Gigi,' Brandon called, the smoke stinging his eyes and catching the back of his throat.

Something darted out from behind a chair leg and rushed back. The floor was hot. Burning through the soles of his shoes. The dog wouldn't be able to cross it.

'I'll get her,' Östberg said, leaving the body on the floor. It was a metre from Brandon and he could see it had been a woman. One of the Missing. One for Chapman.

Östberg was dragging himself around the table to the cowering dog.

'Here, Greta. Here, girl.' He grabbed hold of her by one paw, lifted her up and cradled her in his arms. 'I've got you. Safe now. Safe now.'

As Brandon went to take her, a burning beam crashed down, forcing him to jump back.

'Throw her to me,' Brandon shouted, reaching out, his fingers just clear of the flaming curtain.

Östberg hesitated. But not for long. He hurled the blond ball of fluff over the beam and into Brandon's arms.

The dog's tongue hung out panting. Its little body trembled against his chest.

'It's okay, girl. I've got you now,' he said, brushing a hand over her head and rushing to the door, stamping out a pocket of fire as he went.

'Östberg. Follow me out. Now.'

'I need to get the women out. I can't leave them here. I won't leave them.'

'I'll be back,' Brandon shouted, as he ran from the room, down the passage and out of a side door. He found Jo and Julia out front and dumped the dog in Julia's arms, his head jerking up when he heard sirens.

'Let's hope it's the fire brigade,' he said, turning back to the house.

Flames had reached the turret. The small windows glowed red through black, and smoke seeped through cracks in the glass.

'You're not going back in?' Julia grabbed his jacket as he moved off.

'I can't leave him in there.'

'Don't, Brandon. Please.' Julia's lips were parted, her brow creased, her eyes wide and begging him to stay. She was hugging the dog like a teddy bear.

'I'm coming with you, Boss,' Jo said. She had a car extinguisher in her hand. He smiled. She'd got the one from her car.

'No, you're not,' he said, resting a hand on one of her shaking shoulders. 'You've spent enough time in that hellhole. Keep an eye on things out here.'

Jo handed him the extinguisher and a scarf. 'Don't do anything risky. He's better off dead.' Tears were streaming down her soot-covered face.

'I don't disagree,' Brandon said, going inside.

The fire had spread to the reception and was burning its way up the stairs. Brandon tied the scarf around his face and fought his way through the smoke, extinguishing the flames where he could. He was met by a bank of smoke when he got to the bottom of the basement stairs, but could just make out a mound by the closed door. Östberg must have closed it. He flashed his torch at the mound and staggered back when he saw what it was. Six, maybe seven, bodies, piled up on top of each other. Like something out of a war scene. Victims of Alex Östberg's own war.

He rushed to the door and pushed hard against it. It wouldn't budge. Something was jammed up against it on the other side.

'Östberg! Are you there? I've come to get you out.' He

spluttered the words through a wall of smoke – the heat from the door forcing him back.

'Östberg! If you can hear me get out. Before it's too late.' He heard another beam crash to the floor. But no human sounds. Just the crackle and roar of a furnace.

Brandon ducked below the smoke, and was about to begin his task of dragging out the bodies when four fire fighters raced down the passage.

'Dead or alive?' one of them shouted.

Brandon rose to full height. 'Dead. One man still alive in there five minutes ago. He didn't answer when I called out just now.'

'He wouldn't. No one could survive this. Leave it to us now.'

Brandon leant back down, picked up one of the bodies and carried it out of the door and into the twilight.

'We've got these now, Detective Inspector,' said a fire fighter, bringing out another body.

Brandon nodded. He couldn't say he wasn't relieved. He stood outside, breathing deeply the fresher air.

'Just the three?' Jo had come around the side of the house to look for him. She was trembling.

'The firefighters will bring out the rest. Östberg got them out of the room.'

'How very kind of him,' she said in a hoarse whisper.

'But not himself.'

'He's dead?'

'I would say so. The room's a fireball. The flames were at the door as the men turned up. Östberg had closed the door on himself. To protect—'

'His beauties.' Jo shook her head.

'You okay?'

'I don't know.' She took a deep breath and looked to the side. She felt the back of her neck and looked up at him. 'I've got a sore neck, look a mess and smell, literally, of shit, but I'm alive.'

Brandon wrinkled his nose. 'Maybe the guys will hose you down?'

Jo smiled weakly and jerked her head at the fire engine hosing down the burning building. 'I think they need all the water at their disposal. I'll go get some wet wipes from the car. And I've got a change of clothes in there.'

'Well prepared. Were you a scout?' The war paint made her look more like a warrior. A brave heart indeed.

'Of course,' she said walking away.

Julia was standing by one of the fire fighters when he went around to the front of the house. She was huddled under a blanket, the dog's face peering out. One police car was parked on the forecourt; two more were coming up the drive.

The blades of a helicopter could be heard above. Nice one Stew.

Julia turned a weary head to the sky.

'Your ride to the hospital.'

'Hospital?'

'You and Jo. Just to check you out and give you some attention.'

He thought she might object, but she didn't. Exhaustion was setting in.

'Can I just call Nick?'

'You have my phone.'

'I didn't catch the code?'

'1985.'

She struggled to find it with one hand, the other still clutching the dog.

'Here, let me take her,' Brandon said, reaching for Gigi.

Julia tapped in Nick's number and went to the edge of the forecourt away from the mayhem. The helicopter was making its noisy descent into the walled garden.

Jo walked back over, her hands over her ears. 'They've got them all out. All seven,' she shouted over the sound of the blades.

'Job done for today, DS Menhenrick. That's your lift to the hospital, by the way.'

Jo nodded. Knew the protocol for smoke inhalation and trauma. She had a blanket around her, which she was clutching tightly.

'I just want to go over and see the … Beauties,' Julia said, joining them and passing the phone back to Brandon.

'All good with Nick?' Brandon asked.

'Yes. Yes.' She couldn't say any more. Tears were forming in her eyes. She blinked hard before going over to the line of bodies. She had a word with the officer in attendance and then walked the line, pausing at each one, before standing rigid, head bowed, her lips murmuring what could have been a prayer.

Brandon gave her a while before going over and wrapping one arm around her shoulders.

Julia tilted her face up to him. 'Thank you for saving us.'

'We all played our part. You were brilliant in there with Jo.'

Julia reached for Gigi, who was struggling to get to her. 'You don't know the half of it.'

'I expect you to tell me the whole of it. It's my job to know, after all.'

'Some lucky therapist could make a mint out of me.'

Brandon smiled. 'I'm so proud of you, Julia. Now, let's get you in the helicopter. I'll let Nick know where you are. He can bring you a phone.'

'Thank you.'

'I guess I'm left holding the baby?' He gave Julia an ironic smile and ruffled Gigi's head.

Julia smiled. 'You look good together. Chelsea's going to love her.'

'Now, let's get this clear, the dog is on loan.' Brandon was smiling gently. 'You best get going,' he added, gesturing to the helicopter blades above the garden wall.

'Yep.' Julia reached over and stroked Gigi's head. 'It seems appropriate that I'll be leaving via the garden. This time for good.'

'This time for good,' Brandon said.

'Before you go. Anja Östberg – Alex's—' Brandon paused. 'Axel's sister. Did he ever mention her to you?'

Julia frowned. 'No. But I heard him talking to her on the phone earlier today. I was locked in my bedroom and I heard him through the wall. He was angry with her. Telling her not to visit him. That she should have warned him a long time ago about something. It was as if she couldn't be trusted. Something terrible had passed between them.'

Brandon narrowed his eyes. 'How do you know he was talking to Anja?'

'Because he said goodbye, Anja. It sounded final. And it was.'

Brandon nodded. 'I see. Thanks.' He moved back when he saw Jo approaching. 'I'll call you at the hospital. See how you're getting on.'

'Ready to go?' Jo said, joining them.

Brandon watched them walk over to a side gate and through to the garden. He waved as they rose up above the

wall and turret and turned right to follow the coast to the Royal
Cornwall Hospital in Truro.

Now where was his car?

'Sit still, little lady,' he said, plonking Gigi on the front seat of
his car and steering out of the field. Gigi immediately
scrambled up onto her hind legs to peer out of the window.

A Toyota Prius approached as he turned into the lane. Al
Chapman. A stroke of luck. If they'd met on Postman's Walk
one of them would have had to back up. Brandon stopped the
car as the Toyota drew alongside.

Al wound down his window. 'End of story?'

'I'd like to think so.' He paused before adding, 'We
managed to get the bodies out.'

Al met Brandon's eye. 'Resolution. At last.'

Brandon gave a brief nod.

'And Mrs Trenowden and Jo?'

'They just flew over.'

'The copter? Royal Cornwall?'

'Yes. But they're in pretty good shape.'

'Thank God,' Al said, as he wound up his window and
drove on down the lane.

Brandon

August 4, 2019

Her face was devoid of emotion as she stared out of the screen. It was a one-dimensional facsimile of a woman who, somewhere along the line, had lost the plot. Erik wasn't by her side. Instead, she was flanked by two Swedish police detectives. They'd broken the bad news – if it was bad news – that her brother Alex had died in a fire in the house she'd bought him in 1996. Drowned in 1995. Fried alive in 2019. What a family curse.

It was an hour later in Sweden. 11pm. But, tired as she always was, Anja wasn't going to bed until she'd answered some questions.

'I'm sorry for your loss,' Brandon said, not attempting to sound it.

Anja nodded. 'I lost him years ago.'

'Ms Östberg, I need to ask you some pertinent questions. It is important that you answer them honestly and to the best of your knowledge. I am cautioning you on the basis of potentially aiding and abetting your brother in acts of abduction and murder.'

He glanced at the detectives, confident that, as an EU country, UK jurisdiction applied. But lawyers can get tricksy. Even Swedish ones. 'You do not have to say anything. But it may harm your defence if you do not mention when questioned something which you later rely on in court. Anything you do say may be given in evidence.'

Brandon paused, while Stew, who'd stepped in for Jo, timed the interview in.

'Why did you lie for him, Ms Östberg?'

'I owed him something.'

'A house?' Stew nudged Brandon, who gave him a daggers look.

'I don't understand?' Anja said jutting out her chin.

'Highcliff House in Zennor, Cornwall,' Brandon said, holding her gaze.

She looked down and then rose her head slowly. 'The house in Cornwall. Yes, I bought it for him.'

'Go on.' Brandon edged closer to the screen.

'Alex was going through a difficult time. He'd finished his financial studies in London, but he wasn't happy. He was looking for something else from life. He wanted to take time out to study art at Falmouth Art School. He hadn't his own money at that stage, you see. We had money. And so I bought him the place.'

'That was mighty generous of you.'

'I owed him.'

Brandon leaned forward. 'What did you owe your brother that would make you spend a small fortune on a house for him?'

Anja shrugged. 'The house wasn't so expensive. It was in disrepair. We got it cheap. We saw it as an investment.'

Stew gave him a quick look to acknowledge her change of tone. But, Brandon figured, Anja wasn't unfamiliar with the practical matters of running properties – the family estate and the eco lodge were just two that he knew of.

He pressed on. 'An investment? Did you spend time there?'

Anja hesitated and glanced at her lawyer, an elegant woman in a smart navy suit. 'A little.'

'How much time, Ms Östberg? Were you there at the beginning? In the summer of 1996 when Alex Östberg, your brother, your twin, started abducting and killing women?'

'Yes.'

Brandon inhaled sharply. The two detectives flanking Anja stiffened.

'Were you aware of what your brother was doing? Of the abductions, the murders, the embalming?'

'Yes.'

'Did you assist your brother in enacting these crimes?'

Anja looked to the side. 'I did. But you have to understand why. I took no pleasure from my work. No satisfaction.'

The lawyer moved out of the shadows and into shot. 'I think we need to take a break here.'

Anja waved her aside. 'Alex is dead. I am free, at last, to speak out.'

'Anja, please reflect before you speak. We need to explore all the implications of the UK jurisdiction in this matter,' her lawyer said, her wide face zooming in and frowning at Brandon.

Anja stretched her lips. 'The victims were UK citizens. UK women. I don't want to hide behind a technicality of international law.'

Anja turned back to Brandon. 'I assisted my brother because I owed him. Now he's dead, that debt has been paid.'

She looked to the side again. As if looking for Erik, or someone else.

'Mama told me she was going to kill herself.'

Brandon sucked in a breath but held her gaze.

'I was her confidente. Her little buddy. Her darling Mus. She was all smiles and sweetness with Alex, protecting him, but she burdened me with her fears. Her fears of getting old, of losing her looks, of losing her husband. Of losing her mind. She convinced me the best thing for her to do was die. Die before she "withered on the vine".' Anja looked at her hands. 'I helped her pick the outfit she wore on that … day.'

It was like Brandon wasn't there. Like no one was in the room. On the screen.

'I put the noose around her neck. I held her hand when the life seeped from her body. And I left her there for Alex to find. I did it for Mama. And, later, I did it for my brother.'

'Did what for your brother?' Brandon said, his eyes fixed on her.

'I assisted him. I helped him immortalise those poor women.'

The lawyer shot up. She leant across the table, shielding Anja. 'I suggest we adjourn this interview, while we reflect on the legalities and procedures.'

Brandon nodded. 'Okay. I'll be in touch in the morning. Good evening.'

He watched as the lawyer and detectives moved in on a woman who remained perfectly still, her ice blue eyes staring into the screen and beyond. Before it went black.

'Interview adjourned at 22.20, 4 August, 2019,' Stew said,

clicking off the recorder. 'Fuck-a-doodle-dandy! You need a flight to Sweden, Boss?'

'At some point, probably. But we have the confession. We have a dead killer. And we have Jo and Julia back alive, and the bodies of the Östbergs' victims. Just a few loose ends left. Chiefly, identification and notifying the next of kin.'

'You want me to do that, Boss?'

'No,' Brandon said, looking over his head. 'But thanks for the offer. It's not something I'd wish on anyone.'

Brandon

August 5, 2019

'I can confirm three of the bodies have been identified as Rebecca Morley, Clarissa Bowles and Emily Paxton. We are still working on the older bodies,' Chapman said over the car coms as Brandon drove along the A30 to Truro.

He sighed. 'Good work, Al. How long before you identify the others?'

'I wouldn't like to put a time frame on it. We have some clothing from the missing persons' files dating back to 1996, but, as you know, it will take that much longer to match. It could rely on dental records.'

'Did you identify Alex Östberg's remains?'

'We found a badly-burnt male skeleton. All the signs suggest it's Östberg. But identification of human remains is never easy in the case of fires.'

'The SOCOs found your Stentor, by the way.' Brandon could hear the smile in his voice.

'You know, Al, I think I may give the Stentor away. Donate it to a worthy cause. Or maybe give it to Arvik Larssen.'

'Who he?'

'Curator of the Östberg family museum. An interesting family curio for him.'

Al burst out laughing. 'Christ, that will be one for the True Crime devotees Grand Tour.'

'Talking House of Horrors, what it's looking like at Highcliff?'

'Well, the west wing is a burnt-out shell, as you would imagine. But the fire brigade managed to save some of the rooms on the first and second floors in the east wing. There's a gallery up there. And a studio.'

Brandon turned left onto the road leading to Cornwall Royal Hospital. 'I'll be along there tomorrow. Let you guys finish up first. Have they made it secure for entry?'

'The main staircase is stone. As are the turret stairs. So, in answer to your question, safe enough – if you tread carefully.'

'Good to hear. Thanks, Al,' Brandon said steering the car into the hospital carpark.

August 5, 2019

'What have you got behind your back?'

Nick had come out of the door as Brandon drove onto The Hall forecourt with Julia. The Royal Cornwall had discharged her an hour earlier after she'd convinced them that family and friends were what she needed most.

'Don't look so worried, darling. A nice little surprise for you, after all you've been through.'

'Me? Come here, Mum.' Nick opened his arms and Julia put Gigi down and walked into them.

'You've grown,' she said, after she'd stopped crying and stepped back to examine him.

'And they say stress stunts growth.'

'Do they?'

'I don't know. Sounds clever,' Nick said, smiling. 'You look surprisingly well. You didn't look so hot in that hospital bed.'

Julia hated that he'd seen her wired up and frail. He'd stood there, clinging on to his grandma's hand, like he'd clung onto hers when he was five. Here he was, at fifteen, standing tall, owning the situation. She bit her tongue to stop herself from crying again.

'Stress does age you. I can confirm that,' Julia said, reaching for his hand.

'Age cannot wither her, nor custom stale her infinite variety,' she heard Brandon say from the car.

'Cool, Brandon,' Nick said, bending down to stroke the dog. 'Is he moving in?'

'The dog?'

'Yes, the dog.'

'For a while, at least. She's adorable'

'True. The dog is insanely cute. But is it psycho?'

She heard a guffaw from the car. 'I'll be getting on, Julia.'

Julia turned round. 'Thank you, Brandon. Thank you for finding us and getting us out.'

He smiled. 'I'll need to come over early tomorrow to talk you through things. Nothing to be concerned about. Just need to piece things together. What time suits?'

'Up to you. Early's fine.'

'Nine?'

She nodded. 'There was one other thing.'

'Oh yes?' Brandon said.

'I'd like to go back to the house. After we've run through things.'

'You sure, Mum?' Nick was frowning at her. He took her hand.

'Yes.'

'Do you want me to come along?'

She let go of his hand and cupped his face. 'Thank you, sweetheart. But this is something I need to do on my own.' She glanced at Brandon, 'With a police presence.'

'Cool,' Nick said, 'I understand.'

She looked into his reasonable, intelligent eyes, and she knew he did.

Julia wrapped her arms around him, pulling him close, as they watched Brandon drive away.

Brandon

August 5, 2019

'Cheers, team – here's to finally putting the Sleeping Beauty Killer to bed,' Brandon clinked glasses with Jo, Stew, Suzanna and Al. It was five in the afternoon and they were sitting in the empty first floor bar of the Admiral Benbow having a debrief.

'The Big Sleep,' Al said, taking a big gulp of red. 'Twenty-three years that man has dogged my sleep. And now it's over. Any Shakespearean quotes to wave him on his way?'

'Don't get him started,' ribbed Jo.

Brandon fixed his eyes on a ship figurehead, one of the pub's many nautical curios. 'Is that a dagger I see before me?'

'No, it's a large glass of Malbec,' Stew chipped in. They were all in high spirits.

Suzanna was smiling mischievously. 'We have a present for you.'

Brandon gave her an incredulous look. 'I hope it doesn't come in one of those fancy glass cases?'

'No,' she said, her smile reaching her hypnotic green eyes. 'A wooden case actually.'

She reached down and pulled a package from her tote. 'No points for guessing what it is.'

Brandon took the violin shaped package off her. 'You really shouldn't have. You don't want to see me getting all emotional.'

Jo budged her chair forward. 'Open it, Boss.'

It was brand new – the polished wood case gleamed, the hinges still had paint on them and didn't squeak, and inside was the finest fiddle he'd ever seen.

'Thank you. You don't know how much I've missed my buddy.'

Brandon gave it a fond stroke and replaced it in its case. 'Now, whatever you do, don't let me leave it unattended!'

'Talking of being left unattended, what's happening with Diana Chambers?' Al said.

Brandon sucked in his top lip. 'She's out on bail, with a court case set for October 15th.'

'Is she likely to go to jail?'

'Hard to say. But probably, yes. For a short term. Keep her out of mischief for a while.'

'I wouldn't bet on it,' Al said, taking a sip of wine.

'And Anja?' Suzanna said. 'What's happening there?'

Brandon sighed. 'She's in custody in Sweden. For a shrinking violet that liked to keep out of the headlines, the story is all over the press there, as it is here.'

'She must be suffering,' Jo said.

'Yes,' Suzanna agreed, 'as the sole survivor of the family unit, she's taking the can for them all. But she seems to have developed coping mechanisms. Mainly subordination. The Surrendered Child.' Suzanna put down her drink. 'How's Julia?'

Brandon picked his up. 'She's coping. She was only discharged a few hours ago, but seems set on getting on with things. And she has that dog!'

Suzanna frowned. 'Not sure that's a good thing. A constant reminder?'

'Well, Gigi's there at the moment. Nick likes her, even though he thinks she may have picked up a little of the Östberg spirit. I can't say I recognise it when I look into those baby brown eyes.' Brandon rested his forearms on the table. 'Julia's coming with me to the house tomorrow.'

'An exorcism?' Suzanna was watching him closely.

'Not exactly. We've been going through her trials. Bit by bit. She says she's strong enough to deal with them. And I believe her, with the support of friends.'

Suzanna smiled. 'If she needs a therapist, I can offer my services.'

'Thank you, Suzanna. I'll mention it.'

Jo was fiddling with her bag. She looked dog-tired.

Brandon turned to her. 'You need a lift back, Jo?'

'I don't want to break up the party.' She was looking at the half full bottle of red, and Al and Suzanna's half empty glasses. Stew was on pints.

'You two get back. You've put in the hours. Congratulations, once again, for closing the case,' Al said, standing up to shake Brandon and Jo's hands.

'It was a team effort,' Brandon replied, looking at them all in turn. 'And thanks, everybody, for this beautiful instrument.' He held up the fiddle case and took a bow, before following Jo to the door.

August 6, 2019

More than anything, it was black. Looking at it from across the fields it didn't look big. Just black. They'd decided to park the car at the Gurnard's Head and walk to Highcliff House along the cliff top; open sea and sky on their left.

'We can turn back, you know,' Brandon said, stopping in his tracks and turning to her. The wind was blowing her hair across her face. He reached over to brush it aside.

'No. Let's go on.' But she didn't move. Her eyes on the sea. 'The weather's changeable in Penwith. And yet it was always sunny in that walled garden. It was a haven of sorts.' She thought about the orangery, and how Alex had called it heaven and how, in reality, it was the gateway to hell and the mortician's brick house.

Brandon took her hand and she let him.

'Are you sleeping okay?' he said.

'Yes. Deep, dreamless sleep. But I'm waiting for the nightmares.'

'Well, keep on expecting them.' Brandon squeezed her hand. 'I find nightmares like to sneak up and surprise you when you least expect.'

Julia stopped to look at him. 'You have nightmares?'

'If you prick me, do I not bleed?' He was grinning and she burst out laughing.

'Have you swallowed a Shakespearian anthology?'

'Beaten into me at St Piran's.' Brandon took her hand again and started to walk. 'Östberg was a refined guy. Did you talk much?'

'Not really. It was all artifice. Small chat and gestures. Like a parlour game. A menacing parlour game. I was the lady and he was the gentleman. Until he wasn't.'

'Wasn't?'

'He could get nasty.'

'Did he hurt you?' Brandon stopped walking again and watched her closely.

'Not physically, as such. There was discomfort – that fucking chair that he manacled us to – but he got angry and unpredictable, and that was scary.'

'He bought you the dog?'

'He killed another.'

'He had another dog?'

'The one he used to hunt me down over those fields.' Julia pointed to land to the east.

Brandon slipped his arm around her and she rested against him. 'That must have been the worse time. To escape and be caught.'

'I've had better days,' Julia said, looking up at him. 'You know, the reason he killed the dog was because I was befriending it.'

Brandon stopped and looked at her. 'Really?'

'Made sense. I was sneaking it food. And then one evening the dog was getting upset – it was stationed outside my door – and I heard this howling and the dog led me to him. He was sobbing, stitching some poor woman's decomposing body back together, and just sobbing. At some level, all this was hell for him.'

'You didn't know about his mother?'

'Not until you told me. But I sensed she had a part to play. There's a portrait of her in the first-floor gallery.'

'There's one of you too.'

'You recognised me?'

'I hate to say it, but Östberg could paint.'

'Are they damaged?'

'A little sooty. But, if he was Rembrandt, I'm sure they could be easily restored.'

'But he's not. Wasn't. So what will happen to them?'

'Good question. We will use them, if need be, for identification. Particularly for the women that went missing in 1996. Photos have been taken already.'

They were approaching the iron gate on the right. To the left and fifty feet below, waves rolled onto shingle in Puffin's

Cove. A small boat bobbed in the shallows. She thought of the dog carried on the tide to his watery grave.

'You okay?' Brandon said, his hand on the gate's padlock. Julia nodded.

'Did you climb over when you did the runner?'

'Yes.'

'Nice work, Trenowden. But today, we're entering via the front door.'

They skirted the building to find two uniformed police at the main entrance.

Brandon showed his badge and one of them walked them over to the door and unlocked it.

'I never saw this part of the house,' Julia said, looking around the spacious reception. It didn't have much in it. A pedestal table and chair in the right-hand corner. An ornately framed landscape at the top of the stairs. All covered in soot. It was still very much a crime scene, the stairs cordoned off with police tape.

'What areas did he take you to?'

'The studio and bedroom on the second floor and the gallery on the first, as well as the Orangery – and its … outhouse – and the walled garden.'

'And the dining room.'

'Yes.'

'Did you know there was a small cellar in the dining room? At the far end, beyond the table.'

'No. I never saw him use it. He'd always produce wine bottles – but they'd be on the table already or in the orangery. He had a small kitchen in the orangery.'

'And there's another one at the end of the passage, leading to the dining room.'

'That door was always closed,' Julia said. 'It makes sense that it was a kitchen. It smelt like a kitchen.'

Brandon lifted up the police tape, and they climbed the stairs to the first-floor landing.

'Shall we go in?' Brandon said, when they reached the double doors leading to the gallery.

Julia took a breath before gently pushing open one of the doors. The room, always stuffy, stank of smoke. She walked to the centre of the room, stood under the skylight, and drew energy from the one source of light. Her eyes tracked the portraits on the wall. The Beauties, not so beautiful. Tarnished by events as if human.

Two were missing.

'What is it?' Brandon had read her expression.

'The portrait of me. The portrait of his mother – in the same green dress – they're not here.'

'You're right.' Brandon ran a hand through his hair. 'They darn well should be. Instructions are to keep everything in situ until the final forensic report comes in.'

'How secure is the place?'

Brandon grimaced. 'You saw the uniforms at the door.'

'Why those two portraits?'

Brandon looked at her. He didn't answer.

'I've gone cold,' Julia said, staring at the space where the portraits had been.

'Come here.' Brandon took off his jacket and draped it over her shoulders.

'I'm taking you home.'

Brandon

August 6, 2019

'Dad, that's awesome!' Chelsea was holding the neck of the Stentor up to the light. 'I'm so glad you didn't let the other one back in the house. It would have creeped me out. I could just imagine it playing a death march. On its own!'

'Some imagination, darlin,' Brandon said, although he secretly agreed. He wasn't going to have anything in his house that the psycho had laid his hands on.

'Are you going to play for me tonight?'

'What's the matter with you, girl?' Brandon raised an eyebrow. 'Since when have you wanted me to drown out the sound of your hip hop?'

'Now.' She came over and wrapped her arms around him. Like Nick, she was growing up. Sweet Fifteen. Certainly been kissed – by that toe rag of a boyfriend of hers, Damien Kane. But she was still his little, loving girl.

'What's the matter?' she said, leaning back and scrutinising him.

'Something doesn't sit right.' He took the Stentor from her, picked up the bow and stroked the strings.

'I'm going to Sweden tomorrow,' he said, letting the fiddle fall to his side.

'Sweden? I thought it was being passed over to the cops there?'

'It is – but, as it was a major crime committed in the UK, I have the right to ask further questions.'

'Do you need to, Dad? Didn't she confess?'

'She did.' He gave Chelsea the look. The one that told her she'd reached a line she couldn't cross.

'Shall we get a take-away then?'

'Chinese?'

'Awesome,' Chelsea said, pulling out her phone. 'I'll order."

'You have my card on the app?'

'Duh!' Chelsea said.

He smiled and looked at his own phone, which had just pinged.

Al Chapman: 'The cellar in the dining room. There's a trap door below the wine racks. It opens and leads to a tunnel that goes down to Puffin Cove. There was blood on the stairs.'

Brandon rang him immediately. 'Östberg's blood?'

'Haven't done the check yet, but ... it's fresh.'

'Anything on the boat?'

'The team are going over it now.'

'Want me there?'

'No need. I figure you'll have better things to do.'

Brandon immediately called MCIT to update them and organise a manhunt. To push out to the airports, ferries and borders.

Next, he called Jo. 'It's looking like he escaped.'

'What?'

'Down a tunnel to the cove. The must have clifftop home improvement of yesteryear.'

'He's gained a few days on us.'

'True. But he was badly injured. And he came back, clearly, for the portraits that went missing and, probably, his passport. Or one of them. They're doing checks on all his aliases.'

'Anything I can do, Boss?'

'Lock your doors.'

He heard her gasp.

'I don't want to alarm you, Jo. Just a precaution. I need to call Julia.'

He clicked off his phone and tapped in Julia's number. 'Fancy coming over for some Chinese. You and Nick?'

'Now?'

'Now.'

'Any particular reason?'

'Does there have to be a reason for crispy duck and sweet and sour?'

'No.'

'Shall I pick you up?'

'I'll drive.'

'Well, pack an overnight bag.'

'Brandon? Is that strictly necessary?'

'The attic has a sofa bed and an inflatable.'

'Well, okay …' He could hear the questions in her voice.

He didn't want to scare her. But, darn it, she had to know. 'Östberg. We think he's escaped. Through a tunnel to the cove.'

There was silence at the end of the phone.

'The missing portraits. It did cross my mind,' she replied in a steady voice.

'I've got to go,' he said, seeing MCIT trying to get through. 'See you in a bit.'

'George Nicholson took a flight from Newquay to Stockholm at 11am, 5 August.'

Brandon slapped his forehead. He might enjoy his Chinese after all.

Brandon

August 7, 2019

Anja was sitting across the table from him wearing a garment that resembled sackcloth. He assumed it was a personal choice, as the Swedish prison regime was famously liberal. She sucked the oxygen from the room and he wanted to spend as little time with her as possible.

'Shall we get started?' Brandon looked up at the officer standing in the corner.

He nodded.

'Ms Östberg, your brother, Alex Östberg, escaped arrest in the UK and we have reason to believe is now in Sweden. Your estate and lodge have been searched. Are there any other places you feel he may be using as a hideout?'

She frowned and pursed her lips. 'No.'

Brandon sighed. 'No family holiday homes? Friends' places?'

She stared at him. 'No.'

'I think you can do better than that, Ms Östberg. You have built quite a reputation for withholding vital information until you have no choice. You are doing yourself no favours by hampering police investigations.'

Anja looked around. 'It makes little difference to me what you think and how I can, somehow, help myself. Gain favours. I am here. The Swedish prison service is the most lenient in the world. Too lenient for me. I have nothing to gain by helping you. But I do hope you find Alex. He needs to be stopped. For his victims. And for himself.'

She turned her head to the wall. 'I have nothing more to say.'

Brandon gestured to the officer to end the interview and left the room.

'If she has a revelation, let me know,' Brandon said to Johan Olsson, the Swedish detective in the antechamber. 'I'm done for now.'

Brandon walked out of the high rise detention centre and lit up a cigarette. Was Östberg even still in Sweden? An international manhunt was under way, so it would be hard for him to cross borders. But not impossible. He had a feeling, though, that he was here – licking those copious wounds, laying low, planning his next moves.

He took a long drag. Anja – those ice blue eyes were as unfathomable as a fjord. He took another. Östberg knew the fjords. He was going to take Julia hiking there. Showed her photos of lake houses. Photos. It was a long shot, granted. Arvid Larsson. He dialled his number.

The taxi pulled up outside the Östberg estate in the wealthy Stockholm suburb of Östermalm. It was a swanky pile; a three-story build in yellow stone, flanked by stumpy, two-story wings and crowned with cupolas. Manicured gardens lined the path to the main entrance. Brandon made for the museum in the East Wing. Larsson met him at the door and Brandon followed him to his office. They walked through the displays of manuscripts and costumes, and a miniature of the Royal Palace, which was a bigger and better version of the Östberg estate. That said, you could easily get lost, or lose yourself, in a place like this.

'You wanted to know if the estate has access to lake houses,' Larsson said, gesturing for Brandon to sit opposite him at his office desk. 'We have several, one currently unoccupied.' He handed Brandon some papers.

Brandon looked through them. Soulless modern boxes. They weren't grabbing him. Where would a man like Östberg go? A man who wanted to stop the passage of time. Rewind it, even.

'That photo you showed me in the Zoom interview. Where the twins were playing on a lake. Do you have that?'

Larsson felt down to box by his chair. He brought out a selection of framed photographs and put them on the table.

'May I?' Brandon said.

Larsson nodded. 'Of course.'

They were the same photos he'd shown on screen. The one he wanted wasn't hard to find. There they were – Anja and Alex, messing around on the boat, happy as any kids could be.

'Where are they?' Brandon said, looking up from the photo.

'Blidö. The family had a little rustic cabin there – it was popular with the children.'

'Do they still own it?'

'Yes. But it is rarely used now. Rather run down and dated.'

They looked at each other. 'How far is it?'

'Around 54km east of Stockholm on the archipelago.

'Does it have a landline?'

'No.'

Brandon gave Larsson a long, hard look. 'What are the chances of him being there? And what are the chances of you tipping him off?'

'In answer to your first question. A reasonable chance. The place is deserted and he will have access to it.'

Brandon narrowed his eyes. 'A key safe?'

'A tree trunk.' Larsson shrugged. 'It's as rural as that.'

'In answer to your second question. Zero. I always hated the little shit. That feeling has intensified, as I am sure you can appreciate.'

If Larsson was lying, he was making a fine job of it. Brandon decided to skip the house tour and book a cab to Blidö. It was the perfect place for Östberg to pitch up without the need for ID or cash. The family estate, in comparison, didn't need another skeleton rattling around in it. Brandon was out of the door and on the road within ten minutes, clutching the map Larsson had handed him.

Brandon

August 7, 2019

The wooden jetty where the ferry landed reminded Brandon of a backwater in Alabama – a sanitised one. Blidö was a charming place. Its lake, forests and wooden cabins, nestled between the trees, spoke of serenity.

Brandon checked the map. Ändlös Sommar was 2km west, a short hike along the coast. He moved inland away from the private jetties and decks, and made his way along the road behind the houses that became fewer as he headed west. After twenty minutes he came to the red house Larsson had indicated on the map. It was a grand affair, by island standards, with its own grounds and outhouses. The Östberg cabin was 402 metres west of it. He walked on down the road, not passing anyone, until he reached the towering birch that marked the track through the woods to Ändlös Sommar and the lake. The late summer sun cast sparkles on the water, dappling the path through the pines and birches to the shore.

He hadn't gone far into the woods before he saw the cabin, 20 metres ahead to his left. Trees grouped tight on the approach, light just finding a way through. An apple tree stood out from the rest, forming a silhouette against the lake, one branch weighed down by a swinging object. Brandon stopped walking. He drew a breath, felt for his taser, and proceeded slowly, watching the thing in front swinging back and forth, slicing across the vista. He passed the cabin and walked on to the edge of the clearing that opened out to the shore. He could see clearly now. A tyre swing rocked on the breeze, marking time like a pocket watch.

He turned back to the cabin. It was a miserable looking one-story shack – dark and pokey, fit only for a witch. He could understand why a younger generation of Östbergs might have neglected it for the airy, stilted, glass-fronted houses he'd passed.

He searched until he found the tree trunk Larsson had mentioned, flashing his torch inside, disturbing the bugs, finding nothing. Brandon put away his torch and studied the dark little cabin waiting in the shadows. There were all manner of reasons why the key wasn't in the trunk. A person could have taken it. A magpie could have flown off with it. Maybe it had been lost years ago. Maybe Östberg was sitting in there, watching and waiting.

Brandon's fingers curled around the handle of his taser as he walked up to the door. Unless Östberg was asleep, he would have seen and heard him approach. He could well be viewing him now on a security app. Brandon felt the door handle. It was locked. He bent down to the keyhole and saw the tip of a key. Someone was in the building. Brandon edged away from the door and tried one of the windows. The curtains were drawn, the latch fastened. He squatted low beneath the next curtained window, tapped it with the taser, but it stayed firm. So, he went to the side of the cabin and repeated the exercise until he got to the back door, a slim line of light below it. Brandon felt the handle. It was locked. He took three steps back, took a breath, and launched himself at the door, bashing it open.

August 7, 2019

He was sitting at the kitchen table, a plate of apples to his left, a chopping board and a knife to his right, a pistol in his hand.

'You just don't know when you're not welcome, Detective Inspector.'

'And nor do you, Östberg. Did you think those women wanted you to come into their lives and snuff them out?'

Östberg shook his head lightly. 'You don't get it, do you.'

Brandon kept his eyes on the man; the gun and the knife never out of his peripheral range. 'I get it. I get your warped logic and ideology. But I don't agree with it. I'm sickened by it. And I'm here to stop it.'

Östberg smiled. 'And how, may I ask, do you intend doing that?' He cocked the gun's trigger and pointed it at Brandon. 'Drop the taser and kick it over here.'

Brandon did as he was asked.

Östberg picked up the knife and an apple and began to peel it, all the while watching Brandon, who stood by the door calculating his chances.

'Pull up a chair.' Alex jerked the gun at a chair under the window. 'I could do with a chat before supper.'

'So, what do you want to talk about?' Brandon said, sitting himself down by the table.

'Whoa, back from the table. I didn't invite you to supper.'

Brandon tightened his lips and edged his chair back. 'Better?'

He nodded. 'So who told you about this place? Anja? Larsson?'

'I worked it out.'

'How?'

'An old photo. The one of you and Anja, down there on the lake.'

Östberg looked up at the ceiling and then back at Brandon. 'You went to the museum?'

'I did. Musty old place. Mainly full of boring bric-a-brac. Mainly, that is. The photo was fascinating. And the one at your Dad's funeral. What were you doing there? I heard you didn't get on.'

'Anja?' He shook his head.

Brandon remained silent.

'She betrays me again. I was there to get reacquainted with my father.'

Brandon leaned forward, his eyes fixed on him. 'Reacquainted?'

Östberg smiled. 'Yes. I am so glad I did. He finally came into his own, four days ago – when I introduced him to your forensic friend Chapman,'

Brandon inhaled sharply. 'The skeleton was your father's? Rolf Östberg?'

Östberg gave a mirthless laugh. 'Work it out.'

Brandon stared at him. 'You kept your father's body at the house?'

Östberg shrugged.

'You embalmed your father?'

Östberg's eyes widened. 'Of course not. I took pleasure in watching him rot.'

Brandon rose from his chair. 'I'd like to sit here chewing the fat all evening, but I've got a job to do. I am arresting you for the abductions and murders of Naomi Foster, Esther Baker, Tania Beckingsdale, Lucy Ford, Clarissa Bowles, Rebecca Morley and Emily Paxton, and the abductions and GBH of Julia Trenowden and Joanna Menhenrick. You do not have to say anything. But, it may harm your defence if you do not mention when questioned something which you later rely on in court. Anything you do say may be given in evidence.'

'Why don't you throw in, "the murder of policeman Brandon Hammett". Really go to town.' He was smiling but his eyes were snarling. The left one had a massive bruise. It smarted over a line of stitches on his cheek. Brandon reckoned they were his own handiwork. The right side of his face was mashed in too. Julia had made a fine job of it. The fire had added the finishing touches.

He was looking puzzled – waiting for an answer to his preposterous suggestion.

'You're not going to murder me, Östberg.'

'Why not?' He relaxed back in his chair and Brandon tilted forward a fraction.

'Because the Swedish police will be here any moment. You don't think I came here without a contingency plan? Just rewind to the last one I put in place four days ago. Firearms squad, fire brigade, helicopter. You're going to prison, Östberg, for a very long time. If you're lucky, in Sweden. Do you consider yourself lucky, Mr Östberg?'

'Luckier than you, DI Hammett.' He picked up another apple and started peeling it. 'You go to all this trouble to catch me and you end up dead. You don't even get the girl. You never get the girl. I do. She's in the back room.'

Brandon tilted his head to the side and gave him a hard stare. 'You've got another girl in here?'

Östberg got up from the table, the pistol in his hand, and opened the door. The portrait of Julia was on the wall, next to the one of his mother. He let the door swing shut.

'If you're imprisoned in Sweden, they may allow you the portraits for your cell,' Brandon said. It was completely feasible, although he was sure Julia wouldn't allow it.

Östberg shook his head. 'I'm not going to jail. I've served my time.'

The words reminded him of what Julia had said. How he was punishing himself for not saving his mother.'

'You know, I lost someone I loved very much. Someone I couldn't save.'

Östberg shot him a look.

'She was 27. Had her whole life ahead of her. We were going to grow old together. But she died. And wanted so much to live.'

'My mother wanted so much to die. Ergo, you try to save lives. I try to end them. You see, Detective Inspector, we really have nothing in common. Apart from the timing and location of our deaths. You are going to die on August 7, 2019, in lakeside Blidö. As will I. Nice location, people will say. Shame about the blood and brains staining the walls of the cabin, and the mutilated body of a once handsome man hanging from the branch of a tree by an otherwise tranquil lake.'

Östberg was becoming agitated. Something Julia had warned him about. His effort to empathise had had the opposite effect to what he'd intended.

Brandon tensed. Östberg still had the pistol in his hand. Brandon thought he was going to use it, was ready to dive, when Östberg placed it on the table, a few inches closer to the edge than last time. He wasn't ready yet. Brandon was.

He watched Östberg pick up another apple and then the knife, and prepare to peel. As soon as the knife pierced the skin of the fruit, Brandon roared and charged at the table grabbing the pistol. But Östberg was swift and plunged the knife into his hand, making Brandon reel back with pain and drop the gun on the floor. It rolled under the table and Brandon, the knife still in his right hand, crawled under to get it.

Ostberg crouched behind him, dragging him out by his feet. Brandon kicked back, smashing him in the face. He heard teeth crack, and a cry of pain, as Brandon crawled under the table and up the other side. Östberg was back on his feet, blood gushing from his mouth, streaming down his face and shirt. Brandon's shirt sleeve was drenched in blood too. With one almighty effort, he pulled the knife out of his right hand and cocked the trigger of the gun.

'Hands above your head, now!' Brandon commanded. Östberg wasn't going to do as he was told, so Brandon went round to his side of the table and kicked him in the back of his knees to bring him down. When he was prostrate on the floor, he cuffed his wrists and then his ankles. This man knew his way around manacles. It felt like divine retribution to truss him up. He left Östberg face down on the floor as he searched for a cloth to wrap around his hand to stem the bleeding.

Then his phone began to ring. His hands shook as he felt in his pocket for it – the adrenalin draining from his body like his blood.

'Jo,' he said, when he heard her voice. 'Get me out of here.'

August 9, 2019

'You've been in the wars,' Julia said, frowning at Brandon from the bottom of his hospital bed.

'You can come a little closer. It's not contagious,' Brandon said, his dark blue eyes gently mocking her.

She walked around to the side of the bed.

'Just don't squeeze the right hand.' Brandon was smiling. 'It's outdone the left for major injuries.'

Julia smiled and took hold of his left hand. 'Now, it's my turn to say how proud I am of you. But you should have told me you were coming over here to stake him out!'

'Where would that have got me?'

Julia grimaced. 'Very true.'

'He's just down the road, you know. His detention centre is as pleasant as this hospital ward.'

Julia looked around the room. It was very Swedish, with its clean lines and graphics, and blocks of uplifting primary colours. Alex Östberg, with his fastidious, classical tastes, would hate it.

Julia rested her hand on his brow and pushed back his fringe. 'Let him rot in Ikea!'

Brandon burst out laughing. 'You are a tonic, Julia.'

'Talking of tonics, Jo wanted me to give you these.' She brought out a cake carton.

Brandon opened the box. 'Blueberry muffins. You got these through customs?'

'M&S Stockholm. Special delivery. They heard you were in town.'

'Well, thank you – and Jo – very much. How is she?'

'She's okay. Such a trooper. Taking care of the shop with Stew while you're away. No major crime cases, you'll be pleased to hear.'

'I am that. How are you?'

Julia sat on the chair by his bed and took his hand. 'Still licking my wounds. Still counting my blessings. I can't believe I got out of there.'

'You didn't think I wouldn't get you out of that hellhole?'

'I did,' she squeezed his hand. 'But it was ... hard sometimes to keep the faith.'

'Now you know, eh?' He reached for her with his bandaged hand and she stroked it lightly.

'Yes.' She lifted his hand gently. 'How soon before you can play the fiddle again?'

'Not too long. The sonofabitch missed the tendons,' he said, wiggling the fingers tips poking out of the bandage.

They sat for a while, before Julia mentioned his other visitors. 'Shall we let in the barbarians at the gates?'

'Chelsea and Nick?'

'They're sitting out there, on their phones, waiting to sit in here, on their phones.'

Brandon smiled. 'Well, Chelsea has already brought me in her special rag doll Molly-May for company. I guess I best bring it out from hiding.' Brandon pulled the tatty looking doll out from under the bed sheets.

'Cute,' Julia said. 'Baby toy?'

'Yes. Her lucky charm.'

Julia went out of the room and came back in behind Chelsea and Nick.

'Fancy a muffin, Nick?' Brandon said.

'Cool.' Nick took one out of the box and demolished it in three large bites.

'When you coming home, Dad?' Chelsea said, reaching for a muffin.

'Tonight, most likely. This is a superficial wound. Nothing keeps your old pop down for long.'

Chelsea leaned over the bed and wriggled her arms around him, Brandon keeping his injured hand out to the side. It reminded Julia of the red head's erect arm, the one with the white glove, the one that knocked over the lit candelabra. Emily Paxton. The flashbacks would keep coming, she knew that. But, in this company, with these people around her, she'd heal. They made her feel happy. They made her feel safe.

'I've got an idea,' Brandon said, sitting up in bed, an empty muffin carton on his lap, the kids back on their phones. 'Why don't we take off at October half term? Do a mini road trip round the Southern States?'

'Awesome!' Chelsea said, dumping her phone and wrapping her arms around her dad, clipping his hand as she did so.

'Ouch!'

'Wimp!' Chelsea said, laughing.

'Give me some slack, girl. This hand needs to be fit to drive round the States in two months.'

'What do you think, Mum?' She could see the concern in Nick's eyes. He'd grown so much – physically and mentally. She thought of the old cliché, what doesn't kill you makes you stronger.

'I'm up for it,' she said, smiling at Nick. 'And a little shopping in Östermalm before we leave Stockholm.'

Brandon was smiling at her when she turned to him.

'That's my girl,' he said.

Acknowledgements

I'd like to thank the many people who have contributed to Fairest Creatures. First, my publisher Peter Burnett at Leamington Books and his two editors Ambrose Kelly and Josh Andrew for having faith in me and getting my early draft into excellent shape. Their suggestions brought my DI Brandon Hammett out of early retirement and onto the page. Brandon had been keeping a low profile since I created him on the University of East Anglia Creative Writing (Crime Fiction) MA course several years ago. Course Director Henry Sutton and his department gave me the best possible education in crime fiction and creative writing. So, particular thanks to Henry and Nathan Ashman who were my tutors in the second year, William Ryan, who tutored me in the first year, as well as Tom Benn and Laura Joyce who gave me great practical advice and encouragement.

I would also like to acknowledge my incredible fellow UEA students who were an absolute pleasure and inspiration to work and play with. I'd like to extend my particular appreciation to Elizabeth Saccente, who read the first draft of Fairest Creatures as I wrote it. Her editorial precision and encouragement were invaluable. Also, Jayne Farnworth, former DI at The Met, who not only put me right on police procedure, but was a great source of creativity and laughs.

Thank you, too, Claire Demaine who has supported me over the years and gave useful suggestions and great encouragement. Also, psychotherapist Annette Powell for her insights into the antagonist's behaviour and the effects of early trauma.

The artist, Janine Wing, also deserves much credit. Her work caught my eye at the Penzance Studios Exhibition in the summer. I approached her, and she agreed to create a cover image reflecting the themes of the book. Her artwork's dark, arresting glory is perfect.

Last, but not least, I thank my son Alex Buxton who was locked in the house with me while I wrote the first draft and in the early days of the publishing process. And, also, my sister Yvonne Taylor, who introduced me to the UEA course and supported me throughout, as well as old friends and new ones, including Neil Buxton, Rachel Carnac, Tim Fisher and Roger Manning.